PENGUIN BOOKS
SLOW MOTION RIOT

Peter Blauner was born in New York City in 1959 and, since graduating from Wesleyan University in 1982, has worked as a journalist on *New York* magazine, where he is a contributing editor. However, while he was researching *Slow Motion Riot* he took six months' leave from work and underwent a full training programme as a probation officer, as well as spending time on the streets with the department's field service unit, wearing a bulletproof vest and helping to pick up the most dangerous criminals. He lives in New York with his wife Peg Tyre, who is a crime reporter on *New York Newsday*. *Slow Motion Riot* is his first novel.

D1323916

SLOW MOTION RIOT

PETER BLAUNER

PENGUIN BOOKS

To Peg, who's been there too

PENGUIN BOOKS

Published by the Penguin Group
Penguin Books Ltd, 27 Wrights Lane, London W8 5TZ, England
Penguin Books USA Inc., 375 Hudson Street, New York, New York 10014, USA
Penguin Books Australia Ltd, Ringwood, Victoria, Australia
Penguin Books Canada Ltd, 10 Alcorn Avenue, Toronto, Ontario,
Canada M4V 3B2
Penguin Books (NZ) Ltd, 182–190 Wairau Road, Auckland 10, New Zealand

Penguin Books Ltd, Registered Offices: Harmondsworth, Middlesex, England

First published in the USA by William Morrow and Co. Inc. 1991
First published in Great Britain by Viking 1991
Published in Penguin Books 1991
3 5 7 9 10 8 6 4 2

Copyright © Peter Blauner, 1991
All rights reserved

The moral right of the author has been asserted

Printed in England by Clays Ltd, St Ives plc

I would like to give thanks to the following people: Gerald Migliore, Kevin T. Smyley, Arthur Hudson, God Shammgod, Michael McGuinness, Jane Meara, Liza Dawson, Jim Landis, Bob Mecoy, Clare Alexander, Henry Eisig, Miguel Ibarra, Fran Lubow, Pat McFadden, Todd Siegal, Lovable Dupreme Akbar Physics, Ed Kosner, Troy, Donald Goines, Mark Rosenthal, Brian Walls, Bill Clark, Bob Losada, Reginald Morgan, Vanessa Grant, Mary Anne Sally, Floyd Simmons, Ava Elwort, Lou Shimpkin, Skeeter, Peter Herbst, Father Devine, Wayne Barrett, Jack Newfield, Greg Cox, Joanne Gruber, Charlie, Richard Mayronne, Frances Kessler, Michael Lynne, Wallace Cheatham, Joe Lopez, Thaddeus, and everyone else in or on probation who helped me.

I would also like to give special thanks to Arthur Pine and Lori Andiman for their support and guidance, and most of all to Richard Pine, without whom this book would not be between two covers.

Everything now, we must assume, is in our hands; we have no right to assume otherwise. If we—and now I mean the relatively conscious whites and the relatively conscious blacks, who must, like lovers, insist on, or create, the consciousness of the others—do not falter in our duty now, we may be able, handful that we are, to end the racial nightmare, and achieve our country, and change the history of the world. If we do not now dare everything, the fulfillment of that prophecy, recreated from the Bible in song by a slave, is upon us: "God gave Noah the rainbow sign, No more water, the fire next time!"

JAMES BALDWIN, 1962

What crime and poverty have created is a riot in slow motion.

JOHN V. LINDSAY, 1990

1

Now that the baby was two months old, she seemed to be waking up at least twice a night. But since he was doing a four-to-midnight tour in the city today, the cop named Frankie Page could afford to sleep in a little. He woke up around noon with his dick as hard as a rock. His wife had already gone to work, though, so there was nothing to do, except wait for it to go away and maybe feed the baby again.

It was just after three in the afternoon when the man with the dreadlocks came into the boy's bedroom. All the lights were out and the floor was strewn with fierce-looking toys called Gobots and Decepticons. The boy, whose name was Darryl King, was lying on the bed with one arm thrown over his face.

The man with the dreadlocks knelt over him and put the gun on his chest.

"It's time," he said.

Page liked a lot of things about driving to work on these cold winter afternoons. The stillness of the air and the silence of the other houses as he pulled out of the driveway. The snow on the front lawns. The cars going the opposite direction on

the Long Island Expressway. The Christmas decorations outside the Manhattan stores as he drove north from the Midtown
Tunnel. The only thing that remained unchanged by the holiday was his precinct in Harlem. But nothing ever seemed to
leave much of an impression there anyway.

Darryl King, the boy with the gun, didn't go straight to the
job. It was too early anyway. Instead, he went downtown and
found some friends at the Playland video game arcade in Times
Square. A couple of them wanted to catch a sex show at one
of the nearby theaters, but Darryl, who was seventeen and
good-looking in a blunt way, wasn't interested. He went to the
back of the arcade and stood by the machine that simulated
car crashes. After a couple of minutes, the others came back
to see what he had.

"Thirty-eight-caliber revolver," said Darryl, lifting his coat
flap and showing it to them. "Just like the cops carry."

"Damn," one of the others said.

Why would a wife need an order of protection against her
own husband, Frankie Page wondered as he sat in the patrol
car parked outside a short brown building on 128th Street that
night. To need someone guarding your front door against the
man you married. Snowflakes fell slowly, changing shades as
they flitted in and out of the street light. They landed on the
windshield and melted before his eyes. A family should be
together for the holidays, he thought. He hoped he wouldn't
be on call on Christmas Day in two weeks. Though the overtime
would help pay for the wife's present. They'd already sunk a
fortune into the baby's room. He was going to need that promotion to sergeant next year and the raise that went with it.

He didn't notice Darryl King and his two friends coming
up on the opposite side of the street. It was after eleven o'clock
and below fifteen degrees. The only other people who were
out now were the truly hardy hookers and crack dealers, and

they were all down the block, over on Lenox Avenue.

Darryl walked briskly, a couple of steps ahead of his friends. Smoke streamed out of his mouth and the gun rode high in the waistband under his coat. The police car was only half a block away now, just out of the range of the streetlight.

"You're not gonna do it," the bigger of Darryl's two friends taunted him. "You ain't got the heart."

"Watch me," Darryl King said.

The car's heater was starting to make Page feel nauseated, so he turned it down a little and put his hat on. There was a rap on the window and he looked up. A skinny young black kid with a flattop hairdo and a harelip was staring at him and saying something. Page rolled down the window to hear him.

"Yo," the kid said.

"What's up?" Page asked him.

While they were talking, Darryl King sneaked around the other side of the car. He steadied himself against the doorframe and aimed the gun. Each time he pulled the trigger, the car lit up like a furnace in the snow.

Later on that night, Darryl told his family what happened while they sat around watching a TV ad for an album of Yuletide standards.

"His hat flew off, like 'bing' the first time I shot him," Darryl said. "And Aaron say his eyes got real wide. You know what I'm saying? Aaron was like, 'Oh shit, I seen his hair go up. I seen his blond hair.'"

Darryl's older sister, Joanna, turned slowly to look at him. "Blond?" she said.

Darryl sat up. "Yeah, 'blond hair's what he said."

"But, Darryl, that cop who was ripping off our crack house had like dark hair."

It took a couple of seconds for the news to sink in. Darryl looked up at the ceiling with his mouth open a little. "Shit," he said. "That's fucked up."

"That's right," his sister said, shaking her head and standing up.

"How'd that happen?"

"I don't know," his sister told him. "But you better get some sleep now. Tomorrow's another day."

2

Some mornings at the New York City Department of Probation, I like to play a little game called *What's My Crime?* The idea is to try to guess the crime my client has committed just by looking at the Polaroid clipped to the outside of his file folder. It's one of my ways of relieving the tension and reassuring myself that I don't give a shit anymore.

Delilah, the heavyset black secretary behind the reception desk, puts down the Jehovah's Witness magazine and holds up the first picture.

It's of a Hispanic guy in his early twenties, with a friendly smile and a dreamy warmth in his eyes. His hair is long on the sides and he keeps his chin low, like he was trying to sweet-talk a girl when the shot was taken.

"He looks like a nice guy," I say.

Delilah slips the Polaroid across the desk so I can give it a better look. "I dunno," I say finally. "Forgery or something like that?"

Delilah is already frowning at the file opened on her lap. "This boy's a crack-smoking schizophrenic," she says. "He blew his landlord's head off with a shotgun."

"Oh shit," I say.

Now I have to make space in my life to see this guy. I could have him come by after Maria Sanchez on Friday. But Maria always leaves me feeling wrung out, so I figure I better put him off until Monday.

My union rep walks by. "Mr. Jack Pirone," I say, which is the way I always say hello to people in the morning.

"Mr. Steven Baum," he says to me.

Big Jack.

Two hundred and fifty pounds of interdepartmental wisdom and sheer aggravation in a fedora and a white polo shirt. Before he was my union rep, Jack Pirone was my training instructor. His great line then was "Everytime you reach for a new assignment at probation, you're reaching for your passport to adventure."

He always looks out for me, when he isn't giving me a big pain.

"How you doing this morning, Mr. Baum?"

"Laughing on the outside, crying on the inside," I say.

"Try the other way around," he says, slapping me on the shoulder and ambling on down the hall. "You'll live longer."

The clock on the wall has thin steel bars crisscrossing it, as if they expected somebody to try stealing the hands. Almost nine o'clock. Behind me I hear the waiting room full of probation clients grumbling at each other. I take a quick look over my shoulder and see a bunch of them sprawled out on the wooden benches, like a wayward congregation spilling out of the church pews. The air conditioner is broken, so there's no relief from the June heat in here. The air is dank and it smells of stale smoke. The walls are painted a deep, intense orange. You'd think they would've chosen something a little more calming, like pale blue or ocean green. Instead, this orange is disturbing, maybe even inciting. It's like a "GO" sign for the mentally ill.

One woman is standing up and throwing pieces of a Styrofoam coffee cup around the room. She's probably getting in the mood to see her probation officer. I hope she's not one of mine.

Delilah hands me the last file. "This one don't have a photo," she says.

Instead, it has a sticky yellow note from my supervisor, Emma Lang, on the front. "Special!" it says. "Attention must be paid! Watch this guy." The new client is named Darryl King.

I check the sign-in sheet to make sure he isn't here yet, and then look once more across the smoky civil service purgatory where people are waiting. That woman has finally stopped throwing Styrofoam around. The bleary fluorescent light gives everyone a slightly greenish tint, and there are piles of cigarette butts and suspicious-looking puddles on the linoleum floor. Half the clients look dead this morning, with their eyes closed, and their legs in stone-washed jeans extended stiffly over the sides of the benches. And with my hangover I'm not feeling so great either.

The one thing that picks me up is the hairstyles on the younger guys here. It's been an excellent summer for hair so far. I see one guy has his shaped like an upside-down bottle-cap—a new one on me. I know all about the Fade: that's the flattop with lightly shaved sides. Then there's the Wave, a lopsided ski jump of hair sloping up on one side. And of course, my favorite is the Cameo, a high ebony tower of hair that looks like an Egyptian headdress. I wonder if the bottle cap has a name yet. In a year white kids will be wearing it, which suddenly strikes me as hysterically funny.

Six expressionless eyes turn to stare at me. They belong to three teenage boys with big white sneakers and eerily dulled-out eyes. The term Jack would use is "lacking in affect."

Not that they'd be real intimidated by me anyway. They look at me and see a tall skinny Jew in his late twenties with curly hair and glasses. The free weights are starting to give me broader shoulders and my hands are unusually big, but you wouldn't look twice at me on the beach, I don't think. I guess what they mainly see is just another white authority figure who's got nothing to do with their lives, trying to tell them what to do.

Just then, somebody catches my eye over near reception. An emaciated black teenage girl, with a purple scarf and a gold front tooth. She's squinting at the guard's tiny black-and-white TV. I can't quite tell if she's one of mine. I've got 250 people on my caseload, and I know about half of them by sight. Two small boys are next to her on the bench. One is about five. The other is about a year old. The older one wears thick brown glasses and has big gaps between his teeth. When he thinks no one is looking, he pulls his little brother close and kisses him on the forehead.

I reach into the pocket of my windbreaker to see if I have a piece of candy to give him. Usually I carry my whole life around in the pocket: keys, change, pens, scraps of paper, food. Today I've got no candy, so I just give him a little wink.

The two boys look remarkably similar, except for some ugly scabs and bruises on the older one's face. He clings to his baby brother like he's trying to protect a smaller, unspoiled version of himself. Their teenaged mother suddenly turns and sees the older boy with his arm around the sleeping baby. She slaps him hard with an open hand across his cheek.

"Travis, don't you touch him," she barks.

Travis looks scared and takes his hand off his little brother. The baby wakes up and starts crying.

"You know, he wasn't doing anything," I tell her.

She ignores me and picks at her thumbnail.

"You shouldn't hit him like that," I say.

"Mind your own fucking business," she tells me.

She goes back to watching the television. The baby keeps crying. Travis, the five year old, tightens his body and stares down at his folded hands in his lap. Another client in the making.

I should just forget about it and go look for aspirin. But for some reason, the look on Travis's face sort of gets to me. "What's your name?" I ask the girl.

"Parker," she mumbles.

Definitely not one of mine. "Who's your probation officer?"

"Rodriguez," she says, sucking in one cheek.

A voice in my head is saying, "Forget about it, man, it's not even your case." But my feet take me down the musty marble hall and over to the rickety mailboxes, where I write P. O. Rodriguez a short note. "Dear Mr. Rodriguez, does your client Parker have any outstanding child abuse complaints? If not, she will soon. Check it out. Yours, S. Baum." I drop it in his box and head to my own office.

"Delilah," I say as I pass by the reception desk again, "when are you gonna ditch that husband of yours with the big feet and come slam-dancing with me and my friend Terry at CBGB's?"

She giggles like a flirty schoolgirl. "You too much, Mr. Baum," she says.

"Or not enough."

I start reading the Darryl King file as I walk down the hall. This part of the morning reminds me of descending into an catacomb, probably because of the darkness at the end of the corridor, where nobody's replaced the light bulb that burned out months ago. I pass rows and rows of file cabinets the color of turtles, and peer into the archive office on the right where stooped-over clerks in dust masks are sorting through ancient records of long-forgotten crimes.

Stevie Wonder's "I Just Called to Say I Love You" plays on somebody's radio and a breeze comes from nowhere, rustling the time sheets tacked to the wall.

The information inside the Darryl King file is skimpy. He's on probation for robbing a gas station on East Ninety-sixth Street, but he has an unusually long adult arrest record for an eighteen year old. In the last year alone he's been charged with numerous muggings, burglaries, and assaults, as well as "acting in concert." At one point he was accused of being part of a gang that beat a transit worker with a hammer. Up until the gas station robbery, though, he'd never been found guilty, perhaps because witnesses are reluctant to testify against him. The real danger signal is in the presentence investigation, written by Tommy Markham.

Tommy, a briny little guy, who spent most of his life in the merchant marines, is a soft touch. He recommends almost everyone get probation. This time, he didn't.

He describes Darryl King as intelligent but says Darryl was uncooperative during his intake interview and kept snatching things off the desk. "The defendant seemed to be making a deliberate attempt to intimidate this officer," writes Tommy, who routinely calls vicious mob hit men and drug dealers "misunderstood." There isn't much family or school background in the report. Tommy notes that Darryl showed no remorse about the robbery, saying he only pleaded guilty at his lawyer's urging.

In his evaluative statement, Tommy Markham writes, "The prognosis for his future social adjustment is not favorable." Coming from Tommy, that's like saying, "This guy is definitely going to kill somebody."

I've reached the darkest part of the hallway, so I can't read anymore. Now I know why Ms. Lang put a flag on the assignment. Two months ago a guy on probation killed a young doctor, and the department wants to avoid further mistakes. Ms. Lang thinks Darryl King is a significant risk, and I'm inclined to agree.

Here's the thing about Darryl: Everyone's always bitching about guys like him getting probation instead of going to prison. And my response is usually to shrug and say I don't decide who goes free. Which is true. Then I explain the system doesn't have enough jail space for these criminals, so it's up to people like me to play lion tamer and keep them in line. Also true.

But here's the secret, which I almost never say out loud: Every once in a while, you just might turn one of these guys around.

I notice that the note attached to the file does not say what time Darryl King will show up at the office. Just "soon."

As it is, I have more than a full schedule for today with Richard Silver finally coming in.

Silver is one I've really been looking forward to. He used to be one of the big power brokers in the city, a *gontser macher* as they used to say around my family. He's been ducking his appointment with me for weeks. I had to bombard him and his lawyer with dozens of threatening phone calls and letters before I got any response. Already I have a problem with the guy. Approaching my cubicle, I square my shoulders and throw punches at the air, like a boxer on his way to the ring.

I stop short when I see someone waiting for me by my door. A Puerto Rican kid who looks about twelve with a chipped front tooth and glassy eyes. His dark hair leaps like a flame from the top of his head, crests into a pompadour, and then falls backward slickly. Splotches cover the front of his brown T-shirt and his jeans are too tight. He looks at me and shifts anxiously.

"Can I help you?" I ask.

The kid grunts and hands me a folder. I wonder if he can speak. "What's this?" I ask.

He grunts again and looks down at his sneakers. "They say give you this," he says in a small, hoarse voice.

I open the door and go in. The kid doesn't move. He keeps his eyes trained on the floor. There's something lost and untamed about him. Like the boy in a French movie I once saw who grew up in the woods. Except in the movie, they had five years to educate the boy about civilization, and I've got five minutes for this kid. I gesture for him to come in and sit down.

"Mr. Ricky Velez," I say, sitting behind the desk and opening his file. "Says here you're sixteen. That right?"

Ricky grunts again and nods shyly. In the cubicle across the hall, "the Screamer," an older female probation officer whose name I can never pronounce, is yelling, "WHAT AM I GONNA TELL THE JUDGE!!" at some hapless probationer.

An overhead fan just pushes the humid air around instead of cooling things off.

Ricky squirms around in the chair but can't get comfortable.

The seat's deliberately too hard, because no one's supposed to stay here too long. In the past I've tried to make this cubicle seem more my own, even as I keep telling myself this is my job, not my life. I've brought in plants, cushions, and books, but the place still looks cheap and institutional with those insane orange walls and scuffed-up floors. So now I leave it pretty much the way it was. I don't have my master's degree from Fordham on the walls. It was required for the job—along with two weeks of perfunctory in-house training—but my clients don't need to see it. Instead, I put up two small posters right above my desk: one of Bob Dylan and the other of a defunct theme park called Freedomland. On the other wall, I have the *Times*'s "Help Wanted" section—for my clients, of course, not for me—and a bank calendar that has a color photo of a sandy beach with foamy waves. It seems like a beautiful place where nothing ever happens. And, of course, there's a blackboard in the corner.

I wipe off my glasses and start to read Ricky's arrest report more carefully. "It says you got probation for 'theft of services' and resisting arrest," I say. "What was the theft of services?"

Ricky clears his throat and says, "Just tokens." His voice sounds scratchy, like it hurts him to speak.

"Tokens?" I say. "You mean you robbed a subway token booth attendant?"

"No." Ricky shakes his head emphatically. "Sucked it."

"Sucked it?"

He doesn't respond at all now. For a moment, we both just sit there in our own stupors. I'm too hung over to move. Now I know how old strippers must feel when they hear that familiar drumbeat and see the curtain parting one more time. I rouse myself and get to my feet. Still feeling a little unsteady, I make my way to the blackboard, take the chalk out of my pocket, and draw a small, slightly shaky cartoon of a man bending over a subway turnstile with his mouth on the slot.

"Do you mean to tell me you're one of those guys who goes up to turnstiles and sucks the tokens out?" I say in a loud sort of courtroom voice.

Ricky nods to indicate that is precisely what he did. He's a little young to be a token sucker, I think. I usually see older, scragglier guys puckering up by the turnstiles. "Don't you think that's kind of gross?" I say, pointing at the picture I've drawn.

He smiles and some of the tension goes out of the room. "I mean there's gotta be an easier way to make a living, right?" I tell him. "Those turnstiles are filthy. You shouldn't put your mouth there. You do this by yourself?"

"I got a partner," he says a little louder. "Hector."

I write Hector's name on the board. "Hector suck tokens too?"

"No. He does selling."

"Oh I see, he's like the business manager." I put the chalk back in my pocket and return to my desk. "That was your first mistake. You shouldn't do all the work. You should've made Hector the co-sucker."

"Yeah?" Ricky starts laughing in spite of himself. As quickly and painlessly as I can, I get the necessary information. Ricky lives near me on the Lower East Side with his mother, who's on welfare, and his three brothers. He attends school sporadically and understands English perfectly, but can't concentrate in the classroom.

I've had a lot of clients like this. People who slip from one day to the next without any sense of purpose, all the time sinking deeper and deeper inside themselves. The only time their lives have any structure is when they're out doing crimes. So what Ricky needs is somebody to pull him out of himself. At least that's my considered opinion after talking to him for two minutes.

"Maybe we should try and do like a schedule," I say, jumping back up to the blackboard and starting to write some more. When I notice Ricky staring at it blankly, I ask him if he can read and write okay, without looking at him. It's the best way to ask the question and not make a client feel too self-conscious.

Ricky grunts. Not a yes or a no.

"You know, it's okay if you can't read so well." My tongue sticks out a little as I write on the board. "I've got something called dyslexia myself. Ever hear of that?" I write the word "dyslexia" on the board and underline it twice like it's some crazy new dance we can both marvel at.

"No," he murmurs. "I dunno what that is." Just a few words. But compared to what he's said so far, it's poetry.

"Dyslexia is . . . sometimes when you're reading or trying to write, the letters won't behave in front of your eyes." I start drawing letters upside down and backward on the board, so it looks as if somebody put the alphabet in a kitchen blender. "Like it's some language you can't understand. Ever have that?"

"Sure," says Ricky. "Kinda."

I put down the chalk and take off my glasses. "You know it really helped when I went to this class for people with dyslexia," I say as though I'm confiding in my best friend. "My problem was I waited too long. I should've gone when I was your age."

I hate talking like this, but it seems to be working. He's sitting up a bit straighter and his eyes seem a little more focused. I ask Ricky if he'd be interested in attending a reading class.

"Maybe," he says without much enthusiasm.

"Well, we have to get you into some kind of program," I tell him. "And as far as they go, the reading one's not so bad. It's only twice a week, and they have a place you can go on the East Side, so it's not too far from your house. Okay?"

Now I'm getting determined to break through. I pick up my chair and bring it around the desk so we're sitting side by side. "All right," I say, taking out my notebook. "So what I'm giving you here today is like a list of goals."

I never liked these touchy-feely social work platitudes. But then again, the list does help a lot of people get their lives organized. Ricky smiles when he sees I put his name at the top of the page. "Understand most of what I wrote here?" I ask.

"Most," Ricky says.

"And if you don't understand any of it, do you have somebody in the house who reads all right?"

"Yeah."

"Okay." I pull my chair a little closer, so its arm touches the
arm of Ricky's chair. I can hear him breathing heavily and I
smell something like detergent in his fountain of hair. I hope he
doesn't smell the whiskey on my breath from last night. "So
let's just go over the list here," I say. "We got five goals for now."

"Yeah." Ricky puts his index finger next to where I wrote
"Number one." The nail is chewed all the way down.

"Number one is the reading class," I say, rolling up my
shirt sleeves. "Two nights a week, for an hour. It's nothing.
Okay?"

"All right."

"Number two: Let Hector suck his own tokens." I draw
another picture of a guy sucking tokens and put a line through
it like it's a No Smoking sign.

Ricky laughs and slaps his knee.

"Number three is get up in the morning," I say. "Not the
afternoon. The morning. Do whatever you have to do to get
up. Make breakfast, listen to tapes. Put on like Kool Moe Dee
while you're getting dressed for school."

The kid looks like he's in shock that a white adult knows
anything about rap music. But then he shakes his head. "I like
Madonna," he says.

"Madonna?"

"Yeah," Ricky says with sudden great feeling as he leans
forward in his chair. "I got all her tapes! I got her posters in
my room! I see her boyfriend I fuck him up . . ."

"Okay, okay, great," I say, putting a hand on his arm to
calm him down. "So listen to Madonna for a half hour after
you get up—if it's okay with your mom—which leads us to
number four, which is go to school. And that leads to number
five, which is stay away from the crack guys."

He looks around like I've accused him of something terribly
unfair. But I know our neighborhood and I know where he's

been and where he's going. He probably took the same train
as me to get down here to Centre Street this morning. "Look,"
I tell him, "I know it's a heavy scene on the block. But you
gotta stay clean."

"Aw, man." Ricky twists in his chair to face away from me.

"It's tough," I say firmly. "But you gotta do it. The judge
gave you a break with probation. He could've put you in jail.
So now you have to be careful. That's the deal."

The boy sighs. "I guess."

This is the point where you lose them sometimes. When
they've had enough of the white authority figure. And to tell
you the truth, it's the point where I feel like stopping too. I've
said everything I'm supposed to say, and I've got other clients
waiting outside. But something keeps telling me I have to push
myself a little further.

"Listen, Ricky," I say, moving the chair around so we're
face-to-face. "If you work with me, I'll be your best friend in
the world. I swear it. You call me anytime. But if you fuck
around, and try to get over on me, I'm gonna be mad. All right?
Because that'll mean you betrayed our friendship. And I'll send
you off to jail myself if I have to. Okay?"

"I understand," the boy says.

There's still a long way to go, but I feel like I'm finally
getting through, a little. It almost seems worthwhile to face the
rest of the day. I give him the page with the list on it.

"So where you going now?" I ask.

"Home," says Ricky, standing up slowly. He stretches out
his arms and legs like he's not sure everything still works.

"What about school?" I say loudly. "Remember? Number
four?"

"Oh yeah." He smiles shyly, showing off a chipped front
tooth. "I go to school now."

"How you gonna get there from here? The subway?"

"Yeah." Ricky looks confused.

"Here," I say, taking a subway token out of my pocket and
putting it in the palm of his hand. "Save yourself all the hard
work."

3

"You got to visualize what will be," the big woman said. "Plan for the future. You know what I'm saying?"

"Yeah," the young man mumbled.

"In other words, you got to think about what's gonna happen if you do something." She shut the book, which was called *Visualize Success*, and looked at her younger brother, Darryl King. "You gotta build. Right?"

"Right," he said.

"And remind me I got a message to give you later," said his older sister, Joanna Coleman.

They were sitting on the stoop of a building near Frederick Douglass Boulevard in Harlem. A brutal midsummer sun was overhead. Small children kicked broken glass at each other in the gutter. A half dozen crack dealers did business on the sidewalks. Otherwise, the street was like part of a ghost town, with crumbling boarded-up buildings, vacant lots, and silent, toothless old men sitting on wooden chairs outside the corner grocery store.

Joanna took the large-size cup of Coca-Cola out of her younger brother's hands and drank most of it in two gulps. At twenty, she was turning into a heavyset woman with big thighs and a broad head full of red-streaked hair. In a few years, she'd be taking up two seats on the subway without any problem.

Today she was wearing a white blouse and huge gold earrings with Gemini symbols hanging off them. She'd been following the signs and reading astrology books since she was in her early teens, but now that she and her Jamaican boyfriend, Winston, were getting somewhere in the crack trade, she'd begun picking up business books like *Visualize Success* and *Winning Through Intimidation*. It was hard getting through most of them, though she tried to pass on what she could to her younger brother. The trouble was he never listened.

"So what happened last month?" she asked him.

"What?" said Darryl, closing his Big Mac container.

"With Pops Osborn."

"That was fucked up."

"I know. I saw him after I got back into town last week. He was standing outside his crack house."

"He was alive, right?"

"Yeah."

"So that was, you know, irregular," said Darryl, who had on a pair of snow-white Nike sneakers, jeans, and a T-shirt with the name of the rap group Public Enemy written across the front. "We was on the roof. Right?"

"Who's this?" his sister asked.

"Me." Darryl touched his chest with his finger. "Bobby Kirk. And Aaron. So I give the gun to Aaron."

His sister put down the Coke cup and made a face. "Why'd you do that? Aaron a punk."

"He fourteen," Darryl said, "and I just turn eighteen. So judge won't do nothing to him."

"Okay."

"Except Aaron miss his shot and Pops drove away in his car."

"He fucked up," Joanna said.

" 'S what I said. So I'm like, 'Oh shit, Joanna's gonna be mad at you.' So I come up with another plan."

Joanna belched and asked him about it.

"We went to the gas station," Darryl said.

"Which one?"

"Near FDR Drive. So we go in there and we rob, you know. We take money and Bobby beat up the guy."

"The attendant?"

"Yeah. Then we fill up like three beer bottles, you know, tall boys, with gasoline. Like Winston showed us. And we put rags in them, you know, and we went back to Pops's crack house and we firebombed it." He pounded his left fist into his right palm.

His sister laughed. "You too much, Darryl," she said.

"Yeah, but Pops was gone already, so we didn't get him."

"You get anybody?"

"Just some lady. She came down the steps with her back on fire, you know. And she just like fell in the street. The fire just ate her up, you know. Aaron was like, 'Yo, man, you see that shit. 'S just like the movies.' But I was like, 'No, it's not.' "

A black car with a beefy white man behind the wheel drove slowly down the street. Joanna and Darryl stopped talking and the dealers stopped doing business for a moment. When the car was gone, they went back to work.

"So how'd you get caught?" Joanna asked. "Wasn't no witnesses, right?"

Darryl grimaced and kicked at a discarded Lotto ticket lying near his feet. "See, the guy from the gas station called the police and they charged us with a armed robbery." He shrugged. "But the judge gave us probation, so it was all right."

Joanna stood up. "That was the message," she said.

"What?"

"You're supposed to go in see your probation officer."

Darryl swore and let his head droop between his knees. "I already seen my P.O."

"Well, you got another one, I guess. They say you supposed to report to this one like once a week."

She showed him a piece of paper with his probation officer's name on it. He asked her to read it. "Mr. Bomb," she said.

He looked glum. "That's fucked up," he told her.

"That's what happens when you do shit, Darryl. You got to pay the price."

4

Just as I'm getting into the paperwork, the phone on my desk rings.

"Sending a new client to see you," Roger the guard says.

Most P.O.s like to go out to the waiting room to meet clients; I think it's easier just to send them straight back here. This time, though, I get a strong premonition that Darryl King is on the way. The headache I've been trying to ignore all morning begins to slam away at the base of my skull. I remember what Tommy Markham said about Darryl snatching things from his desk, so I clear off all my papers, remove my glasses, and turn in my chair to face the doorway.

Richard Silver walks right in without knocking.

"It's like a zoo, your waiting room," he says, like he's already in the middle of a conversation. "Some black guy just came up to me with his eyes rolling back into his head and asked if I could spare any change."

"What'd you say?"

"I told him to shine my shoes."

"You got kind of a mean mouth for an old civil rights guy," I tell him, knocking dust balls off my desk.

He exhales and looks impatient. "I'm not a racist if that's what you're trying to suggest," he says, fixing the knot of his yellow Hermès tie. "This is my city too, and I don't like getting hit up for change every goddamn time I leave the house."

The first thing I notice about Richard Silver is that he's a lot bigger than he looked on TV. The image I'd always had of him was as a skinny guy with his tie loosened and a jacket slung over his shoulder, cooling down the streets over the long, hot summers. It isn't just that he's gotten a bit of a paunch since then. He has massive forearms like a wrestler's beneath his tailored suit.

"Since you mention it, perhaps my language was inappropriate with the young man," he says. "Shall I go out there and apologize?"

I can't tell if he's being sarcastic. The small birthmark above his right eyebrow makes it look like the brow is perpetually raised in skepticism. A little unnerving, but probably very effective in negotiations across a conference table.

"Why don't you have a seat?" I ask.

He gets a faraway, annoyed look, like a fly is buzzing in his ear. "This gonna take long? I got other appointments."

"Tell me about it," I say, pointing to the empty chair.

Silver walks around the chair twice, surveying it as though he's considering buying it. Then he stops and glances back at me with his head cocked and a half smile. Very, very slowly he begins to lower himself into the chair. Finally sitting down, but only on his own terms.

"So what do you want from me?" he asks brusquely.

Beautiful. For six weeks, I've been writing letters and leaving messages asking him just to keep his appointment with me. Almost anybody else would get hauled back in front of the judge for acting this way. Instead, he's sitting here like he's on the shoeshine throne and I'm on the footstool.

"Keep your shirt on," I tell him as I look for the papers I put under my desk when I thought Darryl King was coming.

I grew up thinking Richard Silver was a hero. As a city councilman in the 1960s, he was known in the city's poorest communities as "the Enabler." If the community needed garbage trucks or youth programs, he enabled them. I remember my fourth-grade social studies teacher telling us that he prevented the city from burning down in the riots and that we all owed him a debt.

But he changed. First he withdrew his support for a controversial housing project that would've brought low-income people into a middle-class part of Brooklyn. There was a term in Congress and then he left government for a brief whirl through the nightclub business in the late seventies. He wound up opening a law practice, where his main clients were corporations and developers looking for big city contracts. The press celebrated his million-dollar deals and he became a fixture at society dinner parties. Then he suddenly fell from grace. Convicted of a crime so surprising and tawdry that people who'd once clamored to sit next to him denied having ever laid eyes on him. His friend and partner in the scheme, Jimmy Rose, once a great political reformer himself, died of cancer a short time later.

So now I figure I ought to treat Silver the way I'd treat any other client in off the street. I get out my worksheet and ask for a birth date and current address. Silver hesitates when I get to the marital status question. "You better put that I'm still married, okay?"

On a first visit I wouldn't give another client a hard time on that, so I let it go. "What do you do for a living now?" I ask.

"I'm a consultant."

"What does that mean?"

"I consult," he says, loosening his tie. "Y'know. People come to me with ideas. I say, 'This is great' or 'Hey, this stinks.'"

"They pay you a lot of money for this?"

"Well, what do you call a lot of money?" he says, giving me the full eyebrow effect.

He's almost daring me to get into a fight with him. I start squeezing the blob of Silly Putty I keep in the pocket of my windbreaker for just such occasions.

"So who consults you?" I ask.

"Private companies." He gives the picture of the beach landscape a searching look, like his client list is on it.

Before he can explain, I get distracted by some whispering out in the hall. A couple of the probation officers from next door, probably, with their ears to the wall. It figures everyone in the office would get excited about a big deal like him coming in. It's like the first Cadillac rolling into a poor neighborhood.

I go over to the wall and bang on it. "Beat it!" I yell. "Don't you have work?"

"Why don't you sell tickets while you're at it?" Silver says with a smile as they scurry away.

I pick up my pen and papers. "What was I saying?"

"Present employment, stuff like that," Silver reminds me, peeking at his gold Rolex.

"I'll get back to that," I say, holding the pen's cap in my mouth while I write Silver's name on top of a sheet of paper. "Part of your sentence is two thousand hours community service..."

"Yeah, well, we'll see about that."

I check a document on my desk. "My concern," I say, "is that you perform that community service and you do not associate with individuals who were involved in your original offense."

He gets a dark, brooding expression. "Jimmy Rose has been dead a year. What do you want me to do? Raise him from the grave so I can ignore him?"

"I'm just doing my job," I say sharply. "Maybe if you'd returned my phone calls or letters, we wouldn't have to go through all this and I wouldn't be looking at a potential violation."

He doesn't say anything for a long time. He just stares at me. There's something strong and a little scary in his gaze. Like he's done some truly merciless things in his life and hasn't wasted a lot of time worrying about them. I can't afford to look away. It's like an encounter with a wild animal: If you let him see your fear, you're dead. A half minute crawls by.

"You were a lawyer," I say evenly. "You know how it works. If you don't want to cooperate, I have to go back to the judge and tell him you're violating the terms of your probation and he should consider giving you a stiffer sentence."

Silver looks like he's about to start laughing. "Oh that is such bullshit," he says. "Whaddya think? They're gonna send me to jail because I didn't talk to you?"

"Maybe not, but I can run you up some legal bills trying."

"Yeah, yeah, yeah." Silver leans forward in his chair so he's right in my face. He has creases and marks I didn't notice from a few feet away. A deep scar runs from the edge of his chin to the top of his throat. It's as if his face has kept a record of all things he managed to keep out of his written file.

In what first seems like a fatherly gesture, he reaches over and puts his hand on my arm. Then his fingers start to dig into the tendons just above my elbow, and the pain makes me wince.

"All right, you wanna play hardball," he says in a surly voice. "Fine. I been out of government a while, but I still know people. And they know people you work for. So I'd just watch it."

I peel his fingers off my arm and give him a long hard look. "Oh yeah?" I say. "Go ahead. Your friends can do whatever they want. It doesn't matter. I'm already a probation officer. I can't go any lower than that."

A long silence passes. Silver gives me a wary look, like he's seeing me for the first time. The current in the air has subtly changed direction. Both of us move our chairs back a little.

"What the hell is that?" he says suddenly.

"What?"

"That." He points to the blackboard, where the man I drew for Ricky is still sucking on his turnstile.

"It's a visual aid," I say sheepishly.

"A visual aid? It looks like homosexual pornography."

"Well, that's because you don't know what I'm doing here."

"Oh okay . . . What are you doing here?" he says like a card shark looking for an angle.

"Come on. I'm not gonna play games."

"Who's playing games? I'm interested." His manner has changed in the last few seconds. He's smiling now and sounding solicitous. "You're asking me a lot of questions about my personal life. Aren't I entitled to know something?"

He cuts me off before I can protest. "You embarrassed?"

"No, I'm not embarrassed," I say, pushing my fingers into the Silly Putty.

"So what kind of accent is that, anyway? You from Astoria or something?"

I give the ceiling a thoughtful look, but I can't think of a reason not to answer. "Flushing," I mutter. Most people can't even tell I'm from Queens.

"I'm from East Elmhurst myself," Silver tells me. "What street did you grow up on?"

"Blossom Avenue."

There's something a little disarming about the way he's looking at me. "Flushing High School?" he asks.

"Yeah, that's right," I say, putting up my hand to redirect the flow of conversation.

"We used to play you in football. It was a good team."

"Yeah, I guess..."

"You go home much?"

"Sometimes," I say, trying to get back on track. "Anyway..."

"Your name's Baum, right?" he says, closing one eye in concentration. "I knew a guy named Baum once. Maybe he's related to you. What does your dad do?"

My fingers begin molding the Silly Putty into the shape of brass knuckles. "Never mind," I say quietly.

Silver's eyes widen a little. "What're you so touchy about? Something the matter with your dad?"

That's the thing about a guy like Silver. He just works on you until he finds your sore spot. "Nothing's the matter with my dad." I light a cigarette. "We're talking about you anyway."

"Of course," Silver says, nodding seriously. "Community

service. Is he in jail or something, your father?"

I blow a gust of smoke out of the side of my mouth. "Cut it out," I tell him.

"Okay. I just like to know who I'm dealing with, that's all." He leans his head back and smiles slightly, obviously filing away the information for another day. "You know who you remind me of?" he says, turning to look at the small Dylan poster on my wall. "Some of the young guys we used to have doing the community action programs in the sixties. Good people. Did terrific work."

"Is that so?" I say, starting to take notes. While I write down something about what a manipulative prick Silver is, I think about how it would've been nice to know more about that era.

"Yeah," he says, crossing his legs. "Yeah, those were great programs. The antipoverty councils, the rehabilitation centers. A lot of young guys just like you running them..."

"Yeah?"

"Sure... too bad we had to cut all their funding and kick them all out on the street..." He grins and rocks back in his chair. A nice shot, I have to admit. Just his little reminder that he once held the strings over guys like me.

"Well, Richard, we've come a long way since then," I say, putting my glasses back on. "So why don't I just go over the conditions of your probation with you once before you go?"

5

"Awwwwwww, get busy! Get busy! Get busy! Get busy!"

That fucking song again. All summer long it'd been driving Detective Sergeant Bob McCullough nuts. Everywhere he went he heard it. In the tenement stairwells, the school courtyards, and outside, on the street corners. You couldn't get away from it. Not even here, in the detective bureau of the 25th Precinct. Some yo-yo turned on the radio and there it was again. The ceaseless mechanical hip-hop beat, the screeching sound like faulty windshield wipers in the background, and the frantic voice shouting over and over again: "Get busy! Get busy! Get busy!"

Now he was never going to get any work done. He sat with his two meaty arms suspended over the small old manual typewriter, like he was about to give it a good beating. But the noise kept getting between him and the keyboard. File cabinets getting banged around. A sound like an elephant stampede coming up the stairs. Some black kid, handcuffed to a chair, bitching that he hadn't eaten in eight hours. Across the room, some black lady telling two uninterested detectives how her son got mugged. Another cop yelling at a real estate broker on the phone. And a car alarm going off in the parking lot downstairs.

Detective Sergeant McCullough closed his eyes and tried to shut it all out. He still pictured himself as a trim young greyhound leaping across rooftops to chase criminals. But in some obscure way he sensed that he was turning into one of those jowly older guys you always saw huffing and puffing up a stairway. All of a sudden he was forty. For years he'd been looking over his shoulder, expecting to see somebody patting him on the back for all his good work. But his last promotion was a couple of years ago and that transfer to the homicide task force looked like it was never going to come through now. No one was going to notice him unless he made the extra effort. Even his looks were starting to fade a little. There was getting to be more gray than blond in his hair and for the first time in his life he was having to comb it carefully to look presentable. His wife told him he was too old to get away with looking like he'd just rolled out of bed. The next thing you knew she'd be talking crazy about taking the kids and moving in with her mother again.

He glanced up at the clock. Almost eleven o'clock and he still hadn't heard back from the guy at *The New York Times*'s op-ed page. He'd sent them three of his best pieces the week before, "Police Brutality: A Political Football," "Let's Go Auto: In Defense of Police Carrying Automatic Weapons," and "'Have a Nice Day, Officer': On Better Community Relations."

He fixed his holster strap and pounded the typewriter space bar. Writing was like getting sick, he thought sometimes. First he'd get infected by the idea. Then he'd go around for days, thinking about and talking about nothing else. It'd just get worse and worse, until he tried to sweat the sickness out into fifteen hundred words, double-spaced on six sheets of paper. But he'd only feel better once he got one of these fucking things published. It was just a matter of time, he told himself.

The two detectives across the room started telling the black lady how much paperwork her case would generate and how little chance there was of catching her son's mugger. The cop yelling at the real estate broker on the phone started kicking

blue paint chips off the wall. And the song on the radio kept
going, "Get busy! Get busy!" like it was telling McCullough
to work harder.

What more could he do? Everyone knew these pieces he
wrote were good. Even his wife. What she never understood
was why it was so important to get his name in the paper. But
then she didn't know what it was like to sit at a press conference and watch the Chief of Detectives, or the borough commander, or some other fat fuck get up and take credit for an
investigation you'd devoted six months of your life to, like the
rooftop sniper at the Polo Grounds houses or the Schomberg
rapist. And she didn't know what it was like to get laid off
during the fiscal crisis and realize you couldn't depend on the
department to take care of you. And worst of all, she didn't
know what it was like to grow up in a family where everyone
made detective, including your baby sister, and you had to
practically get a fucking movie made about your life before
they thought you were anybody special.

The "Get Busy" song finally ended and the car alarm downstairs stopped yowling. McCullough looked at the black push-
button phone on his desk and wished it would just ring. Why
couldn't those people at the *Times* give him what he wanted?
What he needed. To be recognized. To be reckoned with. The
desire was like a gnawing in his heart. It'd mean so little to
them and so much to him.

Across the room the two detectives had finally convinced
the black lady it wasn't worth her while to have them file a
report about her son's mugging. After she left the room, they
whooped loudly and gave each other a high-five.

McCullough gingerly rolled a fresh piece of paper into the
typewriter. He'd have to try to write another piece, he thought
sadly. He glanced around the room, looking for inspiration.

The cop who'd been talking to the real estate broker
slammed the phone down and began cursing. He got a beer
out of the refrigerator and threw it against the wall. The car
alarm downstairs went off again. Another song came on the

radio, even more annoying than "Get Busy." This one was called "Gettin' Paid."

McCullough put his hands up to his head and started rubbing his temples. All this racket going on, how was a man supposed to stand out?

6

In the ninety seconds between appointments, I cross the hall and stick my head into Cathy Brody's cubicle. "You hear somebody making noise outside my room before?" I ask in a dead-pan voice.

Cathy, who has a long pinched face and bony white knuckles, is always scolding me like a schoolmarm for acting too friendly with my clients. I've heard that outside of work she's in a sadomasochistic relationship. When you run into her at parties, she always seems bored and remote. Like you'd have to let her hit you with a desk lamp before she'd be interested in what you had to say.

But now she starts getting all flustered. "No, I didn't hear anybody outside your office," she says, trying to keep her head-band and glasses perched on top of her head. "What happened?"

Of course I know she was one of the ones trying to listen in on my conversation with Richard Silver. "I don't know," I say. "Somebody was trying to spy on me. Maybe it's one of those union things."

"Why, that's terrible," she says.

"I know I can rely on you to kick their ass if you see them."

"You certainly can," Cathy says with a proud, prim look.

When I go back to my own cubicle, I discover my glasses are gone from my desk. One of my clients must've stolen them. Which confuses me more than it pisses me off. Who wants a pair of used prescription glasses? I try to get accustomed to squinting.

The day goes on. Eleven more regular clients come and go, including a pedophile from Port Authority, a former used car salesman, and a street peddler from Senegal who got in a fight with an American cab driver. It's only 11:15.

Still no sign of Darryl King, though. I see five more people and then step out into the hall to clear my head. As I stand there, smoking a cigarette and listening to the other P.O.s talking to their clients, I think: If this job were a cartoon, it would be a hundred men sitting around with tiny hammers trying to break up huge rocks.

My 11:30 appointment is a homeless guy who calls himself Freddie Brooks or James Stewart, depending on the day he's arrested. By his own admission, Freddie (the name I prefer) has a "very chronic substance abuse problem." He's whippet-thin and his head droops like a rag doll's. He wears a dirty red bandana over his scalp and his eyelids look swollen. He has been arrested almost continuously for ten years on robbery, assault, and disorderly conduct charges, but he's still on probation.

"You know, Freddie, we're just going to recommend they send you to jail next time," I say, balancing his file on my knees.

"I think that's a good idea," Freddie says in a sad, sluggish voice as he sinks down in the chair. "I been to all the clinics for the cocaine and the heroin. But I ain't rehabilitated."

"I thought things were going well in the last drug program you were in." I scratch my head with the bottom of my pen. "You told me it was a good program. Why didn't you stay with it?"

"I drank."

"You gotta do something about this substance abuse. I'm worried about you, Freddie."

"I know." Saliva bubbles gather in the corner of his mouth.

I glance down at his file. "Why didn't you show up at your last court date?"

"I was in the hospital." Freddie closes his heavy lids as if for the last time. The records say he's thirty-three, but he has the face and body of a man in his sixties. His blue-black skin seems to be peeling off in places, leaving rusty patches underneath. I smell something a little funny and hope he hasn't wet himself.

"Well, then how did you manage to get arrested again the very next day?" I ask loudly enough to wake him.

"See, I was standing in front of a liquor store on Pitkin Avenue, around Stone..."

I lean back in my chair and try to get a mental picture of the neighborhood. East New York. I was there maybe once. It reminded me of Dickens's descriptions of nineteenth-century south London. "That's like a really squalid place," I hear myself say.

"Yeah, and it's serious too," Freddie says with an unexpected burst of energy. "I was standing in front of a liquor store with my girl and one of her kids knocked over the sign for the shoe salesman next door. So he comes out and hits my girl in the head with a hammer. So we all jumped in there on him and he bit my finger..."

I hold up my hand like a stop sign. "Freddie, all this sounds a little strange. Why did the guy get so upset about them knocking over a sign?"

Freddie does not have much of an answer for that, or anything else. His days are dissolving into a haze of bad drugs and incoherent crimes. His nights are divided between a shelter on the Lower East Side and the floor of Penn Station. There's no point in using the blackboard or trying to draw up a schedule for him. He's only reliable now in keeping his appointments with me, probably because he knows I care about him as much as anybody else in his life does. Which isn't saying a lot, but we do have a kind of loyalty to each other.

"Freddie," I say, shaking my head, "you're committing suicide right in front of my face."

"That's correct," Freddie says with a certain wasted eloquence. "And I know you don't condone that."

The city doesn't care whether Freddie is salvageable or not. It just doesn't want him taking up valuable cell space in a prison with more deserving people waiting. I try to look out for Freddie, but I refuse to kid myself about what I can do for him.

"The only assurance that he will not end up in jail is the fact that he will probably die soon," I write in my report.

I spend the next few minutes trying to reduce the paper mountain on my desk. I hit Andy Benjamin's file and decide it's time to call him up and hassle him. He answers on the sixth ring.

"Andy," I say. "You get a job yet?"

For the next few seconds I hear what sounds like a dog panting. "No," Andy says a little breathlessly.

"Why the hell not?"

"I'm jerkin' off." More panting. He really is jerking off.

"If you don't knock it off and find a job soon, I'm gonna come over to your house myself," I say impatiently.

He gasps a little. "And do what?" he asks.

"I'm gonna tell your mother what you're doing."

As his gasp turns into a cry of pleasure, I hang up on him.

I use the break to run downstairs and get a new pack of Marlboros, a bag of potato chips, and a Budweiser from the deli around the corner on Worth Street. My teeth ache from chewing on pen caps all morning and my back is in knots again.

When I get back to the office, just after 12:30, my supervisor Emma Lang is waiting. She's a tall, handsome black woman in her mid-thirties, wearing shiny high heels, a long navy blue skirt, and a blazer with shoulders as thick as a linebacker's. She always seems to be frowning, but I've never figured out if that's because she likes me less than I like her or if she's just generally embittered.

The latter is more likely since she's worked at the department seven years longer than me, and she makes less than thirty thousand dollars a year.

She looks around the cubicle and wrinkles her nose. "Two more weeks and then no more smoking in here," she says.

"I know."

She stares intently at my legs like she's about to complain about my wearing jeans again. "There's probably going to be some personnel changes in the next month," she says abruptly.

"Because of the turnover?" I put down the bag with the beer in it and a little damp spot appears on its outside. My stomach flutters. I'd applied for a supervisor's post at the Brooklyn juvenile program weeks before. Maybe she's going to tell me if I got the job.

"Eight people gone and summer's just starting." She leans against the doorframe and studies her fingernails for a second.

I'm not surprised. A lot of people burn out early at probation. You can only stand by and watch so many disasters waiting to happen. The economics of it are enough to drive most people out. Cops, lawyers, and psychiatrists all make a lot more money and get better benefits, though probation officers sometimes do all three jobs.

"You're probably going to be transferred over to the field service unit soon," Ms. Lang says, sounding more like she's giving an order than making a prediction.

My heart sinks. "What about that juvenile supervisor's post?"

"I forgot you applied for that too. Cathy Brody got it. She does have seniority."

I nod patiently, even though I feel like punching something. "But why am I getting field service?" I wasn't aware of any vacancies in the unit, which picks up clients who've violated their probation in some way.

"One of the field guys went over to parole in February and they're still looking for somebody to replace him," she says. "I remember you telling me you were interested in that job before, so I put your name in."

A chill creeps up between my shoulder blades and I reach for the Silly Putty again. I'd have a cigarette if she wasn't standing here now.

"I also put in your name because I think you've done a very good job here," she says.

"I have?"

"Your clients have the lowest recidivism rate in the borough office."

"Luck of the draw." I shrug.

"No, you are my best guy here," she says flatly, like she's looking up a boring fact in the encyclopedia. "I've monitored your cases and read the reports. I told the administration that you can be tough, and you know how to tread lightly, like with this Charlie Simms and Maria Sanchez. You have the gift for connecting."

"Thanks." I clear my throat loudly and blow ashes from my ashtray onto my knees. "I wasn't aware you liked me."

"I don't," she says. "You're a white boy from Queens. Can't like you. Don't like what you are. Nothing you can do about that, nothing I can do about that." Her voice drops into a deep Southern register. "You know what I'm saying. But I am recommending you."

Ms. Lang is not the type to invite you into her office for a heart-to-heart. Like a lot of the black people I know in positions of authority, she's constantly rigid with tension, like she's expecting somebody above her to use any excuse to kick her out. She came from a poor Alabama family and put herself through Columbia's graduate program in social work. She got rid of her drawl and her doubts along the way. But when she went into the city government, she hit a brick wall, mainly because she's black and a woman. Now she lives alone, has hardly any friends, and keeps her part of the bureaucracy running smoothly. Liked by many, loved by few, and only hated by the hard-core bigots in the office.

"I can ask for another six hundred dollars or so for you when you go into the field," she says.

I quickly calculate that with an extra twelve dollars a week I can just about afford to double the number of cigarettes I smoke. "That's fine," I tell her. "But what's going to happen to my caseload?"

"You can hold on to the half who really need you." She adjusts a flap on one of her blazer's pockets. "You're not going out into the field full-time right away. I'd like you to really keep an eye on this Darryl King. We just got a message that he'll be coming in tomorrow instead of today."

"Okay."

"Tommy Markham is still upset from talking to him a couple of weeks ago," she says, "so when King comes in, you might want to lean on him a little. Let him know that he's expected to be a good boy here. Break him in a little bit for whoever gets him after you."

"All right," I say.

But what I'm really thinking is that it'd score me some points if I could turn this guy around myself. Especially since everybody else assumes this is a hopeless case.

There's a rapping sound and then a thirtyish white man in a dark business suit, with thinning pale hair and a raw sunburn appears in the doorway. I recognize him from the hallways outside the administrative offices. Ms. Lang introduces him as Deputy Commissioner Kenneth Dawson. For some reason he reminds me of the cartoon character Deputy Dawg and I have to suppress a smile.

"How do you do?" says Dawson, extending a weak, sweaty hand. "We're so glad to hear you've volunteered for the field unit."

"Well..." I'm about to correct him, but then again, why bother? This is all confusing enough already. I've heard Dawson's name in connection with the department's annual budget report. I didn't know he ever spoke to regular P.O.s like me.

"You're getting a very special opportunity," he says.

"I'm looking forward to it," I answer, for lack of any other inspiration.

"Wonderful." Dawson sways back on the heels of his wing tips and laughs through his nose. "By the way," he says, "when you go out into the field, you know you're going to be required to carry a sidearm."

"Oh yeah?"

"Guns don't scare you, do they?"

"Of course not." I notice that the brown bag containing my beer has turned soggy and is threatening to dissolve while the two of them are standing here. With a trembling hand, I reach for what's left of my third cup of coffee this morning.

All three of us smile awkwardly at each other and then Dawson congratulates me once more on the new assignment. "I'm glad you're going to be part of the magic we do here," he says. It takes me a second to remember where I've seen a phrase like that recently. "Probation—Be Part of the Magic." It's that idiotic new slogan on the stickers around the offices downstairs. Dawson, clearly the man who thought of it, smiles tightly and departs.

Emma Lang lingers in the doorway a moment. She rolls her eyes in Dawson's direction, tilts back her chin, and mouths, "Okay?" She turns to leave, but then sticks her head back in.

"Oh, one more thing," she says. "I got a phone call from that Richard Silver's lawyer a half hour ago."

"Yeah, what did he want?"

"He says you've been harassing his client..."

My beer looks like it's just about sweated its way through the brown paper bag on my desk. The outline of the Budweiser can is unmistakable now. I feel my face burning as she gives me a stern look.

"Keep up the good work," Ms. Lang says.

7

Bobby "House" Kirk, high on crack again, was kicking out the windows and terrorizing the other passengers on the downtown number three train.

"Stop that foolishness and come over here," Darryl King said to him. "I wanna have a talk with you all."

The lights went on and off as a crazy old man with matted hair danced around with his dick hanging out of his pants and the little Puerto Rican guy sitting by the door buried his face in El Diario. "Get Busy" played on a giant radio. Bobby "House" Kirk, who was seventeen, enormous, and psychotic, stood facing Darryl with his back against a metal pole. He had an H carved in his hair, and a gold ring with four finger holes spelled his nickname across his knuckles. A third boy named Aaron Williams, who was skinny and fourteen, with a harelip and a flattop, stuck his head in between them. "Yo, whass up?"

Darryl steadied himself and thought about what he was supposed to say now. There must've been a hundred nights just like this. With the three of them ricocheting back and forth under the city like unguided missiles.

He put his hand through an overhead strap, feeling the train's rumbling power.

The other people in the car were giving him that scared look again. The kind that made him feel all calm inside. A lady with lacquered-up hair clutched her handbag and turned away from him. It would be so easy just to take it right off her, right now.

But his sister said he couldn't do it like that anymore. He had to stop and think about things. Use his mentality. Get into the science of the situation. Start using words like "dividend" instead of "give it up."

The hardest part was telling Bobby and Aaron. "Things's be different now on," he began. "We don't be robbin' nobody for nothin' now. Understand what I'm saying? So don't go shoot nobody over a pair of sneakers no more, okay?"

Bobby was about to point out that it was actually Darryl who'd nearly beaten a boy to death over a pair of Nikes last year, but he got cut off. "We gotta have purpose when we go out now," Darryl said, struggling to remember Joanna's exact words. "We businessmen. Understand. We be doing business."

"Yo, Dooky," Bobby Kirk said. "I don't wanna sell no five-dollar vials for your sister. That shit's small-time."

"Yo, House," Darryl King said irritably. "Don't call me Dooky no more. I'm eighteen, man."

The train grunted to a halt at the 125th Street station and a Spanish-looking guy with a black beard and what looked like a Rolex stumbled on, followed by a well-dressed black woman with a tan pocketbook. "Watch the closing doors," the conductor said.

"Let's go rob," Aaron started whispering to Bobby and Darryl. "Let's go get paid right now."

He began dancing around like the music was getting him in the mood to do crimes.

Darryl grabbed him roughly by the shoulder. "Don't you fuckin' listen, man? We talkin' about the future. You gotta build that shit up. Then one day we don't be riding no subway. We get a car like Pops Osborn."

Aaron's eyes filled with awe. "Cutlass Supreme," he said.

" 'S right," Darryl told him. "So don't be fuckin' around."

Bobby Kirk folded his arms across his chest and looked aloof. "I still don't wanna work for your sister," he told Darryl.

"Then you just be ignorant, Bobby. You too foolish to understand the economics of the situation. I ain't even gonna go see you in jail 'cos I'm gonna be busy flying all around the world."

Bobby turned away from Darryl and started walking to the next car. "You just soft 'cos you on probation now," he said over his shoulder. "You afraida your probation officer. That's all."

"I ain't even met the guy." Darryl followed him with Aaron. "Oh no?"

"No. I'm gonna go in tomorrow and see him."

"Yeah." Bobby smiled and began wiping his face with a Wash'n Dri. "You scared."

Bobby's words started a little fire in his mind. As big as Bobby was, Darryl thought about what it'd be like to kill him right here, right now. Or any of the other suckers sitting nearby. Just to do somebody right now. But his sister's voice came back to him, telling him to chill and consider the situation.

"I ain't got no worries with my P.O.," Darryl said coolly. "He's gonna be scared a me."

"How do you know?"

"I just know."

"Why?" Bobby asked. "What you gonna do?"

"You'll see," Darryl said firmly, like he had it all figured out. "I took care of that cop before. Right?"

The three of them stopped talking all of a sudden. They were standing on the small steel ledges between the cars now. Black space roared all around them. The amphetamized rush of the train rattled the chains and shook them from the knees on up, like a good drug. Nervous faces in the next car watched them through the window in the door.

"Yo, D!" Aaron shouted, jiggling and pulling on his red-and-white Troop shirt.

"What the fuck is it?" Darryl frowned.

"Can we just rob one for old times?"

Darryl snorted and pulled open the door to the front car. Without even thinking about it, he walked in like he owned the place. Shoulders hunched, knees slightly bent, weight up on the balls of his feet. The same charge going between him and the people in the seats. The way they avoided his eyes. Old ladies, white students, punks his own age he wouldn't have thought twice about taking off a couple of weeks ago. And by the empty conductor's booth, sitting with his girlfriend, that Spanish-looking guy who seemed to be wearing a Rolex. "Yeah, all right," he said finally. "One more. Just wait till Times Square."

He went to the head of the car where the guy was and started staring out the front window. The green and red track lights ahead were like stars floating in outer space. He half closed his eyes and imagined he was plunging deeper and deeper toward some distant point without ever really getting there.

8

Standing on the checkout line, I count the items my father just put in the shopping cart.

Seven green-and-red cans of Del Monte sliced peaches. A half dozen cans of Bumblebee tuna in water. Four quart bottles of Mott's apple juice. Eleven jars of Planters peanuts. Five boxes of Band-Aids. Two cartons of Pall Malls.

"What're you doing, having a party?" I ask. I didn't know he had that many friends left.

"Never mind," the old man says with a harsh Eastern European accent that makes the Korean girl at the cash register look up.

I decide to wait a while before I ask him again why he wants all this food. My father is getting more and more eccentric with the passing years, and I ought to try to be as patient with him as I'd be with a client.

When the Korean girl rings up a total of $97.65 for his groceries, he gives her a look of pure loathing.

"You need some cash?" I ask, reaching for my wallet.

"Go away," says my father.

With trembling, liver-spotted hands, he fumbles through the pockets of his blue windbreaker. After a minute, he starts taking out scads of tattered discount coupons clipped from newspapers and magazines. People in the growing line behind us groan loudly. I turn around and smile apologetically.

Fifteen minutes later, my father and I leave the Key Food supermarket on Kissena Boulevard in Flushing and head back to his house. It's half past seven and the sun is just starting to go down.

My father is walking with an exaggerated stoop and a slight limp as we walk down the hill toward Main Street. He has his jacket zipper all the way up, so his stomach pushes out the front of it. His broad rump is bursting through the seams of his gray pants. He's sixty-five, but he looks at least ten years older. His chins dangle before his throat and a small scrub brush of white hair sits on the barren plain of his scalp. His eyelids sag heavily, giving him a look you might take for permanent sadness, if you didn't know him better.

"You got something on your mouth," I tell him.

The old man wipes at it with his jacket sleeve. "What is it?"

"I don't know. It's gone now."

Though his arms are still strong, he seems to be struggling with the one light brown paper bag he's carrying. I take it from him and try to balance it with the four heavy bags of groceries I have in my arms. "You wouldn't consider a cab, would you?" I ask.

"It's just a few blocks," he says. "What are you? Weak?"

I shrug and try to enjoy the rest of the walk.

Here are the streets where I grew up. The rows of identically quaint red brick houses always give me a feeling that's half warm nostalgia and half nausea. Most of the other familiar landmarks are still here. The orange school crossing sign. The temple across the street and the church down the block. McGaskill's Pub on the corner with the woozy neon sign outside. The screech of jets leaving LaGuardia overhead. The smell from the Taystee Bread plant. The way the sky turns to purple and orange at dusk. If you go down a couple of blocks, you can see the giant silver Unisphere on the World's Fair grounds in the distance and just a little bit to the right, the rim of Shea Stadium.

"So you been watching the Mets fall apart this year?" I ask my father.

"What do you want?" the old man says. "They still got that lazy *schvartze* in right field."

"Very nice." I sigh and close my eyes for a moment.

Actually, the neighborhood's changed in a lot of ways, I notice as we continue down Main Street. Every other store on this strip is now owned by either Chinese or Korean immigrants. All the newsstands, produce markets, discount shops, and dry cleaners look the same as they did when I was growing up, except they all have signs with Asian letters out front. The faces on the street are different too. Not just the Chinese and the Koreans, but more blacks, Indians, and Hispanics than I remember from before. Of course, they're getting the same old dirty looks from the same older immigrants like my father, who came to this area to avoid these people in the first place.

"Okay," he says as we turn and make our way down Blossom Avenue. "You can stop with the complaining. We made it home."

Here is the house I couldn't wait to get away from. The chain-link fence around the front yard. The steel gates on all the windows. The blue-and-red stickers on the front door saying the house is protected by security patrols and electronic devices. The old brown rug and the musty, ancient smell in the hallway that I could never quite put a name to. The oppressive stillness of the air. At the end of the hall, the drab, gray light filtering into the kitchen through the raggedy curtains. To the left, in the living room, the rabbit-eared antenna on top of the old Zenith black-and-white television. And the orderly stacks of the *New York Post* and the *Jewish Press* surrounding the green couch as though it were a fortress of conservative opinion under siege.

"Where do you want these, Pops?" I ask. My arms ache from carrying all these groceries.

"Put them down a second," my father says. "If you have to." He's at the other end of the hall already, opening the door to the basement.

I put the bags down by the front door. As I stand up, I notice a thirty-two-ounce Louisville Slugger baseball bat in the umbrella stand. I pick it up and feel its weight in my hands. It's signed by Dave Winfield.

"Hey, Pops," I shout down the hall. "What's this for?"

My father comes toward me slowly as the last rays of the sun stream through the little window in the front door. At first he doesn't seem to grasp my question.

"What's this for?" I ask, slapping the head of the bat into my palm.

"This," says my father, grabbing the handle of the bat with his left hand, "is for them." He points out the window with his right hand.

I look where he's pointing. "It's for the trees?" I say. "You're gonna use a baseball bat to beat up the trees?"

My father doesn't smile. He doesn't seem to have enough lips left for a happy expression anyway. "For the *schvartzes*," he says.

I frown and look away from him. "Come on, Pops, get real," I say, turning on the hall light. My mother's old fixture on the ceiling is so thick and dirty that hardly any light comes through. "You think black people are coming to get you?"

"They're here already." My father looks uncomfortable and moves down the hallway using the bat like a cane. "Didn't you see? From the Bronx I moved you and your mother to get away from them. Now they're in Flushing."

"It's a free country, Pops."

"Hah." My father gives a hacking cough that makes his throat sound like a handball court. "Free for them. Not for me."

"These are middle-class people in this neighborhood. They're not gonna bother you."

"What do you know?" he says sharply.

"You're just being crazy again," I say, prodding one of the grocery bags with my foot. "Anyway, even if they were coming to get you, your setup here is stupid. You've got a baseball bat by the front door. Why couldn't they just grab the bat and go down the hall and beat your brains out while you're sleeping?"

"I got another bat in the bedroom."

"Brilliant." I snort a small laugh as I follow my father down the hall. "I can't talk to you about this. This is nuts."

He stops in the doorway and moves toward me suddenly. "A man does what he does to survive," he says, shaking the bat at me.

I throw up my hands. "Don't gimme that again, please."

"It's true," my father says forcefully.

"You know something?"

The old man ignores me and keeps talking. "Someday, you'll know it's true," he says loudly.

"Hey, you know something..."

"Because one day, you'll do what I had to do..."

"Hey, you know what?" I say, touching his shoulder. "I agree with you. What you're saying makes sense—but only if you're in Auschwitz!"

My father slams the bat against the doorway. "Don't make a joke..."

"I'm not making a joke. You're not in Auschwitz anymore. This is America. Okay? The same rules don't apply."

The argument is always the same and it always leaves me pissed-off and downhearted. It's true that my father has had a hard life, and that at times he had to be ruthless and completely selfish just to stay alive. When I was young, he told me how he almost killed another prisoner over a couple of scraps of bread, and the story has haunted me ever since.

The problem is that my father has applied the exact same logic to life after the camps and he's still paranoid, bitter, and absolutely indifferent to the suffering of the rest of the world. He's ruined his own life and my mother's with his compulsions, and now he's almost done closing himself off.

I'd like to think my own life is the opposite. Even on my worst days at probation, I figure I must be all right since my father disapproves of what I'm doing.

"One day you'll know what I'm talking about," he says

wearily as he props the baseball bat up against the wall and begins shuffling toward the groceries by the front door. "You're just like me, you just don't know it."

"Total bullshit," I say. "I'm not like you. I'm normal."

"Oy," my father says.

"Look, I'm very sorry about what happened to you and to all those other Jews, but I'm not gonna spend my life running scared about something that happened to somebody else forty-five years ago."

My father cries out like he's been stabbed.

"Well, I don't really expect you to go along with that," I tell him. "But I've got my own life. Okay?"

"Yeah, yeah, sure." My father is trying to lift the bags at the other end of the hall. "I got my life too."

"Glad to hear it." I exhale deeply and slap my hands together, ready to move on.

I wish there was another subject I could talk about with him. Cars, sports, women. Just things we could laugh about over a beer the way other fathers and sons do. But then we've never been like other fathers and sons. Sometimes I wonder why I even bother coming by the house at all. My father has driven everyone else away. And he doesn't seem to really appreciate my visits. But I still have a vague, hungry feeling, like I'm expecting to find something I want here.

My throat feels dry. I could use a drink now, but my father probably doesn't have anything in the house, except Mogen David grape wine. Maybe I can pop around the corner to the Irish bar later.

"So you want me to give you a hand with those groceries?" I ask him.

The old man throws back his shoulders and draws up his thick, barbed eyebrows. "You're here, aren't you?"

I lumber down to where my father is and begin picking up the bags. "So you never told me what you got all this for anyway. Are you actually having somebody over?"

"Not like that," he mutters, pushing one of the bags with his foot toward the door to the basement.

"Let me guess," I say as I walk down the hall with the bags, steadying myself against the wall. "When those invading *schvartzes* come through the front door, you want to give them something to nosh on before you clobber them with your Louisville Slugger."

"You're very funny," my father says in a dead voice.

I hoist the bags up and follow the old man down the stairs to the basement. Each step creaks and threatens to snap right out from under me. The hallway smell is here too, though much stronger. There's no light at all. The only reason I don't trip and fall is that I grew up going up and down these steps. When I get to the bottom, I put the bags down and windmill my arms in relief.

My father finally turns on the light. It's a moment before I get my bearings.

I take a good look around and begin to shake my head. What my father has done down here is extraordinary—in fact, it's the most orderly, sustained act of madness of his largely irrational life.

There's a tall stack of Del Monte sliced peaches against one wall. Dozens of saltine cracker boxes are piled against the adjacent wall. In the dim light of one bare yellowish bulb, I can't see all the Bumblebee tuna cans lined up against the boiler, but there are at least one hundred of them. On the other side of the basement, there are rows of Gatorade and Mott's apple juice bottles. It's like he's built himself a kind of fallout shelter in case race war breaks out in Queens.

"Why are you doing this?" I ask him.

"I just have to," my father says. "I just have to."

I try to think of something to say, but no words come to me. A steady drizzle of dust falls from the ceiling and the old pipes make wrenching sounds. I bow my head, turn back to the stairway, and slowly head upstairs toward the faint light.

9

"Let me ask you something," Richard Silver said. "I was sitting in here before and I was looking around—and it's a very nice bathroom, I admit. I paid a lot of money for it. And there's mirrors on the ceiling and there's mirrors on all the walls. Right? There's mirrors everywhere you look. Right?"

Both he and Jessica Riley looked up at their reflections on the ceiling.

"Right," she said.

"So why do I wanna watch myself take a crap?"

"I don't know."

"I don't know either." He seemed genuinely perplexed. "I see myself sitting on the toilet and I think of death."

"Why?"

"Because I look fat sitting on the toilet. I look like Elvis Presley just before he died."

"You're not fat."

"I'm the same age as Elvis Presley."

"No, you're not," Jessica said. "Elvis was forty-two. You're forty-eight."

"I'm forty-nine. Thanks a lot."

"What're you wearing tonight?"

"Green Armani suit, red tie, black shoes I just picked up

at Church's." He looked at himself in the medicine cabinet mirror. "Maybe I don't mean like Elvis Presley. Maybe I mean like a Roman senator about to expire in the baths. You know?" He looked at her. "What're you making that face for?"

"You're thinking about death a lot."

"No, I'm not. I'm thinking about the value of things."

"What?"

"Look at this," he said, taking a gold-backed toothbrush out of the medicine cabinet. "My secretary got this for me the other day as a birthday present from Hammacher Schlemmer."

"Yeah. So?"

"So look at it. Half the bristles are gone already."

"But, Richard," she said with a sigh. "This is a joke. This isn't a real toothbrush. She got you this as a joke."

"Yes, it was a joke, but there's a serious point underneath." She waited three beats before she asked what it was.

"Society is falling apart from the bottom up," he said. "We can't even make a toothbrush with bristles that stay on and people expect us to maintain the infrastructure of the greatest city on earth. It's madness. The fabric that holds society together is tearing."

"You are in a bad mood."

"Yeah, I guess I am." He shrugged. "Get outta here a second, will you. I gotta take a leak."

She stepped outside and let him close the door. She paused at a mirror and pulled down the top of her terry cloth robe to see if her shoulders got tanned. There were faint white stripes where the bikini straps had been. Inside, the sound of his piss hitting the porcelain was like a xylophone solo echoing through the bathroom.

"So how'd things go with that guy downtown today?" she asked.

"That's just what I was talking about."

Jessica stepped back into the bathroom. "What?"

He shook his head. "This kid at probation. I go down there. And it's the bizarro universe, I swear. Twenty years ago I would've had somebody like this guy getting me coffee. Now he's telling me what to do. Like I said, society's coming apart. I gotta get an angle on this guy, though. He's power-mad."

"What does Larry say?"

"Larry says I gotta deal with the guy, otherwise we're gonna have problems." He finished buttoning his shirt and his shoulders heaved in resignation. "Speaking of Larry, he still didn't close that Long Island deal. I'm gonna be an old man before I see any money off it. Jimmy Rose would've never let this thing drag on so long."

"Is that what's been bothering you?" she asked.

"What?"

"That Jimmy isn't around anymore."

He looked hard in the medicine cabinet mirror as though he thought he'd find the answer there. "I don't know," he muttered. "There's just some days . . ."

"Some days what?"

He turned sideways and looked at his stomach in the mirror. "There's just some days I believe life is not what it was." He took a deep breath and let it out slowly.

"You worried about getting old?"

There was a long silence. He loosened the belt of her robe and reached inside. "You know something," Richard Silver said. "If I wasn't making a lot of money and getting laid regular, I sometimes think I'd be a miserable sonovabitch."

10

The sound comes from very far away, moving slowly toward the edge of hearing. A deep, resonant voice describing terrible, nightmarish things. A house on fire. Children with guns. Blacks and whites at each other's throats.

Another cop shot, the radio newscaster says. The mayor announcing a new budget problem. A water main explosion on the East Side. A Brazilian tourist slashed in a Times Square mugging. A real estate magnate's tax evasion trial. A mother of two in the Bronx killed in the cross fire between two drug dealers. Dow-Jones down seventy-five points. A wealthy businessman calling for the death penalty and a tax break. A shooting spree at a midtown disco. A famous fashion designer dead from AIDS. The Mets losing to the Cubs, 5–4.

Another ninety-two-degree day in the city.

Without even opening my eyes, I reach back and slap off the clock radio. Then I just lie there for a few seconds, the heat like a dog's breath coming down on my face.

Every morning you make a choice in life. You can get up and face the world, like most people do. Or, if you're really brave, you can roll over and go back to sleep. I turn on my side. Going out into the world takes no guts really. Because you know no matter what you do or how hard you try, the difference to everybody else is marginal. But to lie in bed, doing nothing. That takes a real man. Like flying without a net. Complete freedom from the dreary realm of responsibility. Or maybe you could end up like my cousin Jerry who sits around the house all day, listening to "I'm Henry VIII, I Am" over and over on the record player.

A long coughing fit forces my eyes open. I look around the apartment and consider whether I could spend a whole day here.

It's hard to believe the rent is going up to $650 a month. What I have is one room, about twenty feet long and twenty feet wide, with a small kitchen off to the side and a bathroom down the hall. Pale blue walls, no air conditioner, and a single light bulb in the middle of the ceiling. My one window looks out on Avenue B and Tompkins Square Park; in the evening I can hear the pit bulls fighting and the skinheads setting off firecrackers. My stereo and speakers are set up near the head of the mattress on the floor so I can blast myself into unconsciousness on bad nights.

Lately I've begun to notice that the floor is a little lopsided, causing everything that falls to roll eastward. Including Barbara Russo's tiny turquoise-colored earring. The earring is still lying under a chair in the corner, where it's been since Barbara slept with me at some point during the Reagan administration. When I discovered it months later, I made a conscious decision to leave it there. Not out of sloppiness or bravado; it's merely a reminder that romance is still possible.

This morning, though, it just depresses the hell out of me, so I figure I'm better off playing it safe and facing the malevolent world outside. Sticking around here is too risky. I roll out of bed, light a cigarette, and take the Sex Pistols record off the turntable. With a rumbling stomach and a hung-over head full of cotton, I put the cap on the half-empty Jack Daniel's bottle and get ready to spend another day straightening out my clients' lives.

* * *

Early in the afternoon I look up to see Jack Pirone, my old training instructor and current union rep, glowering down at me. Big Jack's eyes are darting back and forth, like they've become frightened by the prospect of drowning in his grotesquely fleshy face. His jaw is working furiously, though he doesn't appear to have anything in his mouth.

"Whaddya doing?" Jack says.

"Nothing. Just filling out reports."

"Whaddya doing?!!" Jack says a little louder.

I go back to writing. "I just told you."

"*WHADDYA DOING*?!!!!!!"

I slap my folder down on the desk and give him my undivided attention. "Is something the matter, Jack?"

"What's all this bullshit about you going to field service?"

I start to ask how he knows already, but Jack has spies all over the office and good instincts besides. He eventually figures everything out. He stops chewing and glares at me.

"The membership is not going to be happy, Steven."

"The membership is going to end up feeling whatever you tell them to feel," I say, dropping my pen. "So why don't you just tell me why you're not happy?"

"Precedent," Jack intones with the solemnity of a seminary student. He goes over to my blackboard and writes the word out.

"You're young," he says, "you been here two years, you're not married, you don't know. Your average probation officer makes—what?—twenty-three thousand a year? They're fuckin' fat slobs like me. They wanna sit in front of the tube and eat pasta fazule. They don't wanna run around the streets, looking for some sick fuck who is too busy corn-holing eighty-nine-year-old females to keep an appointment. If your average P.O. wants excitement, he watches *Knots Landing* with the wife, and maybe gets a handjob if she's in the mood."

"So I'm not stopping him."

Jack shakes his head and huffs loudly. "No good, Steven. No good. You're setting a bad precedent for the rest of us.

Office people shouldn't have to risk being in the field. Just because the noble savage asks you to do something, you don't have to jump through hoops..."

"The who?"

"The noble savage—Ms. Lang."

"Ah, knock it off, Jack," I say, frowning. He knows I hate shit like that. "It's not her idea anyway."

"Who then?" Jack asks.

"I think it was this guy Deputy Dawson..."

"He's a fuckin' budget manager! What the fuck does he know? I gotta ask around about this." Jack stops and chews his nails pensively.

"That's all I know."

"So what're you saying, you sold us out?" Jack grabs one of the empty wooden chairs, spins it around, and sits on it backward. Its legs give a sinister creak. "You can't do this. They're not giving us full insurance benefits for the field."

"I get something," I say a little uncertainly. "Don't I?"

"You should get the same benefits as if you were a cop," Jack says, starting to slip into one of his standard union speeches. "The field job is just as dangerous. More, in fact. Because all you're dealing with is convicted felons. You should get full coverage—injury, auto collision, death. The whole she-bang. God forbid one of these bastards should put a bullet in your neck, you should be taken care of. Not just half the cost."

"I'm sure the union will get it straightened out," I say, glancing over at my desk, where paperwork is beckoning to me. "You seem to be on top of everything else."

Jack slowly turns his head to the right and snaps it back. It looks like an isometric exercise for people too fat to consider sit-ups. "How much are they paying you for this move?" he asks.

"None of your business."

"How much are they paying you?!!"

"Never mind."

"*HOWMUCHARETHEYPAYINGYOU?!!!!!*" Jack bellows.

"Not that much. Enough to cover my union dues if they go up." Jack probably knows already. He's just asking to intimidate me.

"Then why are you doing this foolish thing, my boy?" His loud honk of a voice drops to an avuncular timbre. "You know, this field unit is just another fuckin' publicity ploy, so that people won't catch on how fucked-up this agency really is. Probation is a joke. Why are you helping them perpetuate this bullshit?"

"I don't know," I say, cracking my knuckles. "I'm a little bored here. I want a chance to go out and do something. I mean, I talk to a lot of people here, but I don't know if it does any good. Maybe it'd be good to see some action. You were the one who told me that the only time the public is even aware of probation officers is when a client goes out and kills somebody. And then it looks like we blew it."

"Let me tell you something," Jack says. He casts his eyes around the cubicle. "But first gimme a cigarette."

I take a brand-new pack of Marlboros out of my pocket, unwrap it, and offer it to Jack. Before he takes one, he fishes the empty pack I'd thrown away out of the garbage can.

"You see this?" he says, holding up the pack. "You should keep this with you. That way, the next time some bum asks you for a smoke, you can show him the empty pack and say you haven't got any more and keep the fresh pack for yourself."

"What's your point, Jack?"

Jack lights the cigarette, inhales deeply, and blows out a roomful of smoke. "Look, you're a nice kid," he begins. "Everybody likes you and you've got a very good reputation here already. You're obviously very bright and you mean well. I don't deny you any of that."

"But?"

"But if you go out on the street," Jack says slowly, "they are gonna fuckin' eat you alive."

I don't say anything.

"And another thing while I'm at it," Jack says, leaning

forward against the top of the chair. "I heard you talking to your clients the other day. 'I'm gonna violate you personally . . . I'm gonna do this. I'm gonna do that.' Steven! Don't make it so personal. You shouldn't tell clients you're the one who's gonna send them back to jail and all that shit. Just tell 'em you're only doing your job. Some of these guys are kind of sensitive, you know, and you might just get your fuckin' head blown off." The chair legs groan loudly again under Jack's weight.

I start filling out my reports. "We'll see," I say.

"You oughta be a lawyer. That's what you should do." Jack grunts as he begins to get up. There's a sudden squeak and a loud crash on the floor.

"Ah, fuck you, Jack," I say. "Now I gotta get a new chair."

The steady stream of clients keeps up until 3:30, when Maria Sanchez walks in. I call the reception desk and tell Roger, the guard, not to send anyone else back until I'm done with her.

Maria is a seventeen-year-old Puerto Rican girl living with her mother, two sisters, three brothers, uncle, aunt, and five cousins in a tenement on East 106th Street. She's a smart girl and the only person in her family who speaks good English. She gets along with people in the neighborhood and did well in school before she got in trouble. She's a little heavy, but she has a beautiful face with a cloud-parting smile.

She's wearing a short denim skirt without stockings, gold hoop earrings, and a little less makeup than usual. I try to avoid looking into her wide brown eyes for too long. Otherwise, I know I'll be lost.

"So did you go to that word-processing job the counselor sent you to?" I ask as she sits down and crosses her legs. I can't help noticing the way her skirt rides up a little.

"Yes," Maria says with a mild accent and a smile. "It seems like a nice place. Thank you for helping me set that up."

"How much are they paying you?"

"Almost six dollars an hour."

"And how fast can you type?"

"Only about fifty-five words a minute." She looks down at the floor as though she feels ashamed.

"Only?" I say. "What's the name of the place you're working?"

She says the name of a prominent textbook publisher. I tell her that she should ask for at least seven dollars an hour.

"Please don't make me do that, Mr. Baum," she says in a slightly panicky tone. "I need this job. They won't hire me if I ask for that kind of money."

"If you can type fifty-five words a minute, that publisher can certainly pay you the seven."

"No, but they won't..."

"They will," I insist. "Listen, if they don't hire you because you ask for more money, then I will take personal responsibility for finding you another job within a week that pays at least six dollars an hour. Okay?"

"Okay..."

"You still don't sound sure." I put her file on my lap and feel something stirring under it. "Look, Maria, you've got to start having a little higher opinion of yourself. Don't you think you're worth it?"

"I dunno."

"Well I do. You can't allow yourself to be held hostage by your fears..."

I realize I'm gazing at her for too long again. She smiles back at me and doesn't say anything for a minute. She's beginning to see how attracted I am to her. I look away guiltily and squeeze the Silly Putty in my pocket. It just shows the sorry state of my own love life. Not only is it wrong to act this way around a client, but when I think about what Maria actually did, I get a little sick to my stomach.

It happened on a fall night. Her mother noticed Maria had been in the bathroom for a very long time. That's the funny thing about Maria being bright—the rest of her family isn't.

The mother knocked on the door and called her a few times. Maria didn't say anything. She just groaned. The mother went back to watching *Wheel of Fortune*. She didn't understand what they were saying or spelling; she just liked looking at the prizes. During one of the last commercial breaks, Maria came running out of the bathroom, past her mother, and threw something out the window.

An hour later, a neighbor found the newly born baby girl dead in the alley five floors down.

They arrested Maria. The family claimed they never knew she was pregnant. She wouldn't say who the father was. Her lawyer said she was suffering from postpartum depression and the district attorney charged her with manslaughter. The court gave her probation with psychiatric treatment.

Within her first few visits, I learned that her uncle had been sexually abusing her since she was eight and I began to suspect that he was the one who got her pregnant. Then I found out he beat her to make sure she wouldn't tell anyone, but I figure the rest of the family must have known what he was up to and just didn't do anything about it.

With all these confidences going back and forth, Maria and I have built up a good relationship. She always shows up for office visits and I get her appointments with Job Corps counselors. I've even gone with her to their offices a few times to make a good impression on interviewers. I convinced her to stay in school during days and work nights to make money. I also gave her my home phone number, which is what I'd do for any other client, of course.

The one thing I can't get her to do is move out of the apartment where she still lives with her family. Every time I see her, I bring up the subject.

"No, no, no," she always says. "It's not so easy as you think."

She's afraid what her uncle might do if she left. He's capable of coming after her with a gun—he's on probation himself for assault with a deadly weapon. There is also a strong possibility that he might start fucking Maria's eleven-year-old sister. My solution is to get Maria moved out of the house so she can get her life together and then help me start violation proceedings to put her uncle away.

But when I start talking about the plan again, Maria shudders and turns toward the wall. "It's not so easy," she says once more.

As usual, I write down my home number on a slip of paper and give it to her. "Call me," I say.

After dealing with Maria, I go to the bathroom and splash cold water on my face. Trying to take my mind off her. It'd be nice to go by the legal department and check up on that other girl I'm interested in, but there's no time. So I go down to the other end of the hall to get a cup of coffee. I find Jack Pirone holding court around the coffee machine with two other probation officers listening with bemused expressions.

"Look," Jack says. "It's Judas Baum! How you doing, Judas? How's the gold and silver exchange these days?"

"Leave me alone," I say sullenly, picking up a Styrofoam cup.

"What's the matter, Judas? You look depressed."

"I'm all right. Just let me be, Jack."

"Client getting you down?" asks one of the other probation officers, a tall guy named Lloyd Bell, who has no hips and ebony skin like an African statue.

"Something like that," I say, pouring the remains from the tepid coffeepot into my cup.

"I was just telling him that he shouldn't take this shit so personal," Jack tells Lloyd. He turns back toward me, once again affecting a concerned look. "Steven, we see so much human misery and suffering coming in and out of here every day. When you've been around as long as I have, you find a way to deal with that pain."

"What do you suggest?" I say, sipping the coffee and tasting the grounds.

Jack grows contemplative. "I remember a few years ago,

the wife and I shared a house with some people on Fire Island. It was early in the summer. There were hardly any other people around, let alone lifeguards. Some of the other people we were with immediately went out into the water. But there was a strong undertow that day." He becomes very still and his voice takes on a hushed tone. "One of our housemates went out there. And he never came back. We hardly even knew him."

Lloyd looks at Jack and shakes his head with a sigh. "Shit happens," he says.

"I remember a number of us sat around the fire that night, talking about it." Jack pauses, allowing for the impact of his sad story. "*And we laughed like hell.*"

Lloyd and the other guy start chuckling along with Jack. A stumpy, older woman with bright red hair scowls at them as she pushes by. I shake my head. "I don't know, Jack," I say. "I don't find some of this shit too amusing."

"Then you should lighten up." Jack raps me on the arm with his knuckles. "Otherwise, you'll end up like Tommy Markham."

"What's the matter with Tommy?"

"Nothing," Jack says, wiping his hands on the front of his shirt. "He's just an old sap, who don't have nothing going for himself except the job. You know he's retiring, right? We're having a farewell party for him at Junior's in Brooklyn tonight. You should come."

For a couple of seconds I think about whether I could ask the girl from the legal department to come with me, but then I consider what these parties are usually like and decide I shouldn't risk it. I crumple my coffee cup and throw it in the trash. "Does this mean I'm forgiven for going over to the Field Service Unit?" I ask Jack.

"No," he says. "You're still Judas, but you're still my old student."

"I'm still in the union too." I start to go.

"Hey, Baum," Lloyd Bell says loudly. "You got this Darryl King on your caseload?"

"Yeah. What about him?"

Lloyd strokes his goatee with two fingers. "Sounds like a pretty bad guy."

I take two steps toward Lloyd. "Why do you ask about him?"

"I got his homeboy Bobby 'House' Kirk as my client."

The name is familiar from Darryl King's file, but I don't remember the exact details. "Who's Bobby Kirk?"

"Bobby the House was one of Darryl's partners when they robbed that gas station," Lloyd says in a languorous voice, opening the story up to the group. "They hang out at Playland on Times Square sometimes. Bobby's what you'd call a mean motherfucker. He's about six foot four, 280 pounds, and he has a serious attitude, man. He once tore the door of a subway car off its hinges while the train was moving..."

"Why?" I ask.

"No one knows," Lloyd says with a shrug. "All I know is Bobby 'House' Kirk's got his name written in gold across his knuckles, and he once dangled another kid out a window at Spofford. And he's scared shitless of Darryl King."

"So what you're saying," I say, "is that Darryl's gotta be really bad."

"That's what I'm saying."

11

A few minutes after four o'clock, Darryl King stumbled out of the bedroom in his underwear. His sister's five-year-old daughter, LaToya, was in the next room, watching a Yogi Bear cartoon on television with the volume turned all the way up.

"Yo, turn that shit down," Darryl told her.

"Mommy said I could watch," the little girl said, her words whistling through the space in her front teeth.

"And I said, turn that shit down, I got a headache." Darryl frowned and sat down in front of the couch. His niece leaned back on his bare legs.

Paint was coming off the walls in sheets and there were rat-pellets all over the apartment. Wires stuck out from the baseboard where the phone jack used to be and urine seeped in under the front door because someone had taken a piss out in the hall again. There was another puddle in the corner where the ceiling had fallen in the week before. No one from the city had come to fix it, so the King family didn't care anymore.

On the television screen, Yogi Bear was giving his protégé Booboo a set of careful instructions about what to do in their next adventure. Yogi then turned and walked right smack into a tree trunk, flattening his entire face.

"Yo, what's up with that bear?" Darryl said.

LaToya squealed with delight and shook her pigtails. She had a sweet gap-toothed smile and a light in her eyes that no one else in the family had. "He funny, Dooky!" she said.

"He's not funny," Darryl said. "He be acting ill."

He leaned forward to nuzzle her head affectionately. A clarinet played on the sound track while Yogi sat on the ground watching stars go around his head. Darryl and his niece laughed as the bear jumped in the air and his feet whirled like propellers. The sun was coming through the broken window and an opened pack of Oreos sat on the table. Next to it was the Rolex he'd taken off the Spanish guy in Times Square last night. Only one small dot of blood marred the glass over the dial. He was starting to feel better now.

LaToya suddenly whipped around to look at him. "Grandma says don't miss your pointment," she said in a high voice.

His face coiled up. "Moms said I got an appointment?"

"She say be downtown."

"For my probation officer?"

She smiled widely and nodded up and down vigorously. "And what if I don't wanna go?" he asked her.

She made an angry face and balled up her fist like she was going to clobber him. "You better."

"Shit." He grabbed her fist and stood up. "You don't have to tell me nothin'. I'm all ready for my appointment."

He hopped around on one leg, doing karate kicks and kung fu chops, like he was warming up for a big fight. LaToya just stared at him. In the bedroom down the hall, something fell over and one of Darryl's children started crying. Darryl tried to ignore the sound for a minute, turning back to the TV screen.

Yogi Bear had just run smack into another tree and now he was desperately trying to straighten out his snout again.

"Bear must be on the pipe," Darryl said.

12

After getting all worked up about Maria, I'm grateful that the next appointment is somebody I don't know. A skinny kid with hair down to his ass and studded leather wristbands. His name is Gary DeStefano and he plays bass in a heavy metal band called Sodomy and Gomorrah. He's on probation for breaking a beer bottle over another musician's head outside a bar.

"There's a lot of frustration and anger in our music, you know," he explains, sinking so far down in his chair that he's almost looking straight up at the ceiling. His legs are splayed out before him like octopus tentacles.

"Why're you so frustrated?"

" 'Cos we're not too good," he says after giving it some thought. "People don't understand how hard it is to play your instrument when you're wearing eighty to one hundred pounds of fur and armor."

"I'll bet." I start to take notes.

"And what's really like a bitch is moving it around between gigs, you know."

"Where do you play?"

"Around. Wherever. L'Amour's in Brooklyn and Queens. CBGB's. You know that place?"

"Sure." I smile.

"The place is a dive, dude," Gary says. "And we once even opened for a crucifixion."

"I beg your pardon?" I put my pen down.

"Oh yeah," says Gary, happy to have any kind of audience. "We were playing to a biker club in Bay Ridge and after we were done they decided to have a sacrifice. I guess they really liked us or something. So they got this kid, you know. And they got him to put on a harness and a hood. And they put him up on a cross."

"You're kidding," I say, trying to keep my mouth from falling open.

"I'm not. He wanted them to do it too, you know. He was like this really weird dude. Anyhow, they whipped him and put a votive candle up his butt. Which was okay with him, you know. He liked it. And then, you know, they brought him across the street . . ."

I can't decide whether I'm appalled or fascinated. "While he was still on the cross?"

"Oh yeah, absolutely. They carried him on the cross across Fourth Avenue. It was like midnight and there was some traffic, but the cars waited for them to go by. So, anyway, they brought him across the street to the clubhouse and they began the ritual, you know. They started the music and a couple of guys dripped blood into a cup. And they were really gonna do it. They were really gonna like crucify him . . . But at the last minute they decided to spare his life."

"And how did you feel about all of this while it was going on?" I ask, leaning forward in my chair.

"Wow," says Gary. "Like I was really glad we didn't have to follow that act."

As the day winds down, I find myself tensing up. I scream over the phone at a car thief who got a job at a parking garage and I take a call from a client's mother, who says her son is shooting heroin again. What am I supposed to do?

I'm not sure if it's the new field assignment or the seven

cups of coffee jangling my nerves. My stomach is cramping itself into a ball. I hate these days on the emotional roller coaster, going from angry to sorry to hopeful and then back again. Still the clients keep coming. By 7:30, I've speeded myself into a numb blur and I can't remember what anyone said. My limbs feel heavy and useless from sitting here all day.

The old anxieties start to creep over me: You're not helping anyone. You're wasting time. You're burning out. Life is passing you by.

Outside my cubicle, I hear the sounds of briefcases shutting, footsteps in the hall, voices grumbling down by the elevators. I don't want to stay here much longer, but I'm not quite ready to go back to my cubbyhole on Avenue B. I sit at my desk, staring up at the photograph of the beach landscape, as though I could will myself into the picture.

Sometimes I don't think I understand my clients at all. I only see them for a fleeting moment, less than 1 percent of their time. And once they're out of my sight, they're going on with their lives while I'm still stuck in here, beating around the inside of my skull. I wonder if the things we talk about in here mean anything to them after they leave. Sometimes I wish I could just break down the walls and find out for myself.

It's a little late to be worrying about all that now, though. I clear off my desk and get ready to head out the door when I hear something strange out in the hall.

At first it's a faint, high-pitched tone. It gets a little louder and I recognize the sound as violins. The strings begin to swell and a police siren wails. There's a silence and then the beat kicks in. The joyless, insistent rhythm grows louder and louder outside the cubicle. Somebody is coming for me. A young man's voice cuts in, ranting in angry rhymes. "Don't try and outgun me/And this is a threat/There ain't been a motherfucker who can do that yet."

He comes in. A solid-looking black kid with dark eyes that glimmer like precious stones under his heavy brow. I wonder if he dressed specially for the occasion to intimidate his probation officer. He hasn't just embraced the racist stereotype—he's perfected it as the ultimate "fuck you." He wears a black Kangol hat, Guess jeans, ropes of gold chains around his neck as well as rings on his fingers, and a brand-new pair of Nikes with the tongues sticking out at obscene angles. A beeper for phone messages is clipped to his waistband. He cradles a black forty-eight-inch-long Sony radio cassette player in his arms as tenderly as a mother would hold a child. Its silver knobs and panels gleam from loving care and maintenance, and a rapper keeps declaring his virtues from its huge speakers. The rhythm pounds in my ears.

He glares at me defiantly, but doesn't say anything at first. An overpowering sweet, musky smell fills the cubicle.

"What can I do for you?" I say.

When he still doesn't answer, I ask for his name.

"Darryl King," he says in a small nasal voice.

"Have a seat, please."

I got my work cut out for me, I think, as he throws himself down into the new chair replacing the one Jack Pirone broke. While I search for his file, Darryl mutters along with another rap song, putting special gusto into the line "Sucker-ass nigger I should shoot you in the face."

"Yo, where's this at?" he asks, looking at the picture of the beach landscape on the bank calendar. "You live there?"

I ignore him and look at his record once more. "I see you've got like almost a dozen arrests in the last year or so."

He doesn't respond at all.

"Would you mind turning that radio down a little?" I say in a reasonably friendly voice. "I've got a little bit of a head-ache."

He leaves the radio on and keeps glaring at me.

"Hey, Darryl, what's the problem? Turn the radio off. I wanna talk to you."

He finally snaps it off. By now, most sensible people are long gone and the lights are dim around the rest of the office. Darryl looks past me and farts powerfully. There's something strange about this guy. He's clearly not happy to be here, but he doesn't seem to be in any hurry to go anywhere else.

"You know you're coming in here a little late in the day," I tell him, trying to maintain an even tone.

He shakes his head and makes a disgusted ticking sound with his mouth, as if I'd just told some outrageous lie about him. "Man, why you clockin' me?" he says. "I don't have time for this shit."

I find the pink office slip about what time he was supposed to come in and slide it across the desk to him. "What does that say?" I ask.

Without even looking at it, he shoves the slip right back at me.

"It says you were supposed to be here yesterday morning," I say, picking the note up and putting it in his file.

Darryl becomes very still. At first I'm not sure if he heard what I said. "Fuck that shit," he says finally.

"Fuck your shit," I say. "What's your excuse?"

Darryl looks away from me and bursts into hysterical giggles, as though he's sharing a joke with a small invisible friend in the corner. I write "Inappropriate responses" on his evaluation sheet and make a brief notation that he might have smoked crack before coming in here.

My instinctive reaction is to be a little nervous. But my job is to try to turn him around. They used to have a saying in my social work program: Everybody likes the easy victims. The people you can really feel sorry for, because they haven't done anything wrong. The little kids with AIDS. The sweet-tempered homeless woman. The forgotten old man in the nursing home. But it's the hard ones that count for more sometimes. You know the people I'm talking about. The ones who spit in your face and really dare you to give a shit.

So in spite of all the voices in my head telling me to get away from this guy as fast as I can, I force myself to give him another chance. I look him right in the eye without saying anything for a moment. I remember how Tommy Markham said Darryl had tried to intimidate him during their interview, and I wonder if he might be putting on an act for me too.

"I think we're getting off on the wrong foot here," I say, trying to get some warmth into my voice. "I just wanna get some sense of what's going on in your life now."

He draws his head back skeptically and a little fold of skin appears under his chin. "Why?" he asks.

"So I can find out why you're doing these things."

"What things?"

"The things that brought you here. You know. Robbing the gas station." I check his rap sheet. "This arrest for assault with a deadly weapon. Burglary. More robbery..."

"Arrests." He hisses the word. "Not convicted."

"Yeah, yeah, I know," I say. "The only guilty plea is on the gas station robbery. But you know what I'm talking about, even if you're not getting caught."

His eyes sweep across the ceiling as if he's barely hearing me, but I go on anyway. "You know, a lot of people would look at your record and say you're just a bad guy and they should lock you up," I tell him. "But it's not my job to judge you like that, necessarily."

Darryl just looks at me. Though he doesn't say it, the word "sucker" hangs in the air as vividly as a neon sign.

"You don't know me," he says in a slow, belligerent voice. "You don't know what I can do with my mentality." He puts a little polish on the last word to show he's good at picking things up.

"All right. Let's get to know each other then."

He folds his arms and half closes his eyes.

"I see you have a Harlem address on your arrest report," I say. "Do you live with your parents?"

"My mother."

"Your parents divorced?" A form question.

Darryl smirks. "They were never married."

"Where's your dad now?"

The smirk disappears. "I dunno," Darryl King mumbles.

I light a cigarette and ask for a daytime phone number for his mother.

"She was here before. You could've asked her..."

"She dropped you off?"

"She was seeing her officer..." he murmurs.

"Uh-huh. She's on probation too?"

"She was framed, just like me."

"What was the charge?"

"They say she stab Mark," Darryl says.

"Is Mark her current boyfriend or something?"

"No. Mark my friend at the projects. He fifteen."

Another note: "Home environment not condusive to re-habilitation." I correct it to "conducive." His answers seem to be getting less composed as they go along. I might not have gotten an honest response out of him yet, but the act is definitely slipping. Maybe I can get through to this fucker. "So why would she want to stab your friend?" I ask.

"Homeboy tried to get bad with me," he says impatiently.

"Why?"

"See, Mark got mad 'cos he say I throw his mother down the steps. Right? He threatened me with violence. So my moms don't like him."

I'm not sure what to believe now. "Let's back up a second," I say. "Why did you throw Mark's mother down the steps?"

"Bitch say I get her pregnant. She say I threw her down the steps. I don't. No arrest, no indictment, no grand jury. Nothin'."

I give the Silly Putty in my pocket a squeeze and try to stay cool. Jack says that if they see they've gotten to you emotionally, you're no longer an effective probation officer. But if I don't get myself psyched-up, I don't see how I'm ever going to reach this guy.

The beeper goes off on his waistband, but he doesn't bother checking to see what number is on it. He just starts acting agitated, like he already knows who's calling him.

"What's that?" I ask.

"My fuckin' job, man," Darryl says absentmindedly.

"What job?"

He stops and gives me a disingenuous smile. "I don't be discussing that. The court didn't remand me. I'm in your custody for supervision, not investigation," he says, slipping into the practiced legalese he's learned through years spent going in and out of the criminal justice system. "You don't be asking me questions like that. You ain't no cop. You're just a social worker, that's all. I know what time it is."

"Oh no? Well I disagree."

"Well, suck my dick."

He folds his arms across his chest and defiantly puts his feet up on my desk.

"Would you mind putting your feet down?" I say to him.

"Why should I?"

"Because I asked you."

His feet remain on top of my paper tray. "I'm comfortable," he tells me.

It's time to deal with this guy on his terms. After all, Ms. Lang wanted me to lean on him a little. I reach across the desk, lift his right foot an inch or two, move it over, and drop it over the side. "My house, my rules," I say.

I come around the desk and sit on the front of it, leaning forward so my nose is just an inch or two from Darryl's. His features remain absolutely still. His mouth is closed so tight that it's hard to believe that it'll ever open again. His eyes are bloodshot. From the smell of his breath, you'd think a little man had crawled up inside him and died.

"Listen to me," I say loudly. "You have to give me a full account of all your activities. Where you live, what you do, and who you're doing it with."

Darryl waves his hand and turns away, like I'm nothing.

"Don't give me that," I say. I'm starting to really get pissed off now, with the veins pumping up in my neck. "If you don't do the right thing, and I find out that you're doing more shit out there, I'm gonna personally send you to jail. And since it'll be a violation of probation, you'll do serious time."

"Shee-it," Darryl King says.

"I expect you in here next week at a reasonable hour. Like nine in the morning next Friday would be nice." I rest my chin on my clenched fist. "I'm telling you now, Darryl. You work with me, I'll be your best friend. You work against me, I'm gonna come down on you as hard as I can."

He turns up the left corner of his mouth and tightens his facial muscles. "Anybody ever wasted a probation officer?"

"What?"

"I'm just askin'. You know. 'S just a question," he says lightly, as though he's just being philosophical.

"You kill a probation officer and your life is over, okay?" I light a Marlboro and then notice I already have one burning in the ashtray. "That would be murder one..."

I suddenly realize I'm shouting. I've never lost my temper like this with a client before. Richard Silver bothered me yesterday, but this is different. This guy is really getting under my skin. The thing is that he knows he's crossing the line. I have no idea why he's making it into a personal thing between us. But now I can't back down. And neither can he.

"Man, don't try to front on Darryl," he says violently. "I know what time it is. They save murder one for cops. And if I was still a youthful offender, they wouldn't say shit, no how. I know the courts. I know 'em better than my lawyers. I could be a cop. I could do that..."

He jumps to his feet, throws his left arm straight out, points his index finger like a gun, and steadies it with his right hand. "MOVE IT—MOVE IT—MOVE IT!" he yells. "THIS IS A FUCKIN' RAID! GET YOUR BUTT ON THE FLOOR! YOU ALL UNDER ARREST! THAT'S RIGHT, THAT'S RIGHT. FORTY-FOUR MAGNUM FIREPOWER, BABY! NOW SPREAD 'EM. I SAID, SPREAD 'EM, PUSSY! YEAH, YOU LOOKIN' GOOD. WE GONNA PARTY DOWN. BEND OVER AND SPREAD 'EM. HERE I COME!"

At first I think he's talking to me, but then I realize he's off in his own angry world. Light still pours into his eyes, but now nothing shines out. I write a note: "Possibly psychotic."

"JUST SHUT UP NIGGER! I'M IN CHARGE HERE!" he says, pacing back and forth. "WHAT WE GOT HERE? A coupla dope fiends. Motherfuckin' crackheads. This place smells like shit. You gotta get some Glade lemon air freshener. I SAID, SIT YOUR ASS DOWN. Yeah, you take her in the back, Jefferson, I'm gonna have me a discussion with this nigger. WHERE'S THE MONEY? JUST SHUT UP. YOU THE PERP, I'M THE COP." He cocks his head to one side like he's listening to somebody. "What? Ain't gonna tell me? Well, CHECK THIS OUT."

He brings his hands down fast like he's slamming someone with the gun butt.

"I split your head? I'm sorry, man. I'm really crushed. I think you better tell me." He clicks, waits, and makes a firing sound. "DAMN! Boy, your arm is all fucked up."

He waits and then slams the butt down again. I cross out the "possibly" next to "psychotic."

Darryl grows still and puts a finger to his lips. "Yo, Jefferson," he calls out in a schoolyard voice. "Yo, this nigger bought it. He's dead. He bought the fuckin' farm, man. I dunno ... Just chill, awright ... This don't look too good, you know." He pauses and looks around. "Yo, we gotta make this look like a rip-off or something. Shit ... Just take the fuckin' money on the table. We gotta find us some rope, so we can tie up his hands and feet. Now you go down to the car and get back up some gasoline ... Nah, I don't wanna torch the place. I wanna pour it down his throat. Make it look Colombian an' shit." He makes a holstering motion. "The girl? She thirteen? We better waste her too."

He takes a long pause and then his beeper goes off again.

I can't think of anything to say. It doesn't matter if all of this was an account of true events or a performance for my benefit. The feeling is the same either way. Darryl smiles at me once more.

"Yeah," he says quietly. "I coulda had me a career in law enforcement."

He leaves the cubicle a few minutes later. It's almost eight o'clock and my day is over.

I take out my evaluation sheet and write three more words under Darryl King's name: "He scares me."

13

"Why y'all beeping me when I'm talking to my probation officer?" Darryl King wanted to know.

"How do I know who you're talking to?" said his sister, Joanna Coleman, looking up from the horoscope chart on her refrigerator. "All I know is that I got business to discuss with you right away."

She wore a gold cable as big as an arm around her throat. Two brown incense sticks burned on the kitchen table, wafting a sweet, overpowering odor through the room, and there was a "healing" crystal on top of the refrigerator. A pile of self-help and astrology books sat on the counter.

Joanna's two children, Howard, the six-year-old boy, and LaToya, the five-year-old girl, were running around the cramped apartment like wild Indians. The boy was like a little man. He walked around with a stern expression and his shoulders back, turning his body from side to side as if he was ready for a fight at any angle. The little girl followed him, with her pigtails flapping. She threw her arms over her little brother's shoulders like she wanted him to give her a ride.

"LaToya, you mind your brother," her mother warned her. "Else he'll turn around and smack you one..."

Aaron Williams, the fourteen-year-old with the harelip, sat

on the sofa, watching the Mets game on the television. Darryl's large friend Bobby "House" Kirk sat next to him and a catatonic-looking boy Darryl had never seen before sat on the floor staring at Bobby's size sixteen sneakers.

"What's so important?" Darryl asked.

"Him," his sister, Joanna, said, pointing to the catatonic boy. She said his name was Eddie Johnson and he was sixteen years old. Darryl King glanced over at him. The boy had hair that stood straight up and no physical energy. He was like a piece of furniture. Joanna explained that Eddie Johnson usually woke up at noon every day and sat up in bed about two hours later. By early evening he'd come as far as the front room, where he watched TV until it was time to go to sleep again.

"They think he's depressed," said Joanna.

"So what?" Darryl said.

"But he listens good," his sister told him. "That's the thing. You say something, he hears it. He never forgets it. He notice everything ... Even though he's a Scorpio ..."

Darryl glared at the blank-faced boy on the sofa. Then he clapped his hands in disgust and pivoted away from all of them. "Joanna, I don't believe you called my beeper for this ..."

"So listen, listen, part of the time Eddie live with his sister in the Bronx," Joanna said, pointing a long red nail at her younger brother. "The rest of the time, he live around here, with his mother. Right next to Pops Osborn."

She was still after Pops Osborn and all his crack houses. She and her Jamaican boyfriend, Winston, were getting obsessed with killing him and taking over his business, and Joanna had never stopped giving her younger brother shit about blowing the first attempt on Pops's life.

"You hear what I'm saying?" she asked Darryl. "Eddie here lives in the apartment right across the hall from Pops. He hears when Pops comes in with a guy and when he's alone. So he can get us into Pops's place, and you can get another shot at Pops."

"Oh." Darryl gave the kid on the sofa a sideways glance. "How you doing?"

"It's like I said," his sister told him, picking up her well-thumbed copy of *Visualize Success* from the dinner table. From the book's black cover, the pair of intense blue eyes seemed to be staring right at Darryl.

Eddie continued to stare straight ahead at the television as though he were a zombie. Next to him, Aaron Williams was biting the red cap off a crack vial and pouring the beige chips into a pipe with a Jack Daniel's label on it.

"So how'd you do with that guy anyway?" Joanna asked her younger brother.

"Who?"

"Your probation officer."

"Aw, he's a sucker like that other one," Darryl said. "But he's a little younger...a little more...like..." He couldn't think of the word he wanted. He shook his fist.

"Like energized?" his sister suggested, rolling her hips to a rhythm no one else could hear.

"Whatever." He shrugged. "Better watch his ass, else he'll end up like that cop got shot."

She looked over his shoulder and out the window. The lights from the other buildings in their housing project were shining brightly. LaToya, the little girl, ran up to her mother and buried her face in Joanna's thigh.

Darryl laughed. "What I did, I made up all this crazy shit to tell the guy. You know, I told him like I was going around like a cop." He dropped his hands and swung his shoulders in a macho swagger. "Like I bugged out in his office, you know. I told 'im I was like the maniac cop..."

He stomped around the apartment shouting like a madman and waving his hand like a gun. Bobby Kirk and Aaron Williams were almost doubled up with laughter on the couch. The two little kids hid behind chairs as Darryl lurched around. Joanna Coleman frowned and said she thought her brother and his friends were all idiots. Aaron was giggling so hard that he could barely keep his lighter flaring at the crack pipe.

"The guy was sitting there like this," Darryl said as he imitated his probation officer's squint. "Then I told him how

I was a cop and we was busting in on drug dealers and taking their money and then pouring gasoline down their throats."

His friends roared with laughter again. This time even Eddie Johnson, the catatonic kid, seemed amused. At least he was paying attention.

Joanna was less impressed. "You told him what?" she said loudly, stuffing her hands in her back pockets.

"I told him like I was a cop..."

"You told him a story about a cop and pouring gasoline down somebody's throat?"

Darryl grabbed the crack pipe from Aaron, who he felt was taking excessively long draws. "That's what I just told you."

"Since when are you smoking that?" his sister asked.

"This is only the second time," he lied.

"What am I gonna do with you, Darryl? You starting to smoke that shit. You not thinking straight."

"Shut the fuck up. Why do I take orders from you? What you know?"

"I know you're stupid to talk about that shit with your probation officer. That's playing with fire after what you did. You just daring him to catch you now."

"Nah," said Darryl, taking a hit off the pipe. The clean strong ether smell filled the room, drowning the incense odor. "I was just fuckin' around with the guy."

His sister got up and glared at him with her hands on her hips. "Darryl," she said, "why didn't you just tell that man you were behaving and have him leave you alone? What did I tell you about visualizing. You have to think about what happens after you do shit."

Darryl King didn't answer. He was busy taking another pull on the pipe. His right arm waved frantically like a drowning man's as the pulsing surge went through his body. He closed his eyes and raised his brow.

"That's why you be taking orders from me, Darryl," his sister said.

14

Walking down Flatbush Avenue toward Junior's, where they're having Tommy Markham's farewell party, I find I can't stop thinking about Darryl King.

I'm not sure what it is that bothers me so much about him. Maybe it's just the wear and tear of the job. I mean, it's demoralizing enough putting most of these poor bastards through a system that hardly ever helps them or anybody else. But there's also a matter of macho pride involved. When somebody like Darryl pushes you, you push back.

I try to be a good guy and all, but I'm starting to hate this wimpy social worker image. I'm somebody who barely made it through the two years of Erik Erikson, developmental psychology, and clinical training you need for a graduate degree. And after that, you don't get many opportunities to swagger around bragging about the job: "Yeah, I listened to that boy's problem real good. We achieved some fuckin' *empathy*!"

Just before I go through the front door of Junior's, a woman coming out gives me a strange look. I realize I've been talking out loud to myself again. I've got to try to spend less time alone, or I'm going to turn into one of those guys you cross the street to avoid.

Inside, regular customers sit around the front counter near

a glass display case full of cheesecake. Some of the lights are dimmed and an easy-listening radio station plays in the background. Tommy Markham's farewell party is under way in the section on the right. Jack Pirone is once again holding forth to a group of a dozen P.O.s. around the side tables. Tommy, who is a little guy in his late sixties with a gnome's face and thick glasses, sits by himself near the back. He has a half-eaten piece of strawberry cheesecake on his plate and a pink party hat on his head with a rubber chin strap. He's trying to look happy, even though nobody's paying attention to him.

I sit down next to Tommy and ignore Jack, who is swigging from a bottle of beer as he tells the other officers, "And the last time I saw her, she was giving head to a bunch of Shriners in the elevator!"

"Mr. Tommy Markham," I say as the guys behind us roar with laughter. "You getting ready to take it easy a while?"

"Oh sure, sure, kid," Tommy says in a salty little tough guy voice that makes him sound like the sergeant in a foxhole in an old Warner Brothers war movie. "It's gonna be swell. Just swell."

It's always struck me as funny the way Tommy can sound so hard-boiled, yet still be the biggest bleeding heart in the department. I notice, in fact, that somebody has draped a white T-shirt with a picture of a red bleeding heart across the seat next to him. I ask Tommy if it's one of his going-away presents.

"Oh yeah, yeah," he says, a forced smile creasing his knobby face. "It's just the fellas havin' some fun with me. Y'know, Steve. They're just havin' some fun. Y'know. 'Cos they call me a bleeding heart. Y'know. 'Cos I feel sorry for everybody. Y'know. I always say everybody was once somebody's baby. Y'know what I'm saying, Steve?"

"I know." I try unsuccessfully to get the attention of a waitress going by.

"Even the guys who killed somebody, Steve. They was somebody's baby too. Y'know what I mean? I used to go down to the cells to talk to them. I remembered one guy who killed his whole family. He looked at me through those bars and you know what he said, Steve? He said, 'I need help.' Y'know. It does something to you inside when you hear stuff like that."

I put my elbow up on the table. "I know, Tommy."

I've always thought Tommy was a very nice man, but his penchant for repeating trite and obvious things is really irritating. The sad truth is that Tommy is not too bright, and while everybody likes him, almost nobody respects him. Jack and the others are using the gathering more as a union meeting and a drinking session than as a chance to say good-bye.

"So, Tommy, what're you going to do with yourself now that you're retiring?" I ask, taking a cigarette out of my shirt pocket and thinking about a stroll over to the cheesecake display.

"I dunno, kid. Y'know . . ."

"Are you gonna travel?"

"Nah, kid, I was in de merchant marines. I seen the world already."

"Oh. Do you have family you're gonna stay with?"

Tommy tries to keep his chin from sagging and his eyes from dropping. "Nah. I really don't have much family around, Steve. Y'know. I got a room around the corner from here. That's where I'm gonna be most of the time."

I start to get depressed as Tommy explains that he's actually looking forward to spending the rest of his days in the tiny room. "It'll give me a chance to catch up on a lot of things," he says, like he's trying to convince himself it won't be so bad. "I gotta catch up on watching television. They got some good programs on now . . ."

I don't know. It seems like a frustrating end to an unsatisfying life. I hope I don't wind up like Tommy. I wonder what, if anything, he has to show for all his years on the job.

"Tommy, can I ask you something?"

"Sure, sure, kid. Fire away. Anything you want."

"Well, you've been a probation officer a long time, right?"

"Long time, Steve. Very long time. Y'know. More than

twenty years. Ever since I got outta de merchant marines."

"Okay." I put up my hand to interrupt him. "And you've seen a lot of clients in that time. Probably thousands of them..."

"Sure, thousands, kid." Tommy bobs his head up and down furiously like a doll on a car's dashboard. "Thousands..."

"And a lot of those people were in terrible trouble when you met them, right? Like they'd really messed up their lives. They were really at the end of their rope..."

"Absolutely, kid, absolutely." With the way he's bobbing his head, I worry Tommy's about to sprain his neck.

"So tell me something, Tommy. How many of those people did you really help? I don't mean giving them bus fare, or getting a summer job for a kid who didn't commit that serious a crime in the first place. I'm talking about actually turning somebody's life around. Giving hope to somebody who was in total despair. Do you know what I'm talking about?"

Tommy's head stops bobbing and he gives me a hurt look. "Yeah, I know what you're talking about," he says slowly.

"So I was just wondering what you had to show. Can you name one person who you really helped that way? Did you ever change somebody's life?"

Tommy looks glummer than ever. He pokes his cheesecake a couple of times with his fork and then puts the fork down. "I dunno, kid," he says after a very long silence. "I guess I gotta think about it a little. I never thought about it like that."

I'm sorry I asked the question. I didn't mean to make Tommy feel so bad. I only wanted to know what I might have in store for the future. Better to leave it alone now. I try once more to get the waitress's attention, but she still won't look at me.

"Excuse me a minute, Tommy. I'm gonna go to the counter and get a beer. You want anything?"

"Nah, kid," Tommy says, still looking down at his cheese-cake. "I got everything a man could need."

I get up from the table and walk down the aisle past Jack

Pirone, who's sweating profusely, gesturing wildly, and telling a stupid joke.

"Hey, Judas," Jack says as I try to squeeze by him.

"Jack," I say, "I'm not Judas, and you sure as hell ain't Jesus. You're too fuckin' fat. You'd break the cross. So get off my back."

The other P.O.s laugh as I keep going toward the counter. I turn to see Jack bowing and smiling as though acknowledging my point. I lean over the counter and order a Budweiser and a slice of regular cheesecake.

"Hey you," says a familiar voice.

I turn and see Ms. Lang looking at me, with a glass of vodka in her hand. A couple of buttons on her blazer are undone and her hair is out of its bun. Her eyes seem a little glassy and she's even smiling a little. She's not quite drunk, just a bit more relaxed than usual. Lloyd Bell, looking trim and handsome in a dashiki and jeans, is sitting on a stool between her and me.

"So what're you doing here?" Ms. Lang asks me.

"Just saying good-bye to Tommy."

"Oh." She gets quiet and puts a finger to her lips. From the back of the place Jack Pirone's voice is saying much too loudly, "So the tribal chief says, 'We will grant your request and put you to death, but first, a little Boom-ba.'"

"Keep it down, Pirone!" Ms. Lang suddenly shouts. "Show a little respect for Tommy."

There's an abrupt silence. She looks more surprised than anybody by her outburst. In two years I've never seen her lose her cool this way. I've never liked her as much.

"I think I'll be going to the ladies' room now," she says softly, turning around on her stool and getting off.

"All right," says Lloyd.

"Sure you don't want to join me?" she asks, running her fingers along Lloyd's taut, muscular arm.

"My wife would prefer that I don't," Lloyd says gently.

"Suit yourself."

She smiles crookedly and goes teetering off toward the bathroom. Lloyd looks after her, shakes his head, and sighs. Then he takes a long sip of water.

"She's a good woman," I say.

"She's special."

"Yeah."

"I'd be interested," Lloyd says, twisting the watchband on his wrist. "Except I'm married, you know."

"Yeah."

"And she's a little old for me."

I stop and give Lloyd a good look. He doesn't seem that much younger to me. He already has wrinkles around his eyes and his neck. The guy behind the counter sets my beer, dessert, and check down in front of me.

I ignore the food for a moment to watch Tommy, Jack, and the rest of the scene around the restaurant. There's something a little strange and a little sad about a lot of the people from probation, I decide. So many of them started off wanting to do something else with their lives and then got waylaid. I remember how Jack once told me he'd wanted to be a chef years ago. I see Cathy Brody standing near Jack with a drink in her hand and her arm wrapped around her waist. She wanted to be a psychiatrist. And Lloyd Bell, sitting next to me, wanted to be an actor. For a moment I'm glad I didn't set out to do anything else. There are already too many disappointed people running around.

"So did you see my homeboy Darryl King today?" Lloyd asks me.

"Yeah, I think he's a psychopath. You want him on your caseload? I'll trade you him for two chain snatchers and a token sucker to be named later."

"Not necessary." Lloyd leans back with his elbows on the counter. "I already got his friend Bobby 'House' Kirk as my client. Remember? Anyway, I just heard something I wanted to pass on to you."

"What's that?"

"Well, you can't believe everything you hear on the street, but the word is Bobby had something to do with setting a fire at a crack house the other night."

"Oh yeah?" I fumble with my wallet.

"It had to do with a fellow named Pops Osborn," Lloyd says calmly, turning around and tapping the counter with his long fingers. "You don't know if Darryl had anything to do with it, do you?"

"No, but maybe we should put our heads together and see about violating both of these guys. We could call the local precinct..."

"Whoa, boy," Lloyd says, putting a hand on my shoulder like he's trying to calm a bucking bronco. "We can't do that."

"Why not?"

Lloyd stands slowly and turns up his hands. "It's just word on the street, man. It's just smoke. Might not even be true. No one reported nobody starting no fire. It's just people talking. I just thought you might want to know about it."

"So what am I supposed to do, Lloyd?" I ask.

Lloyd shrugs and checks his hair in the mirror behind the counter. "Ours is not to reason why," he tells me. "Besides, all this might be bullshit. Your boy Darryl may be a Boy Scout after all. He wouldn't be the first black youth who got pegged wrong by the system." He's smiling uneasily.

I'm about to say something else to him when somebody starts poking me in the back with a sharp finger.

I whirl around and see it's Tommy Markham. His eyes are moist and he's licking his lips. "I thoughta somebody," he's saying. "I thought about what you asked and I thoughta somebody, y'know."

"Somebody who you helped?"

"Yeah, yeah." Tommy closes his eyes and rocks from side to side. "You asked if I ever changed somebody's life and I thought of a guy."

"Who?"

"Augusto Ramirez."

"Augusto Ramirez?" The name sounds familiar, but I can't quite place it. "What did he do?"

"Ah, he was in a mess of trouble. Y'know. I helped him plenty, Steve. I tell you. I got him a job, and a place to live, and I even introduced him to his wife. He's doing great now. He writes to me all the time."

"That's great, Tommy." I'm still not sure where I heard the name Ramirez before. But Tommy is smiling and his head is bobbing up and down again as he limps to the bathroom. I don't want to break his mood by questioning him too closely. I pick up my beer and cheesecake and start to walk back to the booth where we'd been sitting.

Along the way, I step directly into Jack Pirone's path. "Hey, Jack, I got a question. You ever hear of somebody named Augusto Ramirez?"

Jack snorts and smiles cynically. "Of course. What do you want to know about him?"

"Who was he? I asked Tommy to name one guy he'd ever really helped in his career and he said this guy Ramirez. And I can't think of why I'd heard that name before."

"That guy was a cop-killer," Jack says with a sigh. "He was Tommy's client a few years ago and Tommy got him out of jail and the guy walked up to some cop in the street and blew his fuckin' head off." He shrugs. "Fuckin' Tommy never could keep anything straight."

15

Just before midnight a stumpy woman with a microphone stood at the base of 1 Times Square on Forty-second Street. The headline parade of the day's news stories revolved on the brightly lit "zipper" sign over her head.

"Brothers and sisters," she said. "You don't have to go to hell."

A tall man wearing a short sequined dress, high heels, and a blond wig paused to stare at her.

Richard Silver, driving a navy blue Audi across town, was stopped at the nearest red light. He rolled down his window to watch the scene that was unfolding across the street on his left. "Homosexuals," he said. "Another thing I don't understand."

Jessica Riley, sitting beside him in a Tiffany necklace and a short black Galanos dress worth five thousand dollars, said nothing. In the backseat, his son, Leonard, wiped his nose with his shirt sleeve.

"I mean, how could you allow such a thing to be done to you?" Richard Silver said without taking his eyes off the man in the sequined dress. "It's humiliating, some of the tnings they do."

"Well, I don't think you'd have much choice if you were

in prison," Jessica said pointedly. "You know, some people go to prison when they do bad things, Richard."

"Thank you for saying that in front of my son," Richard Silver told her.

Leonard wasn't listening anyway. He was too busy pressing his nose against the back window, making the pig face for the people in the car behind them. Jessica checked her makeup in the mirror and crossed her skinny legs.

"So did you hear back about the Long Island thing?" she asked.

"I gotta meet the guy on July Fourth," Richard Silver said. "Can you believe that?"

"Couldn't you do it another time?"

"They're gonna have a hemorrhoid in Chicago if we don't do this soon," he explained. "They're already worried."

"So what'd you tell them?"

"I told them to relax and avoid impure thoughts," Richard Silver said. "What am I supposed to do?"

The eastward traffic wasn't budging. He stuck his head out the window and saw tightly packed cars for at least two blocks ahead. On the far corner a crowd of people were gathered in front of the Off-Track Betting outlet. In the rearview mirror Richard Silver saw a movie marquee that said "Desire Me Wet." A neon ad for a Japanese camera company splashed green light over the street.

"You don't have to be unclean or live a life in darkness," the stumpy woman with the microphone shouted. "You don't have to buy or rent pornography."

The transvestite, who was standing there listening to her, moved his purse from his right shoulder to his left shoulder.

"Let me ask you something," Richard Silver said to his son. "You understand that play tonight?"

"Yes," said Leonard Silver, who had brown bangs, braces, and his father's eyes. He had just turned thirteen. "I think it was about imperialism."

"What?" His father winced like he'd been hit on the head by a frying pan.

"Like the Oriental guy who was dressed like a girl, he was like China, you know?" Leonard said in a thin voice that meandered up and down his vocal register. "And the French diplomat, he was like the symbol of Western imperialism, trying to colonize her."

"Hey, Leonard," his father said, "all I want to know is how you could sleep with a guy for twenty years and think it was a lady."

Jessica Riley shook her head dismissively. "Did you like the play, Leonard?" she asked, turning around to look at him in the backseat.

He slumped down a little when she spoke to him. "It was okay, I guess," he mumbled.

"I thought it was filth," Richard Silver volunteered.

"Mom said she liked it," Leonard said tentatively.

"Oh she did, did she?" said his father.

"Yeah." Leonard made squeaking noises on the windows with the tips of his fingers. "She thought I should see it."

"I told you she was poisoning him," Richard said angrily to Jessica.

The light changed once more, and traffic still did not move. Across the street, a car pulled up near the preacher woman and a group of young white men wearing tight T-shirts and hair that was carefully sprayed back and shaved on the sides got out. The transvestite did not notice them. He was too busy looking through his purse like he wanted to give the woman with the microphone some money.

"You don't have to be depraved," the stumpy woman cried. "You don't have to be a drug addict. Or homeless."

"She's trying to turn him against me," Richard Silver told Jessica. "She'll do anything to hurt me."

His son banged his knees together in the backseat. "Dad, we're missing *Friday Night Videos*."

"Leonard, what do you want me to do? Get out and push the other cars out of the way?" Richard Silver turned to Jessica and lowered his voice. "You see what I mean? She's spoiling him too."

Leonard stared silently out his window. On the other side of Forty-second Street, one of the young white men with sprayed-back hair got a tire iron out of the trunk of his car and approached the preacher woman and the transvestite. His brow was knit and his arms were like sides of beef hanging off his shoulders.

The transvestite saw the young white men coming and began to edge away. "You don't have to give in to temptation," the preacher woman said.

"I'll tell you one thing, Leonard," his father said as traffic finally began to move. "It's a free country and you can grow up to be anything you want, but if you turn out to be a homosexual, I swear I'll cut my own throat and hold your mother personally responsible."

The transvestite broke into a run with the pack of well-groomed men in pursuit. He clattered across the street on his high heels and almost got hit by Richard Silver's car as it rolled forward. "Fuckin' imbecile," Richard Silver said.

The transvestite made a left at the Travelers Aid bureau and then ran across Broadway. As the light turned red again, he tried to disappear into the three-card monte crowd standing in front of Off-Track Betting, but the man with the tire iron and his friends followed. The crowd quickly parted and then the men with the sprayed hair were all over the transvestite, kicking him and beating him with the tire iron.

As Richard Silver drove by, he saw the transvestite lying in a bloody, burbling heap of sequins on the sidewalk.

"You don't have to be a sinner," the stumpy woman's voice said over a loudspeaker somewhere behind him.

"What a life," Richard Silver said.

16

Having convened with the likes of Darryl King and Tommy Markham earlier in the evening, I am in no mood for brie wheels, corny Motown tapes, and long discussions about interior design. What I need is a slump-breaking drunk and a lively fuck.

Instead, I get belligerently stewed and nearly ruin my ex-girlfriend's engagement party. I can't seem to get along with anybody anymore. Most of my old friends are in business now and our lives have nothing to do with each other. They're all busy moving to the suburbs where they'll be safe from people like my clients. I get into a stupid argument with the fiancé about coddling criminals and nearly take a swing at him.

I wake up on Saturday afternoon alone in my apartment with my pants off and my shoes still on. My mouth feels sore and I can't remember how I got home. In my left hand, I'm clutching a miniature Grenadian national flag.

I think I need to make some changes.

I shower, shave, drink two cups of coffee, and swallow three aspirins. Calling to apologize for last night will probably just make things worse, I decide. I put on side two of the Ramones *Road to Ruin* album and try to get myself reanimated. The phone rings in the middle of the second song.

Maria Sanchez, finally asking if I'll help her move.

"When?" I ask in a groggy voice.

"Right now," she says.

A girlfriend from school is going to let her stay with her and her family on Edgecombe Avenue until Maria gets settled. But we have to do it immediately. Her uncle, who's sexually abused her for all these years, will be home by five. If he finds out what we're up to, he'll be good and pissed, and he might not hesitate to use his gun.

I call my old pothead friend Terry Greene and wake him up. After twenty minutes of threatening and cajoling, I convince Terry to borrow his parents' Toyota.

By 3:30 Terry, wearing a pair of shades and a "Butthole Surfers" T-shirt, is waiting outside with the car. One thing about Terry: He never went upscale. While my other friends are making their way up the corporate ladder or working out of some back office in Bergen County, Terry is still straggling along as a free-lance photographer, specializing in pictures of bar mitzvahs and cockfights. A half-smoked cigarette dangles from his lips as he holds the passenger side door open for me.

"You look like shit," he says as I get in.

Catching my dark red eyes in the rearview mirror, I have to agree. "Go pretty slow, all right. Otherwise, I'm gonna throw up all over your inside."

"Y'know you better watch it with that drinking," Terry says, peering at me over his sunglasses as he eases the car over a beer can and a dead bird on Avenue B.

"Tell me about it," I say. "The last thing I remember last night I was quoting Lillian Hellman to you about anti-Semitism and professional ice hockey."

"What's the matter? Why'd you get so fucked up?"

I stick my head out the window and inhale deeply. "I dunno. I'm kind of having a hard time at work, you know. Just a mild case of the doubts, I guess."

"I thought you liked it so much," Terry says, aiming the

car uptown. "With the interestingly dysfunctional people and all."

"You know what I wish sometimes?" I say, lighting a cigarette and blowing a trail of smoke out the window. "I wish I had a really simple job. Like drilling holes for a car's transmission or something. Just stand there all day with the machine. Then after it's done, you got a car and it just goes. And then after five years, it breaks down like it's supposed to, and you get another one."

"Oh, you don't know anything about cars," says Terry. I notice he has a new purple streak going down the back of his hair. "I had a Honda Accord after college and I had it in the shop every other month, and that's supposed to be like the most reliable car in the world."

"I thought you drove a Chrysler."

"Honda Accord," he tells me. "Stick with being a probation officer."

"Well, I'm probably not gonna be doing that forever."

"Since when did you start saying that?" Terry asks in a surprised voice while he switches lanes and his glasses start to slide down the bridge of his nose.

"Long time ago," I tell him as the jackhammer in my brain gets going. "Between the time I left the curb and when I got in the car."

Traffic is bad going north, so we get on the FDR Drive. Right away, a dark blue Cressida starts threatening to shove us off on to the shoulder. There's a furious argument going on in the yellow Mercedes ahead of us. The woman in the passenger's seat keeps hitting the guy driving in the back of the head with the back of her palm. Off to the side, the East River shimmers turbulently and a barge full of new cars sails by. The sun makes the old upholstery stink in Terry's car and I have to lean out the window again to get a good clean breath.

"So what else are you gonna do?" Terry asks, pushing the shades back up on his nose.

"There's a lot of things I can do," I say, flicking my cigarette out the window. "I'm going into this Field Service Unit, so that could turn into something. And you remember I used to talk about becoming a lawyer." Some of the ashes fly back in my face.

"Sell out, sell out, sell out," Terry chants as he grips the steering wheel.

"It's not selling out," I say, more than a little defensively. "I'm just thinking maybe there are other ways to do good work without getting burned out."

"Yeah," says Terry. "Like not getting fucked up so much. You know you got a real ugly side that comes out when you drink. That was really stupid that fight you had with Jamie's fiancé..."

He fiddles with the radio until he gets a station playing "Institutionalized" by Suicidal Tendencies and I decide that maybe I will look into those law school applications. Not committing myself: just checking it out.

Traffic has come to a complete stop for some reason. I'm starting to feel the future bearing down on me. Once I thought I could do anything with my life. Even if things looked bad at any given time, there was still a chance I might pull myself together and be somebody. But I'm almost thirty now and every day I'm getting a little closer to becoming the person I'll always be. Which scares the shit out of me.

As traffic lightens, we shoot past the heliport, the imposing Waterside Plaza apartment complex, and a high stone wall with an empty playground on top. It's like a fortress for the rich, well out of reach for the Bronx-bound. On the horizon up ahead, I catch a glimpse of one of those obnoxious glass towers Richard Silver helped put up. I think it's blocking the view of another smaller building that I used to like, but now I can't even remember what it was.

When we come off the Ninety-sixth Street exit, though, time seems to stand still. The taller, newer buildings are all behind us. What's ahead are old anonymous gray projects and tenements. I spot the name "PACO" spray-painted in huge black letters on a brick wall. It's probably been there since the 1950s. Paco was probably a brash young stud when he wrote it. I'll bet he's a doddering old fool now.

"What I don't understand," Terry is saying, "is how you can tell your clients how to run their lives when you drink like that?"

"Enough with the drinking!" I say, slapping the dashboard as another skinhead anthem blasts from the radio. "You do drugs, don't you?"

"I did Ecstasy last night," Terry says with a smile.

"Doesn't that affect your ability to reason?"

"Not at all." Terry shakes his head violently. "I had a perfectly coherent conversation with somebody about God and the Druids."

"And would you have had that conversation if you hadn't taken Ecstasy?"

"Well," says Terry. "It might not have gone on three or four hours."

Just before four, we arrive at the building on 106th Street, where Maria and her family live. Upstairs, everyone is in hysterics. They're sure the uncle is about to show up with his gun and blow them all away. He is said to be especially angry with me. Maria, Terry, and I manage to get the car loaded with her stuff in less than twenty minutes. But then she spends an hour crying and hugging people in the doorway. It's very sweet, but Terry and I are hopping up and down with fright, because the uncle is supposed to show up at any minute.

We're lucky to get rolling before sunset, I figure. But halfway to the new address, I'm looking up at the rearview mirror and swearing to Terry that a green Mazda is following us.

"My uncle drives a green Mazda," Maria says.

"Fuck him."

I'm sweating, Terry's cursing, and Maria can't stop crying. The car bounces wildly over potholes and through detours around Sugar Hill and West Harlem. A group of windshield-washing kids surround us at a stoplight. I try to fend them off with my department badge, but they spray the glass anyway and don't bother to wipe it off.

Finally we arrive at Maria's girlfriend's house. It's just after six. We bring everything upstairs and the family welcomes us like heroes. Their home is a warm, comfortable place. Salsa plays on the stereo, a large blue, red, and white Puerto Rican national flag hangs on the wall next to the front page of *El Diario*. An elderly couple plays on the living room floor with five very young grandchildren. Two televisions blare in English and Spanish. The smell of rich, spicy food is in the air. Maria's girlfriend calls Terry and me into the smoky kitchen and serves us red beans, yellow rice, and green plantains. We eat standing up against the counter, and for the moment everyone is very happy. End of the story, I hope. We'll do the violation on the uncle and then Maria will be on her way in life.

"Call me if you hear from your uncle," I say, turning toward the door. "You got my number at home."

"Can I call you if I don't?" Maria asks.

I don't know what to say. "Sure," I mumble. "I'm around."

She hugs both of us good-bye. Terry holds on to her for a little longer than is necessary, I think. I slap his back and we race each other down five flights of stairs and burst out laughing at the bottom.

Walking outside, I get a settled feeling inside I haven't had in months. It looks like it's going to be a cool, starry night, I'm with a friend, and for once I've done a single, unambiguous good thing with a tangible result.

"Ayyyiyii, ave Maria," says Terry, opening the door on his side of the car. "How come you never told me what a babe she was?"

"Come on, Terry, she's one of my clients."

"Yeah, right. I heard that business about calling you at home."

I blink twice. "All my clients can call me at home."

"Yeah, right."

"I speak the truth." I give him the scout's honor salute.

"You mean to tell me you'd just as soon take a call at home from one of those drooly guys who hang around the bus terminal as from that beautiful babe upstairs."

I take the safety belt off the seat and sit down in the car. "Sure," I say. "That's what I'm supposed to do."

Terry puts the key in the ignition. "Then some of you probation officer types must be more fucked up than your clients."

I stare at him for a long time before I slam down the lock on my door. "No shit, Sherlock," I say.

17

When the firecrackers exploded near his feet, Pops Osborn dove into the back of his Oldsmobile Cutlass Supreme. He told his driver to get going and sank down like he was trying to hide his skinny body between the cushions of the black leather seats. Just as the car jolted forward, he noticed one of his brown lizard penny loafers was ripped and he cursed in a high, whiny voice.

"Don't worry, boss," said the driver, who was called Sunshine. "Those kids just dissing you."

"Just drive around the block for an hour or so," Pops said.

Pops had been going downhill ever since Darryl King's posse took a shot at him. He started losing heart a little bit at a time. First his nerves went. It got so whenever he stepped outside, he'd start looking around like someone was about to kill him. Eventually he hired Sunshine, a tall Trinidadian man, for five hundred dollars a week to drive him around and guard him with an Uzi.

Business was suffering. Brash young punks were showing up on his corners and in the crack houses he once controlled. They were know-nothing kids—some as young as fourteen—though they often had Uzis of their own. They were taken care of easily enough. Pops killed two of them personally with his

9 mm. But they kept coming. They were like cockroaches. Every time you got rid of one, there were two others crawling up your bathroom wall.

The world seemed to go around a little slower in the old days, the year before, when Pops, then a confident nineteen year old, took over his small portion of the crack trade from his uncle Paul "Stewy" Harris. Pops had been brought along the right way, learning about the trade one day at a time. He didn't get to be a lookout until he was as old as fifteen. He hung around his high school until it was time for yearbook pictures. Then Stewy had him call in sick. "You don't wanna make it too easy for the police to get a picture of you," he told Pops.

The size of the business was steady back then, four spots around Harlem and the Fortress, a tall redbrick building in a housing complex near the East River. Stewy had inherited the business from a guy named Breeze, who took it over when it was a heroin racket from someone named Frank, who got it from an old numbers guy called Morris, who was hooked up with the Genovese crime family in an operation going back to about World War II.

But the order of succession had broken down since the crack explosion of the mid-1980s. People lost their memories and their sense of reason. Old alliances were abandoned. Young kids blundered onto other people's territory and shot off their automatic weapons without regard for the consequences. They lived only for the sensation of the moment, like the customers who bought their crack. Everything happened in the present tense. The rap song everybody was listening to in their cars one day was forgotten by the next. The jewelry and clothing that everybody wore Friday night was thought ugly by Saturday afternoon.

"Even the way they talk," Stewy Harris was heard to complain shortly before he was killed. "When they say, 'I be downtown,' you can't tell if these kids mean now, before, or later. It's all the same to them."

Because crack was so cheap and easy to make, everyone was a player. One ounce of cocaine equaled almost four hundred vials of crack. So any kid with a little coke, a box of baking soda, and enough balls to squeeze a trigger could go to the corner and sell five-dollar vials. Anarchic, primitive battles were waged for each small piece of turf. To gain any real foothold, a crew had to be willing to go anywhere anytime and kill anyone, whether they were a bystander or a rival, a cop or a social worker.

From what Pops was hearing, the crew that took a shot at him was the wildest one yet. But it seemed like nobody could give him a name to work with. Otherwise, he would go out and kill the punks himself. Several of his salespeople stopped working for him and one of his crack houses got boarded up by the city. Now he would not be able to finish paying for the customized Mercedes and the ranch-style house in Elmont, Long Island, in time for the fall. And he still wanted to get married. To whom, he was not sure. One of the women who used to come by the house would have been all right.

He looked out the backseat window of his Cutlass as his driver kept circling the block. The Sunday night crowd was out on the streets. At one of his most profitable locations, near First Avenue, a crew of little kids he'd never seen before were selling crack to people in cars. The oldest one might have been twelve. The world was going around faster and faster all the time and Pops felt his place in it slipping away.

18

When you're having a lot of doubts about your job and the way your life is going, the first thing you think to do isn't to go up to some godforsaken swamp in the Bronx, slap muffs over your ears, and start firing a .38-caliber revolver at a plastic target.

I mean, if I heard one of my clients had done that, I'd tell him he wasn't being honest with himself. Or some bullshit like that. But since I'm getting trained to go into the Field Service Unit, I have no choice.

It's not so much the trip I mind. In fact, I sort of like getting out of the office for a little while. And I think I can handle some bullet-head instructor telling me what a high-powered rifle can do to your skull. What I don't like is the whole idea of being a cop.

It's not that I have anything against cops, although I've never met one who felt any loyalty to anyone who wasn't connected to the department. It's just that I'm doing something different. I'm supposed to be concerned about all the people the cops arrest and then forget about. I'm the garbageman whose job it is to recycle these people. It's not the most respected profession in the world, or the most popular, but somebody's got to do it and it might as well be me. Besides, if I was going to be a cop, I'd have gone to the academy years ago.

At least that's what I used to think. On the other hand, if there are a lot more guys like Darryl King running around now, who am I to say there shouldn't be more cops? And who's to say that even some of your social worker types like me shouldn't learn which end of a gun fires. I'm not saying that I'm ready to walk a beat or anything. I'm just saying the world's a different place from the nineteenth century when that bootmaker John Augustus bailed some drunk out of jail in Boston and invented probation. You change with the times. That's all I'm saying.

Anyway, it turns out that the Police Department's training facility is in a remote part of the Bronx called Rodman's Neck, off the City Island exit on the New England Thruway. To get there, you drive along a twisting country lane, passing woods, open fields, and little lakes. It's enough to make you forget that you're still in the city. In fact, it's a bit of a shock to turn around and see Co-op City on the horizon behind you.

When we first get to the checkpoint of the police training facility, it looks like a military compound in the middle of the wilderness. There are armed guards at the front, chain-link fences everywhere, and a dozen low-slung barracks with aluminum roofs off to the side. But once we start to walk around, the place seems more like a summer camp for overage boys.

There's a little hut where the guns get fixed. Just across a stretch of grass, a set of gray plank steps leads up to a small bathroom with both doors open, as if the boys inside might need a counselor's help to zip up their pants. The painted wooden signs hang from posts with a little burnish around the edges and Boy Scoutish axioms like *Be Professional* and *Listen to Instructions* printed in earnest yellow letters.

The three of us who've been driven up here from the Probation Department are led into a large barracks where two dozen young police recruits sit listening to a captain lecturing them from the front of the room. The captain is a ruddy man in his mid-forties, wearing a khaki uniform and a green base-ball cap. His back is ramrod-straight, but his stomach hangs over the front of his pants.

Since I've come in late, it's hard to figure out exactly what he's talking about. He keeps pointing to a white chart on a nearby easel that says "Post-Entry Level Training or PELTS," which I always thought was a derogatory term for women. But then again, these are cops, so you never know.

The young police recruits in the audience look like soldiers without a war to go to. Most of them are younger than me. Their faces are pasty and a little unformed. I figure the majority are from Rockland County or Long Island and have never been on a subway before. I briefly convince myself I have the edge on them because of my experience.

As the captain's lecture goes on, I still can't get a handle on what he's saying. The one phrase that keeps jumping out at me is "Avoid reflective action."

Avoid reflective action. Typical cop talk. Not just gram-matically incorrect, but hopelessly blockheaded. Avoid reflec-tive action. Shoot first and ask questions later. " 'Don't think' is what they're telling us," I mutter to the guy next to me in the front row.

I find myself resisting the message and wanting a drink. What the captain is saying goes against everything I've tried to do at probation. If you don't think about what all this means, how can you expect to understand the people you're locking up? How can you understand the community you're supposed to be protecting?

But the fourth or fifth time the captain uses the phrase, I realize I've had it all wrong. What he's been saying is "Avoid reflexive action." I sink back in my chair, feeling more than a little naïve.

Over the next few days, they put us through almost forty hours of tactical training and instruction on the use of lethal and nonlethal force. The hardest and most intimidating part is a trip to what they call the "Tactics House."

"The House" is actually a small airplane hangar about a half mile up the road from the barracks. Inside it has a stage set that's been made to look just like a South Bronx prewar apartment with a "Beware of Dog" sign on the front door, a busted television in the living room, and a doorway to a dark, mysterious back bedroom, where anyone could be waiting.

We're told that we'll be playing cops in a series of training skits, with cops playing the criminals. The premise is that we'll be given the same amount of information a cop would get on a radio call, and we are expected to respond appropriately.

I feel a little tightness in my stomach as my instructor, Sergeant Hammerslough, a heavyset guy wearing chains, a mustache, and a sweatshirt that's two sizes too small, tells me what to do.

"I want you to pretend this is real life," he says with a mildly belligerent Bronx accent. "Me and the other officers are gonna be citizens in this. Some of us are gonna be the bad guys, but we're not gonna tell you who beforehand. You gotta figure it out. All right? You gotta be ready for anything."

The only information I'm given before my skit is that there's been a call about a domestic dispute and someone inside the apartment has a weapon. My partner is a twenty-four-year-old Rockland County cowboy named Greg, who has red hair and buckteeth. Greg immediately establishes his claim as a high-blood-pressure candidate when he starts banging on the front door and yelling, "Come on out with your hands up!"

There's a slight rumble of laughter from the spectator galley above the set, where the twenty or thirty other recruits are watching us. I start to roll my eyes in embarrassment as the door swings open and a middle-aged cop, playing a citizen, sticks his head out. "Oh thank God, you're here," he says with convincing urgency. These guys really throw themselves into the roles, I notice.

"What seems to be the problem?" I say, stepping into the apartment and slipping into the old reliable social worker's tone.

Meanwhile, my partner, Greg, is standing in the middle of the living room, screaming at three other people: "Get against the wall! I wanna see you all spread-eagle!"

"Easy, man," I say. "Let's just find out what's going on from these people."

Greg ignores me and looks toward the doorway to the back bedroom. A mean-looking Hispanic dude in shades comes out and snarls at him.

"Don't gimme that!" Greg screeches hysterically. "Get up against the wall."

"Calm down," I say, turning to address the Hispanic guy, who's already pointing and cursing me out in street Spanish. Another guy is shaking his fists at us and raving about how we've violated his constitutional rights. The testosterone level in the room has been rising steadily for the last minute. All the guys are shouting at us and acting fired up. It's like standing in the middle of a bullring with everybody waving a red cape at you. Even though I know this is just playacting, my heart is beating faster.

"Sir, we had a report of a problem here," I say to the Hispanic guy, trying not to lose my head. "We just wanted to find out what it was."

The Hispanic guy looks me up and down, as if he's beginning to find all of this a little tiresome. Then he lifts up his shirt, revealing a gun in his waistband. He pulls it out and fires a blank at my partner, Greg. Before I even have time to look down at my own gun, the guy turns and shoots me.

The scene is over and the spectator galley explodes with laughter.

"You're both dead," Sergeant Hammerslough grumbles as he wanders onto the set. I notice the twenty or thirty other recruits who've been watching us are clapping their hands and are almost all doubled over from giggling at our incompetence.

"Hell," Greg, the Rockland County cowboy, says.

"Now what did these yo-yos do wrong?" Sergeant Hammerslough asks the assembled recruits.

"The one with the red hair shouldn't watch so many *Hunter* re-runs," someone calls out once the laughter starts to die down.

"Good point," says Hammerslough, his arms folded across his chest. "What about this guy?" He points to me.

"Too laid-back," says one fat-faced recruit.

"He acted like a social worker," Greg whines.

"Exactly," Sergeant Hammerslough says, putting his face right up to mine so I can smell how much garlic he had at lunch. "You gotta leave that namby-pamby shit at the office. This is the real world. You make a mistake and a split second later you're dead. You got that? And for Chrissake, keep your eyes on where everybody's got their hands."

I step off to the side, feeling thoroughly humiliated. As other recruits and probation officers go through their skits, I promise myself that I'll be more alert if I get another chance.

The last phase of our training is on the outdoor target range. The targets are cartoons of fifty-year-old guys with square jaws and crew cuts, who look like they ought to be called Sluggo. Remnants of another era. I've never had a client who looked anything like that.

I step up to a line twenty-five yards away from the targets. An instructor hands me a pair of earphones and goggles. It's a good thing I started wearing contact lenses recently; they wouldn't have fit over my old glasses. Then he gives me the .38-caliber Smith & Wesson service revolver. I'm not so much surprised by its weight, but the shape feels pleasing in my hand. I somehow thought it would have rougher edges or less balance. Instead, it has a certain solidness, a rightness; it re-minds me of the first stone I ever cast into a lake. The instructor shows me how to grip it and look down its sights.

I know I should reflect on what I'm about to do. I've spent so much time trying to steer other people away from violence that I can't believe I'm going to fire this thing. But I'm anxious to get it over with, the way a boy wants to lose his virginity, just so he can say he's done it. I raise the gun and stare down the barrel. Out of the corner of my eye, I see my instructor step away. My hands shake a little. A plane flies by. The sun is white. I pull the trigger.

It's hard to describe what it feels like the first time. The gun bucks. It rears back. It revolts against you and tries to throw you off. And once it's gone, you see dirt getting kicked up behind the target.

"Try holding it steadier," says the instructor. "You almost missed the target completely."

The second time I put my whole body into it. I stoop and bend a little at the knees, like they told me to. I have a feeling it makes me look like I'm taking a dump, but it helps my aim. I squeeze the trigger once more. The power surges up and down my arm and then out of my hand again. Even with the headphones on, the sound is piercing. But I haven't heard enough gunshots in my life to automatically think of people getting hurt.

"Straighten it out a bit," says the instructor, squinting at my target. "And next time you'll put it right through his heart."

19

Darryl King was sitting in the seventh row of the Apollo Theatre, next to his sister, Joanna. On the stage a handsome woman in a frilly black dress was singing a snappy Ella Fitzgerald song. Darryl ignored her and grabbed his sister's arm.

"What I wanna know," he said, "is when do I get to run the show?"

"Why don't you shut up and watch her sing?" his sister hissed at him.

Darryl sank back in his seat and twisted up his mouth as the woman finished her song to warm applause. It was Amateur Night at the Apollo and Darryl felt uncomfortable sitting there. Almost everybody else in the audience looked legitimate. Black middle-class families in suits and skirts. Scandinavian tourists in denims. Older poor people who must've been saving their money for weeks to afford the fifteen-dollar tickets. Darryl didn't see another crimey in the place, which had a beautifully maintained interior with red velvet curtains and gold designs on the walls and ceilings. Squirming around in his seat, he ignored the older guy in the gray suit onstage, who was saying something about how Billie Holiday and Sarah Vaughan got started here.

"Joanna, why'd you ask me to come if you didn't wanna

say nothing about the business?" Darryl asked.

"We'll talk," she murmured.

"I don't wanna talk," Darryl said a little louder. "I wanna better job."

Without taking her eyes off the stage, Joanna reached over with one large hand and grabbed her brother by the throat. "You behave now," she said.

The next act was a thin man with a ponytail. The booing started before he even touched the microphone. By the time he sang the opening notes of "God Bless the Child," people in the audience were on their feet, shaking their fists at him and telling him to get off. He stayed for two verses out of sheer defiance, his bum notes resounding like a foghorn through the great old theater. Finally, a man dressed like a clown came on the stage and chased him off with a broom.

"That sucked," Darryl said.

" 'S right," his sister told him, turning one of her Gemini earrings. "You're not so dumb for a Taurus."

She said that as if it might be worth her while to take him to more nice places like this, so he'd know how to act in public. He smiled a little to himself. In the meantime, a Japanese girl and boy had walked onstage, dressed completely in black. A rumble went through the crowd like they were about to start booing again. But then the band started the old rhythm-and-blues hit "Me and Mrs. Jones" and the Japanese couple began singing with so much soul and such tenderness that the audience forgave the way some of the lyrics were getting mangled and began cheering. A lanky young guy in a brown-and-black warm-up suit walked up one of the aisles, stopped in front of the stage, and threw a handful of money at the singers.

"Who the fuck is that?" Darryl wanted to know.

"I dunno." Joanna shrugged. "Maybe the brother's selling drugs in the Bronx or something. I ain't seen him around here."

"Shit," said Darryl, following the guy with his eyes back down the aisle again. " 'S what I wanna do."

"Then save yourself some money."

"But how am I gonna save the money when you won't let me do the shit I gotta do?"

"It's not time," his sister told him firmly. "I looked at the book. You got a unfavorable lunar aspect right now."

Whenever he heard his sister talk like this, Darryl didn't know what to say. She didn't seem to understand what he was capable of. Otherwise she and Winston would let him do more. All this ambition was giving him a headache.

The next act made him feel better though. Nine girls in white T-shirts and striped pants gyrating wildly to a Big Daddy Kane song. "I could do that," said Joanna, watching one really sexy girl at the front of the stage who was thrusting her pelvis at the men in the first row.

"I hate to see it," her brother said.

Before she could turn to hit him again, there was another shower of money coming at the performers. This time, the bills were fluttering down like autumn leaves. They were being thrown from the red-trimmed opera box less than ten feet above the left side of the stage.

Darryl looked up and saw Pops Osborn standing there, in a navy blue warm-up suit with a gold Mercedes-Benz symbol hanging around his neck. He was grinning down at the crowd like an aristocrat, while the big West Indian bodyguard glowered at his side. When the sexiest dancer glanced up at him, Pops threw down another fistful of dollars and put the sunglasses with the rhinestone frames back on top of his head.

"Fuckin' faggot," said Darryl.

"He just be showin' off," his sister told him. "He ain't nothin'."

Darryl started going through his pants pockets, looking for stray dollars. When the next act came on, a buxom woman in a tight spandex outfit, singing almost as well as Aretha Franklin, Pops started throwing even more money. And as stagehands rushed on to clear it off, some of the people in front started saying they weren't twenty-dollar bills, but hundreds.

By the last verse, Darryl had had enough. He found thirteen

one-dollar bills in his pocket and carefully crumpled each one into a ball. Then he stood up and began to throw them, one by one, at the stage. But somehow his trajectory was off and none of the bills reached the singer. They seemed to lose momentum around the first row and fade into the pit just before the stage, like snowflakes dying before they hit a damp street.

20

At noon on one of those summer days when it feels like a dome of fur has descended on the city, word reaches me at Rodman's Neck that they need a gun downtown. The problem is they're short of weapons at the Probation Department's Field Service Unit, so they need to borrow one from the police. And since I'm due downtown anyway, they figure I might as well drop it off.

I'm only too happy to oblige. I'm tired of being up in the Bronx and I have paperwork to catch up on back at the office. But most important, I haven't had a chance recently to check up on this girl I'm interested in.

Her name's Andrea Clinton. She works in the legal department, which is in the same building as the Field Service Unit. She's a law student from NYU doing a summer internship with Probation. A beautiful light-skinned black woman with delicate features and luminous gray eyes. Nearly every man in the department has noticed her, but she's spoken about much more often than she's spoken to.

When I get to Probation, I don't even bother stopping by the Field Service office on the first floor. I go right upstairs, looking for her. I find her by the water cooler just outside her office.

"I haven't seen you around here in a while," she says brightly. "What brings you our way?"

"A case," I lie.

I have to justify my presence on this floor, since I normally only come up here to hand in the paperwork for violations. "Nothing too heavy, I hope," she says, glancing over her shoulder at me as she heads back into the office.

I follow her in. I'd be intimidated as everybody else by the way she looks, except for one thing: Just below her mouth to the right, she has a mole. That changes the situation. It's like some cheap Hollywood makeup man thought he'd jazz up her somber beauty with a sleazy Marilyn Monroe touch. In fact, that mole is the one thing about her face that makes you feel like you could ask her to a ball game or buy her a domestic beer.

The other secretaries in her office smile when I come in after her because they know what I'm really here for.

"So what's your case?" Andrea asks, sitting down at a nearby word processor. "Are you violating somebody?" She straightens her back and her fingers fly across the keyboard, inputting furiously.

I realize I have to come up with a reasonable-sounding excuse. "Yeah," I tell her. "I'm thinking about getting rid of one particularly bad guy I've got on my caseload."

"What's his name?"

"Darryl King."

On the other side of the room, Miriam, a stocky secretary with a Clark Gable mustache, does her nails and talks on the phone in Spanish. "Whaddeedo?" Andrea says.

"Excuse me?"

She swallows hard and laughs. "I'm sorry, I was just eating a peanut . . . I meant to say, 'What did he do?' "

I hadn't been counting on her asking this. What did he do? I try to make up the case against Darryl on the spot. "Well," I say, "he showed up late for his appointment . . . And then he wouldn't cooperate and directly answer the questions I was asking . . ."

She can tell I'm stumbling around to gather my facts. Taking another peanut from the paper cup on her desk, she leans back and places it between her soft lips. She looks very sexy, holding her hair back with her hand. "What else?" she says.

"He, uh, kind of threatened me."

"How?"

"He asked how much time someone would get for killing a probation officer," I tell her. "And then he went into this whole sick fantasy riff about being a cop and pouring gasoline down people's throats . . ."

Somehow when I say this, it doesn't convey how scary it was sitting there listening to him. Andrea doesn't seem impressed. "Is that it?" she asks. "Why don't you just recommend him for a psychiatric exam?"

She may be new here, but she's clearly smart enough to know that nothing I've said constitutes more than a slight technical violation. Certainly not enough to stand up in front of a judge. I have to say something to avoid looking like a complete fool here.

I hitch my pants and try the honest approach. "I guess what it comes down to," I say, "is that I just have a bad feeling about the guy."

"A bad feeling?"

"Yeah."

"A bad feeling." She repeats the phrase disdainfully, as though it were the name of her least favorite song.

Across the room, Miriam the secretary is winking at me and pulling on her right cheek. I'm not sure what the gesture means exactly, but I suspect it's derisive.

"Darryl may not have done anything that bad yet, but I know he's going to," I add a little lamely.

"Hmm." Andrea glances over at the clock. Half past noon. She draws her chair back, slips off her high heels, and puts her black stockinged feet on the linoleum floor.

As she stands up and smooths her plaid skirt, she stops to

stare at the left side of my windbreaker. "Are you wearing a gun or something under that?" she asks.

I get embarrassed, realizing I still have the gun from the target range in my shoulder holster, without any bullets in it. I should've stopped downstairs and dropped it off before I came up here. Maybe I was doing some dumb-ass John Wayne daydreaming. "How could you tell?"

"The way it was bulging," she says, reaching into her black leather shoulder bag and pulling out a pair of white running shoes. "Walk me to the elevator," she says, putting them on. Out of her high heels, she moves with limber, athletic grace.

As she tells Miriam she's going to lunch, I take a deep breath. I figure I'm finally about to get my shot at asking her out. Miriam waves and keeps talking on the phone. I think I hear her say the words "marital aid" amidst all the Spanish. When Andrea turns her back, Miriam puts her thumb under her front teeth and flicks it at me.

We walk to the elevator bank and Andrea pushes the down button. I get ready to ask her what she's doing on Saturday night, but she starts talking first.

"I wanted to ask you something," she says.

"What?"

She tosses her hair back and gives me a cool appraising stare. She turns me on the same way Maria Sanchez does. They both have this thing that tells me I have no business trying to make it with them.

"How can you try to violate somebody just because you have 'a bad feeling'?" she says.

"I don't know. I've been doing this awhile. You can tell sometimes."

"Is that right?" She narrows her eyes. "Now this boy Darryl wouldn't be black, would he?"

"It happens that he is."

"And is that why you have 'a bad feeling' about him?"

"No," I say calmly. "I get bad feelings about white people all the time too."

"You know," she says, closing her bag, "I always thought guys like you became P.O.s because you wanted to help people."

"Yeah," I say. "That's right. I really like most of the people I work with."

"Then why is it you're walking around with a gun and talking about 'bad feelings'? Would you rather be a cop or something?"

Somehow when she says all this, it doesn't come off as bitchily self-righteous. It's more like she's young and into provocation. Pushing you a little, just to see where you really stand. That's okay. In fact, it reminds me of somebody I used to know.

"Things are a little more complicated than you're saying," I tell her.

"So explain it."

I scratch the back of my neck and think about it. "Sometimes you have to be your client's friend," I say finally, "and other times, you gotta be a hard-ass."

I hear the whining sound of the elevator coming down the shaft. It stops a couple of floors above us.

"But when you blame Darryl, you're just blaming the victim," she says. Now I know who she sounds like: me, about a year ago.

"No, I'm not blaming the victim," I explain patiently. "I'm blaming the guy who robbed the victim's gas station."

"Yeah, sure," she says. "I'll bet you treat your rich white clients exactly the same as you treat a poor boy from Harlem."

It's gonna be hard to ask her out on a date after this. I try to think of a way to turn the argument around.

"Look," I tell her. "Why don't you work with me on one of these violations? Then you'll understand what I'm saying."

She gives me a long, searching look. I hope what I said about Darryl King before didn't sound racist. A lot of people think she's white because of her skin tone, but I wonder if it just makes her more sensitive to slurs.

"Listen," I say, using a softer voice and rubbing my eyes

because the new contact lenses are still bothering me. "If you're so sure this Darryl King is going to get a raw deal from me, you should report me to my supervisor."

"And tell her what?"

"Tell her I'm being unfair and discriminating."

She considers what I'm saying. "Your supervisor is Ms. Lang?" In other words, she's asking, is your boss a black woman?

"That's right," I say.

She runs a delicate finger along the outer rim of her ear. "I don't know," she says distantly. "I don't know."

"Hey," I say abruptly. "What do I have to do to get through to you?"

"What?"

"You know, I'm doing and saying all these things just to get you to notice me and you just look right through me."

"Well, I . . ."

"You know something?" I say, putting a finger on my chest. "Every day I sit upstairs in my little cubicle and I talk to these people who've done these awful stupid things. And you know what I do with them? I give them a break. Each and every one of them. They've all screwed up terribly, and I give them another shot. So you know what? You should give me a break. All right? I haven't even done a crime. I just want you to give me a fair first chance. That's all."

The dazed look Andrea's been wearing through most of this speech turns amused. As the elevator doors open, she reaches over and shakes my hand. Her manner is grudging, but her touch is warm. I don't know if I'll be able to get her interested in me now, but I'm going to try anyway. "Do we have a deal?" I ask. "I mean, to work on the case."

"Well," she says as the elevator doors slide back together again. "I suppose everybody deserves a chance."

21

"Who is that?" Darryl King's mother asked.

"Just some kid," Darryl grumbled. "Keeps following me."

They were in a Harlem boutique/electronics store called Big Anthony's. Eddie Johnson stood by the front counter, staring up at the surveillance camera. The security guard by the door paid no attention to him or the constant buzzing from the store's alarm system for shoplifters. The muscular brown pit bull by his side strained at his leash and growled indiscriminately. Dozens of young men walked in and out of the store with ropes of gold chains and designer canvas jackets, which they wore off-the-shoulder style like 1940s movie starlets wearing mink stoles. A sleek soul ballad by Whitney Houston played over the public address system.

Darryl's mother looked down at the jewelry case and slapped her son on the arm. "When're you gonna buy me this necklace?" she said, pointing to a long, twisting chain of stones the color of rubies and sapphires.

"After you pay for my coat," he said.

"You're making money now too," she said.

He gave his mother an uneasy look. At thirty-five, she was a rail-thin, hollow-cheeked, and snaggletoothed woman who had an even longer criminal record than her son. She had a pending indictment for criminal sale of a controlled substance in the seventh degree to go with her conviction for stabbing Darryl's fifteen-year-old friend Mark. She'd started shooting heroin when she was thirteen, and now many of the veins in her arms, legs, and neck were dead and discolored from her needlework. Her career as a prostitute began a couple of years later, shortly after the birth of her children. These days she was often quiet and preoccupied, though she could turn vicious without warning. She lived for drugs, money, and her children, in that order.

"Hey, Moms," Darryl said. "Look at this."

She turned and saw Eddie Johnson making scary faces for the surveillance camera. When he saw Darryl and his mother glaring at him, he tucked his head down inside his unseasonably heavy blue parka and began to convulse. They couldn't tell if he was laughing or crying uncontrollably.

"Something very strange about that boy," Darryl's mother said.

"He just do everything he see me do," Darryl explained. "He got arrested last year in the Bronx, 'cos he was throwing rocks at cars. And he just do it 'cos he see another kid do it. He don't think for himself."

His mother hugged herself and rolled her eyes. "Why you let him hang around?"

Darryl told her that Eddie Johnson had actually been moderately effective as a steerer and a lookout when they'd recently taken over two of Pops Osborn's corners. Since that night he'd seen Pops at the Apollo, Darryl had been paying more attention to the family business. They'd made more than eight thousand dollars the next week and they were just getting started. Now he was starting to see the importance of little things. Like saving money and making long-term plans. Like the fact that tomorrow night, Eddie would be in the apartment next to Pops Osborn. He would give Darryl and the others the signal when Pops was alone and vulnerable. Then they could kill Pops and take over the rest of his locations, including the Fortress.

"Sounds all right," Darryl's mother said in a spaced-out voice.

There was a commotion at the back of the store. Darryl's custom-made jacket was ready. It was made from smooth white leather. An eight-point star adorned the back and there was a large Louis Vuitton symbol on the front. The price was three thousand five hundred dollars. Big Anthony, the store's proprietor, stood behind Darryl and draped the jacket over his shoulders as though it were an opera cape.

"I look nice," Darryl said, studying his reflection in the store's full-length mirror.

"Yes, you do," said his mother. "Very handsome."

Eddie Johnson came over and began to meekly pet the jacket. Darryl made a fist like he was about to sock him.

"Darryl, don't," his mother said. "He just wants to feel it."

"Next, he's gonna wanna wear it home," Darryl complained.

"So what would be the harma that?" his mother said. "Didn't I always teach you all to share shit?"

22

The Friday before the long weekend goes slowly. I feel blocked and useless behind my desk, and I wish for the millionth time I had a window in my cubicle so I could at least see if there's a sunny day going on outside. I have to settle for the photograph of the beach landscape on my wall.

This is one of those days when I long to be there. It seems like all my clients are trying my patience. Darryl King doesn't show up for his scheduled appointment, and to add to my frustration, Andrea gives me the cold shoulder in the hall when I come by her building to turn in some papers. And then there's Scottie Austin, a short and jittery twenty-four-year-old mugger, who normally hangs around Port Authority but has just been arrested for robbing an old man in his Washington Heights building for twenty-five dollars.

Scottie has gotten all the breaks he's going to get. "You're definitely getting violated this time," I tell him.

"But I didn't do it," he protests. He appears to be pulsating in his chair. A long dark scar marks the back of his hand and an even uglier one runs across his cheek.

"Oh yeah? What happened."

"Okay. I'm gonna tell you what happened. Okay? This is what happened. Here it comes: The old man just dropped his money on the ground." Scottie sits back and folds his arms, like he's just finished a formal presentation.

I raise my eyebrows. "And then?"

"Yeah," Scottie says. "He dropped the money twice. The first time I'm like, 'Yo, whass up with this shit? You drop your money.' And I give it to him. And he say, 'No, I don't want it,' and then he throw it down again. So then I pick it up."

"I find that very hard to believe," I say, grimacing and examining the arrest report more carefully. "Especially since it says here the old man caught a pretty bad beating from you. You broke his nose and two of his ribs when you threw him on the ground. I think I'm gonna have to violate you."

"Oh no. Don't do that. I can't go to jail. I'm not a career criminal. I'm a good guy."

I flip back and forth through the two dozen pages in Scottie's file.

"I'm just a jolly-going fellow," says Scottie, sitting back in the chair and musing on his place in the universe.

"You're a menace," I say, closing the file. "If it's not this arrest, it's just gonna be something else. The scams you were pulling at Port Authority were bad enough, but then I look at your rap sheet and all I see is you getting arrested for more and more serious crimes all the time. And the reason is that you're still smoking crack."

"I only smoke crack at night," says Scottie proudly. "And maybe in the afternoons. But only sometimes in the morning."

"Why not then?"

"I gotta sleep."

Maybe I'm getting a less tolerant attitude from hanging out with cops at the target range, but there seem to be more and more clients who get on my nerves the way Scottie and Darryl King do. It's all these serious felons with serious crack habits. I guess, for one thing, it's harder to empathize with them than with the other clients. What I really wonder is why anyone would want to smoke that shit. Don't they have enough problems? I know I do.

I mean I did a little bit of experimenting with sex and drugs when I was in school, and I certainly still remember what it felt like the first time Jack Daniel's took off the top of my head and let the pressure out. The only problem is, you can never quite get that first high back again. You have to try something harder each time. And eventually you stop feeling anything at all.

I'm just thinking about having a drink when Richard Silver walks in for his second appointment. He's a little more casually dressed this time, wearing brown loafers with gold buckles, a new pair of chinos, and a white linen jacket. With his hands clamped in his pockets, like he's carrying the most valuable lint in town.

"Hi," I say.

"Hi yourself," he grumbles.

The last thing I need is a big fight with this guy to start off the long weekend, so I just get out the file. But flipping through my notes, I see I left a lot of items blank during our last appointment because he had me distracted.

He sits back, legs crossed and hands laced up behind his head. His eyes never leave me. If you were just taking a glance, you might think he's waiting patiently. But I know that he's just coiling himself up, like a cobra waiting to strike.

"We got a lot of things to cover today," I say in the voice I use when I don't want a client to trifle with me. "We never really talked about your current job or your community service requirement."

"Is that so." There's absolutely no change in Silver's expression.

"We never even talked about what you got convicted of," I go on, needling him a little. "And I always ask people about that."

Silver stirs an inch or two and clears his throat. "My conviction?" he says darkly.

"Yeah," I say. "Your crime. Why'd you break the law?"

Silver smiles thinly at the insolence. "Why did I break the law?"

He gives me a sad, magisterial look that seems to say, *oh, but only a couple of years ago I could have broken you in half and stuffed you in a garbage can.* "Why did an untalented prosecutor have to get his name written in the newspaper with my blood?"

"That's not really the point, is it?"

"The hell it isn't. My one mistake is that I failed to properly delegate responsibility."

"In other words," I say, "you didn't hire somebody else to get caught holding the bag. I mean what kind of sleazy shit was this? Paying off somebody from the Board of Estimate with a million dollars in a bowling alley and hookers in a hotel room? That's just sad, that's all."

Silver's reaction is hard to gauge. His eyes bug out a little and he rises about a half inch in his seat. It looks like he's smothering an explosion inside himself. "Let me tell you..."

There's a knock at the door. Two Puerto Rican boys stick their heads in.

"Yo, man, we waiting all day," says the taller one, who wears a green hooded sweatshirt with nothing underneath.

The younger, smaller one wears a clean white shirt. He's not old enough to shave, but he's grown as much hair as he can on his upper lip. "We wait since lunch," the young one says. "Now we miss lunch. You should buy us lunch."

"I'm sorry," I say. "Who are you?"

"You don't know?" says the tall one in the sweatshirt, bouncing up and down with nervous energy. "Oh, man..."

"Gimme a break. I got two hundred and fifty other clients. I can't know everybody on sight."

"Morales, man." The tall one puts his hand to the side of his mouth like he's about to whisper something to me. "Unauthorized use of motor vehicle."

I know the name and I vaguely recall seeing the tall one before. Silver stares up at the ceiling, holding on to a thought.

The two Puerto Rican boys keep bumping shoulders with each other.

I look for my master list in a desk drawer. "Both of you aren't my clients, are you?"

"No, just me," says the tall one in the sweatshirt. "This be my baby brother, but I take him everywhere I go so he don't get in trouble at home."

I hold up a finger. "Can you just wait outside a couple of more minutes please?" I ask.

"We not the only ones waiting, you know," the taller, older Morales says.

The two boys leave, slightly annoyed with me. I write down the name Morales on a pink message slip and then turn back to Silver. "You were saying?"

"You know there's a thing the old-time pols used to call 'greasing the public weal.'" From the way he pronounces the words, the pun is clear. "Are you familiar with that expression?"

"Not entirely."

"Either you are or you aren't." The birthmark on his eyebrow makes him look more skeptical than usual.

"Okay, I'm not."

"All right," he says, standing up and looking at my posters. "You got Bob Dylan on your wall. Here's a little history lesson. This is what it was really like. The sixties. I'm in the City Council. You're in Romper Room. Or something. Wetting your pants. Whatever. City's about to blow up. We got war protesters up at Columbia. Martin Luther King getting popped. They're going apeshit in Newark and Los Angeles. In the ghettos here too. We're talking Mau Mau rebellion. They're gonna burn New York down. What do we do?"

I'm not sure if I'm supposed to answer, so I light a cigarette without saying anything.

"Frankly, we paid some of those ghetto guys off," Silver says, pointing and looking down at me like a college professor addressing a student. "A guy called Muhammed. Another one named Hakim. Threw everything at them. Money. Jobs. Grants. Know what? No riots in New York. You know what else? People who wouldn't have had a shot were able to get civil service jobs and move to better places. Completely legal? Maybe not in every single case." He smacks his right hand into the palm of his left. "Necessary for our survival? I think so." He doesn't mention Sullivan Houses, the low-income project he stopped supporting a short time later.

"By the way," I say, leaning forward in my chair. "How did you do with those voters you paid off?"

"Very well," Silver says, pacing back and forth and glaring at me combatively. "Call it gratitude."

"That's gotta be the highest-minded excuse for bribery I've ever heard," I say. "Correct me if I'm wrong, but you and your buddy went downtown to Bowlmor Lanes with a shopping bag full of money because you had a client who wanted to tear down some nice landmarked buildings on the Upper West Side and put up a condo..."

"The thing with Jimmy Rose was a serious thing," Silver says loudly, interrupting me. "There is a lack of affordable housing in this city. My client wanted to build fifteen hundred new units. Go ahead. Smirk. I would make money. True. But it would be for the common good."

He puts his hands together like a man begging for absolution. "Of course, the bureaucracy and the approval process move so slowly that it's hard to get investors to hang in there. So Jimmy and me. We did it. We greased the public weal. Guilty as charged."

Throughout the monologue Silver has been on his feet dramatizing, laughing, bullying. But when he gets to the part of the story where he gets convicted and his friend Rose kills himself, he seems drained. "You know the rest," he tells me. "Crime and punishment... Am I gonna do it again? No. My friend is dead. My life is nearly ruined. Did I have to do it in the first place?"

He takes off his jacket and slings it across his shoulder in the "man of the people" pose he must've copped from an old Frank Sinatra album cover. "We're all whores, you look at it that way. You wanna make a difference? You accept what they call 'corruption' in school. Only they don't tell you that." He raises his voice and then drops it suddenly. "Steven, you can't say anything to those Puerto Rican boys just in here that's gonna change their lives. To change lives, you need resources. You want resources, you buy into the system. You buy into the system, watch out for the prosecutor, my friend.

"See, you may not be doing anything wrong now, Steven, but you're not doing that much right either." With that, he puts the jacket under his arm, bows his head, and walks out the door.

23

"This is a guy who buys his wife a television antenna for an anniversary present," Richard Silver said.

"You should give him a chance," his lawyer, Larry McDonald, told him.

The two of them were sitting in a Long Island restaurant called Captain Nemo's Seafood Bar and Grill. All the wooden chairs had anchors on the back and legs shaped like dock ropes. Live fish tanks were built into the walls and each drink had a plastic swordfish stirrer. The lighting was dim and a little musty, like an underwater grotto. Larry McDonald and Richard Silver kept watching the door to the men's room.

"He's been in there a long time," Richard Silver said. "What's he doing, writing the Torah?"

"He's just nervous," Larry said in his airy singsong voice. "He's never done anything like this before."

Larry was not a bad lawyer, but he was no Jimmy Rose. There was something a little off about him. The paleness of his skin, the thinness of his wrists. His habit of sighing and letting his voice trail off. Richard glanced at the men's room door again as the boy dressed in a first mate's uniform brought him his tuna fish sandwich.

Richard told the boy to hold the rest of the food until the

third man in their party came back to the table. The boy left
and Richard shook his head.

"Captain Nemo's Seafood," he said. "With Bobby Kennedy
I had dinner at '21.' You believe that?"

Larry sighed. "Life is very funny..." his voice trailed off.

"Now, I'm spending July Fourth with a forty-thousand-
dollar-a-year bank manager from Syosset. What kind of world
is this?"

"I don't know..."

"Yeah." Richard turned his eyes to the bathroom once more
and then leaned across the table. "Listen, Larry, you sure about
this guy? The last thing I need is a pain-in-the-ass federal
probe. I already got this probation thing."

Larry held up his wrists, like he was offering to let Richard
slash them. "This is my second cousin. Practically my blood."

"Then why do I have to be here?"

"He wanted to meet you, Richard. The last time he was in
Manhattan, I showed him some of the buildings you put up.
He was very impressed."

Andy Altman finally came out of the bathroom. Richard
sized him up all over again. A small-boned man in his early
forties, with a boy's sparse mustache and a few strands of black
hair stretched, hopefully and impractically, across an expanse
of pink scalp. Sears blazer, purple Izod shirt, cheap loafers.
The kind of guy Richard used to beat up for his lunch money
and his baseball cards when he was a kid. Taking small steps,
Andy returned to the table and sat down between Richard and
Larry.

"I'm sorry," he said shyly. "My stomach's been bothering
me."

"It's all right," Larry said, patting his hand. "We had the
waiter hold your food."

"So, Andy," Richard said in a low voice. "You thought
about what we were saying?"

"Well." Andy cleared his throat and peered over at the
waiter to let him know he wanted his food now. "There were

a couple of things I wasn't quite clear on."

Richard's brow furrowed. "What don't you understand? You have the easy part."

For the third time, Larry took the napkin with the diagram on it out of his breast pocket. "It's just like we said before, Andy," he said in a voice that was just a bit above a whisper, "you hardly have to do anything. When Richard's friends bring in the deposits, you just don't fill out the IRS report. Don't worry about the Cayman Islands. Somebody else will go down there to handle things..."

"Larry, Larry, Larry." Andy shut his eyes and nodded. "I know how money laundering works."

"Sssh." Richard Silver looked like he was about to leap across the table and clamp a hand over Andy's mouth.

"I understand all that," Andy said in a softer voice. "What I don't understand is where Richard's friends get the money from. Are these Mafia people or something?"

There was a long silence. Richard waited until the waiter put down Andy's seafood platter and left before he spoke again.

"Why would you wanna know a thing like that?" he said in a quietly intimidating voice.

"I don't know." Andy seemed to shrink a little in his seat. "I just wanted to know. I thought it'd help me make my decision."

"Listen, Andy, when you get an opportunity, you take it. If the men who built Long Island had hesitated, we'd be sitting in a potato field now, instead of this fine restaurant." Richard looked over at the waiter and tapped his empty Diet Coke glass.

"That's right," Larry said. "You never know when something's going to come along and change your life."

The waiter brought Richard another Diet Coke while Andy held a skewered shrimp over the flame in the middle of his platter.

"I remember something that happened a few years ago that changed my life," Larry said, a long gray hair protruding out of his nose. "I had a very powerful client with a lot of friends in what the newspapers call the organized-crime community. Anyway, he was very fond of me and he invited me to a big party at his penthouse on the East Side. And I wanna tell you, it was the wildest thing. He had a swimming pool built into the roof of his penthouse. And when you went downstairs, there was a window so you could watch people swimming from under water. So I looked in, and he had all these naked boys in the pool."

Richard scratched his head. "You talking about Frank Raggi?"

"This is somebody you don't know," Larry said. "Anyway, I went downstairs and I'm watching this. And these boys were like dolphins the way they swam. A lot of the time, they had their heads out of the water, so all you saw were their legs and torsos. But every once in a while, one of them would swim by and take a little nibble at another guy's cock and balls. It was like the Aqua Show. The most erotic thing I ever saw in my life."

Richard shifted uncomfortably in his seat. "And then what?"

"What do you mean, 'Then what?'" Larry asked.

"What'd you tell your wife when you got home?"

"I told her I'm a fag."

"What?" Richard nearly spit out his soda.

"You didn't know that? I'm gay. Sure. And I never would've known it if I hadn't of gone to that party. That's what I was saying to Andy here about opportunities."

"Shit." Richard sat still for a moment, watching an angelfish eat a baby minnow in a nearby fish tank. "I never knew that about you, Larry."

"I only brought it up to make the point with Andy. I know it doesn't have any effect on our relationship."

"Of course not," Richard said, covering his mouth with a napkin. "So what do you say, Andy? Are you gonna be with us?"

Andy had done nothing but eat for the last few minutes.

His seafood platter, which started off with twelve items, had just two mangled pieces of calamari left. He sat back, rubbing his stomach.

"Could work out, I guess," he said.

"What's the problem?" Richard Silver asked.

"The ten percent you were talking about. That only comes to a thousand dollars if I help you wash ten thousand."

Richard put his glass down and looked at Larry again. "So?"

"So," said Andy, loosening his belt a couple of notches and suddenly sounding more confident. "I was thinking you could probably afford to add on another five percent."

"I see you already know all about opportunities," Richard said. "We'll see about your five percent. That's more than we were thinking of."

"Well, at least, throw in dessert tonight," Andy said. "I think I still feel a little hungry."

24

I don't suppose there's much I can say to explain why I call Maria Sanchez for a date on the Fourth of July. I guess I could claim that I care so much about my job that it spills over into my personal life. But the truth is that I'm kind of drunk and horny and I've been thinking about her a lot lately. Besides, it's the holiday and I've got nothing else to do.

My hand shakes a little as I'm dialing her new number, because I know I'm not supposed to be doing this. But I got one drink past my inhibitions a half hour ago and I figure I have to seize the moment now or let it pass forever.

By the second ring, though, I suddenly realize I could be making the mistake of a lifetime and blowing my job on a drunken whim. I'm about to hang up when I hear somebody picking up on the other end and immediately recognize Maria's voice saying, "Hola."

Hanging up now would make me feel like I was making a dirty phone call or something. "Yeah, Maria," I say, fumbling for a cigarette and trying to figure how to get out of what I'm about to get myself into. "How you doing?"

"Mr. Baum," she says in an excited voice. "I can't believe it's you calling."

"Yeah, neither can I."

"What are you doing?"

I put the cigarette down and start mashing up my Silly Putty. "Well, I, you know, like to check in on my clients over the holidays. Because, um, they can be really stressful times, you know. So I want to make sure everything's okay."

There's a long pause. I try to think of an excuse to get off the phone right away, like an airplane is about to hit my apartment.

"What are you doing, Mr. Baum?" Maria says in a very calm, deliberate voice.

Panic bounces my heart around like a basketball. She's on to me, I think. This is the end. On Monday she'll tell my supervisor, Ms. Lang, that I called her up and asked her out on a date, and then I'll get fired. And I'll end up on the street, begging for quarters and trying to sell old copies of *Freud on the Unconscious* and *Penthouse Forum* on sidewalk blankets like the scuzzy guys in my neighborhood.

"I told you what I was doing," I say, backtracking furiously and praying it's not too late. "I'm just calling all my clients and making sure they're all okay."

"No," Maria says firmly. "I mean, what are you doing tonight?"

I stop and take a deep breath. "Nothing, I guess. What're you doing?"

"I'm not doing nothing neither."

The words come out of my mouth without my permission. "So," I say, "you wanna see some fireworks?"

By ten, we've made our way to the Battery Park esplanade in lower Manhattan. Behind us, yuppie couples walk arm in arm and high-rise buildings glitter like too much expensive crystal jammed onto a narrow shelf. Down the river, toward the Verrazano-Narrows Bridge, fireworks deliver a series of shocks to the sky.

Maria is standing right next to me. She smiles and bounces up and down when a particularly colorful rocket scatters over the skyline. The mother-of-pearl smell coming from her keeps me by her side and reminds me I don't have any real excuse for being here with her.

"Oh, look at that one," she says. "It's just like a flower."

The rocket bursts open right over our heads. It's red at the center and the petals are blue and it keeps opening wider and wider until it seems like it's going to take over the whole sky. Only it doesn't make me think of a flower. It makes me think of pussy. Which just goes to show how long it's been.

"I'm so glad I came tonight," she says as the sparks in the sky fade.

"I am too."

That's the strange thing. I *am* glad she came with me. It's so obviously and so unambiguously wrong that I can't help being turned on by it. Her hair shines in the promenade lights and her pupils reflect the sparkle of another rocket going off. I find that I can't keep my eyes off the curve of her lower lip.

"Maria, I wanna ask you something," I say haltingly.

"Yes, what is it?" There's something sweetly eager in her voice that breaks my heart and makes me want to take her in my arms right now.

The whiskey haze in my head lifts a little, so that I may more clearly hear the tiny devil I imagine on my right shoulder and that boring harp player on the left. "Maria," I say. "Do you ever think about our meetings after you leave the office?"

For a moment, her mouth hangs open and though I can't see the rest of her face in the evening light, I have a feeling she's blushing. "Yes," she says. "Yes, of course, Mr. Baum."

I decide I don't like it that she keeps calling me Mr. Baum while I'm using her first name. It reminds me of the office, which in turn makes me think of her original crime. And that makes me even more uncomfortable than I was in the first place. So I start mashing up the Silly Putty in my pocket. A green rocket streaks across the sky and fragments in front of the Statue of Liberty. "What do you think about our meetings?" I ask.

"I think about the things you say." She looks up brightly as though someone was murmuring something exciting in her ear. "I remember everything you tell me."

I'm feeling that heady rush, like I'm about to either get laid or punched out. The harp player on my shoulder keeps telling me she's seventeen, but who asked him? "What parts do you remember most?"

She puts her fingers on her lips and looks thoughtful. "I think about how you tell me to work on my typing and to go to the Job Corps interviews..."

"Yeah, yeah, I know all that. But I mean..." I watch a yellow rocket shoot by and make a wish on it that I sort of hope won't come true. "Do you think about me?"

"You?" She gives me a smile like a Beach Boys' song in the dead of winter—a promise of something better ahead. "I think about you always. You're like one of *los angeles guardianes*."

The yellow rocket fizzes out. "What is that?" I say. "A minor league team or something?"

"No," she laughs. "It's a guardian angel. You're my guardian angel."

A second ago, her guardian angel wanted to stick his tongue down her throat. Now, I'm nodding my head like I know what the hell she's talking about.

"When I was young," she says, "and all the bad things happened to me, when my uncle would come to my bed, I always prayed for the guardian angel to come and make everything all right. Because otherwise no one would save me."

"Uh-huh." I am now three feet tall and shrinking because of the things I've pictured her doing in graphic detail over the past few hours.

"And now I have my guardian angel," she says, taking my hand and kissing me chastely on the cheek.

"Hey, Maria," I say, flushing with embarrassment and making sure my fly is still zipped up. "I'm just a regular shmo. You know?"

"I know you won't let anything bad happen to me," she says, skipping down the esplanade and looking over her shoulder like she wants me to follow.

I suppose I could chase after her, hoping vainly some spark might strike between us, but I chose to bring her here and as Maria's guardian angel, I choose to bring her home in a cab which costs $23.75. Then I take the subway back to my neighborhood and stop at the bar on Seventh and Avenue B for two scotch and sodas, a favored drink among disappointed guardian angels, I believe.

25

"What're you looking for?" Bobby "House" Kirk asked.

"Car keys," said Darryl King.

"For what?"

"Oldsmobile Cutlass Supreme."

Darryl King rolled Pops Osborn's body over and checked the left hip pocket. Blood was spreading from the gunshot wound in the back of Pops's head and staining the white carpet. Eddie Johnson stood in the corner, quivering, with his head tucked into his parka. A bottle rocket went whistling off a rooftop somewhere outside. Darryl told Aaron Williams to stop counting the cash for a minute and look in Sunshine's pockets for the keys. As Aaron went through the dead West Indian's clothes, Darryl began to sniff.

"Yo, man, I smell something," he said.

A thick pile of twenty-dollar bills and a money-counting machine sat on the table by the window, surrounded by containers of Chinese food that Pops had ordered. There was half an egg roll left on a paper plate nearby. Bobby Kirk picked it up and put it in his mouth.

Darryl looked over at the fat key chain Aaron was jangling. "One of these gotta be for Pops's Cutlass," Aaron said.

Darryl snatched the keys. Bobby asked him why he wanted

them so badly. "That's my ride," Darryl said, stuffing the keys along with two vials into his pants pocket. He figured that if his sister and her Jamaican boyfriend, Winston, were going to take over Pops's business, then he was at least entitled to the car.

"You remember the license number?" Darryl King asked Bobby.

"No, why should I?"

"Then we're just gonna have to try every Cutlass parked downstairs."

Bobby threw up his hands angrily and let them fall gently to his side. "Yo, I ain't with that, man," he said.

"Fuck you, Bobby," Darryl said. "Let's go."

Aaron said he would stay behind with Eddie Johnson for another minute or two to wipe the place down for any fingerprints and grab any extra guns they could find. They did not have to worry about witnesses. The neighbors already agreed they did not hear the nine rounds of gunfire.

Darryl headed for the door. "My head is going like this," he said, making a pulsing motion with his hand.

"You smoke too much of that shit," Bobby said, following him.

"Don't go judging me, Bobby. That's fucked up."

26

On Tuesday morning, I'm coming up the hall to my cubicle when I notice my door is already open. Immediately I start thinking somebody must've broken in and gone through my papers. There's been constant tension between management and the union these past few weeks, and all kinds of weird things have been happening. As I get closer, I hear papers rustling and a chair squeaking inside my cubicle, so I know whoever it is still is in there.

I pause outside the doorway and wonder if I should go get help in case things get rough. But decide it's my office after all, so I come belting in, shouting, "What the hell is going on in here?"

Andrea Clinton almost falls off my chair. Her papers go sliding off her lap and flying on the floor. "You frightened the shit out of me," she says.

"Sorry," I say, bending over to pick the papers up. "No one's supposed to have a key for this office except me."

"Your supervisor let me in," she says. "I told her I had a surprise for you."

I know she can't mean this the way it sounds, and I look at her carefully.

She's dressed a little more casually today, in a blue oxford shirt and a khaki skirt without stockings. Her ponytail is tighter than before, giving her a severe, judgmental look. Like she's so beautiful that she doesn't have to forgive the people who cross her. The rest of us can't afford a lot of grudges, because life's too short. You have too few friends. But a truly gorgeous girl can write off anybody, because somebody else will always be interested. I better watch what I say here.

My stomach's jangling as she hands me the file without looking at me. The top sheet is a new "hit notice" generated by the New York State Identification System computer in Albany. It says:

King, Darryl. Male. Black. NYSID #04606670N. Eighteen years old. Originally sentenced to probation on June 2. The above individual using the name Daniel Kane was re-arrested on July 4 for a crime committed earlier that evening. The charges were attempted grand auto theft, unauthorized use of a motor vehicle, burglary third-degree, possession of burglary tools, and resisting arrest.

"Shit, man," I say, checking out the rest of the file.

"I thought you'd be pleased," she says coldly.

"Why should I be?"

"It proves you were right about him all along."

True enough, but in another way I'm kind of disappointed. There's no denying that Darryl's a bad guy, but I was looking forward to trying to turn him around. It would've been a challenge, kind of like a hunter getting a prized lion's head to go over his mantelpiece. But now that will never happen. Maybe just as well though, I think, looking at his file.

"He was trying to steal an Oldsmobile Cutlass Supreme," I say, checking the arrest report. "I guess the arresting officers charged him with everything they could think of. Where is he now? Are they still holding him?"

"Look at the next page," Andrea says in a curt voice.

The next page says Darryl was arrested two nights ago by

officers from the 25th Precinct, and then arraigned in Manhattan Criminal Court before he was released on his own recognizance.

From this point on, it should be cut-and-dried. Darryl was arrested and now it's my job to go to the judge and tell him that he's a violator who should go to jail. But I notice Andrea looking upset. I hope she's not going to hit me with that whiteman's-justice-black-man's-grief argument again. I feel myself tensing up inside at the thought of fighting with her.

"What's the matter?" I ask.

"What's the matter?" she says. "What's the matter is that they gave this guy probation in the first place."

I take off my windbreaker and squint at her like I can't believe I'm hearing her right.

"How could anybody let this guy go?" she says. "Didn't they look at who he was? Didn't they see what he'd done?"

I can tell she's about to launch into a full-fledged rant, so I cut her off right away. "Wait a second," I say. "The other day, you were giving me a hard time about the way I was talking about my clients."

"Well, that was before I saw the rest of this case."

Andrea has come up with the files for both Darryl and his mother, Kimberly, including her conviction for stabbing Darryl's fifteen-year-old friend Mark. "I heard about this," I say, turning the page.

She's also managed to get hold of Darryl's previously sealed juvenile record, which says Darryl has been arrested at least four times a year since the age of twelve for muggings, beatings, joyrides, sexual abuse, chain snatchings, and drugs. The earliest recorded incident happened when he was six, just after he was placed in a foster home. He was on his way to his first grade class one day when he found a hypodermic needle on the sidewalk outside the school. He took the needle into the classroom and began stabbing his little classmates. He was sent home for a week and then taken to a counselor.

"It's like he's one of those guys with the extra Y chromosome," Andrea says furiously. "He just loves to do crime..."

I know just what she's feeling right now. I remember the first time one of my clients left my office and went right out and did another crime. It felt like a bucket of cold water in my face. But as I'm reading Darryl's file, I sort of get a sad feeling too.

"Look at the kid's mother," I say. "They had to take him away from her when he was six and put him in a foster home."

"Yeah, but look at the report; she got him back when he was twelve."

"That's still a long time," I tell her. "A lot of bad things happen to kids in those foster homes . . . and where's his father? He never really stood a chance." Just the old social worker in me talking again.

I guess I feel sorry for Darryl in an abstract way. When I think about the guy who was actually standing here, bellowing out his insane fantasy, I get frightened and angry.

Andrea has also uncovered the obscure detail that Darryl King was once nicknamed "Dooky."

"I gotta remember that," I say. "I always like to know people's nicknames."

Andrea frowns as I look at the arrest report for the recent case, which involves Darryl's attempt to break into the Oldsmobile Cutlass Supreme parked near East 124th Street. The name of the arresting officer, Ron Kelly from the 25th Precinct, is typed at the top. "Let me give this cop a call," I say. "If you can get the arresting officer, he can give you some nice details to put in your violation report."

She hands me a cup of coffee as I dial and listen to the phone ring at the precinct. You almost never get these cops the first, second, or the third time you try because they all have these weird schedules. I leave one message for Kelly, and then a half hour later, Andrea and I go down to the legal department and try him again. This time we get lucky and the sergeant catches Kelly going out the door for the day.

There's a sound like the receiver being beaten with a hammer and then he picks it up. "This is P. O. Kelly," he says with a raw Queens accent. "What can I do for you?"

I look over at Andrea, who's listening in on an extension a few feet away, and quickly explain who I am. I ask Kelly if he can spare a minute to tell me about Darryl's arrest.

"Ah, I don't know about any of this," Kelly says. "Didn't you get what you needed from the D.A.'s file?"

"Sometimes an arresting officer can pass on the kind of detail that will convince a judge to lock a guy up."

There's a long pause. Background noise roars on his end of the line. "You know," Kelly says finally, "the relationship between your department and our department is not the most cooperative in nature, if you hear what I'm saying."

I give the phone the finger and mouth "Fuck you" several times while Andrea looks on, appalled at what he's telling me. Some cops hate probation officers beyond reason. They're sure that we're protecting criminals and that we love putting them back on the street after they arrest them.

There's also an element of class snobbery. A cop's starting salary is about ten thousand dollars higher than a probation officer's; the gap in pay and benefits increases with each year on the job. So a lot of cops don't like to consort with lowly social workers.

"Maybe you should have your superiors reach out for my superiors," Kelly says. "Let them sort it out."

"Oh, c'mon, man . . ."

"Hey, that's the way it is . . . yeah, just a minute, I'll be off," he yells to somebody else at the precinct. "Anything else I can do for you, Mr. Baum?" Kelly's voice grows fainter as he prepares to put the phone back on the hook. Andrea shakes a fist in frustration at the phone.

Figuring I got nothing to lose, I try one more angle. "That's Byrne," I say.

"Your name's Byrne? Not Baum?"

"Yeah."

"Why didn't you say so?" Kelly says in an I-didn't-know-you-were-an-Irish-guy tone. "Hold on just one second, I got that mutt's file right here."

Andrea's mouth drops open and she has to cover her receiver as she begins laughing hard. When she regains her composure, she gives me a thumbs-up sign.

Kelly reads the notes about the arrest. Just after midnight on Sunday, they arrested Darryl King and another young man named Robert Kirk trying to break into an Oldsmobile Cutlass Supreme parked near a big housing project by the East River. I smile and put my hand over the receiver.

"Bobby 'the House' Kirk was his codefendant on the gas station robbery," I tell Andrea in a soft voice. "He violated another condition of his probation by hanging around with a 'disreputable person' like Bobby. We can use that in the hearing."

I scribble notes as Kelly goes on to say that Darryl was carrying a sharpened screwdriver. He took a swing at Kelly when he was arrested and used "abusive and threatening language," though Kelly won't or can't give me the exact words.

The hearing for the arrest is a month and a half away, so Kelly's worried that my violation proceeding will ruin his collar. I assure him it will be okay.

"So how'd you pick him up?" I ask now that we're on slightly more friendly terms. "Were you just going by the building on patrol?"

"Oh no, we were already up there as backup to the homicide detectives. We just saw this guy King and his buddy getting behind the wheel of the car when we came out."

"Oh yeah?" The air around me suddenly seems to get very still. "So what was the homicide up there?"

"Ah some fuckin' thing," Kelly says. "They killed two of the fuckin' crack dealers who were running the fuckin' building."

I flash on the thing that Lloyd Bell was telling me the other night at Junior's: that Darryl's friend was trying to firebomb some crack dealer in Harlem. Because of the hazy way Lloyd told me the story, I'd just let the whole thing hang out in the back of my mind.

"Who'd they arrest for the murders?" I ask, letting him hear the urgency in my voice.

"They didn't catch anybody yet. They found a pile of clothes in the apartment with the bodies and a forty-four with the prints wiped off near the incinerator down the hall." He lowers his voice. "It sounded a little hairy up there. A lot of blood and Chinese food lying around."

"Did you ask Darryl about the dead guys?"

"Whaddya," the cop says, "that kid's just a car thief. That's not his thing, killing people."

"I don't know about that," I say as forcefully as I can. "The kid came into my office wearing a beeper, like he works for a dealer. He was acting out, like he was gonna get violent. So that's one thing. And then the other day I heard a story about his friends setting fire to a crack house uptown. You caught him across the street from a drug killing. It doesn't seem so stupid to me to bring him in and ask him about it. He might at least know something."

Andrea nods as if the idea makes sense to her too. But Kelly snorts. "You hear about all kinds of things you're on the street long enough."

This time, Andrea is giving the cop the finger into the phone. "Okay," I say. "By the way, which detective caught the homicide case?"

"I think it's McCullough upstairs. Or somebody. Yeah. Detective Sergeant McCullough. You want me to have him call you?" Kelly's tone is getting remote and bored now.

Andrea is gesturing that she wants to take care of this part of it. "Yeah, would you?" I tell Kelly. "I'd appreciate it."

I put the phone down and ask Andrea what's up.

She's already fussing with her hair and rolling up her sleeves like she can't wait to get to work. "I'll go see Detective McCullough," she says.

"Why?"

"Well, maybe now I have something to prove to you, Steven."

27

"I still don't believe you tried to break into the wrong car," Joanna Coleman said to her brother, Darryl.

"And got arrested," his mother added. "Don't forget he did that too..."

"Didn't you visualize what would happen?" his sister said, pointing to the book *Visualize Success* on top of the TV.

Everybody else started laughing as Darryl stared dumbstruck at the letter from his probation officer telling him to show up for a violation hearing. "I don't visualize taking no more of this shit," he muttered, ripping up the paper.

They were back in the narrow apartment his mother shared with her grandmother Ethel, Darryl, and occasionally, Darryl's girlfriend, Alisha, and their two small children. Ganja smoke drifted through the wind chimes suspended over an unmade sofa bed by the window. Joanna's boyfriend, Winston Murvin, who had watery red eyes and long dreadlocks, held up his hand and waited for them to be quiet.

"Now listen up all you people," he said. His light Jamaican accent made the last word sound like "pee-pell," even though he was from Jamaica in Queens, not the Caribbean island. "I am going to show you how to do this once and only once, then that's it."

Winston asked Aaron Williams to bring over the bag of cocaine he'd taken from Pops Osborn's apartment. Aaron put the bag on the table next to a hot plate, a large bottle of water, and a yellow-and-red box of Arm & Hammer baking soda. A slow reggae song lopped along in the background. Joanna and Winston's two kids did a silly, arm-swinging dance on the bed a few feet away.

Darryl knelt down by the side of the table. Winston put the bottle on the hot plate and turned it on. Then he dropped the baking soda and the cocaine into the water. "This is how you do it when you don't have a tank of ether to use for the purifying," Winston explained.

It seemed to take a long time for the coke to boil down to its oily base. The baking soda sopped up its impurities. What was left, after Winston added cold water, were hard white balls of cocaine base.

"This is a business like any other business, mon," Winston told the assembled group. "We live by the law of the supply and de demand. So don't be getting high on our supply."

" 'S right," said his girlfriend, Joanna, staring accusingly at her brother, Darryl. "Just like any other business."

"And the ones who come out on top are the ones who understand the laws of the economics," Winston went on. From the incantatory way he was speaking, he might've been talking about the world of spirits instead of the business of selling cocaine. "Now we can buy a kilo for thirty thousand dollars from our friend in Miami. And what does that mean?"

Darryl looked at him and shrugged uncomprehendingly.

"That means we have at least a hundred and twenty thousand worth of crack," Winston explained patiently.

Darryl smirked and waved his hand. "I know all that," he said.

The Jamaican gave him a cool, level glare. "Then why are you not in business for yourself, Darryl, mon?"

Darryl got embarrassed and didn't say anything. He hated getting disrespected in front of the whole family like that. He wondered if it would be possible to kill Winston without everybody getting pissed off at him.

"Remember," Winston was telling everyone. "The first sample you give the customer must be the purest hit he's ever had. That way he'll keep coming back for more."

"Then you step on the shit with baby laxative or inositol," Darryl's mother added helpfully.

"Thank you," Winston said. "That is the first rule for any salesman. Get the customer hooked on your product." He glanced over at Darryl. "Will you remember all of this later, Dooky?" Winston asked mockingly. "Are you a good student?"

To show his disgust, Darryl made a ticking sound with his tongue and the roof of his mouth, and then he refused to look at the Jamaican. Darryl's girlfriend, Alisha, sat by the television rocking the baby to sleep. The older child, Toukie, was running back and forth with Joanna's two kids.

Winston spooned the white balls onto a sheet of paper on the table. He showed Darryl, Aaron, and the others how to measure the hardening coke and chop it into chunks the size of a penny. "And that is what we call cracks," the Jamaican man said, like a magician revealing a trick.

"Gimme some of that shit," Darryl said, stuffing a couple of chips into his glass pipe and flaring his huge butane lighter.

"Darryl, mon," Winston said. "You'll never get rich that way."

They laughed again. Hours went by. Darryl, Aaron, and Bobby took turns with the crack pipe. Alisha took the two children back to her mother's house. Darryl's mother chased her grandmother out of the apartment, once more telling her that Darryl would beat her old face in if she didn't stay out of the way.

As she came back in and settled down on the unmade sofa bed, Darryl's mother talked about how the local dealers used to test the purity of heroin in the old days. "They'd find theyselves some junkie and take 'im back to the apartment, and shoot 'im up, and if they threw up and got all sick, they knew the shit was good," she said.

"Is that so?" asked Winston.

"I should know," said Darryl's mother proudly. "I was the prime testee on my block."

"Damn." Darryl gave his mother a stern look.

"Back when I was your age, Darryl, I was shootin' up heroin for five years," she told him. "We didn't have it as easy as you all. Drugs cost more, they was harder to get, and they was harder to take. You understand what I'm saying? That's the problem with this country now. The youth have it too easy."

In the meantime, Winston was trying to demonstrate to Darryl and the others how to stuff the crack into the small glass vials and put rubber caps on them. He did a dozen vials himself and then he told Aaron to try.

"Very good," Winston said. "Aaron is a good factory worker. This is our factory now, and we are a corporation."

Winston explained that while he was busy dealing with his suppliers in Miami and the Kennedy Airport area, the posse should have somebody making crack twenty-four hours a day in the small apartment. He designated Darryl King's mother to be the financial comptroller at the factory, paying workers five hundred dollars a week. He gave his girlfriend, Joanna, responsibility for overseeing the street peddlers, who made roughly one thousand dollars each. The more industrious ones could make ten times that amount in a week. Winston told Joanna to be wary of ambitious young dealers trying to slice off a piece of the territory for themselves.

"Only give it to them on consignment," he said. "At the very, very most, a hundred and fifty capsules at a time. We don't want them to run away on us."

"What about me?" Darryl said. "After what I did, I should get to be more than just enforcer."

"Darryl," said Winston Murvin. "You are our first and most loyal customer."

28

I take time off around lunchtime to finish some of the paperwork for the Darryl King violation. I call Judge Bernstein's chambers to set up a court date and then slowly type a second letter to Darryl, whiting out all the words I misspell along the way. He didn't respond to the first one I sent, so there's no reason to expect he'll answer this one either, but I don't mind the extra work. If I don't cover myself now, the judge will find the hole in my case later and throw me in it.

"Make sure you touch all the bases," Jack Pirone used to say in our training sessions. "The system can afford to fuck up; you can't." I find Darryl's home phone number in my file and dial it. I don't particularly want to speak to him again, but there's a regulation that says I have to make every possible effort to reach him before the date of the violation hearing.

The line has a tinny, unnerving buzz. I let it ring nearly a dozen times before somebody picks up. Then it's another thirty seconds before I hear anyone speak.

"Hello?" says a meek, high-pitched voice.

"Ah hi," I say. "Is Darryl King there?"

"I don't know." She sounds like a sweet, older woman. She doesn't say anything for a moment. From her steady breathing, I can tell she has not moved an inch away from the phone.

"Hello," I say. "Are you still there?"

"Yes."

"Can you please check if Darryl is there for me, ma'am?"

"Oh, of course, I'm sorry." She makes her voice even smaller and wispier. "Darryl...Darryl...Darl..."

She's just holding the phone a little ways from her mouth and whispering to herself. Darryl King could only hear her if he was three inches high and standing on her shoulder. She clearly doesn't want to find Darryl even if he is there.

"I'm sorry," she says in a voice that's said "sorry" more than any other word over the course of a lifetime. "He doesn't seem to be here right now."

I explain who I am and why I'm calling.

She keeps saying "uh-huh" in a happy, agreeable tone. Anyone listening to her end of the conversation would think she was being offered a free magazine subscription and a weekend in the Bahamas.

I ask her if she's Darryl King's mother.

"I'm Darryl's great-grandma, Ethel."

"Um, I don't like having to do this, Mrs....uh, ma'am," I say. "But you must tell Darryl it's very important for him to come to court on the date I gave you. Otherwise, he's going to be in even more trouble than he is right now."

"I understand."

"See, because..."

"Darryl is a good boy," she says suddenly. "He is actually a very nice person...He just do have...his little moods sometimes."

"What kind of moods?"

She doesn't answer.

"Does he have moods from taking drugs?" I ask.

Still nothing.

"What does he do when he's in these moods? Does he break things? Ma'am? Does he steal things? Does he hurt anybody?"

She seems to realize I'm trying to gather evidence against her great-grandson because she maintains her silence. A fly buzzes around my cubicle and lands on my desk directly in front of me. I go to swat it, but the fly jumps off quickly and I bang my hand on the edge. It takes several seconds for the pain to subside.

"Well, Darryl isn't in right now," she says. "I believe he's gone downtown to see his friends at the video arcade."

"Is that right?" She must be talking about Playland, the place on Times Square that Lloyd told me about.

"Maybe I should have Darryl call you," his great-grand-mother finally says in her smallest voice. "Could I have your number please?"

I give it to her and then she does something unusual. She asks me to give her my office address. "Thank you very, very, very much, Mr. Baum," she says. "You take care."

Normally, that would be enough. But this time, Ms. Lang comes marching right back into my cubicle with the "violation of probation" papers I'd just dropped on her desk.

"You touch all the bases?" she says. "You talk to Darryl?"

"I called his house, but he wasn't there," I tell her.

"Did they say where he was?"

"Well . . . sort of."

The Playland video arcade is next to a television studio and a Wendy's fast-food restaurant in Times Square. In its windows, there are monster masks and signs advertising that photo IDs and authentic military dog tags are available here. Just standing on the sidewalk outside, you can hear it's a noisy place, but when you walk in, it's like entering a fire zone in Beirut. The air is thick with electronically produced sounds of gunfire, car crashes, and women screaming.

I glance around and take in the names of the video games making this racket: Street Fighters. Shadow Warrior. Operation Wolf. Two Crude. Ninja Star. Castle of the Dragon. Crime City. Basket Brawl. The titles alone are an assault on the senses. A sad-eyed girl with a ring through her nose slouches against a machine called Forgotten Worlds. Next to her a bullnecked boy in a backward baseball cap is ignoring her and holding on to a loud game called RoboCop. He's so riveted to the screen that you'd think it's giving him electroshock therapy. In fact, the whole atmosphere of the arcade is so intense and obsessive that it's easy to forget there's actually daylight outside.

"Happy Motherfucker's Day," someone walking by me mumbles.

On the whole, I'd rather have piano wire wrapped around my neck than be here, but I have no choice. Ms. Lang wants to take special care with this case, so she won't let me file Darryl's violation unless I've actually made contact with him before the court date.

After a couple of minutes of searching, I spot Darryl King near the back of the place. He's wearing a couple less chains than the last time I saw him and a pair of jeans that look just a little loose on him. The game he's playing is called Devastators. Just standing behind him, I can see he's very good at it. The game is essentially a cartoon version of the movie *Rambo*: A burly Sylvester Stallone-type figure stands at the bottom of the screen, waiting to be attacked by an army of men in gray uniforms. Using a lever and two buttons, Darryl maneuvers the Stallone figure with great skill, deftly evading half the men in gray and killing the rest by stabbing them and shooting them. Eventually, the Stallone figure reaches the top of the screen and blows up the gray army's ammo dump. The whole screen explodes in celebration and flashes Darryl's score of fifteen thousand points over and over.

"Well, all right," says Darryl.

He almost steps on my foot backing away from the machine and then turns around abruptly.

"Remember me?" I say.

For a split second, his features come together in the middle of his face, like he's about to get mad and punch me out right now. I remind myself that we're still on neutral territory here, halfway between my office and Darryl's home, so I shouldn't have anything to worry about.

"I'm Steve Baum," I remind him. "Your probation officer."

A few more seconds pass while he decides how to react. The Pac-Man machine behind him plays a cheerful ditty and an old guy with smelly hair walks by pushing a broom over the blue-and-white checked floor. Whitney Houston smiles at me from a poster on the wall. Slowly, Darryl begins to smile too.

"Yeah, I know you," he says to me. "You my nigger."

Now I'm sure he's confused, but he sidles up next to me like we're old friends who haven't seen each other since high school. I notice for the first time that we're about the same height, though his forearms are about twice the size of mine.

"What's up, Mr. Bomb?" he asks. "I didn't know you was coming here."

He says this like he would've prepared hors d'oeuvres if he'd been alerted. When he's grinning this way, his face has an open, boyish quality. If I was just meeting him now, I'd take an instant liking to him. He seems like a charming, normal kid. I have to force myself to remember what he was like that night he came into my office.

"You know you've missed a couple of your appointments," I tell him.

He looks abashed, like a child confronted with a toy he's just broken. "I know," he says. "I was ill."

"You were ill?"

A machine called Elvira screams and a dumpy, effeminate man brushes by me on his way to the fake jewelry counter on the south side of the arcade. Darryl looks me right in the eye for a moment and then dips his head shyly. "I'm sorry," he says in a quiet voice.

I figure this is a guy who's been through the criminal justice system enough times to know when he's supposed to put on a good boy act. So the surprise isn't so much that he's behaving himself now, but that he acted so violent when he was in my office before.

"You know we still have some unfinished business to discuss," I tell him. "Our first appointment was not what I'd call very satisfactory."

He nods as though he'd been thinking the exact same thing and it'd been keeping him up at night. "Can I speak with you?" he says, putting a light hand on my arm and leading me toward a quiet corner of the arcade. At that moment, his touch is so gentle and his tone is so reassuring that the idea flashes into my mind that maybe all of this has been a terrible misunderstanding and he is just a victim of circumstance after all. I wonder if it's possible that I judged him too quickly. I think of the thing I saw in his file about him being raised in a foster home.

But then we pass a skinny boy with a harelip and a flattop and he looks at Darryl like he's waiting for some kind of signal. I get a peculiar tightness in my gut that reminds me of the training session I had at Rodman's Neck. I wonder if I'm about to get jumped here. From Darryl's arrest record, I remember he's got plenty of experience with assaults. The front door is only about thirty yards away, but with all these machines and all the noise they're making, it's doubtful that anyone would see me or hear me if anything bad happened back here.

Darryl is standing in front of a video game called Gang Wars. He fishes around in his pants pockets and then pulls out two quarters and puts them into the machine. Without taking his eyes off me, he pushes the button allowing two people to play the game.

"So now you've got yourself in all this trouble," I tell Darryl. "Why've you been fucking up so much?"

"I got so much confusion on my mind," he says.

On the Gang Wars video screen behind him, a narrative is unfolding. Yellow letters appear against a black background, saying: "New York. The 21st Century. A girl is kidnapped by someone unknown." The letters fade and an animated street scene appears. A run-down cityscape of abandoned tenement buildings, craggy sidewalks, and sinister garages. Another Rambo-type guy in a tank top and a headband walks across the screen. Darryl turns and starts controlling his movements with the lever and buttons on the machine.

Darryl keeps talking even as he's playing the game. "See, what I need to do is get some place where I can get all the shit out of my head. You know what I'm saying? 'Cos like, see, what I wanna do is try to get my own self into a position to take advantage of the opportunities in the marketplace."

What the fuck is he talking about? It sounds as though he's been reading up on those business training schools on the matchbook covers.

On the screen, the Rambo guy is being set upon by three or four other steroid cases. The object of the game seems to be punching them and kicking them senseless so you can reach the kidnapped girl. I notice that Darryl is very good at having his Rambo guy beat people up, but he doesn't seem to be making much progress in finding the kidnapped girl.

"Like I know I'm fucked up," Darryl is saying. "But I got shit I wanna do. You know what I'm saying? It takes money to make money...work. I wanna expand. You know. Make contacts. I just need time to work it out, and then I'd have my shit together. Right? But now you come by my crib and that fucks me up all over again."

"Well, the problem is not that I came by your crib," I tell him as he continues to beat the crap out of people on the screen. "In fact, this isn't your crib, it's a public place. The problem is that you didn't show up for your appointments, and when you did show up, you were acting out. So what am I supposed to do?"

He pushes a button and the Rambo guy on the screen punches someone twice his size in the face and kicks him in the nuts. "'S what I'm saying." Darryl steps away from the machine as it flashes his score. "So step off, all right?"

"Step off?"

He waves his hands at me. "Gimme a break."

"You got a break, and you went out and tried to steal a car."

He makes this little ticking sound with his mouth and looks ever so slightly annoyed with me. I can tell he's trying to hide his anger. A couple of other kids who seem to be friends of his are hovering nearby. I tell myself once more that I have nothing to be afraid of.

"So you got my letter, right?" I say.

"What?"

"The letter I sent you about the judge. You have a violation hearing in court next week. You know that, right?"

"Right," he says. "It's your turn."

"What?"

He points to the video game. The Rambo guy is standing in the middle of the screen, waiting to be directed. A couple of his pumped-up enemies are approaching. One of them looks a little like the cartoon character Thor, with his flowing blond hair and huge hammer.

"Listen, Darryl, I don't have time for this. I gotta get back to the office."

"Still your turn," he says, eyeing the game.

I halfheartedly put my hand on the lever and glance at the screen. My Rambo guy moves toward Thor and his hammer. Almost reflexively, I touch one of the buttons and my guy punches out Thor.

I turn back to Darryl. "So you got all that, right? You know you're supposed to be in court next week. You should make sure you have a lawyer."

"See, I was meaning to speak with you on that," he says with a small smile.

"Yeah?"

"I was thinking maybe you could talk to the judge."

"I can't do that. It's out of my hands now."

"Who give the papers to the judge?" he asks.

"I did."

"Then it's not out your hands."

I happen to look down at the screen and see a man in a turban about to smash my Rambo guy over the head with a rock. I push a button labeled "jump" and my guy gets out of the way just in time.

"See, you took things out of my hands when you tried to steal that car," I tell Darryl. "You broke the rules at probation and now you're gonna have to pay the price. And if you get violated, it's gonna be twice as bad as it would've been if stealing the car was your first offense."

"So it's like that," he says. "Huh."

There's something disturbingly cold about the way he says the words. I recognize the tone. It's the same one he used when he first came into my office. Before he started ranting. Like it wouldn't bother him if I burst into flames now and burned to a cinder right in front of him. *It's like that.* After all the nodding and smiling he's been doing today, it's as if the curtain has finally gone up, revealing the real guy who's been standing up there all along.

"It's like that," I say.

He takes a deep breath and shakes his head. A white guy who looks like he could be a cop starts playing the machine next to me called Special Criminal Investigation. For a second, I get bold and say something to Darryl I almost immediately want to take back. "Of course things might be different if you were going to tell me about those guys who got done across the street."

"Where?" he asks.

"From where you tried to steal the car. Those two crack guys who got killed across the street. If you were going to tell me something about that, I might be able to talk to the judge."

The long pause in our conversation quickly gets filled up by beeps and screeches from the nearby machines. Darryl just looks at me. Once again I can't read his expression. He might be thinking anything. He could be bored. He could be hungry. He could be in a homicidal rage. Looking at him is like staring into a deep, dark cave.

"I guess I see you in court," he says.

Just then, I hear a man's voice shouting. I whirl around looking for the source, and then realize the sound must've come from the video screen. My Rambo guy is under attack again and he's crying out for help. This time he's surrounded by three ferocious-looking guys with Mohawk haircuts. I look up to say something else to Darryl, but he's already walking away from me. His left hand is jumping and jerking at his side, as though it has a mind of its own.

No point in going after him. I've done my job here, which was to inform him personally about his court date. Now it's up to him to show up. I turn back to the game. Two of the three Mohawked guys have disappeared, and the one remaining is now locked in a mortal struggle with my Rambo guy. I push a button and pull the lever. The two figures on the screen tumble over each other, punching and kicking. After a couple of seconds of fighting, they stop and just lie there facedown on the animated New York sidewalk. Nothing happens for a few moments. Then, little animated bloodstains slowly appear on each figure's back. Somehow, they've managed to kill each other.

Two days later, I'm looking through my mailbox when I find an old torn envelope with my name on it among the interdepartmental memos, notices for union dues, and new case files. The letter inside is written in spidery black ink on dirty blue-lined paper with a laundry list on the back. On first glance, it looks like it's from a child. But when I read it, I realize it's from Darryl's great-grandmother, who I'd spoken to on the phone the other day. Any doubts I'd had about violating Darryl evaporate. It says:

"I, Ethel McDaniels, the great-grandmother of Darryl King is a seventy-six-year-old individual who cannot continue to live with my great-grandson Darryl who have been making My Life a living Hell Due to his crack abuse and cryme. Will the Court please help me. I give this letter to Probation Officer Steven Baum."

"P.S. Please do not tell Darryl I wrote you."

29

Detective Sergeant Bob McCullough got gas pains every time he looked at the file for the Pops Osborn homicide. This guy was a piece of shit when he was alive and he was a piece of shit dead. Whoever killed him did the world a service, except that McCullough now had to fill out another DD5 Supplementary Complaint Report, giving an update on the investigation.

Everything in the New York City Police Department was a fucking ritual. Filling out forms. Going to promotion ceremonies. Talking to inspectors. Attending mass and the Holy Name Society. Getting drunk at parties. If they made it a ritual to give the assistant chief a blowjob, he'd have to do that every week too. Maybe there was a piece in it, but probably not for a family newspaper.

A better piece might be something like "Why the Police Department Is Like the Church" with all these fucking rituals. If only the department had a ritual for resurrecting the dead. Then this Osborn motherfucker could tell McCullough who killed him and he could close out the case. But then this Osborn would be walking around again and somebody else would have to arrest him as a drug dealer and they'd have even more paperwork.

"Efforts to interview reltives of the decedent were met with negtive results," McCullough typed with his index fingers on the old gray Royal manual. "Recnvss of the plce of occurrence ws lso negtive."

He read it over and grumbled, "Oh, fuck me royally," when he realized the a key was sticking on his typewriter and he'd have to fix the report with liquid Wite-out and a pen.

The only reason he was having to write this thing up was because that blue-eyed jerk from Narcotics was bothering him. The one who kept saying, "If you're Captain Willie's boy, you gotta be all right."

Fuck him. If that lazy Narcotics hump didn't need the statistics so badly just to look like he was doing something in front of his chief, he would never have bothered McCullough about this. And McCullough was backed up enough with work anyway. That poor old lady strangled with her own bridgework shoved down her throat, that robbery at the Citibank on Second Avenue, that forty-year-old guy who got blown away with a 9 mm because he stepped on some thirteen-year-old's red suede sneakers.

Not that he was going to make lieutenant off any of these cases. It would just be nice to clear some of the deadwood away.

What a thing this job was. Day after day, seeing people at their most wretched and vulnerable. Confronting them with their despicable and intimate secrets. Where were you last night anyway? Who were you with? Why'd you beat your kid up like that? Why'd you kill your wife?

The worst part was looking through homicide victims' apartments. You always ended up seeing things they'd never shown anybody while they were alive. Their diaries. Their unmailed love letters. Their intestines splattered against the walls. What a thing it was to find out so much about these people, and then to come home and not be able to tell the wife where you wanted her to touch you.

It got him thinking about the girl on cable television. Even as he sat there with the phones ringing and the de-

tective at the next desk talking to somebody, he could picture
her curled up, with her luminous white ass in the air, licking
her rouged red lips and saying those dirty things that she
promised to put into writing: "First there was Harry—I slam-
fucked him and wrote him a letter. Then there was Sam, I
sucked his cock, Roto-Rootered his ass, and wrote him a letter.
Then there was Bob..."

He felt like calling her right now. Right here in the precinct.
He wanted her to say those things to him. Right here in front
of everybody. He had the number. Who was going to know?
As far as the guy at the next desk was concerned, he could be
talking to his wife or the Crime Scene people.

He dialed the number and waited. After the fifth ring, her
voice started, "Hi, big boy, why don't you take off your clothes
and get comfortable right now? I wanna suck your big, hard
throbbing dick..."

Under his desk top, he was getting a massive hard-on. It
was a good thing no one was watching him. "I'm getting all
wet just thinking about it," the girl on the phone was saying.
"I just want you to fuck me harder..."

His hard-on was demanding his attention now. It was
threatening to burst through his desk top unless he gave it a
light petting. Who was going to see it? As the girl on the phone
declared she'd never been so horny in her life, he began to
reach down.

"Come on," the girl on the phone said. "Give me every
inch."

At that moment, he felt a tap on his shoulder. He looked
up and saw a beautiful young woman staring at him. She was
like his fantasy made real, except she was black, carrying a
briefcase, and looking impatient.

"Detective, I'm Andrea Clinton from the Probation Department," she said, holding out her hand like he was supposed to shake it instead of using it to jerk off. "I'd like to talk
to you about the Pops Osborn case and Darryl King."

He tried not to panic or come on the spot. He covered the

receiver and calmly said, "Can you wait over there a second? I'm talking to the captain."

She nodded and he was about to make up something about sending a sector car around, when he took his hand off the receiver and the girl on the phone let out an orgasmic cry that everyone within ten feet of his desk could hear.

"You're too much, big boy," she moaned. "Fuck me again?"

30

"I don't know about that detective," Andrea is saying. "He got this weird look when I walked in."

"Did he tell you anything about Darryl?" I ask.

"No, he wasn't too anxious to tell me much of anything," she says, stepping around a pile of books on the sidewalk.

We're walking through the East Village after spending most of Saturday afternoon at the office working on the Darryl King violation.

This is the neighborhood where I always wanted to live when I was growing up. I used to take the train in from Flushing every weekend, just so I could wander up and down St. Marks Place, looking at the freaks, the punks, and the girls dressed in black. I guess that wasn't much more than a dozen years ago, but the place seemed so much stranger and more romantic then. I remember how even the air seemed headier and more intoxicating than it was in Queens. My favorite thing then was to buy pot from the hippies around the Third Avenue Gem Spa, get stoned, and gawk at the drag queens and punk girls outside the Trash and Vaudeville Boutique.

Now about half the village is gentrified, all the drag queens are dead from AIDS, the pushers are shady-looking guys chanting, "Crack-it-up" from the doorways, and the only punk girls left are way too young from me. Still, I like living here.

There's no other place in this city where you can feel so much a part of all the people who aren't part of anything.

"WHITE FOLKS!!!! HEH! HEH! HEH! HEH!"

This wild-eyed, skinny black guy with a scraggly, devilish beard keeps sneaking up behind us and yelling, "WHITE FOLKS!!" as though it were an embarrassing accusation.

"I'd tell him he's only three-quarters right in our case," Andrea says as we cross Third Avenue, "but what's the point?"

The energy on the street tonight seems a little different to me. It's up over ninety degrees again. Everyone's walking a little too fast and talking a little too loud. It's like all sense of distance and civility have evaporated in the humidity. Car horns are honking and arguments are breaking out on the sidewalks for no reason. Dogs lunge at each other's throats. A punk kid spits at a lady in pink jogging shorts going by.

Just ahead of us, a short Oriental man and a big blond Swedish guy are walking with their arms around each other, oblivious to the orchestra of bad vibes surrounding them. Rounding the corner of Third Avenue and heading down St. Marks Place, they trip and stumble into the pack of sidewalk vendors selling bottles of incense and back issues of *Stud* magazine.

The wild-eyed black guy, who was taunting us, sneaks up on the big Swede and his Oriental friend. "WHITE FOLKS!!! YEEEEEAHHHHH!!!!"

The two men shuffle away with guilty expressions. "Come on," I tell Andrea. "All this tension's making me hungry."

We find a loud, dim restaurant with vague Tex-Mex overtones. The lighting is indirect and so is most of the conversation here. The couples seem more interested in their food than each other. The front window looks out on an entrance to Tompkins Square Park, where a crowd is beginning to gather.

As she stares out at the street, I notice that Andrea looks even younger than twenty-four tonight, with her "Be-Bop

Café" T-shirt and her halo of curly hair tied back in a ponytail again.

"Is that some kind of protest starting?" she asks.

"I'm not sure," I say. "I heard something about a neighborhood demonstration. Something to do with the yuppie condo and a curfew to keep the homeless out of the park."

"That's the kind of thing I wanted to be involved in this summer," she says with some mild disappointment. "I was trying to get an internship with one of the tenants' rights groups down here, but I applied too late."

"Is that how you ended up at Probation?"

"No, I was interested in that too," she replies, maybe just a little defensively.

"But it's not the kind of thing you want to do when you get out of school, right?"

"I'm not sure." She shrugs. "I've got offers from a couple of the big firms already, but I want to make sure they'll let me do some *pro bono* work if I join them."

Pro bono. I wonder if that's actually Latin for "this isn't what I really do for a living." Andrea's a lot more middle-class than I am, it turns out, which embarrasses me a little. She's from Princeton, New Jersey, where her father is vice president of a software company and her mother teaches art history at the university. She looks very serious when she talks about them.

"You get along with them okay?" I ask. "You like your parents?"

"They're fine," she says with a warm smile.

Through close questioning I find out she majored in English at Yale and spent half her time getting involved in politically correct causes and the rest having affairs with people she didn't particularly like. "I had two long-term, serious relationships with guys, and a short one with a woman," she says, laughing. "Why do I feel comfortable telling you this?" I shrug and she takes a sip of her beer.

"It's because you're a good listener, right?"

"I practice at home in front of the mirror," I tell her.

As she orders the house wine, I notice she's wearing an ebony bracelet and a gold necklace. Not a spoiled girl, exactly, just used to the good things in life. I fire a dozen more questions at her and what started as a slight shaking around her shoulders soon erupts into a full-throated roar of laughter. She slaps the table as she rocks back and forth.

"What's the big joke?"

"Nothing," she says, taking a deep breath and still smiling. "You're just so ... so ... so ..." She beats the table with her fist a couple of times. "Intense is the word, I guess. You're acting like you're my probation officer."

"I'm sorry." I look down at my beer. "I just get so used to talking to people that way ..."

"I didn't mean to make you self-conscious," she says, reaching across the table and brushing my hand. "I just thought you were being funny, that's all."

She is truly a knockout, I tell myself for about the hundred and second time since I met her.

She orders the chicken fajitas and I ask the waitress to bring me another beer. "So I was sorry I gave you such a hard time the other day before I read Darryl's file," she says.

"It's okay, I'm used to it. It's just that after a while, I think you just get to be a little more careful about your sympathies. Otherwise, your heart gets broken too often and it doesn't work as well ..."

This strikes a bum note and she gives me a suspicious look.

"That's a great excuse for giving up," she says. "Is that why you're going into this field unit?"

"No, it is not," I say, tapping the table for emphasis. "I'm doing it because it's an assignment. I still have plenty of good clients who I care about."

While an old Neil Young song plays on the jukebox, I start to tell her about Maria Sanchez. But then I remember that I tried to take Maria out on a date the other night and I decide that's not such a good example. Instead, I tell her about Charlie Simms.

Charlie's remarkable, I tell her, the closest thing I've got to a complete success story so far. I met him a couple of years ago when I was just starting off at Probation and he was just starting off as a thief. Neither of us knew what we were doing. He'd been arrested for trying to steal a radio from an off-duty cop's Buick when the cop was standing a few feet away. I was still trying to figure out the difference between a felony and misdemeanor.

Charlie first came into my cubicle wearing a Confederate army cap and a giant watch around his neck. Right away, we started talking about how the only role models in his neighborhood were the guys who had the best cars. I tried using social work bromides to convince him that the problem wasn't that he'd gotten caught trying to steal the radio, but that he'd broken the law.

Over the last couple of years, Charlie and I have done a lot of growing up together, I tell her. He's taught me something about the street and I've helped him in the straight world. He tells me the new drugs on his block and I give him books by Claude Brown and Malcolm X so he can get a better sense of his own people's history. Now he wears leather Back to Africa medallions, he's almost done with school, and he's planning to marry the girl who had his baby last month. He's also out looking for a job. Though it's too condescending to say out loud, I'm proud of Charlie. His progress is a measure of how far I've come in doing my job.

"If I spent all my time trying to turn around hopeless cases like Darryl King, I wouldn't have any energy left for people like Charlie," I tell her as Neil Young keens about a friend who died from a drug overdose and beer sloshes around in my mug.

"I wasn't defending Darryl," she says, leaning forward on her elbow. "I just wonder if you're finding excuses not to care anymore."

"That's not true!" I say loud enough to be heard over the music. When I see people at the nearby tables are looking at me funny, I lower my voice a little. "I really get into it with some of these people," I say. "Like this kid came in the other day, Ricky Velez. He's a token sucker. But I noticed that he couldn't really read what I had on my blackboard. Like he had a reading problem. Just like me. I pick up on these things because I'm dyslexic."

"Really?" She looks up.

"Yeah, sure. I know what it's like to be on the outside looking in."

She seems a little skeptical.

"I've been through the same kind of rejections my clients have been through."

"You have, have you?" She still isn't convinced.

"I mean, you could look at these people and you could look at me and say nobody could be further apart. But I'm just like a lot of these people," I say, touching my chest with my fist. "I'm just like them."

"No, you're not," Andrea says firmly. "You're white."

I feel like somebody just slapped me across the face. I look down, feeling stupid and gravely embarrassed. "Yes, of course, you're right," I mumble.

She stares at me for a long time, her eyes at exactly the same level as mine. Her expression seems to say, *I know what it's like, you never will.* I hope she isn't about to get up and walk away in disgust.

Instead, she lets a couple of silent seconds pass and then changes the subject. "You know you still never told me why you became a probation officer," she says.

"You really wanna know?"

"That's why I asked."

I don't answer right away for fear of saying something else foolish. "It's kind of hard to say." I put my chin on my fist and try to force the idea into a coherent shape. It's strange, but hardly anyone has asked me this so directly before. "I guess I started off like I wanted to help people. You know. Other people join the Peace Corps, but I don't like to travel ..."

She shakes her head like she doesn't quite believe me. "There must've been another reason ..."

"Yeah. There must."

It's hard to recall how I ended up where I am. I guess it started off as a process of elimination. I didn't want to go into business. I didn't want to work out at the airport as an engineer or anything. But I guess the biggest thing was that I didn't want to be someone like my father. So I did the thing that I thought would displease him the most. I tell Andrea most of this, but I leave out the fact that the old man would probably have a heart attack if he saw me trying to make time with this beautiful black woman.

"You know what I like?" she says suddenly, sitting up straight.

"No, what?"

"I liked what you said to me before about giving people a break."

I'm caught a little off guard. "What'd I say?" I ask as the Ray Charles song with the same name starts playing on the jukebox.

"You said I should give you a break," she tells me. "Because every day you give somebody upstairs a break. And I thought to myself, this is a nice man."

I slug down the rest of my beer, feeling a little bit like a fraud. Outside the front window, the crowd near the park's entrance is growing steadily. Pale skinheads and punks in heavy black boots, old bearded hippies, stocky Puerto Rican women in tank tops, elderly Ukrainians, and various people without clear connections to each other or anyone else. Signs say things like Die Yuppie Scum! and Fuck Tha Police! A dozen or so cops stand around the park entrance. Something's definitely about to happen.

"So I was going over a couple of your cases who needed to be violated the other day," Andrea is saying.

"Who?"

"Oh. This guy, I think his name is Freddie Brooks or something..."

"Oh no." I frown. "Don't violate Freddie."

"Why not? He just got arrested for disorderly conduct."

"Yeah, but that's bullshit." I lean across the table to her. "Freddie gets into fights all the time. He lives in Grand Central. If you look at the arrest report, you'll see the complainant is probably another homeless person. That's what they do. They fight each other over space. It's terrible, but you shouldn't violate him for it. Freddie's a good guy."

Andrea looks amazed. "You really like these people?"

"Yeah! That's what I said before. They have a lot of...I guess, variety in their lives. Not like yuppies or anything."

"I guess not."

"Don't send Freddie to jail," I say. "He just wants to get drunk and ding people for quarters. He doesn't want to hurt anybody. He's a sweet guy."

She seems simultaneously amused and touched. "And he likes you too?"

"Sure," I tell her. "I mean, I guess so. We're friends. There's plenty of other people you could violate instead."

"Like who?"

I think for a moment. "You ought to violate Scottie Austin. He's a pretty bad guy."

The smile still plays on Andrea's lips. "Oh yeah? What does he do?"

I hesitate, not quite believing she wants to hear all of this. "His big thing is hanging around the Port Authority bus terminal when he's not robbing old people at his house. He's into all the scams."

She seems interested. "Like what?"

"Everything," I say. "He hangs around the phone booths and when he sees businessmen making calls with their credit cards, he memorizes the numbers and sells them to the other hustlers for twenty dollars. And then he likes to put on a tie and stand by the Greyhound ramp where the buses come in so the people coming off think he's like a porter. Then he takes their bags and walks them to a deserted part of the terminal where he either beats them up and robs them or makes them pay fifty dollars before he'll give back the bags."

"Oh yeah?" Now she's fascinated. She orders another glass of wine and settles back in her chair. "Who else do you have?"

"You really want to hear this?"

"Yes, of course."

I tell her about Mo Armstrong. Mo is a guy in his mid-seventies who liked to take pictures of himself having sex with other elderly people in his senior citizens home. His big thing was using the photos to blackmail their grandchildren. I've actually seen a couple of the shots myself. In one of them, another old man is on his hands and knees in front of Mo, fellating him through the bars of his walker, while Mo affects a look of serene, almost regal indifference. I could understand how the pictures were part of the blackmailing scheme. What I never quite got was why Mo felt the need to enlarge each shot to poster size so he could hang them on the wall.

"I'm a dirty old man," he once told me, "and my masculinity is fading. I wanted something to remember it by."

Instead of gasping in horror when she hears this story, Andrea grins strangely. "People are so interesting," she says.

I realize I've never been out with a woman who wanted to hear about my job before. We're starting to hit it off and I hear myself telling stories I haven't told in years. I'm excited about being with Andrea. I hope I do something for her.

"Can I ask you one more question?" I say, realizing I'm a little looser than I expected to be after two beers. "Are you, you know, seeing anybody right now?"

She breaks off from smiling. I get scared I might have pushed too far and asked the wrong question. I wish I was somebody like Richard Silver, who knows just when to stop pushing people. She looks as if she's remembering something unpleasant.

"I was seeing Joel until the start of the summer," she says.

"What was he?"

She crosses her arms and looks over at the neon sign for a defunct gasoline company on the wall. "Joel is a very ambitious young man who just graduated," she says. "Now he's going to be a nasty yuppie and make lots of money . . . One of my friends said he had the looks of a movie star and the manners of a Visigoth."

"That's better than the other way around, right?"

"You certainly do not remind me of Joel."

"Is that good or bad?"

She raises her glass. "It's all right with me," she says.

After a few more minutes, we pay the check and head for the front door. She asks me to hail a cab. It's unclear if I'm invited along for the ride.

The point's moot anyway, since a riot's beginning outside.

The first thing I notice is the helicopter hovering low over the park. I turn and see about two hundred cops lined up near St. Marks Place. It's hard to make out their faces under their helmets and visors, but you can tell they're good and pissed from the way they're standing. About one hundred freaks and demonstrators are taunting them on either side of the street.

"PIGS OUTTA THE PARK!"

"DIE YUPPIE SCUM!"

Suddenly a bottle gets thrown and it shatters in front of several officers.

Pandemonium breaks out. Now everyone's running. More bottles are thrown. M-80 firecracker rockets explode under the park's dense, twisting trees. Riot cops shove their way down the middle of the street as people scream and bubble gum lights sweep over the building. Sirens howl. Odors of horseshit and fire fill the air.

Andrea's about to say something when she gets caught up in a stampeding crowd and almost dragged away from me. I grab her around the waist and pull her back to my side. "Let's head toward Avenue B," I say. "This is getting a little too scary . . ."

"Where are we going?"

"I live around here," I say. "It might be safer just to hang out inside awhile."

She stares at the nihilistic ruckus on Avenue A and gives me a worried look. "Shouldn't we try to do something?" she says.

"Like what? Call the cops?" I put my hands in my pockets and start walking east toward my place.

She lowers her head and comes trotting after me. I put my arm around her shoulders and guide her to the doorway of my building. For the first time, I feel heat passing between us.

A couple of old homeless men are taking refuge in the foyer. Andrea and I pass them and go up five flights of warped old steps to my apartment. I get the door ajar, reach in to remove the "police protection" pole that keeps it shut, and turn on the lights.

"You live like this?" Andrea says right away.

"Something the matter?"

She blinks in wonder. "Well." She shrugs. "Nobody can say you live better than your clients."

She takes a good look at the mattress without the box spring and the stacks of probation folders and albums in the middle of the room. I know I should be more concerned about her seeing the place in its current state, but I've been living this way for so long that I honestly do not give a shit anymore. The only thing I hope she doesn't notice is Barbara Russo's turquoise earring, still lying near the corner of the room.

"There's no place to sit in here," Andrea says, still short of breath.

"Try the mattress."

She laughs quietly to herself, as if to say, "Yeah, right, buddy."

"Can I look at your records?" she asks.

"Help yourself." I go into the kitchen and open a beer.

"Get me one too," she says.

I look through the cupboards for a clean glass to pour her beer into. I hear her rummaging around in my room.

"Hank Williams," she says. "Mom has this. Can I put it on?"

"Go ahead. Do you know how to..."

I hear the long, painful squeal of the needle scratching across the length of the album side. I wince and after clearing my voice of all irritation, I tell her to just push the first button.

This time the needle settles easily into the grooves and Hank Williams starts singing about honky-tonking. I step into the room. Andrea is sitting on my mattress. I still feel the heat coming from her. Her right leg is stretched out invitingly. Her left leg is drawn up as if to say "not so fast." She leans back on her elbows, displaying the fullness of her breasts and the roundness of her hips. The ponytail is gone and her hair falls in a seductive curtain over the left side of her face. She turns up the corner of her mouth and gives me a look that makes my knees go weak.

"Thanks for pulling me out of that herd," she says. "I thought I was going to get trampled."

"Yeah, that would've been a bummer."

I sit down and hand her the beer. I hope she won't notice my hands aren't quite steady. She sips from the glass once and then puts it down. Leaning back so that our bodies are parallel, I start to say something, but think better of it. Hank Williams sings a few more songs, including a real strange one about a cigar store Indian who falls in love with the wooden maiden across the street.

"You're touching me," Andrea says in a soft voice.

I look down. The knuckles of my left hand are barely brushing the knuckles of her right hand. "So what're you going to do about it?" I say. She smiles and leans toward me. We kiss.

She pulls her entire body toward me and I feel something melting around my heart. I draw her onto my lap and hold her tightly as I kiss her lips, her smooth jawline, and the nape of her neck. She reaches down the front of my shirt to stroke me and nerve endings I forgot I had awaken.

There's a flapping sound in the distance. A slight breeze

comes through the window bars and stirs the drapes. Hank Williams sings "Settin' the Woods on Fire."

She raises her arms and smiles dreamily as I pull her shirt over her head. I slide off her sneakers and massage her feet. She makes a small sound. I pop open the buttons of her jeans and her body springs forth. She has a lovely young figure with firm abundant breasts, slender thighs, a long back, and a heart-shaped ass.

I take off my shirt and slowly make my way down her body. I kiss her lips, her throat, her shoulders, and the tops of her breasts. I move my tongue in prolonged orbits around the areolas, making smaller and smaller circles as I close in on her nipples. I lick them until they get hard, and then I move down to her pussy.

I explore the sides and top with my finger and tongue. As her pussy gets wet, I catch a powerful, salty smell. I locate the sensitive spot near the top and she begins to moan loudly. Voices call out from the street below as though they're answering her. Her first orgasm is brief but intense; she pulls my hair in the back as she shakes and then cools herself down for a moment.

It doesn't take long before she's kissing me again and pulling my pants off. My cock leaps from my boxer shorts like a dangerous lunatic finally out on parole. I quickly find one of the condoms I buy occasionally as articles of blind faith and I slip it on.

"Do you wanna fuck me?" she says.

"Definitely."

I raise myself over her and feel my way around the outside of her pussy and its lips with my cock. Then I begin to move in. I start with short, gentle entries before making more profound, soulful thrusts. She grinds her hips against mine, pushing my cock farther and farther into her body. I don't think I've ever been this deep inside a woman before.

The flapping sound has grown louder just outside the window. It's like a couple of burly angels are beating their wings out there and watching us. Andrea sits up on the bed and straightens her spine so that we're face-to-face. We drive ourselves together harder as something inside her sucks my cock onward and squeezes it tight.

Andrea starts to tremble again, more violently this time. Her low, steady moans turn into fierce, ecstatic gasps. Her mouth opens wide and her eyes shut. As she comes again, my own hot spreading sensation begins.

The flapping sound is so loud now that it seems to be coming from inside my head.

Finally, I realize it's the police helicopter hovering over the park and Avenue B. A strong wind blows in the window. The whir of the helicopter's blades and the force of our orgasms shake the room. Our clothes and the papers from the floor are swirling up into a whirlwind at the foot of the bed. Dust and ashes fly against the walls. The sheet is tugged up from under us. Andrea cries out as her eyelids flutter and she grips the back of my neck.

Then as suddenly as it started, the great wind subsides and everything lands. The helicopter draws away and Andrea lies back on the mattress, with her eyes still closed and a smile on her lips.

The riot is over.

31

"I assume the boy doesn't have a father," Goldfarb, the lawyer, said.

"Well, you assume wrong," Darryl King's mother told him.

"Where is he then?"

"I dunno." She shrugged. "But he somewhere."

They were standing outside a courtroom at 100 Centre Street. The air was heavy with stale smoke and discount ammonia. With its worn marble walls and its dulled brass railings, the lobby had retained just traces of its 1930s art deco glamour; it was a little bit like the slatternly old hooker walking by just then, who still had good legs and a pair of stylish stiletto heels. Goldfarb, who was in his late sixties with a shock of white hair and a breast pocket full of shiny silver pens, looked after her with a wan smile that turned into a leer.

"You know, it's been quite some time since I've had sex," Goldfarb told Darryl King's mother. "My wife died five years ago. A lonely man can start to have some desperate thoughts."

"Well, keep them to yourself till you get my son off," she said, scratching the front of her brown slacks.

"Where is the dear boy anyway?"

"Who?"

"Your son, the defendant," Goldfarb said, taking a pen and

a small notebook from his breast pocket. "I need to speak with him. He should be here. I barely have anything to work with. This is a violation of probation hearing, is it not?"

"I guess so," Darryl King's mother said, putting her right hand on her left arm, which was only slightly thicker than a policeman's nightstick. "He just don't get along with his P.O. That's all. That man wouldn't let him be. That's all. Darryl didn't do nothing wrong. He's a good boy. It's just that man."

Goldfarb clicked his pen several times, wondering if he should bother writing any of it down. He put the pen away and glanced at his watch. "About the payment," he said.

"What?" Darryl King's mother began to raise her eyebrows but gave up before she got halfway. "I haven't got no money with me."

Goldfarb looked deeply chagrined. "How do you expect me to defend your son without a retainer?" He was peering around frantically now, like he was hoping a bank would suddenly pull up. "Why didn't you get a Legal Aid lawyer?"

"You'll get paid," Darryl King's mother said.

"With what? A man of my age needs security. What collateral can you offer? What incentive is there for me to defend your son?"

"Well, what incentive do you want?" she said, putting a hand on her hip.

He checked his watch and looked around furtively. "Are you suggesting what I think you're suggesting?" Goldfarb asked.

Both of them seemed to notice at the same time that the janitor had left the door open to the broom closet at the end of the hall.

"Well I don't know," said Darryl's mother.

32

At a quarter past ten, I see Andrea walk into the courtroom wearing a demure white blouse and a red skirt. It's the first time I've seen her since we slept together and she almost doesn't recognize me because I have on a jacket and tie and my hair is neatly combed. I put my hand on the seat next to me in the first row so she'll sit there.

She seems shy and a little distant. "I guess I should say I'm sorry for leaving like that the other night," she murmurs.

"I guess." She was gone by the time the Sunday morning birds woke me up. No note, no phone call.

Now she's glancing around the spectator section to see if anyone can hear us. Two little energetic Hispanic boys are chasing each other between pews. "Mikey, I'm gonna kill you, man," one tells the other. An old black woman is weeping in the fourth row. In the back, a young white guy in a khaki suit and glasses with tortoiseshell frames reads *New York Newsday*.

"I'm just not sure if I'm ready to get serious about someone like that," she says and then hesitates.

I don't know what "like that" means. Is it that she's not sure she wants to get serious in a particularly intense way? Or does "someone like that" refer to me being just a probation officer? I'm a little pissed off, but I know I'll never get anywhere with her by acting sour. Instead, I ask if we can have dinner and talk it over.

"I'll get back to you on that, Steve."

"Sure," I say, trying not to sound too dejected.

I pan around the courtroom, looking for a familiar face. "Where is the court liaison officer?" I ask Andrea. "I'm not going to prosecute this violation myself. That's not my job."

Court liaison officers act as prosecutors at violation hearings, which are somewhat less formal than trials. If no court liaison officer is available, regular probation officers sometimes prosecute the cases, though I've never done that myself.

"I don't have time for this," I say. "I'm supposed to be training with the Field Service Unit so I can go out with them tomorrow."

"Ms. Petrocelli said she'd be by to do this case," Andrea says.

"Shit. She hasn't even called me to talk about it. She doesn't know what the fuck's going on."

"That's what she told me to tell you."

More people stream through the big oak doors to the side and fill up the spectator benches. A male and female pair of court officers stand around comparing muscles and firearms. Most of the new arrivals in the courtroom are defendants with family members and Legal Aid lawyers in tow. I take Andrea's folder off her lap and start going through the papers quickly. Then the side doors slam and several voices mumble tensely.

"Is this Darryl King?" Andrea whispers.

He walks slowly past the wooden balustrade right in front of us. What he wears is nothing special: a red T-shirt, black jeans, and sneakers. But something about him puts sweat on the back of my neck. He has the fearless "b-boy" swagger down to an art. Other defendants swivel in their seats to look at him. He gives Andrea and me a bored smirk as he passes the first row and turns down the center aisle. The court officers hitch up their gun belts and try to look a little more alert. A woman who looks like she might be his mother follows. Then comes Ross Goldfarb, a wily old defense lawyer I know, who seems to be having a problem closing his fly.

"You never told me why Darryl got probation," Andrea says.

"It's the numbers. Everybody wants numbers. Prosecutors get rated on how many cases they get convictions on, right?"

"Of course," she says, getting a notebook out of her bag and starting to write down what I say.

"And so do judges and defense lawyers. So it's in everybody's interest to dispose of these cases as quickly as they can, without going to trial. And the easiest thing to do a lot of the time is to get the guy to take a plea, so he'll get probation and be out of everybody's hair."

Judge Bernstein comes out of his chambers and makes his way to the bench. He's a bent-up man in his sixties without a hair on his head. His face, with its deep creases and broken blood vessels, is like a map of war-torn Gaza. He wears his black-framed glasses far down on the bridge of his nose. On the few occasions when I've stood near him, I could swear the judge's glasses do not have lenses.

As the first case of the morning is called, the male court officer yells at the well-dressed white man in the back row to put down his newspaper. When he obeys, the male officer smiles at the female officer and mutters something that sounds like, "I showed him."

The first defendant has his case called and steps forward with his Legal Aid lawyer. He's a short, chunky Hispanic guy in his mid-thirties.

"Why didn't you show up for your last hearing, Mr. Hernandez?" the judge asks.

"I had an excuse from God," Mr. Hernandez says in a forthright voice, giving a court officer a piece of paper to give to the judge.

"I see," Judge Bernstein says, looking it over. "And do you have any witnesses?"

"Yes. God."

"Oh." The judge glances around the courtroom. "Is he here?"

"Yes, Judge," Mr. Hernandez says earnestly. "He's in my body and he's using my voice."

"And why's he doing that?"

"He's embarrassed," Mr. Hernandez explains. "He has a funny voice."

Jeff Washington, the judge's clerk, is waving for me to join him at the table to the left of the bench. Jeff is a tall, young black guy who's a sometime drinking buddy of mine. We have a steady exchange of inside information about the courts and probation flowing back and forth.

"We're gonna get to your case this morning," Jeff says, laying a hand on the folder I gave him earlier. "But the judge has gotta see a couple of people before you. All right? So just sit tight, we'll get you in."

"No problem."

"Who's handling the violation?"

I check the room once more. The spectator seats are more than half full. Andrea's giving me that appraising look again from the first row. Four rows behind her, Darryl King glowers and folds his arms across his chest. Ms. Petrocelli, the court liaison officer, still isn't here. "I guess I'm going to be doing it," I say.

"How interesting," Jeff says. "Are you nervous?"

"I'm starting to be. Do prosecutors ever get stage fright?"

"Oh yeah, absolutely. It's terrible sometimes. You want a Valium? The judge has a jarful in his chambers."

"No thanks, I guess."

As I go back to my seat, I notice Darryl King watching me with furious concentration. Trying to unnerve me just by staring.

I try to smile back at him, but my heart isn't in it. Darryl isn't the only thing bothering me. It's that I'm going to have to make a lawyerly presentation right here and now and I don't want to make a fool out of myself in front of everyone. Especially not in front of Andrea. My throat starts feeling dry and parched. I could use a stiff drink and a long smoke right now. "You all right?" I hear Andrea say. "You look a little pale."

People are moving and talking in front of me; I can't quite hear them. It's like watching television with the sound turned down. The images pile on top of each other, making increasingly less sense as you can't follow their meaning. I try rereading some of the court documents, but that just makes things worse. The words and letters appear backward and out of order to me. I get that old feverish panic I couldn't control or understand when I was younger, before they told me it was dyslexia. Everything's blurring. In the middle of the crowded courtroom, I feel absolutely alone.

The next sound I hear clearly is Jeff Washington calling my case. I turn and look at the clock on the back wall. It says almost 11:30. The last time I looked, it was 10:25. Andrea touches my arm lightly. "Good luck," she says.

I button my jacket, straighten my tie, and stand up to approach the bench.

I stop at the district attorney's table on the left. Sergio Rivera, the assistant district attorney handling the regular cases this morning, steps aside to give me some room. Darryl King and his mother are standing near the defense table with Ross Goldfarb, the lawyer. Darryl puts his hands behind his back and crosses his wrists, assuming the classic defendant's pose, as though he were still wearing handcuffs. Darryl's mother searches through her handbag. "Mr. Baum," the judge says. "You're looking very handsome today in your jacket and tie. To what do we owe the pleasure of your formal presentation?"

Bernstein has a harsh voice; I picture his throat being like a rusty old pipe. Everything he says has the singsong rhythm of ancient Yiddish wisdom and a knife's edge of bitterness.

"Judge, we have a probationer who needs to be violated here." I sound strange and disembodied, like my mouth is on one side of the room and my ears are on the other.

The judge stops shuffling papers and peers down his long nose at me. "What's the problem?"

"Judge, since you gave the defendant Darryl King probation earlier this year, he has violated a number of his conditions and I believe he is quickly moving into a high-risk category. He has repeatedly failed to report to his assigned probation officer. When he has reported, he has been uncooperative and he has refused to answer all reasonable inquiries."

Darryl King makes that disgusted ticking sound with his mouth as I pause to look at my notes again. "In addition, Judge, the probationer here continued to associate with his original co-defendant, a Robert Kirk, of 209 East 105th Street, and I have evidence that Mr. King is persistently using drugs. He appears to be becoming a menace within his own household . . ."

I protect Darryl's great-grandmother's identity, as she asked me to, by not mentioning her name in court. But I put a copy of the note she mailed me in the judge's file.

"Finally," I say, "Mr. King was recently arrested again, this time on multiple charges involving car theft and resisting police officers in Harlem. And . . . I have reason to suspect he may be involved in much more serious criminal activities . . ."

Darryl whips his head around to glare at me. I deliberately avoid meeting his eyes. I don't need to know exactly how much he hates me right now.

The judge looks down again at the papers on his desk. He rocks back and forth in his chair as he reads for the next few seconds. He reminds me of the film I once saw of Orthodox Jews davening before the Wailing Wall in Israel.

The file, which Andrea helped assemble, includes Officer Kelly's statement, notes from my interviews with Darryl, the formal statement of charges and the violation complaint, and an affidavit that Andrea got from a nonpolice witness to the most recent arrest. Goldfarb, the defense lawyer, asks if he can have a word with the judge.

I don't have enough experience to know whether I should object to the judge and Goldfarb having a private conference.

Goldfarb faces the bench and at one point, he jerks his thumb over his shoulder to indicate he's talking about Darryl and me. I can't hear a word they're saying. It's like trying to eavesdrop on a conversation in a tomb. The judge keeps looking back and forth between Darryl's side of the room and mine. From the corner of my eye, I see Darryl's mother blowing her nose into an old tissue while Darryl impatiently bounces up and down on his heels.

Finally, the conference breaks up and Goldfarb returns to the defense table. "Mr. Baum," the judge says. "Do you ever go to the track?"

I lean forward, not sure I'm hearing him right. "No, Your Honor."

"Have you been to Atlantic City?"

"Um, no, sir."

The judge clears his throat with a loud revving sound. "Then let's become gamblers, you and I, Mr. Baum. Not in Atlantic City, not at Aqueduct, not on the roll of the dice or how fast a horse can run—but an enlightened form of gambling. Let's gamble on a human being."

The judge seems to be giving a campaign speech, though as far as I know, he is not up for renomination any time soon. "I am not one who believes that there is no such thing as rehabilitation," the judge declares. "I believe human beings are capable of change. So I say, let's be gamblers, Mr. Baum, and let us use probation as our track."

"Your Honor, with all due respect, I think Mr. King has already shown himself to be a very bad bet." A few people chuckle behind me.

Without meaning to, I find myself making a speech too. "Judge, you were talking about racetracks before. I wonder if I could change metaphors on you for a moment. Because sometimes I think poor neighborhoods are more like river streams and the people struggling to get out are like the salmon making a run for it. Felons like Mr. King poison that stream. And his victims are often the best people in those communities, and he makes it harder for them to get out. If I might switch back to your racetrack analogy, giving Mr. King probation is like blowing all of your money on a doped-up horse, Your Honor. Which leaves you nothing else to gamble with."

All this sounds like a lot of shit to me as I'm saying it, but everybody else seems impressed, including the judge. I turn my head slightly and see Andrea nodding. I don't know how all of this came out of my mouth. The judge asks me to step forward.

"That was very eloquent, Mr. Baum," he says with a low rumble. "I'm surprised you did not become a lawyer..."

I'm too confused and nervous to manage a decent response. Bernstein takes off his glasses and rubs his eyes. People in the spectators' galley shift in their seats. Darryl and his mother murmur to each other. "Man, why are these motherfuckers clockin' me?" someone says.

The judge ignores the growing restlessness. It feels like a big fist is closing in my stomach, taking my guts in its grip. Bernstein gives me a mean look as he pushes his glasses back up on the bridge of his nose. "Mr. Baum," he says, "do you remember when you were in investigations two years ago?"

"Certainly, Your Honor." My first job with Probation was writing presentence investigations, which supposedly help judges decide what sentence to give a defendant.

"Do you remember an individual named Claude Briggs?" the judge asks.

"Not offhand, Judge."

"Let me refresh your memory," Bernstein says. "I promised Claude Briggs probation. He was a young man of eighteen. Not the smartest youngster I have ever seen, who dropped out of school and impregnated a girl. He became the sole support of his paramour and his mother, who was a junkie and badly in need of treatment for drug abuse, and a couple of siblings. He had a job. He worked as a manager of a pizzeria. He met someone older than him—a street person—who took this young man and encouraged him to go on what he thought was a burglary. He entered the apartment in a building near St. Nicholas Avenue, ready to steal, when the complainant witness came home..."

"And they beat the crap out of him," I say. "I remember the case now." And I remember Claude Briggs too. A big slow-talking kid with huge hands.

"And do you remember what you recommended?" the judge asks.

"I believe I recommended jail time for this Briggs fellow." Almost as soon as I say this, I remember that I did so despite the judge's early promise of probation for Briggs. In those days I did not know better.

"That was indeed your recommendation!" The judge slaps his desk so hard that sleepy eyes around the galley pop open. "And do you know what Claude Briggs is doing now?"

"No, I don't."

"I ignored your advice and gave that young man probation," the judge says. "He responded beautifully. I gave him youthful offender treatment, which means that as far as his criminal record is concerned, he has no criminal record. He is doing spec-tacularly well in his job. He is going to buy his own pizzeria. He saw to it that his mother entered a methadone program and is doing fine. And he was trying to attain a high school equiva-lency diploma. He did not succeed! But he enrolled in the course again! He's going to keep taking that course until he fi-nally masters it!"

I hear Darryl King make the angry ticking sound with his tongue again and then mutter, "Bullshit," as Judge Bernstein glares down at me for his triumphant summation.

"By being placed on probation that young man assured society far more protection because we now have an individual who can be productive," the judge says, smiling and shaking his head in wonder. "And you wanted him locked up."

"Judge, nothing makes me happier than a story like that. I went into this field to help people. But this...individual is different." I point to Darryl King, who looks like he's ready to explode and take everybody else in the room with him.

By the time I finish speaking, I know it's too late. In Judge Bernstein's mind, this is no longer a typical case. If it was, he'd be happy to violate Darryl King and pick up another disposition for his scorecard. But now the judge has to teach me a lesson. I made a terrible mistake, challenging him with my little speech, and now I'm going to pay the price.

"I have already gotten one bum steer from you, Mr. Baum," the judge says in a steely tone. "I don't intend to get another."

He indicates he wants me to step back to the prosecution's table. Then he looks over at Goldfarb, Darryl, and Darryl's mother. Goldfarb is writing something in a date book. The mother has her head down; she appears to be asleep standing up. Darryl has his broad shoulders back and his bottom lip curled.

"Mr. King, I'm very disappointed to hear about these violations from Mr. Baum," the judge says. "Probation is a privilege and it should not be abused. Now, I don't expect to hear anything else about you getting in trouble. But if I do, rest assured the full weight of the law will be brought to bear on you. For the moment, though, I'm impressed by your mother's involvement in your rehabilitation, as Mr. Goldfarb has explained it to me, and I am restoring you to probation ... You should continue reporting to Mr. Baum as assigned."

My heart sinks. Goldfarb clicks one of his pens, closes his briefcase, and walks away. Darryl's mother thanks the judge and sniffs back the tears that never came.

Darryl King is already sauntering past the balustrade and heading for the door. He gives his shoulders an exaggerated roll and pumps his arms into the air victoriously. After what just happened, why shouldn't he feel indestructible?

"OUTTA HERE!" he shouts as he hits the doors.

An elderly, well-dressed black woman in the fifth row looks after him with pure hatred in her eyes, like she's just seen a parent's worst nightmare go by.

In the first row, Andrea looks hurt and bewildered. "What went wrong?" she says. "I thought you did great."

"Well, that's what they do." I loosen my tie. "What can I tell you?"

Jeff Washington is already calling the next case. A kid with two gold-plated front teeth—one of them with the Mercedes-Benz insignia—smiles as he passes me on his way to the defense table and Judge Bernstein.

"Come on, let's get out of here," I say. "This place is getting me depressed."

Andrea takes my hand and accompanies me through the big oak doors. The old marble corridor has that peculiar sweaty scent that people give off when they're desperate.

Every few yards, variations on the same scene are being played out. The lawyer is almost always an older man wearing a three-piece suit despite the vicious heat. He's usually talking very fast and gesturing extravagantly as he tries to delineate the plea-bargain procedure to the clients, who are almost all under twenty-five and often have small children with them. Few seem to understand the deals their lawyers have made, but most are resigned to the result. It's a little like walking down an assembly line at a movie studio. The dialogue and individual characters are all a little different, but the basic scenario rarely changes.

Andrea and I round the corner to the elevators and almost walk right into Darryl King, his mother, and their lawyer. The confrontation unfolds so suddenly and unexpectedly that I don't have time to collect my thoughts or react properly.

Darryl points one finger at me and closes the rest of his hand into the shape of a gun. Something seems to catch fire behind his eyes.

"Fuck you, man," he says. "You dead."

His words are nothing. They're banal. Schoolyard stuff. It's just the way he says them that hits me like a punch in the face.

The elevator doors open and Andrea pushes me in. "Your next appointment is Friday," I tell Darryl before the doors close. "Don't be late . . . Dooky."

33

"You hear what that motherfucker called me?" Darryl King asked, pushing through the clumps of people standing outside 100 Centre Street, with his mother and lawyer trailing behind him.

"What?" His mother could barely keep her eyes open.

"He call me 'Dooky.' Man, I ain't with that. You know what I'm saying? Motherfuckers got killed for saying less."

"That's right," his mother said.

"Motherfuckers got killed for saying nothing at all. Like last Christmas..."

His mother suddenly became alert and gave him a look that said: Stop talking. They kept going along the curve of Centre Street, heading toward the great stone edifices of New York's federal courthouse and the municipal building. Small Chinese women scurried by them, plucking soda cans out of the steel-mesh garbage receptacles.

Darryl was still indignant, spitting and clenching his fists, as if he'd lost the case. "Man, he shouldn't be acting like that," he said.

"Who?" his mother asked.

"Mr. Bomb. He's supposed to be my P.O. Why's he all over my shit?"

Goldfarb, the lawyer, was silently trudging along beside them with his heavy briefcase. Even in the day's bright sunshine, he seemed gloomy and bewildered, like an old magician who'd accidentally conjured up an unwieldy beast. Now he finally spoke.

"Excuse me, young man," he said. "But I would say your probation officer is the least of your troubles."

Darryl's face got tight. "Say what?"

The lawyer put down his briefcase and smoothed his shock of white hair, like he was preparing to perform one final trick to bring the curtain down. "If you get arrested again, you are going to find yourself having a very hard time raising bail," he said, wagging a finger at Darryl. "I've seen many young men just like you, and the courts will not look kindly on your next appearance. I'm sure your poor mother has already lost hundreds of dollars in bail money because of your prior arrests and it will be very difficult to find another bail bondsman who'll be willing to stake you."

Darryl and his mother had been listening patiently to his sidewalk lecture, but now Darryl put up his hand like he'd heard enough. "'Scuse me, Mr. Goldberg."

"Goldfarb . . ."

"I know," Darryl said pointedly. "You best go back and study your book. In New York State, you get all your bail money returned once you go in probation. That don't have no effect on future bail application."

"Is that true?" Goldfarb looked stunned. He scrambled to recover the high ground. "But you know, you still may have trouble getting a bail bondsman."

Darryl handed his wallet to his mother. "Show 'im, Moms," he said.

She started taking business cards out of the wallet and flashing them at the old lawyer. "Rothman and Sons Bail Bonds," she read in a droning voice. "Jacobs and Sullivan.

Max Miller. Hagen and Seligman Bail Bonds..."

"Those are my homeboys," Darryl interrupted. "My credit is good with any of 'em. Is yours?"

His mother handed him the wallet back and he put it in his pocket. "So don't you be giving me a lecture too, Goldberg," he said. "I got enough from my P.O."

Passing cars stirred old newspapers and paper cups in the gutter. Darryl and his mother were moving faster now, leaving behind Goldfarb, who was still staggering along with his heavy briefcase. The old lawyer shifted the case from one hand to the other, cleared his throat, and kicked a pigeon out of the way. His shoes seemed to sink into the hot asphalt with each step he took.

Darryl King and his mother were about one hundred yards ahead of him now. He just barely caught sight of the two of them as they crossed the street and disappeared into the rage of cars, people, and colors around Foley Square.

34

My first day with the Field Service Unit begins at 4:30 on a Tuesday morning. Something about the way the pinkish-gray sky breaks over Manhattan at that hour always makes me melancholy. And *really irritable*. Another day is beginning and the fact that I'm up so early means that I didn't accomplish what I set out to do the night before. Which usually means getting laid or getting obliterated.

In the shower, I think about Andrea as the mortifyingly cold water streams down my back. I wonder if she'll ever take me seriously. She'll probably just find another boyfriend when she goes back to law school in the fall anyway. I dry off and get out the big blue bulletproof vest I was issued yesterday. It looks like an apron for a chef at an industrial barbecue. I fasten the Velcro straps and pull a black T-shirt on over the vest. Then I put on a pair of jeans, black sneakers, and my windbreaker.

Unfortunately, the train downtown doesn't have air-conditioning, and I start sweating as soon as I sit down. A homeless woman with a collapsing face stares at me from across the car. The old man beside me babbles on graciously like a guest on a talk show for demented people.

I arrive at headquarters on Leonard Street just before 5:30.

For my first tour, I get two experienced partners.

Bill Neill is a heavyset, dark-complexioned black guy in his forties, who served with the infantry in Vietnam. He has a thick Brooklyn accent, practically chain-smokes cigars, and votes Republican whenever possible. Because of a bad shrapnel wound in his left knee, he has to elevate the entire leg at a peculiar angle once every ten minutes or so.

He also has a ridiculously overconfident way of speaking that makes almost everything he says sound instantly suspect. "You know they got a lot of us addicted to monkey tranquilizer in Vietnam," he tells me within ten minutes of our first meeting. "Just 'cos they ran out of morphine. Now there are over ten thousand monkey tranq addicts in the United States. You knew that, didn't you?"

I find Bill slightly intimidating and immensely likable. His partner is a thirty-six-year-old former gang leader named Angel Vasquez. Angel, who has a lean, athletic build and high cheekbones, has boxed professionally and studied developmental psychology. I quickly learned that he is equally at ease quoting Clint Eastwood movies and *The Drama of the Gifted Child*.

Bill and him are constantly arguing about politics, but they have an easy, jokey rapport and a long-standing friendship.

"I been with this unit a year," Angel says as he shows me to a locker. "And I'm telling you that you're gonna like being out on the streets, man. You don't have to mess around so much with other people's superegos and that family therapy bullshit."

"But I don't know if I'm quite ready to give up being a regular probation officer. I still have a lot of paperwork to take care of and people to see..."

"How long you been with the department, man?" Angel asks.

"Two years."

"You would've burned out sooner or later."

I think about my recent encounters with Darryl King and shake my head. "Yeah," I say. "I guess maybe you're right."

"You know it, baby." Angel slaps me on the back. "It's real simple in this unit. You don't have to go through that psychic torture. If we have a warrant for the clients here, that means they had their shot and they blew it and we go out there to lock 'em up. Nobody gives us any static. If they come from a dysfunctional background, it's not our fault. And the best part is you don't go home worrying about someone else's problems."

Bill Neill ambles into the locker room a couple of minutes later and presents me with my first department-issued .38-caliber service revolver. He helps me put the gun belt through the loops in my jeans and secures the holster on my hip.

"Don't look at it so funny," Bill tells me. "It's not gonna bite you."

"I know," I say, touching the handle gingerly.

"It might blow your balls off, but it definitely won't bite you."

I manage an uneasy smile.

"What're you anyway?" Bill suddenly demands.

"How do you mean?"

"Are you one of them phony white liberals? Are you one of those types who goes running around telling niggers to feel sorry for themselves because society's at fault and they aren't to blame when they do a crime?"

The way he's talking is confusing. I can't tell if it's a test to see whether I'm a bleeding heart or a racist. Since we've just met and he seems pretty conservative, I decide to play it safe.

"I think I see things for what they are," I tell Bill.

"Whatever that means," he says harshly. "What they let these goddamn kids get away with now. When I was a kid and I wanted a pair of new sneakers, I went out and I worked for 'em. And if you got in trouble, you went to jail or you went into the army."

"That's right," Angel pipes in.

"And if you got Article Fifteen'd for insubordination, the

sergeant was allowed to hit you in the nuts with a rifle butt," Bill says. "You knew that, didn't you?"

"What?"

Bill slams shut a locker door and looks at me in stunned disbelief. "You didn't know that?" He glances over at his partner. "Angel, what kind of yo-yo have they assigned us here? Next you're gonna tell me that you didn't know Ho Chi Minh went to Bronx Science. You know that, don't you?"

I'm beginning to sense I'm being put on. "I'd rather not say right now."

"That's very smart," Bill says in a gravelly voice as he lifts his leg and places my hand firmly on the gun on my hip. "Congratulations. You are now a peace officer for the City of New York. You knew that, didn't you?"

As Bill walks out of the locker room, Angel pulls me aside one last time. "Hey, don't worry about Bill," he says. "He may talk tough and he may whack guys around now and then, but deep down he's just as conflicted as the rest of us."

By five to six, we're in a black Aries K car cruising up toward Harlem. "Brilliant that they give us these cars, right?" says Bill in the front passenger seat. "A black guy, a white guy, and a Puerto Rican guy. People on the street corners make us for cops in about three seconds."

The deadening humidity is still in the air. This must be what Calcutta is like in the summertime.

We follow two other K cars—carrying four more Field Service officers—past the el tracks near La Marqueta. A young woman with puffy eyes and a twisted mouth stands near one of the pillars. She wears high heels, a very short skirt, and torn stockings.

"Tell her there isn't any bus that stops here," Bill says to Angel between drags on his second cigar of the morning. The smoke fills the car and makes me ill.

"I think she knows already." Angel taps his fingers on the steering wheel. "Business must be slow."

"Hey, Baum," Bill says. "You fuck her, your dick will fall off three days later."

Bill chuckles to himself and pulls out his Motorola walkie-talkie. "Hey, Turner," he says into the radio. "Who the fuck are we going to see first?"

There's a blast of static and then Probation Officer Jocelyn Turner, a stout black woman in the car ahead of us, replies, "James Ferguson."

"What's his claim to fame?" Bill asks.

"Nothing," Turner says sullenly as though she doesn't want to bother looking at Ferguson's file.

"Nothing?" Bill takes another long drag on his cigar. "Do you mean to tell me that we are going to arrest an innocent person?" he asks.

"There are no innocent people," an unidentified voice says over the walkie-talkie.

Bill and Angel laugh all the way to the first address, an old squat apartment house on 167th Street. If this building was a person, it would be a wino. It seems to rear back from the sidewalk in drunken revulsion. Bill gets out of the car first and heads for the front door without looking back to see if the rest of us are following.

"First door right on the second floor," Angel calls out to him after checking the apartment number with Turner. "The guy's a chain snatch. He's probably not armed."

I trail my two partners into the building with the four other officers coming up behind us. The lobby, decorated with broken marble and mirrors, is silent. This must've once been a nice place to live, I think, as I follow Bill and Angel up the cracked staircase. But the landlord let it go to hell. There's a smell like a bus's exhaust in the air and dust flies into my contact lenses.

"The good thing about coming out at this hour is that all the crackheads are still asleep," Angel whispers over his shoulder to me. "They've all been out late partying last night."

Bill is already standing on the second-floor landing, nonchalantly cocking his leg in the air like a dog about to relieve himself. "They never live on the first floor," he says with a grimace.

"And they hardly ever have working elevators," Angel adds.

"Yeah, so let's fuck 'em up," Bill says.

Officer Jocelyn Turner, who moves gracefully and wears her hair in braids, sighs as she joins the rest of us on the landing. "The way you talk," she says.

Bill begins hammering the apartment's front door with a blackjack. The sound is so loud and insistent that I start to get a headache. If they knocked on my door like this at six in the morning, I'd call the cops. There's a thumping sound from inside like somebody falling out of bed. Then the door creaks open.

A small, fiftyish Dominican man with a creased face and deep-set eyes peers out. He looks exhausted, frightened, and bewildered.

"James Ferguson here?" Bill asks gruffly.

The man just stares at him. He seems unable to speak for a moment. "No," he says finally in a weary, confused voice. "No hablo..."

Angel steps forward and says something in Spanish to the man, but Bill is already pushing past him into the apartment. "Yeah, bullshit," Bill is saying as he takes a flashlight from his belt loops. "We'll see for ourselves."

Angel, Turner, and the others push in after them. I reluctantly follow. The apartment is completely dark. I can't discern its size or shape. All I can see is what the beam of Bill's flashlight illuminates. I glimpse the small man who opened the front door. He wears only a pair of old boxers and black socks. I feel embarrassed for him as the light swings away. We bump through a short, narrow corridor into a side room. The flashlight falls toward a bed on the side.

"Let's see. What do we got here?" Bill walks over and pulls down the bed sheet. A stocky woman wearing only a hairnet rolls over quickly and tries to hide her breasts. I get queasy like I would reading violent pornography. Bill shines the light under the bed and then crosses the room to check the closets.

"All right, he's not in here," he announces to the rest of us. "Let's see what other rooms they got in the house."

As he sweeps the beam around the rest of the room, I manage to briefly catch Angel's eye. "This is awful," I murmur.

"I know," Angel says as he follows the others out of the room and into the hall. "But you can't take any chances doing this. If somebody moves, you better know where they're going."

Bill and the others are already in another room down the hall. "Stop fucking around, Baum," Bill growls. "Get in here already."

I arrive in the room to see one officer on his hands and knees looking under a bed while Turner and the others rifle more closets and pull a chest of drawers out from the wall. I hear the whoosh and creak of water pipes overhead. It takes my eyes a moment to adjust to the slightly better light in the room. Then I notice a six-year-old boy cowering on the bed. He holds an old stuffed gray rabbit with one of its eyes missing. I glance up and see his father, the small man in the boxer shorts and black socks, looking at his boy imploringly from the corner. He seems to be asking his son's forgiveness for allowing all this to happen.

James Ferguson is not here or anywhere else in the building. We can't find anyone who's even heard of him.

"Well, what do you think so far?" Bill asks me in the car afterward.

"It's not exactly an exercise in civil liberties, is it?"

"Ah, get over it," Bill says, lighting another cigar and tossing the next warrant into the backseat where I'm sitting.

For the rest of the morning, we stop by a dozen different buildings, starting at the northern tip of Manhattan and working our way down. But most of the people we're looking for are not around. At noontime, we get assigned to check in on a transfer case, a young Italian woman in Queens. She got arrested last year for buying crack and we're supposed to make a home visit to make sure she's still living at the same address. We find her sixty-five-year-old father-in-law sitting on the steps outside the two-story house in Forest Hills where he lives with the woman, his son, and their five-year-old daughter.

"Stick around," the old man tells me and Bill as he looks up at the midday sun and strokes a panting brown Chihuahua. "She comes home for lunch this time every day. Can't stand to miss her soap opera."

Bill pokes me in the side with his blackjack, cuing me to ask a question. "Is your daughter-in-law staying off drugs?" I say.

"Ask her yourself," the old man says, closing the top button of his light blue bowling shirt.

Ten minutes later, his daughter-in-law shows up wearing too much lipstick and distressed blue jeans. "What the fuck're you guys doing here?" she says, barging up the steps and into the house. "Don't I got enough problems with my regular probation officer?"

"We just wanted to ask a few questions," I say.

She's already in the house, with the Chihuahua trailing her and the screen door closing behind them. Angel, Bill, and I bound up the steps and in the door after her.

The house is neat and clean with an orderly kitchen to the left of the foyer and a spacious living room to the right. The woman is already turning on the TV and lighting a cigarette with trembling fingers. She puts the wrong end in her mouth first.

"So ask, ask, ask," she says irritably as she collapses on a sofa and the Chihuahua yaps around her feet. "What do you want from me?"

"Baum," Bill murmurs. "Take a look around the place. Make sure she's still living here."

I start to argue, but think better of it. I'm definitely out of my element and I decide there's no harm in verifying that this

is the woman's true home. I make a quick tour of the seven
rooms. Most of them look exactly like any other room in any
other suburban house I've ever visited. Andrea must've grown
up in a place like this. No wonder she was so dismayed by
my apartment. I wander into the little girl's room; there're
stuffed animals and a down quilt on the bed and pictures of
Mickey Mouse and Snow White on the walls.

The shock comes when I go into the room where the woman
sleeps with her husband.

It's like stepping into another universe. Or a third world
country. The walls are bare and scraped in places. Clothes are
strewn all over and two filthy, smelly mattresses, without blankets or sheets, are laid end to end on the floor. I wonder if this
is the kind of place Darryl King comes from. On my right, the
closet door is open a little bit. It's dark in there and for a second,
I think I hear something stirring inside. The sound leads me
into a daydream of what it would be like if Darryl King was
hiding in there, waiting to jump out at me. I can see his angry
eyes and his hand coming up at me. When I find myself reaching for my gun, I decide it's time to get out of there.

I take a quick look in the closet and step back out into the
hall. It's confusing and disorienting to see that the rest of the
house has remained unchanged and suburban.

I go back into the living room. Angel is trying to talk to the
woman, but she's just staring straight ahead at the soap opera
on the television.

"So who takes care of your daughter?" Angel is asking.

"He does." The woman points at her father-in-law standing
in the doorway, but doesn't turn her eyes to look at him.

"Are you still taking drugs?" I ask. I'm surprised to hear
some anger creeping into my voice.

"Just the methadone," she says nonchalantly. "And cocaine
like once a night."

"Why're you doing that?"

"Because the methadone makes me so tired that I'd go to
sleep otherwise," the woman says as if she can't believe what

an idiot I am for not understanding immediately. She's so out of it that it doesn't even occur to her to lie.

A beady-eyed actor on the screen is kissing a blonde actress. The father-in-law glares at the woman from the doorway. I can tell the old man truly despises her for being a bad mother. Just then, Bill moves to my side and gives me an elbow in the ribs.

"Hey, Baum," he mutters. "Check out the dog."

I scan the floor and finally spot the Chihuahua squatting near the woman's knee. Amazingly, the dog, who can't be more than eighteen inches in length, is harboring an eight-inch hard-on and quietly working himself into an autoerotic frenzy.

"Oh shit," I say.

The Chihuahua, seeming to sense everyone looking at him, slinks behind the sofa, toting his grotesque erection. The woman briefly glances after him.

"Aw, he's all right," she says. "He just needs a girlfriend. That's all."

35

Here was the new thing on the street: When the police came to arrest you, you didn't run. You just stood there and gave them attitude. *Yeah. What's up? What you gonna do? You gonna shoot me?* Stupid teenage macho shit.

But the kid they picked up outside the bodega robbery on East Tremont was different. The ones who'd actually jumped the guy behind the counter and taken the money were across the street already, strutting around and flashing their new rolls at everybody like they'd earned it themselves. But the kid in the unseasonably heavy parka was still hanging around by the mangoes and the melons at the stand. He kept tucking his head inside the coat and quivering, as though he was laughing or crying to himself.

In fact, Eddie Johnson wouldn't have been taken in at all if the patrolman hadn't bothered to pat him down and find the unregistered handgun, the marijuana, and the chicken bones in his pockets.

36

That night, I try to call Andrea, but she's not around, so I leave a message with her roommate. With these new hours, it's hard to keep up with anybody.

I dig up my photographer friend Terry Greene and we go to have dinner at an Upper West Side coffee shop and maybe catch a movie. I have tuna on rye, which is what I always eat, and Terry has ice cream and seven-layer cake. I don't know why he never seems to gain weight, though I notice he's more jittery than usual these days. I hope he's not doing heroin again. Afterward, we go for a walk around Lincoln Center.

"I don't know about this field job," I say as we circle the fountain in the middle of the complex. "I'm way behind on my paperwork now. What I'd really like is to see a couple of my old clients again. That way I'd feel like I was still doing serious work."

"I thought this was what you wanted," he says, scratching the purple streak in his hair, which he's accentuated into a kind of a Mohawk. It looks a little pathetic since he's almost thirty. "You're actually getting to see where these people live, instead of just talking to them in the office." He stops and tries to light a cigarette, cupping his hands protectively around the flame.

"Yeah, I suppose I am getting closer to the source."

"Hey," he says abruptly. "What about *My Life as a Dog?*"

For a second, I think he's talking about the aroused Chihuahua I saw earlier today, but then I see he's pointing to a movie poster with that title in the window of a nearby video store. "We could rent it and go back to my house," he says.

I shake my head. "I really don't feel like seeing a foreign film right now."

"Okay," he says wearily as he stops scratching his arm and goes back to scratching his head.

"It's just this field job makes me wonder if we're accomplishing anything. I mean, we just go marching into people's houses and start ordering them around. I don't know if that's so great..."

I notice that he's wearing a pin on his lapel for Peru's Shining Path movement. But when I ask him about it, he gets very defensive. "I just been reading about them," he says. "I think what they tried to do is really interesting."

"But aren't they kinda right wing?"

"So?"

"I thought you said you were a socialist."

"I said I was trying to develop anarchist tendencies," he insists. "That's why I stopped reading the TV listings..."

"Anyway," I say, rubbing my eye where the contact lens was poking it, "I was getting a little fed up with the way things were going in the office, but that doesn't mean I want to become a full-time cop."

"Is that what's bothering you?" He looks at me the way he'd look at an alarm clock waking him from a peaceful rest.

"That's part of it."

"What's the other part?"

"That I might start liking it."

37

"All I'm looking for is a little comeback," Richard Silver said. "You know what I mean? Just a little comeback."

He clenched his teeth and all of the tendons and veins in his neck stood out. Slowly, he lowered the 350 pounds of weight he'd lifted while on his back.

"You look stiff," said his personal trainer, Sandy, a blond-haired, blue-eyed former surfing champion and Vegas body-guard.

"Stiff? I got pressures like you wouldn't believe."

"Keep your back straight," said Sandy, kneeling by the Nautilus machine.

Richard Silver looked straight up at the ceiling and did five quick reps with the 350 pounds. While he was catching his breath, a buxom redhead in black nylon stretch pants paused in front of his machine and pulled up her white T-shirt, exposing a smooth flat stomach.

"Jesus Christ," Richard Silver said.

"Is that enough weight for you?" Sandy asked.

"Hell no." Richard sat up for a moment and twisted from side to side. Sweat matted his hair and ran down the front of his blue T-shirt. "Gimme four hundred."

"I thought you already had too much pressure."

"Hey, Sandy, do me a favor. Don't be funny. Help me get big, all right. That's what I pay you for. Jesus Christ. As if I don't have enough problems."

He lay down on his back again as Sandy added more weight. On the other side, a dozen lissome women were bouncing up and down to a frenetic disco beat in their aerobics class.

Richard Silver caught sight of himself lifting the weights in the floor-to-ceiling mirror while Sandy stood there admiring his own biceps. It made him think of an old bull trying to pull a cart past the new stud on the farm.

"You got business troubles?" Sandy asked, throwing back his mane of blond hair.

"The worst," Richard Silver grunted between reps. "There's gotta be ten people now devoting themselves to making my life miserable. You go out of the picture awhile and everybody tries to change the rules on you. They turn everything upside down."

"Yeah," said Sandy, who had no idea what Richard Silver was talking about.

"Hey, Sandy, you don't know anybody who's into offshore banking, do you?"

"I don't know." Sandy reached down and ever so subtly realigned the position of his balls in his jockstrap.

A refrigerator of a guy was standing by them now, waiting to use the machine.

"And then there's my wife," Richard Silver said, extending his bulging arms.

"What's the matter with her?"

"I should say my ex-wife. She wants to give me a hard time about seeing my son. You believe that? She goes around saying things about me. In front of my son."

"It's not right," said Sandy, turning to give a wide smile to a slim-hipped blonde passing by.

"Ah, what do you know?" Richard Silver dropped the weights with a loud crash and went over to the next machine, which looked like a medieval torture device with red cushions.

Sandy adjusted the weight to 425 pounds as Richard put his back to the machine and started lifting. He stopped after ten reps. "The head of the investment firm you train, can he do that many?"

"Almost."

Richard Silver did ten more reps quickly. He stood up and held on to the hems of his shorts while he caught his breath. His biceps strained against the sleeves of his T-shirt. "I'll tell you something, Sandy," he said. "The more time goes by, the more you find yourself doing things you never thought you'd do in a million years. Just to get by. That's the sad part."

"Huh," said Sandy.

"If you could put yourself in a time machine twenty years ago, you'd never recognize yourself now. That's how things change."

Sandy wasn't listening. He was too busy staring at a full-lipped brunette, who was wearing hot pink shorts and lifting at least three hundred pounds by spreading her legs on the Y-shaped machine across the room.

"Hey, Sandy," Richard Silver said. "Tell me something. You fuck a lot of these girls?"

"A few, I guess."

The girl in the hot pink shorts smiled at Sandy and closed her eyes as she kept lifting.

"Jesus Christ," Richard Silver said. "Jesus Christ."

38

The next day in the field begins a little more promisingly. Just before seven, we arrive at a tall, red brick housing project that takes up an entire block near West 134th Street.

As dark clouds gather overhead, Bill, Angel, and I have a conference with the four other probation officers in the plaza outside the building. Officer Jocelyn Turner takes out a manila folder and reads from the file about the guy we're seeking.

"This mutt has really been acting out lately," Angel says in his peculiar mixture of cop talk and social work jargon.

His name is Cecil Shavers. A twenty-two-year-old male black with a long history of drug arrests and violent behavior. His regular probation officer set up a violation hearing after Cecil got rearrested and then failed to report. Of course, Cecil did not show up for the hearing either, and the judge issued a warrant for the unit to pick him up. According to the reports, Cecil's father is wheelchair-bound and lately Cecil has taken to tying him up and beating him to get crack money. The report also mentions that Cecil's mother works as a cleaning woman and his younger brother has cerebral palsy.

Turner shows me the file photo of Cecil. He has a bony face, cornrowed hair, and eyes set far apart. Suddenly, playing *What's My Crime?* at the office seems like a long time ago.

We walk through the plaza to the building's entrance. Bill warns us all to look up at the roof and make sure nobody is throwing anything down on us. A light rain is starting to fall. From the old green benches, two old women, four little kids, and a man in a wheelchair watch us approaching.

"Should we show them the picture and ask them if Cecil still lives here?" I ask Bill.

"No way. The old man over there is probably his father," Bill answers. "Fuck 'em, we don't want them to know we're coming..."

The glass in the front door is cracked into a spiderweb pattern. Jocelyn Turner tries to check the apartment number in Cecil's file with the directory by the aluminum mailboxes. She gives up after a few seconds. "If the name is still on the directory, that usually means the people are gone," she says. "And if the people are still here, they've probably ripped their names off the directory. Same shit, every time."

The building is about thirty years old. The lobby smells like piss and motor oil. There are a few graffiti scrawls on the walls and a couple of crack vials on the floor. A little boy in a New York Mets cap sits outside a first-floor apartment and asks us if we can fix his family's air conditioner.

We have a bumpy ride up to the twenty-seventh floor in the steel elevator. At one point, I make the mistake of leaning on the wall with my hand. A mysterious brown liquid gets all over my palm. My fellow probation officers convulse with laughter.

Jocelyn Turner walks up to the door of 27K and starts knocking with her blackjack. The door is covered with a large black-and-white poster that says "Crack Shatters Lives" in bold letters surrounded by broken glass. It takes two minutes of continuous pounding before a woman's voice from inside shouts out, "Who is it?"

"Police. Open up," says Bill loudly. He gives me a conspiratorial grin. "That always works better than saying we're probation officers," he explains quietly.

Turner pounds on the door again. "Let's go, ma'am. Open it up, now."

The door finally opens. A round-faced, fiftyish woman in a white housedress stands there, rubbing her eyes. Turner shows her the shield. The woman doesn't bother to look at it.

"Is Cecil here?" Turner asks.

"I dunno...No."

"Are you his mother?"

"Uh, well...yeah."

"Then make it easy on all of us," Turner says. "Where is he?"

"I don't think he's here," Cecil's mother says with a bit of confusion. "I ain't seen him in a long while."

"That's a lie," Bill mumbles to me. "He's right here."

"Ma'am, we're gonna have a look around here for ourselves," Turner says, pushing past the mother and heading through a narrow corridor with her gun drawn.

"What makes you so sure he's here?" I ask Bill.

"Believe me, I know," Bill says. "These people just get into the habit of lying. They do it every time. Once you do this a few times you'll see. They never tell you when a guy is there."

I follow Turner and the others around a corner and into a dark blue room. In the bed on the left, Cecil Shavers is naked and lying on his stomach. His head is turned just enough to the right so I can see his eyes are closed and his mouth is half open, revealing a gold front tooth next to a chipped one. Under him, a fragile-looking young woman in a ripped pea-green nightgown seems to be struggling for comfort and air. I can't tell if they just got done fucking or are about to get started.

They're being watched from the bed across the room by Cecil's brother. He's about a year younger than Cecil. All his limbs are withered. He looks both horrified and fascinated by what his older brother is doing to the girl in the bed. A triangle-shaped bar hangs over his head. He's naked, except for the bed sheet covering his lower body up to the start of his pubic hair. His right hip bone protrudes at an unnatural angle and his left arm is about a third the size of his right. He twists his head as though he's in great agony.

There's a poster on the wall between the brothers' beds. It shows a teddy bear in a slumped position with a bottle in his paw and a slogan scrawled over his head, "I have a drinking problem—Only one mouth and two hands." I assume Cecil was the brother who put the poster up.

"Come on, Cecil, get up," says Turner.

"Whass up?" He opens his eyes slowly.

"You're getting a free ride to court."

"Why?" He sits up. "What did I do?"

"You didn't go to court on your violation hearing," Angel says. "Now the judge wants to see you."

Cecil's mother steps into the room behind us. "What are you doing here?" she howls. "He's a good boy. Why don't you leave him alone?"

"Sorry, ma'am, we're just doing our job," I say.

"Hey, Baum, we're not holding a discussion group here," Bill snaps. "Save your sensitivity training for your girlfriend."

"Come on, Cecil, get dressed," says Turner.

Cecil leans out of bed and grabs a pair of dirty blue sweatpants off the floor. His girlfriend wakes up briefly, looks around at all the people in the room, loses interest, and then goes back to sleep.

"Can I take a shower?" Cecil asks.

"No time," Bill says as he cases the room for guns.

"Keisha, where my Reeboks at?" Cecil grumbles. His girlfriend remains unconscious. From across the room, his brother looks at him with an expression of infinite sorrow and suffering.

"Can I brush my teeth and all?" Cecil asks.

"See how clean he is?" his mother says.

"Yeah, but one of us will have to go to the bathroom with you," says Turner. "Baum, get his shoes, will you?"

I look under the bed and find a brand-new pair of black Reeboks. I bang them together to see if there's a shiv concealed, but only dust flies out. Cecil takes the sneakers from me and walks into the bathroom. Angel follows, leaving the door ajar in case Cecil tries to attack him.

The rest of us go to the living room to wait. There's a nice river view, but the pale green paint on the walls is filthy and peeling. The furniture consists of two couches with stuffing overflowing from their upholstery, a small brown table in the corner, and a Sony twenty-four-inch color television with a VCR. A videocassette of the film *The Principal* lies on top of the machine. That movie is probably as close as this family can come to having order in their lives.

I look over and see Bill in the middle of the room, raising his wounded leg at a peculiar angle. For a moment, it looks like he's going to make like Chuck Berry and duck-walk across the floor.

"You know it's a funny thing, Baum," Bill is saying. "Sound doesn't travel too well in this kind of building. That's because they put bags of sand between the walls. You knew that, didn't you?"

Before I can answer, Bill points to a *Just Say No to Crack* sticker above the table in the corner. Then he smiles and picks up a small crack pipe from the table under it.

"Why do they have that *Just Say No* up there?" I ask. "Are they being ironic or something?"

"You're looking at it all wrong, Baum," Bill snarls. "These people aren't capable of any kind of intellectual reasoning. They're like animals."

If I heard a white guy say this, I'd probably pick a fight with him. But since it's Bill, I just feel mixed up again. I wonder what he'd say if he ran into Darryl King. Maybe he could've done a better job of controlling him than I did.

He clears his throat and holds the crack pipe up like it's a rare scientific specimen.

"What are you going to do with that?"

"Well," he says, "I could bring it to court and present it as part of the violation hearing." He tests the pipe's sturdiness with his fingers. "But the judge might throw it out as an illegal seizure. So I think we'll exercise a more basic kind of enforcement."

He crushes the pipe with his left hand and flicks cigar ashes on the floor with his right. "You know, it's funny about this crack business, Baum," he says. "It's a little bit like dealing with the villagers in Vietnam. They want you to clean up their town, but they don't want you to take their sons away."

Just then, I hear Angel calling my name from the bathroom. I go down the hall and meet him at the entrance. "Hey, man, I gotta use the other can in the house," Angel says. "Keep an eye on Cecil here, will you?"

Behind him, Cecil is standing at the sink, still shirtless, with his toothbrush in his mouth. Angel departs and I move into the bathroom. Cecil ignores me and gazes admiringly at his reflection in the bathroom mirror. I step around him to the other side of the cramped room and find myself standing by the bathtub. I'm considering whether I should take a seat on its ledge when I hear water dripping and look down to see a sickening brown ring around the tub. I raise my head to say something to Cecil. Suddenly, he slams me hard on the head with the medicine cabinet door. I'm completely unprepared— barely able to catch a hold of the bathtub ledge and avoid falling over backward into it.

I look up in pain to see Cecil snatching a red Swiss Army knife out of the cabinet and brandishing it at me. With the toothpaste foam still around his mouth, he looks a little rabid. I don't know what to do. I'm paralyzed. Cecil advances on me with the knife. "Oh shit," I hear myself say. "Oh shit." It seems to take an eternity for me to remember I'm carrying a gun.

I finally pull it out and yell, "Don't move," in a high, squeaky voice. Cecil drops the knife and stands still. By now I'm so scared that I start hitting him around the face and shoulder with the butt of the gun and shouting: "WHY'D YOU DO THAT, YOU DUMB FUCK?! WHY'D YOU SCARE ME LIKE THAT?!"

When he puts up his hands to protect himself, I just start hitting him harder.

Eventually I feel Turner pulling me off the kid as Bill and the others charge into the room. My pulse is racing and blood is pounding in my ears. As much as anything else, I feel humiliated about getting caught so off guard like that. After the training session at Rodman's Neck, I should've known better. Bill puts his hand on my head and I hear someone laughing. "Take it easy, man," Bill is saying. "Everything's copacetic."

While I get my breathing and temper back under control, Bill and Angel shove Cecil to his knees in front of the toilet and make him put his hands behind his back. Bill takes his handcuffs out and beckons to me.

"You can put these on the skell," Bill says. "It's your first collar, tough guy. You lost your cherry. I knew you were more than a social worker."

I put the cuffs on him and walk out into the living room, rubbing my head where the medicine cabinet door hit it. I notice one last strange item on the wall above one of the couches. It's one of those novelty posters made by stores around Times Square. It says *Wanted: Dead or Alive* and offers a million-dollar reward. The black-and-white picture is of Cecil Shavers and his brother. The photo seems to be a couple of years old, from a better time, before Cecil started smoking crack and his brother was crippled by palsy.

It looks like something their mother did as a way of saying: "Look out world, here come my boys!"

Angel leads Cecil out of the bathroom in handcuffs and takes him out of the apartment.

I guess only one of the brothers lived up to the poster's promise.

39

"You know this isn't right," Detective Sergeant Bob McCullough was saying. "I mean, you know the difference between right and wrong, don't you?"

The boy didn't say anything. He kept his head tucked inside his parka and quivered like a small frightened sparrow. The other detective in the room threw a paper clip and swore loudly.

"Now let's not be impatient," McCullough said in a nice voice. "Eddie here just needs a chance to get accustomed."

Very slowly, Eddie Johnson took his head out of his coat and looked around. His eyes followed the border where the blue paint met the white paint about five feet up the wall. He was watching that border like it was a waterline and he was drowning underneath it, McCullough thought. In a way, he was drowning. With the new charge he was facing for carrying the unregistered handgun, and the old probation term he had for throwing rocks at cars in the Bronx, he could get as much as four years in prison. His only chance now was to make a deal.

"These things that you do," McCullough said softly. "You can't keep doing them. It's not a life." He shook his head.

Eddie Johnson grimaced a little as the other detective brought his fist down hard on the desk. "Enough of this shit," he told McCullough. "Let's just lock this mutt up."

"Our friends at Narcotics wouldn't be happy to hear you say that, Lou," McCullough said, getting out of his chair and walking around like he'd just gotten off a horse. "They think Eddie here can help us out. They have a lot of faith in him."

"Ah, he can't even fuckin' talk," said the detective named Lou who had enormous thighs and hair on his head that looked like it belonged in his armpit.

"Yes he can," said McCullough. "Can't you talk, Eddie?"

"Yes," Eddie said in a quiet, blunted voice.

He looked at both detectives warily, as though he sensed they were trying to confuse him. After a couple of seconds he put his head back inside his parka. The detective named Lou picked up a copy of the Manhattan telephone directory and began waving it around menacingly.

"You know what I think?" McCullough said, facing Eddie. "I think getting arrested the other day is gonna turn out to be the best thing that ever happened to you. I really think so."

Eddie brought his head out of his coat and looked at McCullough curiously. "When you put your head in your coat like that, you're chewing on something, aren't you?" McCullough said.

Slowly, reluctantly, the boy began to nod.

It took just a little while longer for McCullough to get Eddie to open the coat and show him the chicken bones that he carried around in his pocket and chewed on when he got scared. Then the detective sent out for a ham and cheese sandwich. Eddie gobbled down half of it and stuffed the other half in his pocket.

"Before you didn't have anybody looking out for you," McCullough told him. "Those people who were supposed to be your friends didn't help you out when you got arrested the other day. So now you have us. And we'll look out for you. Okay?"

"Okay," Eddie mumbled, sitting forward in the steel chair that badly needed to be oiled.

"We're like your family now. Okay?"

"Okay." The kid looked like he was about to start crying again.

"So tell us exactly what you told those detectives up in the Bronx," McCullough said. "Tell us about your friend Darryl King."

40

I'm standing behind a building in Washington Heights, waiting for the action to begin. Bill and Angel have gone in the front, looking for an old breaking-and-entering guy who's missed three appointments with the judge. In all likelihood they'll just grab the guy and haul him out. But Bill says that given his case history, there's a chance the guy will try to make a break for it through the back entrance, so I better be ready.

Sure enough, within two minutes, I see a runty little white guy with his hair in a ponytail and wearing a lot of jewelry climbing down the back fire escape. He looks like a renegade from the 1960s, except his face appears to have been run over by a tractor. He jumps down off the fire escape and I go chasing him across a vacant, rubble-strewn lot. Just like TV. He's not too young and not too swift, so I catch him and tackle him easily, as though we were playing touch football in the park. The guy doesn't even seem too angry with me. He's probably been caught and locked up so many times that it doesn't make much difference to him. In fact, he gives me a little wink, like he admires my technique.

I've got to admit that I'm starting to like this job a little. After two years of heart-wrenching cases that never seemed to end, it's a pleasure being liberated from the glum social work

pieties and bureaucratic snares. I like having people respond
when I order them around. And I like getting out into the field
and doing physical work, instead of sitting behind a desk
all day.

The worst part of the job is not having any time to catch
up on my paperwork and see Andrea. The best part is getting
to hang out with Angel and Bill. When I was in school, I missed
out on things like cruising around with the boys on a Saturday
night. Now, for the first time in my life, I feel like one of the
guys.

After we process the breaking-and-entering guy, they take
me on a sightseeing tour through Harlem and the rest of Upper
Manhattan, even though I could use the time to knock off some
of that paperwork and see some of my old clients.

Driving without any particular pattern or direction, they
start off at the Audubon ballroom on West 165th Street, where
Malcolm X was murdered, and then decide to race down to
the Abyssinian Baptist Church on West 138th Street, where
Adam Clayton Powell, Jr., once preached. We take a detour
over to P. T. Barnum's old house near Sugar Hill, with its weird
cornices and gables, and then head south past the apartment
building on Edgecombe Avenue where Duke Ellington re-
hearsed his band and sometimes watched baseball at the Polo
Grounds from his window. I've actually been around here before because I went to City College, but I don't let on because
Bill and Angel are obviously having a good time playing tour
guides and local historians.

We swing by the beautiful old houses on Striver's Row and
then drive past the Apollo, where Bill says he saw James Brown
and Bobby Blue Bland perform years ago. Finally they show
me the old whorehouses and numbers joints on St. Nicholas
Avenue and encourage me to have a look inside for myself.

"They love white meat in there," Bill says, pointing to a
shabby tenement. "Jack Kennedy used to go in there, you
know."

"What?" I give him a dubious look from the backseat.

"You knew that, didn't you?"

"Yeah," says Angel.

"Sure," Bill says, putting his left leg up on the dashboard. "Jack Kennedy went to that whorehouse every time he was in Harlem. Right, Angel?"

"Right."

"Sure." Bill gestures with a lit cigar. "He was having an affair with Josephine Baker. You knew that, Baum, didn't you?"

"Josephine Baker?"

"That's right," Bill says in a deadpan voice, rolling down the window. "And Moms Mabley too. You knew Kennedy was fucking Moms too, didn't you, Baum..."

Behind the wheel, Angel is starting to shake with laughter. Bill continues to insist that the president was having an affair with an eighty-year-old black female comic.

"Kennedy was fucking Moms Mabley?" I ask.

"Of course," Bill says with utter confidence. "She gave him head..."

"What about Slappy White?" I say. "Was Kennedy fucking Slappy White?"

"The old guy who was on *Sanford and Son*?" Bill asks.

"Yeah." I lean back in my seat and open the beer Bill gave me. "I heard Slappy wouldn't have JFK..."

The two of them start laughing and slapping my hand. "Pretty funny for a white guy, Baum," Bill says.

We pass a bunch of middle-aged guys standing outside a tenement, polishing BMWs and Mercedes in the afternoon sun. Given the neighborhood, you'd think they might be drug dealers, but they seem a little old and ratty. Drugs are supposed to be a younger man's game. Maybe they're just paid to wash the cars. In the meantime, Angel fiddles with the radio, trying to find a station we can all agree on. Most of what he gets is static, except for one station playing a reverberating electric guitar introduction.

"What is this shit?" Angel asks.

"'Welcome to the Jungle' by Guns N' Roses," I say. "That's old already."

Angel and Bill both turn their heads to look at me. "The young generation, Angel," Bill says. "We need them to be our eyes and ears."

I shrug. I'm having a good time now. I've even succeeded in putting Darryl King out of my mind for the moment.

"You know what I like?" Bill says as we pass Sylvia's Restaurant, the Casablanca Bar, and Beeper World on Lenox Avenue. "Country music."

"Is that right?" I rest my elbows on the back of his seat.

"Sure," says Bill. "You knew that, didn't you? Some of it's like poetry, you know, the way it tells a story. That's all we listened to around the Mekong Delta 'cause I had all them hillbilly rednecks in my unit. Who's the guy who does 'Okie from Muskogee'?"

"Merle Haggard," I say, drawing on my own country record collection.

"Yeah." Bill chomps down on his cigar. "I knew a guy from Muskogee over in Vietnam. Only he didn't like that song. Henry Lee Oliver. Blond-haired white boy about your height, Baum. Man, he hated that song."

"Why?" I ask. I've always sort of liked that song in spite of its belligerent, hippie-baiting lyrics.

"That's what I always wondered too," Bill says. "You'd figure a guy from Muskogee would consider that song his national anthem. But he never wanted to be around when they played that song. He said it made all the people where he came from sound like rednecks and he wasn't like that. Taught me a lesson."

"What?" I ask.

"That you can never know what to expect from people. I'll tell you, up until then I thought all white people were rednecks."

"It's just most of them," Angel says, looking over from the driver's seat.

"Yeah," Bill tells him. "But not Henry Lee Oliver. He was all right. He hated that 'Okie from Muskogee.' He liked, you know, whaddyacallit ... 'Ruby.'"

He starts to hum the melody. After a couple of bars I recognize it as "Ruby, Don't Take Your Love to Town," a terribly sad song about a guy who comes back from the war as a paraplegic and winds up lying in bed helpless and alone while his wife goes out on the town with other men. Angel and I join in for the chorus, and we sound pretty good within the confines of the car.

Bill stops singing and for once he looks somewhat reflective. "Yeah, Henry Lee used to hum that song over and over when he went to sleep at night. I guess it must've spooked him or something. He used to say how awful it would be if something like that happened to you. You know, getting crippled in the war and coming home to see your woman fucking somebody else."

"So whatever happened to Henry Lee?" I ask.

"He got shot in the head outside a rice paddy," Bill says, casually throwing his cigar butt out the window. "So he shouldn't have bothered worrying about the whole thing..."

As we make the turn onto 125th Street, two things hit me. Number one is that there's a lot more to Bill than I'd thought. Angel's right about him: He talks tough, but he's just as mixed up as the rest of us. I wonder if there's some level of self-loathing going on when he calls black people "animals" and stuff like that. The other thing that strikes me is a vague sense of unease. But that slips out of my mind quickly as we pull up to a row of Senegalese peddlers selling umbrellas, wallets, and vinyl handbags on the sidewalk. From the Senegalese guys on my caseload, I speak enough of their native tongue, Wolof, to negotiate a good deal for Bill and Angel to buy their wives some nice scarves.

Bill starts to give me the thumbs-up sign, but then the walkie-talkie on his belt blasts static. He picks it up, says a few words into the receiver, and then listens for a few seconds.

He raises his bushy eyebrows at me and then signs off.

"That was for you," he tells me. "You're supposed to give some cop a call."

"Oh hi, how you doin', Mr. Baum. This is Detective Sergeant Bob McCullough from the two-five..."

"Oh yeah, I tried to reach out to you before." I put a finger in my ear so the noise from the street doesn't drown out what he's saying on the pay phone.

"Your name is Baum, right? Not Byrne like you told Kelly?" I admit that's true and McCullough has a good laugh.

" 'Kay, listen, buddy boy, you and your friend gave us a good tip there about this Darryl King guy. So the other day, we picked up an individual name of Edward Johnson in the Bronx. He's like...not retarded, you know. Just weird. Anyway, the first point of the thing is this guy Johnson can connect King to those crack dealers who got popped in Harlem."

"That's great," I say. "Now you can put the guy away."

"Well, not so fast," McCullough says. "This guy, Johnson, our informant. He's had some problems with your people." From the insinuating way he says "your people," I wonder if he means the Jews.

He soon disabuses me of that notion. "Johnson is on probation in the Bronx for a rock-throwing thing," he says. "But he's been a bad boy. He just got picked up again carrying an unregistered handgun and a quantity of marijuana. So that could get him...whaddyacallit?"

I hear the click and put another quarter in. "Violated," I say.

"Yeah, violated."

"I think I catch your drift. He'll cooperate with you if he can stay on probation."

"Kee-rect," says McCullough.

"However, you need to convince him that the threat of the violation and the revocation of his probation are real..."

"Exactly."

"I'll talk to my people."

SLOW MOTION RIOT ·

I spend another quarter and call Ms. Lang with the information. She'll call the assistant commissioner for the borough, who'll call the assistant commissioner in the Bronx, who'll talk to her branch chief, and eventually it'll all come back to Eddie Johnson's probation officer in the Bronx, who probably has no idea his client's been rearrested. In the end, Eddie Johnson will agree to cooperate with the police and a warrant will be issued for Darryl King's arrest.

This puts me in a good mood, and I come bounding back to the car where Bill and Angel have been waiting patiently with these odd-looking smiles.

"What's up?" I ask as we pull away from the curb.

"Well, we've been doing nothing but our cases the last few days," says Angel. "So we went to your old supervisor Ms. Lang and got a couple of your old cases."

He hands me a file over the back of the seat. Richard Silver's name is written in bright red letters across the top. I feel my face instantly start to crumple. "Oh fuck! I wanted to get rid of this guy."

Bill and Angel burst out laughing, as we pass a glossy waterfall of a high rise in the East Nineties and keep going down Second Avenue. I get a picture in my mind of Richard Silver giving me that patronizing raised eyebrow and I feel like getting out of the car right now. "What do we want with this case?" I ask.

"He's another one of your bad boys, Baum," Bill says. "He missed an appointment with his new P.O. and still hasn't done his community service requirement."

We pass a bus that has a picture of a girl who looks like Andrea in the scotch ad on the side. I wonder why she hasn't been returning my calls and then I start to feel empty inside. I reach for my Silly Putty, since I can't bear the stench of a cigarette with Bill's cigar smoke in here.

I glance through my old reports on Silver and see, for once, I haven't made any serious spelling mistakes. "So he's not getting violated?"

"No. No. Just a gentle reminder to keep his appointments."

Bill checks his watch. We've been working for nearly ten hours and the overtime is starting to pile up. That may be the most important thing Bill and Angel have taught me: how to put in for overtime without drawing undue attention from your supervisor.

"So we're going to Sutton Place now, right?" Bill asks me, his brown eyes amused in the rearview mirror.

"That's the address Silver gave me," I say, closing the folder just as I start to feel carsick.

I ring the soft, chiming bell next to the mahogany doors of Richard Silver's apartment and try to think of a snappy comeback to however he's going to put me down. For a few seconds, "yeah, your mutha" are the only words that come to mind. One door opens and a stout Hispanic woman with close-set eyes looks me over and checks out Bill and Angel. She wears a white maid's uniform and has no expression.

"Hi, the doorman just rang us up," I say. "Is Mr. Silver here?"

Nothing registers on her face. I get a strong feeling that she doesn't speak English. Then Angel talks to her in Spanish and she steps aside. We walk down a long foyer and into an entrance gallery with a marble floor and a high, rounded ceiling. The air-conditioning keeps the temperature comfortable, around sixty-seven degrees. To the left, a pair of ivory-colored doors with gold handles open with a sound like a thoroughbred's hooves hitting the ground. An attractive woman with long brown hair stands there smiling. She wears a blue silk bathrobe and black high heels.

"I'm Gloria Silver," she says in a husky voice.

We awkwardly introduce ourselves and shake hands with her. Up close, she still looks good, just a little older than she first appeared. At least forty-two, with sharp worry lines on either side of her mouth and a few rings around her throat. The skin under her eyes is a little tight, possibly from premature cosmetic surgery.

"Richard isn't in right now," she says. "But please do stay awhile."

There's something a little needy in her voice, and something else strange in her eyes. Flaky lady. She *really* wants us to stay. And she doesn't even know us. We give each other confused looks. This whole trip downtown has been for nothing, especially since we could've gone home early today. After a few seconds' hesitation, Angel and Bill excuse themselves.

"Mr. Baum can handle this himself, ma'am," Bill says. "We have to be off for the weekend." I give them both irritated looks, but Bill just flashes a sly smile at me, like he's saying, "Go get 'em, tiger."

Now I have to stick around for a few minutes, just to be polite. I decide I'll ask a couple of questions about Richard Silver and leave at the first chance. She guides me through the living room into her den. The walls are covered in salmon silk moiré and the carpet is a delicate Oriental tapestry. The tables and chairs are nineteenth-century French antiques. The Donahue show is just ending on the giant TV screen. She goes to the bar, picks up a crystal glass, and fills it with Sprite and ice.

"Would you like something to drink?" she asks me, and then nervously looks over at the maid, who is standing there, still absolutely expressionless, in the doorway.

"Just water, please."

She fumbles around the bar until she finds the ice bucket and the stainless-steel pitcher of water. Haphazardly she pours it, and the maid doesn't move an inch. "We're just going to be in here a little while, Iris," Mrs. Silver says to the maid. Her voice is tentative, as if she's dying for the maid's approval.

Iris barely acknowledges that she's been spoken to. She puts her hands on her hips, takes a deep breath, and then slowly walks away.

"I think she likes you," Mrs. Silver tells me.

She must be kidding, I think. "I'm worried Iris is angry with me," she confides in a low, anxious voice. "She gave me a look this morning as she was changing the bed..." She shakes her head and turns the TV volume down with the remote control.

I sit down at the end of her long gray sofa. She sits a foot or two away, the slit in her bathrobe revealing a pair of skinny legs wrapped around each other. One black high heel wiggles on her foot. The scent of strong, expensive perfume is in the air; it reminds me of something much older women would wear to a funeral. A long, uneasy silence passes and she sniffs three or four times. I never would've thought Richard Silver was married to such a strange lady. I guess I imagined him zipping around town with a redhead in a sports car or something.

"So what time are you expecting Richard to get home?" I ask.

"I'm not."

"I don't understand."

"Our divorce was finalized last week."

"Huh...I mean, well...I'm sorry."

This whole scene is starting to get a little too strange for me. I try to figure out a way to get up and leave immediately. She looks me straight in the eye and starts singing, "Put the blame on Mame, boys, put the blame on Mame..." She gestures for me to sing along with her. I smile nervously and look down at my water glass.

After a verse or two, she stops singing. "I actually haven't seen Richard in a few months," she says. "Not since he took up with that blonde chippie..."

I have no idea who or what she's talking about. I didn't know any of these things about Richard Silver before. But that just shows how little you find out about anybody from sitting in a cubicle with them for five minutes.

"Do you know Richard well?" Mrs. Silver is asking.

"Not really."

"Richard is a very...dominating personality," she says, scratching a spot near the side of her nose and then leaving her finger there. I pray she's not about to start picking it. "He's very good at getting something when he needs it. Of course, you know he did very well in our divorce."

"Is that so?"

"Well, my dear, he should have." She straightens her spine. "He paid off the judge and my lawyer..."

Oh boy. I think, she is really nuts. "It looks like things didn't work out too badly," I say in a voice that's supposed to settle things down so I can leave gracefully. "After all, you got this great apartment..." I rock back on the sofa and prepare to flee.

"But that's all I got," she says, raising her voice suddenly and bitterly. "That and a lousy thirty-five hundred a month for alimony and child support. How am I supposed to live on that? I ask you. Do you know what Richard did?! He went to..."

Her voice is just a decibel or two shy of hysteria when Iris the maid appears at the door again. This time her lips are pursed and her eyebrows are raised.

"Oh, Iris," Mrs. Silver says apprehensively. "Everything is just fine."

Iris leaves again, without a word. "What do you think she meant by that look she just gave me?" Mrs. Silver asks.

"I have no idea."

As she chews her knuckles and talks on frantically, I start to get a glimmer of understanding. Mrs. Silver doesn't work. The signs are that she stays in the house all day, thinking about her divorce. I mean, it's past five and she's still in her bathrobe. Other than her son, Leonard, who's in school all day, the only human being she sees on a regular basis is her maid, Iris, who speaks no English. So in Mrs. Silver's mind, they've built up an intense, complicated relationship. Days can be ruined by the tilt of Iris's head or an ill-timed cough.

In an odd way, Mrs. Silver reminds me of some of the poor women I've worked with. It's that same sad inertia. Getting up late, watching television all day, no good reason to look for-

ward to tomorrow. From the way she keeps rubbing her nose,
I have to wonder whether she isn't doing as much cocaine as
some of my old clients. Of course, she can afford to languish
in much more pleasant surroundings than her counterparts on
public assistance.

"And now, Richard is trying to turn Leonard against me,"
she's saying about their son as she finishes her Sprite and fixes
herself a vodka tonic. "It's a terrible strain on a boy his age . . ."

I start to say something about leaving again, but she's already ruminating obsessively about another sordid point in
her divorce proceedings.

"I knew Richard was running around even then," she
drones on, lighting a cigarette and letting the ash fall down
the front of her robe. "And he always had those shady business
deals, like the ones he has now . . ."

Something about the offhanded way she says this catches
my attention. "What shady business?"

"Well, like the money laundering," she says, clearly not as
interested in that subject as in Richard's philandering. "He
always liked blondes . . ."

"Wait a second," I say to her. "Are you telling me you think
your husband's involved in money laundering?"

She looks offended. "Of course," she says, throwing back
her shoulders and pushing out her chest. "I can prove it too."
She walks off on swaying hips and disappears into another
room.

This whole thing sounds like a crock and I'm anxious to
get this afternoon over with so I can go home and feel anxious
about Andrea not calling me. And Darryl King running around.
Finally, Mrs. Silver comes out of the bathroom. She seems to
be in a much better mood now, like she just got high or something. The high heels are gone, and she's put on a blouse with
a floral design and a dark skirt that looks just a little tight on
her. I notice a lipstick smear across her front teeth.

"Hi, handsome," she says in a loud party girl voice. "I have
something special for you . . ."

She shows me two large shoe boxes she's been holding behind her back. She offers them to me, but when I reach for them, she backs away flirtatiously. She sashays across the carpet in her black-stockinged feet, singing "Put the Blame on Mame" again.

"What's in the shoe boxes, Mrs. Silver?"

"Gloria to you, big boy."

"Okay," I say. "What've you got in those shoe boxes, Gloria?"

She's on her knees on the other side of the room, opening a black oak cabinet and turning on some electronic equipment. There's a soft hiss from hidden speakers and then a steady wallop of drums playing in four/four time. Gloria is on her feet, dancing with a shoe box in either hand.

"Got to go disco!" she cries out as the song begins.

It's a shopworn old Bee Gees tune I haven't heard since *Saturday Night Fever* came out. She sings along in a silly falsetto and does twirls around the carpet. She's really getting down and getting funky, but who am I to criticize? It's a tough job, but somebody has to be nostalgic for the 1970s.

"C'mon, D-A-N-C-E!" she shouts. "Are you gay or something?"

"No."

"I've slept with gay guys," she says with not entirely sensible confidence.

As the song ends, I manage to get one of the shoe boxes out of her hands. What's inside is like a bag person's treasure trove. Old, torn-up receipts, inky credit card carbons, and photocopied bank statements from accounts in the Cayman Islands. "All this is supposed to have something to do with money laundering?" I say.

"I started making copies of everything back in the seventies, when Richard was in the nightclub business," she explains, standing behind me and breathing on my neck. "Richard even put some of the accounts in my name. I just thought it might come in useful one day."

I don't know about that. It just seems to be an incoherent blizzard of old documents to me, most of them with the name Goldman Resources, not Richard Silver. "Why didn't you use any of this in your divorce case?" I say, giving her the shoe box back and putting my hands in my windbreaker's pockets.

"My lawyer wouldn't enter it as evidence," she says, following me around the room. "He said it was too hard to follow. Can you imagine? I only found out later that Richard paid him off too. On the first day, he told the judge..."

She starts to drown me with more obscure details about her divorce but I hold up my hand. "Wait a second," I say. "I looked at those papers just now and I don't think I could follow them either."

"But you didn't even try," she says, flopping down on the sofa and pulling out some of the documents. "It's all right here."

I have had enough of this insanity for one day. It's time to go home and get drunk. "You know, even if I take the information you have here, it's probably not going to get you a big divorce settlement or anything," I say. "It'll just mean giving your ex-husband a tremendous pain in the ass."

She sits right up and her eyes brighten, like this is the happiest moment of her week. "Do you think so?" she says. "Do you really think so?"

41

On the nineteenth night in a row with a temperature of ninety degrees or more, a dozen New York City police officers gathered in the plaza outside an East 116th Street apartment house.

One of them, Detective Sergeant Bob McCullough, carried a warrant for Darryl King's arrest for the murder of Pops Osborn and his bodyguard. It had been a long day. Sweat began to seep through the armpits of his yellow T-shirt as he looked in the file and saw a note from Darryl's probation officer, Steven Baum. He described King as "psychotic" and said "he scares me." McCullough smiled to himself, thinking it did not take much to scare these social worker types. He wondered why this Baum thought he had enough psychological training to call somebody psychotic. The guy sounded like a know-it-all on the phone. Maybe it was worth writing a piece about the proper role of probation officers in police work.

As eleven o'clock came and went, Emergency Service Unit officers got out of their truck parked near the courtyard.

"Listen, we're not gonna have any problem with this thing," Lieutenant Roger Keefer told McCullough. "We're all set ... We know about this guy. We just knock on the front door, the guy will come running out one of the side entrances and we'll grab him. Okay?"

Just before eleven-thirty, McCullough entered the building, accompanied by Lieutenant Keefer and Officer Jenkins from his precinct and Officers Morales and Esposito from the Emergency Service Unit. During the slow elevator ride up to the second floor, Lieutenant Keefer discussed the upcoming election, Officer Morales's physical attractiveness, and the general sorry state of the world. Detective Sergeant McCullough realized Keefer was drunk just before the elevator stopped and the door opened.

Later McCullough would blame himself for not moving more quickly to stop Keefer from running down the dimly lit corridor to 2C, where Eddie Johnson, the informant, said King often stayed with his girlfriend, Alisha. Keefer knocked on the door twice and then pushed it open. McCullough and the others followed him through the front door. The apartment's living room was now empty, but someone had obviously been there moments before. A quart bottle of Olde English "800" beer was lying sideways, spilling its contents into the beige carpet. An open pack of Marlboro Lights rested on the slip-covered arm of the couch. A crack pipe was next to it. *The Honeymooners* played on the enormous television with a fracture in the middle of the screen.

"Come on out, Darryl," Keefer shouted. "I know you're here."

A minute seemed to pass. The other officers spread out around the room and edged toward the doorway that appeared to lead to a back bedroom. Their walkie-talkies bleated. On the television screen Jackie Gleason patted his stomach anxiously and chanted, "Homina, homina, homina," as though it were a mantra.

A little girl emerged from the back bedroom and stood in the doorway. She wore fuzzy blue pajamas with feet and her hair was in pigtails. Her eyes were glazed and watery and her lower lip trembled. She looked as if she'd just seen a monster.

"Come here, sweetheart," said Officer Lucy Morales of the Emergency Service Unit, reaching out to the little girl with both arms. "Everything's going to be all right."

"I have one at home her age," Keefer said to McCullough.

Since they were all facing the back bedroom, they did not notice that Darryl was actually standing right behind them in the front doorway. He aimed his 9 mm Browning automatic and squeezed the trigger. There was a loud pop and Keefer fell over sideways with a geyser of purplish-red blood spurting from the back of his neck.

The other cops spun around fast, but Darryl had backed out into the hall. While Keefer lay on the carpet making low groaning sounds, a hand reached out from the bedroom doorway and pulled the little girl back inside. McCullough asked Officer Philip Jenkins to look after Keefer's injuries and call for backup. Then the detective sergeant told Officer Esposito to give him cover so he could peer out into the hallway and maybe take a shot at Darryl. But before any of them could move, Darryl's 9 mm peeked in through the front door again and fired four times.

All four missed, but Darryl was not about to bring himself out into the open, McCullough realized. He was just pointing the gun around the doorway and firing randomly into the apartment, without showing himself. His invisibility made him even more frightening. He was like a disembodied, irresistible force.

Then there was an abrupt, eerie silence. Ninety seconds passed. It was as though Darryl had evaporated. A deodorant commercial played on the TV. McCullough crawled slowly across the damp carpet toward the front door. He hesitated for a moment and then took a quick peek down the hall. There was no sign of Darryl. Officer Marty Esposito was beside him now in the doorway, holding a 12-gauge shotgun. McCullough wondered what made Emergency Service officers more qualified to use such weapons than regular cops. He heard a door slam at the north end of the hallway and he leaned out of the doorway a little farther so he could get a good look.

Without warning, two more rounds from Darryl King's gun

rocketed past his head and pierced the grayish cinder block wall a few inches behind him. It was like a cannon had gone off right next to his ear. For a few seconds, he was deaf. The shots seemed to be coming from the south end of the hall, but McCullough still couldn't see where Darryl was standing.

Officer Morales stepped out of the apartment with her gun drawn. Before McCullough could tell her to look out, a third and fourth shot from Darryl's end of the hallway spun her around and dropped her to her knees. Morales cried out and clutched her bleeding right hand. Her .38 was on the floor now. As Esposito moved to help her, McCullough saw something that looked like Darryl's head peering out of a doorway at the south end of the hall. McCullough stepped toward the middle of the hall, assumed the shooter's position with his .38, and fired. It was a difficult angle, and he recognized the low whistling noise he heard next as the sound of a bullet's ricochet. He ducked and backed up against the wall. Darryl fired back and McCullough turned and saw Officer Esposito sway back on his heels and melt to the hallway floor in a heap, like the Wicked Witch of the West. The shotgun fell from his hands and blood spurted from his abdomen, just below his bullet-proof vest.

In a panic, McCullough fired two more shots down at Darryl's end of the hall. Again, there was no response. Once more, the long silence started. "Let's get the fuck out of here!" McCullough screamed at no one in particular.

Officer Morales was not hurt too badly and she was able to give McCullough one hand's help in dragging Esposito some thirty yards toward the north end of the hallway where the elevator was. The stairway door was too far to go. They fell down several times trying to pull the body along. Esposito's wound was not quite as bad as McCullough first thought, but he was going to need immediate attention.

While he was examining the injuries, McCullough heard footsteps and scampering coming toward their end of the hall. But when he looked up again, he still did not see Darryl, though he knew he was watching them. McCullough rang the elevator bell a dozen times in a row.

The wait seemed like hours. There was still no sign of back-up. McCullough pleaded for help into his walkie-talkie. Morales and Esposito were both bleeding and gasping. The elevator was groaning and moving as slowly as an old elephant waking up. Just as it arrived, McCullough saw Darryl pointing a 12-gauge shotgun from a doorway some twenty feet up the hall. The shotgun wavered for a second and aimed at the cops. Darryl fired another blast over their heads.

As he ducked once more, McCullough heard a .38-caliber service revolver being cocked and suddenly realized that Darryl was picking up each officer's weapon as it was dropped. His arsenal was growing as he advanced on the cops. McCullough looked down and saw to his horror that his own gun was missing. It must've slipped out of his holster while he was dragging Esposito along the floor.

McCullough pulled the elevator's outside metal door open. He rolled into the car with Morales and Esposito tumbling in after him. They were all breathing hard as the door paused on its hinge and slowly began to close. Watching it was agony.

McCullough heard the clip-clop of sneakers coming down the hall quickly toward the elevator. The first door finally closed, but the second sliding door had not budged and the elevator did not move. Slumped in the corner, McCullough looked up at the porthole window in the first door. Through the wire-screen squares in the glass, he saw Darryl King's face. Darryl glowered at him. He looked just like his picture in the file, only meaner. Then as suddenly as it appeared, his face was gone from the window.

McCullough closed his eyes and sighed as the sliding door finally began to close. A tremendous shotgun blast ripped through the first door. Double-aught pellets ricocheted and clattered through the car. Two rounds from a .38-caliber service revolver followed. McCullough felt a burning sensation up and down his leg. As the second door slid into place and the elevator descended, McCullough checked to see how bad his wound was. He'd been hit in the right leg with buckshot and splintered wood. His pants were torn and bloody. His left leg seemed to have caught at least part of the shell from the .38.

He was all right physically. But by the time they'd reached the first floor, he was becoming dimly aware that he'd been shot with his own gun.

There was a stone pathway along the grassy knoll behind the building. Three young officers stood on its pavement, talking to each other and turning the knobs on their walkie-talkies. Old sodium vapor lights cast weak shadows around the plaza.

The shortest of the three cops was holding forth about fly-fishing on Long Island Sound. His partner, a skinny man with a long nose and sunken eyes, flapped his shirt collar to cool his sweaty chest. A third cop named Simmons smoothed his mustache and ignored the fisherman.

All three looked up when a rear window on the second floor opened and a young man with close-cropped hair stuck his head outside and stared straight ahead.

"Hey, man, you better get your head back inside," said the cop named Simmons. "There's a wild man running around with a lot of guns."

"Thanks," said Darryl King.

He ducked his head back inside and reloaded three of the five guns he was carrying. He leaned back out and began firing the 9 mm and the .38. The cops scattered. The fly-fisherman and his partner briefly took positions near some broken green benches and returned fire. But when Darryl's shots came too close, they ran for cover.

The one named Simmons fell to the pavement, yowling in pain with a bullet through the back of his right knee. Darryl came down the fire escape quickly. He jumped from the last step and fired one more shot at Simmons's prone body, missed, and then ran off into the night.

Over the next two hours, hundreds of police officers swept through the neighborhood. They turned apartments upside down, questioned possible informants, and watched street corners, but they could not find Darryl. The police commissioner assigned several units to keep up the search for the next few days or however long it took to catch him.

Just after 3:30 in the morning, Darryl arrived at the apartment where his sister, Joanna Coleman, was staying.

Joanna and her boyfriend, Winston, were watching a video-cassette of the film *Escape from New York*. Their two small children, LaToya and Howard, were running around naked and firing Lazer Tag guns at each other.

When LaToya saw her uncle Darryl with his bloodshot eyes and sweaty T-shirt, she ran at him with open arms and hugged him around the knees. "I was ascared for you," she said.

"They ain't got me yet."

Instead of patting her head, Darryl looked around the place in a daze. Three men and two women were smoking crack and having sex in one of the back bedrooms. Ida Montgomery, a tiny sixty-six-year-old woman, tried to sleep on a cot in what used to be the kitchen. Her crack-addicted daughter gave use of the apartment to her dealer, Joanna Coleman, after she fell behind on payments.

Darryl walked over to the couch and collapsed. He was exhausted from running so hard and being so scared. After a minute, he realized nobody was paying attention to him anymore. He took Detective Sergeant McCullough's gun out of his belt and laid it on a cushion. Its chambers were empty now. He began to weep softly. His sister looked up from the television and glared at him in disgust.

"What's the matter with you now?" she asked. "Why you crying? Ain't you a man?"

"Nobody loves me," Darryl King said.

42

For about the last three nights running, the lead story on the eleven o'clock news has been the Darryl King shoot-out and its aftermath. The format's almost always the same. First they show a clip of those wounded cops being carried out of the building on stretchers. Then they cut to the regular patrol car parked outside the building on Frederick Douglass Boulevard where Darryl usually lived with his mother. Then they talk about how at least 125 officers are taking part in a massive manhunt around the playgrounds, courtyards, bars, lobbies, friends' homes, and street corners where he was known to hang out.

In the meantime, the rumors have been getting started. The first one came out of the police public information department. I think what happened is that somebody there thought he saw Darryl standing behind the police commissioner in a picture of an outdoor awards ceremony. They actually investigated this, on the theory that Darryl was following the police commissioner around because that was the least likely place for anybody to look for him. That lead turned out to be false, but then another rumor started that Darryl had been seen walking the streets of Harlem in drag. That tip turned out to be wrong too, and I read somewhere that the cops picked up one very ugly and angry woman, who's filed a $1.5 million lawsuit against the city for harassment.

But what really turns up the heat is something that happens two days after the big Darryl King shoot-out.

Early in the morning, police got a tip that Darryl had been seen hanging around the housing projects behind Mount Sinai Hospital on the Upper East Side.

A team from the Emergency Service Unit was sent over with rifles and bulletproof vests, and several officers came from the Technical Assistance Response Unit. A hostage negotiator was dispatched and a dozen squad cars were assigned as backup. In one of them was a rookie named Bryan Hopkins.

At twenty-one, Hopkins was still trying to get over the fact that he couldn't be a lifeguard for the rest of his life. He'd grown up in outermost Suffolk County and spent so much time on the beach that when he did bother showing up at school, he had to go straight to the infirmary to deal with all the little skin cancers and windburns he'd developed. In his entire life, he'd talked to perhaps two black people, and one of them was an instructor at the Police Academy. His uncle Artie, a homicide detective in Queens, had helped him get into the department. And every day that Hopkins found himself patrolling these strange ghetto streets, like a visitor to another planet, he cursed his uncle silently and swore he'd never forgive him.

As he sat in the patrol car now, listening to his partner and the radio shows talking about Darryl King, he cursed again and felt himself tense up inside. He would've preferred to stay there parked by the curb all morning. The other teams seemed to be doing a good enough job searching the first three red brick buildings in the project without his help. And when word came over the walkie-talkie that there was no sign of Darryl here, Hopkins relaxed a little. Now, he figured, he could get back to the serious business of hanging out in the back of a bodega, drinking beer with his partner, a twelve-year veteran named Franco who claimed to have relatives in the Mafia.

But then the sergeant came by and said people on the first floor of one of the buildings had reported a couple of burglaries the night before and they suspected one of the kids who lived in the building might be responsible. The sergeant told Hopkins to go take some statements from them. The rookie swallowed twice and blinked nervously, like a man about to be lowered into a shark tank.

Jamal Perkins lived on the first floor of the third building. Every morning when his mother saw him off to school, she thought of the bumper cars she used to ride at the Coney Island amusement park. Sending her son out into the world was like trying to navigate a car around that track without having someone smash into you. He could get hit from any angle. Somebody in his class could start him selling drugs. There could be a scuffle on the subway platform and he'd get stabbed by a mugger. A stray bullet might hit him when he was just talking to somebody on the corner. Or he could end up like his uncle James, tied up with a bunch of low-life winos and thieves, in and out of prison all the time, and dead from cirrhosis of the liver at twenty-eight.

Just watching him cross the street in the morning sometimes, she'd get so scared that her asthma would act up on her and she'd have to sit down awhile.

But if it hadn't been smooth sailing so far, at least nothing had happened that couldn't be undone. At sixteen, he was turning out to be a tall handsome boy with a dazzling smile that the girls all liked. If he was mainly interested in hip-hop and basketball now, that was all right because he was doing well enough in school to make college a real possibility. That foolishness with the stolen car was a long time ago, now, and the judge had understood it was the other boy's idea and Jamal was just along for the ride. Once he was out of the city, she could stop worrying. She knew she shouldn't expect too much from him, because he hated pressure. He had the brains to be a lawyer if he ever applied himself. But she'd be proud if he could just get an apartment of his own.

Hopkins, the rookie, was talking to people down at the south end of the first floor, but his mind was on what he'd heard on the radio about Darryl King. Six cops he'd shot and they still hadn't found him. These black people Hopkins was talking to now were acting like they wanted him to help them with their burglaries, but he just knew they hated him too and would shoot him the second he turned his back. He smiled uneasily and didn't take in a single word they were saying.

Out of the corner of his eye, he noticed someone leaving an apartment at the other end of the hall. He turned and saw a black kid. Thinking as fast as he could, Hopkins tried to size up the situation. The kid seemed to be about the same age as Darryl King and he was black for sure too. Hopkins made the decision right then. He'd tell the kid to stop and if the kid looked like he was reaching for a gun, Hopkins would draw his service revolver. You only had a second to react to these things the older guys said. Better to be tried by twelve than carried by six.

Jamal Perkins was listening to Bobby Brown's "My Prerogative" on his Toshiba Walkman when he saw the people at his end of the hall gesturing wildly at him. They seemed to be telling him to stop. A voice behind him was yelling something too. He figured he better turn off the music so he could hear what everyone was saying. He reached into his pocket and felt around for the stop button on the tape player. Then he turned toward the flash of light coming from the other end of the hall.

I guess part of what's exceptional about this case is that the kid was only wounded, instead of being killed like a lot of the other black youths over the past few years. That's a good thing in the long run, of course, but what's funny is that the day after his shooting I start noticing that the myth of Darryl King is getting out of hand. In the beginning, it's just a couple of pieces of graffiti around town saying things like *Darryl K. All the Way* and *Free Darryl King* (though there's no way to free

Darryl King since he's not in prison). Then I get home, turn on the radio, and hear a black college station dedicating Public Enemy's rap song, "Don't Believe the Hype" to Darryl and wishing him Godspeed from Allah.

I suppose I can understand this in a way. People are upset about that Perkins kid getting hurt, and given the history of the criminal justice system in this town, they don't expect a cop to be convicted for shooting a black youth. So they figure Darryl was just evening the score ahead of time. But if you really think about that, it doesn't make sense; Darryl didn't know that kid and he didn't shoot those cops out of any sense of justice. He did it because he didn't want to get locked up.

But at the moment, you can't tell that to anybody. Despite their offer of a ten-thousand-dollar reward, the cops aren't getting much cooperation from the community in their search. Everybody's too busy going to rallies and marches for Jamal Perkins and protesting the Manhattan D.A.'s reluctance to press for an attempted murder indictment against that bone-head cop who shot him. Now there's a rumor going around that Darryl is getting shelter and food from strangers in Harlem and Brooklyn.

As for me, I've been keeping my head down, hoping no one will remember that Darryl was my client. I've gotten a couple of decidedly cool looks in the locker room in the morning, but other than that, nothing. Andrea didn't even mention it when I saw her in the hall the other day, but then again, things have been a little strained between us and a lot's been left unsaid.

Out in the field, though, we've been hearing about Darryl all the time. One decrepit apartment on Adam Clayton Powell Jr. Boulevard is like a shrine to him, with his black-and-white mug shots from the newspaper up on the walls next to the headlines. A shot of that kid Jamal Perkins is taped to one of the other walls, and looking at it, I'm glad the kid's going to be all right. The guy we're looking for isn't here, but we stick around to watch the beginning of the noon newscast on Channel 2. As soon as the announcer says a story is coming up about Darryl King and the police, the two eight-year-old boys watching the show in the apartment give each other high-fives.

"He smoked their shoes," one says to the other excitedly.

"Fuck the police!" says his little friend.

It doesn't do any good to yell at them. These days Darryl gets respect. "The only thing black folks hate more than drug dealers is cops," Bill tells me later in the car. "And your boy Darryl done shot both of them."

This whole notion makes me distinctly uncomfortable. I wish I could tell people what Darryl was really like the times I've met him. But I wonder if it would do any good. "I guess people have their own reasons for identifying with Darryl," I say, working out a backseat rationalization as a bus steers by us. "I'd be pretty upset about the cop shooting that Perkins kid."

"Why?" Bill asks with a completely straight face.

"The kid didn't have a gun."

"What would you have done?" Bill says irritably. "You're standing in a dark hallway and homeboy reaches in like he's packing an Uzi or something. You got one second to decide if you wanna live or not. I know what I'd do."

"That wasn't a bad kid, Bill."

"Never a doubt, Baum," he says. "Never a doubt."

I keep expecting him to turn around and tell me this is all a put-on or a litmus test to see how I'll react. But he doesn't. He just gives me that same look my father gives me when he talks about how he survived the Holocaust. Like I just don't know anything. I start squirming around and trying to find a way to change the subject.

Fortunately, Angel does that for me. "I know somebody who's talked to the cop who shot the Perkins kid over at Psych Services," he tells us. "She says he may have a narcissistic personality disorder."

"What a crock of shit," Bill says to him. "The guy's got kitty litter for brains."

They both laugh. As the afternoon sun burns on, Angel steers the car east on 125th Street past the Apollo and the State

Office Building, a sheer slab of concrete and glass stubbed down haphazardly in the middle of Harlem. Bill turns and asks him if he's going to stop by the house over the weekend for a cookout. The Four Seasons song "Let's Hang On (to What We Got)" plays on the radio. Bill, the black Vietnam veteran, and Angel, the Puerto Rican ex-gang member, sing along with the old white group's hit record.

For a moment, I feel kind of left out. Over these past couple of weeks, I've developed real affection for these guys. They've taught me how to get myself in and out of dangerous situations and treated me almost like a baby brother. I wouldn't mind seeing them outside of work, but now I'm beginning to realize there are too many barriers. They're black and Hispanic; I'm white. They live in the suburbs; I'm in the city. They came of age in the 1960s; I'm still learning. They're both married with families; I'm on my own. I guess it's unlikely that we'll ever really be friends.

Just to make conversation, I ask Bill how he thought people would react if the cops Darryl shot had died.

"They'd have a statue for Darryl up by tonight," Bill says, lighting a fresh cigar and propping up his injured leg on the dashboard.

They nod and give each other knowing looks. I feel more white and ignorant than usual.

It happens that on this day, we actually have an assignment at a housing project near the one where that Perkins kid got shot. A guy called Bill Blass was arrested for possessing a small quantity of marijuana there last week and was let go. But since he's already on probation for a robbery, we get to pick him up as a violator.

There are signs of trouble almost as soon as we park the car. From the backseat, I can see a bed sheet hanging out the window of the front building with "Darryl K. ALL THE WAY" scrawled on it. It reminds me a little of the old Banner Nights at Shea Stadium.

The three of us get out of the car. "This skell's in the building at the back," says Bill, pausing on the sidewalk to put out his cigar and double-check the file.

The project is made up of six five-story buildings that started off red brick, but have been turned almost gray by the New York City air. Some municipal architecture genius has arranged them into an odd, cluttered hexagonal configuration, so that we have to walk through a courtyard past the five other buildings to get to the one in the back. Something about the courtyard tile under our feet and the baking sun overhead makes me think of a giant oven.

Bill points out the building we're going to and I lead the way. As I pass the first building, I see "JustICE for JAmal" drawn in chalk under a window and I hear a man calling out something to us. At first, I think it's "go away please" that he's saying. But then his words get more distinct.

"GO AWAY, POLICE!"

"He thinks we're cops," Angel says with a weary smile.

A bottle of Heinz 57 Varieties comes flying out of nowhere and smashes into 114 pieces near my feet.

"Watch it!" Bill stops walking and looks up, as if he's expecting to stare down any of the five buildings the bottle might've come from. "Who did that?" he calls out.

"Fuck you, Uncle Tom!" a voice calls out from a high window behind us.

We're almost in the middle of the courtyard now, equidistant from each building and the street. I look up and see dozens of people hanging out the windows of all the buildings. We're surrounded by hostile faces. Boys. Girls. Old ladies in curlers and floral gowns. Chunky guys in sleeveless shirts, drinking beer. It's just after noontime. What's everybody doing home? Before I can say anything to Angel or Bill, I hear a low grumbling sound that gradually gets louder and louder. People are chanting something in Spanish.

"MAMÓN! MAMÓN! MAMÓN!" it sounds like.

I've got to ask Angel what that means when I get a chance.

Somebody hurls a beer can at us and it wings me on the knee.
I look around again and see people ahead of us, behind us,
beside us, and above us are leaning out their windows, yelling
at us and giving us the finger. Their chanting is a wall of sound
that completely surrounds us; it's like we're in the middle of
a Roman gladiator arena.

"Let's get the fuck out of Dodge," says Bill as somebody
else narrowly misses us with the smelly garbage they're throwing out the window.

We make a run for it back to the car and manage to get
away after being pelted with only rotten eggs and fruit. The
odor is awful when it's mingled with our sweat, and for once
I ask Bill if he'll light up a cigar.

"To hell with 'em," Angel says as he starts the car and pulls
away. "We'll have to call the office and tell them they gotta send
somebody out here much earlier in the day to pick that guy up."

"Yeah, but, Angel, what the fuck was that about?" I ask.

"People be pissed off, Baum," Angel replies, breaking off
from his usual social-work-speak to give me some straight street
talk.

"About what? The Perkins kid?"

"Not just that," Angel says, barely avoiding a mover's truck
that comes barreling through an intersection. "They be angry
about their air conditioner not working and the paint coming
off the walls and how nine-one-one don't come when they sick
and the school's no good and they can't get a bigger apartment
with the kids . . ."

"Yeah, yeah, yeah," I say. "But we're here to help. Why
are they picking on us?"

"Why are they picking on us?" Bill slowly repeats with an
incredulous smile. "Because we're here."

43

The rain was coming down in sheets on the first Sunday that Richard Silver decided to go up to the country.

"I don't understand why we're doing this," his girlfriend, Jessica, said loudly as she opened up the back of the car to put their bags in. "Couldn't we have waited until next weekend?"

She was getting soaked in the downpour and her blouse was sticking to her back. She looked like a bird drowning in the middle of Park Avenue. Richard Silver closed his umbrella and got in on the driver's side. He leaned across the seat and opened the passenger's side door for her.

"We have to go up this weekend," he told her as she got in. "Otherwise, we'll waste all of next weekend opening the house up. And if it's nice out, we won't want to lose the day. And I'll have Leonard . . ."

"I thought you didn't like going to Greenwich," she said. "Wasn't part of the settlement that Gloria got to be there every other weekend?"

He winked and grinned as he turned the key in the ignition. "Larry got an injunction against her," he said.

The rain beat steadily on the windshield as they drove north across Eighty-sixth Street. A cloud of steam rose from a hole in the street, like an explosion was building underground.

"So what do you hear from your friends in Chicago?" Jessica asked.

"Still very nervous," Richard Silver told her. "They're talking about a lot of investigations with these savings and loan associations, you know. But to tell you the truth, I don't think anything's really doing with it."

"So let me ask you something, Richard," she said. "Why don't these savings and loan people use someone they know in Chicago to wash their money for them?"

He let out a long breath and the dark circles under his eyes seemed to get a little bigger. "They can't do that," he said. "It's too much of a straight line. They need somebody who's a little bit out of their circuit to set some of that up."

She pushed back her wet hair with both hands. "So why do they come to you? Everybody knows about you already."

"Yeah, well, we gotta watch out for that too," he said. "In fact, one of these days, we're gonna have to find somebody to make a trip to the Caymans for us."

He told her to turn on the radio so they could hear a traffic report. But all they could get were Madonna songs and news updates. The latest one said that the Perkins kid who'd been shot by the cop was going to pull through and get out of intensive care, but there were still plans for community protests. In the meantime, there was no sign of Darryl King turning up.

"Another long, hot summer," Richard Silver said sardonically, as if reciting some old piece of verse he'd been forced to memorize as a kid.

The cars directly in front of them seemed to have come to a dead halt. Richard put on his left-hand signal and tried to switch lanes, but a maroon Le Baron cut him off. He honked his horn in frustration and then moved over. But by then the light had turned red and he found himself stuck halfway in the crosswalk. An old lady, trying to walk past the front of his car, struck his hood with her cane.

"Do you think there're going to be riots?" Jessica asked.

Her question caught him off guard and he blinked like he'd just been awakened from a sound sleep. "What?"

"Do you think they'll have riots?" she said.

"Well." He cleared his throat. "You know, I have a theory about that," he said.

"Just a second."

Jessica turned up the radio and began singing along with Madonna. Even with her hair all wet and her face red, she was lovely. But Richard had heard cats in the rain making nicer sounds. He turned right on Ninety-sixth Street and headed toward the entrance to FDR Drive.

"See, people only riot when they want the attention of the institutions," he told her, "because they think that's how things get changed. But most people in the ghettos here don't believe in the institutions anymore."

They were going north toward the Willis Avenue Bridge. Traffic had lightened up, but the road was still slick and the gray curtain of rain coming down on the East River was so thick that Ward's Island was invisible on the other side.

"So you think it won't be as bad this time?" Jessica asked.

"No, I think it'll be much worse," he said. "With the riots everybody got angry all at once and got it over with. Now things get broken down a little bit at a time. Instead of one big riot, people are angry all the time. And since they figure they got nothing to lose, they might as well burn the city down block by block."

They made the turn and headed across the Willis Avenue Bridge, a humpbacked metal beast reaching across the river. The road was pockmarked and bumpy. On the left, a cigarette company's clock said it was 1:02 and seventy-four degrees. Richard Silver glanced over to his right at the useless smokestacks and abandoned factories, where generation after generation of immigrants had held down their first jobs. It didn't matter if you even spoke the language. Of course, his own father hadn't done anything of the kind, but there were millions of others who had. All that was gone now anyway.

He made the turn off Bruckner Boulevard and got on the expressway. Off to the side, old tenement buildings and housing projects stood like forgotten sentries in the rain.

"So what can anybody do?" Jessica asked.

"What do you do?" Richard felt around in his pockets for change to pay the first toll. "What you do is get a nice house in Connecticut so you can get out of town and not have to look at this mess."

44

Slowly, the mainstream media began to concentrate on finding out how Darryl King had managed to slip through the cracks in the system.

For the first few days after the shoot-out with the police, Judge Philip Bernstein took most of the blame. He had, after all, decided to release Darryl on his own recognizance after a violation of probation hearing in Manhattan Supreme Court. The headlines about Bernstein went on for two days and the uproar was such that the head of the Patrolmen's Benevolent Association, who was normally too much of a snob to talk to anybody except *The New York Times* and TV reporters, actually had a press conference to denounce the judge and call on the governor to take disciplinary action.

When stirrings and rumblings began to be reported in Albany, the judge, who'd maintained a stony silence in the face of all the criticism, finally went on the offensive. As a former head of the district attorney's rackets bureau, he was shrewd about the press, and particularly sensitive to the needs of reporters on deadline. He waited until after five o'clock on a slow news day and then picked up the phone in his chambers to call a reporter he knew at one of the city's major tabloids.

Speaking with a confidence honed from years of courtroom

experience and back room wheedling, he spent fifteen minutes ripping into the Probation Department and blaming its officials for Darryl King's release.

"If I had to single out any one factor, I'd say it was the probation officer who presented the violation in my courtroom," he told the reporter. "Never in forty years in the criminal justice system have I heard anything so sloppy and self-serving! He neglected to give me any of the facts that would've allowed me to make an informed decision about the defendant. My hands were tied! What am I supposed to do if I don't have the facts?"

When there was a long silence on the other end of the phone, the judge asked if he was talking too fast again. The reporter said no, it was fine, he was keeping up with him. The judge went on to say that if he'd still been at the D.A.'s office and the probation officer Baum had been on his staff, he would've been fired immediately for incompetence. He then broadened his attack to include the entire Probation Department and even suggested the mayor was at fault for allowing such mismanagement.

"Don't you think that's a little over the top?" the reporter asked meekly.

"No, I do not!" the judge thundered back. "What I am telling you is that at the racetrack of justice we are betting on a lame horse and the losers are all of us . . ."

The judge's rant went on with such ferocity that the reporter thought smoke was going to come out of his end of the receiver. Finally he told the judge he thought he had quite enough for a story, thank you very much. There was less than ten minutes until deadline and it would probably be impossible to get a full response out of anybody at Probation on such short notice, which of course had been the judge's intention all along.

"Do you need a picture of me?" the judge asked.

"No, I think we have something in our files, Your Honor."

"Don't use that one where I'm wearing the hat again," the judge said before he hung up. "It makes me look like Francis the Talking Mule."

* * *

An hour after the tabloid hit the street with the headline "THEY TURNED HIM LOOSE!" and the subhead "Judge Blames Probation for Releasing Darryl King," Steve Baum got a call at home, telling him to be in the deputy commissioner's office first thing in the morning.

"Bring a second pair of underwear," the guy calling said.

"Why?"

"Because they are going to rip you a new asshole."

45

The Probation Department's administrative building on Leonard Street is a misconceived hunk of modern architecture that somebody left in lower Manhattan. At first it appears to be an imposing gray edifice with jutting angles—at least an octagon. But on closer inspection, it's just a horrible mistake. Even though the building is not that old, its marble surface is crumbling and for the past few years the entrance has been surrounded by protective scaffolding to keep passersby from getting bonked on the head by the falling pieces. Somebody has scrawled the name of the anarchy group "MISSING FOUNDATIONS" in white spray paint across the dark scaffold boards. I guess it's meant to be ironic, but it comes off as more of an understatement.

Upstairs, Deputy Commissioner Kenneth Dawson is waiting for me in his office. His walls are cluttered with those idiotic *Probation—Be Part of the Magic* stickers and pictures of him shaking hands with various assemblymen and clubhouse politicians. I remember how Big Jack told me that Dawson got this job because his father was hooked up with the Staten Island Democrats. He has a copy of the newspaper with the headline about Probation letting Darryl King go on his lap. It's already so well thumbed that it looks like a vintage edition.

He chews his upper lip furiously and glares at me. "I want you to tell me what happened here," he says.

The clock on his desk reads 8:08. A cup of coffee would be nice, but with the look he's giving me I know I shouldn't expect any small kindnesses. Deputy Dawson. For once, I don't think of Deputy Dawg.

"You wanna know what happened with the violation hearing?"

"I didn't call you here to congratulate you on your sharp work," he says in a nasty, insinuating voice that would earn him a good beating from some of my clients.

I rub my eyes and try to get my thoughts in order. I should be used to getting up at this hour from being out with the Field Service Unit, but it still takes me a while to get going.

"Well," I say slowly, "it's not at all like the judge said. I handed in my V.O.P. papers..."

"Your what?"

V.O.P. stands for Violation of Probation. I thought everyone who worked here knew the term. But then again, this guy Dawson is mainly supposed to be in budget, so he may not be up on all the shop talk.

"I touched all the bases," I say. "I pulled together all the papers and the evidence and the judge made his own decision. What else was I supposed to do?"

He shakes his head like he hasn't heard a word I've said. "Why did you leave it up to the judge?"

"I'm not sure what you mean. It's his decision."

"But why did you put this guy King on probation in the first place?"

I look at him skeptically, not sure if he's putting me on or not. Can he know that little about the way this agency works? He's been here a year, I think.

"I didn't put Darryl King on probation," I explain.

He picks the newspaper off his lap and reads out loud. "The judge said the Probation Department had originally recommended King not be sent to jail..."

"First off, they're talking about the presentence investigation, which I didn't write. Tommy Markham wrote it and he certainly didn't recommend probation. I read the report."

He rocks back in his chair abruptly. "All I know," he says, "is that so far this morning, I've gotten calls from City Hall, the PBA, the criminal justice coordinator, and three newspapers all wanting to know how it is that one of our officers is responsible for six cops getting shot..."

I just look at this guy a minute, with his sunburn, and his Sy Syms suit, and his little political clubhouse mementos spread across his desk. What a hack. I used to think those descriptions were unfair and two-dimensional. But this asshole can't see beyond the doorway of his own office. Here's a guy who doesn't know the first thing about probation and is just serving time until another administrative job opens up at a city agency that pays better. I suddenly feel a surge of admiration for Richard Silver; he's what this guy can only aspire to be.

"I just told you what the situation was," I say as evenly as I can. "I went in to the judge and I gave it my best shot, and the guy got out anyway."

"And that's not good enough." Dawson turns slightly red and shakes an emphatic finger at me. "The people we have to work with want to know that there's some accountability in this department. And I've had to assure them that the officer responsible is going to be disciplined."

"What'd you do, give 'em my name?"

"In some cases, that was necessary."

"Well, you know, I'm not gonna be the fall guy for this."

"Well, somebody's responsible and it certainly isn't me."

Of course, I think. It couldn't be. To be responsible you'd have to have some idea of what's going on.

"So as of today we're starting dismissal proceedings," Dawson says matter-of-factly.

"Against who?"

"Against you. I've already told the people at City Hall that you're being let go."

It takes a couple of seconds for what he's saying to sink in. Two years of hard work are disappearing just because the judge was in a bad mood that day. For a couple of seconds, my mind goes blank and I can't think of anything to say in my own defense.

"We both know all about severance pay and administrative procedures," he says. "But you'd be doing everyone in the department a great service if you'd start clearing out your desk today."

A half hour after I storm out of his office, I'm still bouncing around the locker room downstairs in frustration. I keep smoking cigarettes and asking myself how I wound up in this mess.

Do they think they can just make me the scapegoat for the whole system? After a while, I stop and try to think about whether it could be my fault. I start going over the Darryl King case step-by-step in my mind, trying to figure out what I could've done differently. I know this is going to eat at me for years. Maybe if I'd been a little firmer with him the first time he came into my office, it might've turned out differently. It could be that Bill's been right all along, and I have been too soft on these people. Maybe I shouldn't have acted like such a social worker, arrogantly thinking I could persuade Darryl to change.

I haven't even gotten to the question of what I'm going to do with the rest of my life when Jack Pirone shows up and asks me what's the matter. Before I'm halfway through telling him about my getting fired, he's barreling out of the locker room like a pickup truck without brakes and heading upstairs to Dawson's office.

"I want you to tell me something," Big Jack says, his girth pushing against the arms of the most comfortable chair in Dawson's office. The deputy commissioner is looking at him, like he's afraid of Jack coming across the room to sit on him. "Did you read the transcript of Mr. Baum's violation hearing in Judge Bernstein's courtroom?"

Dawson shifts the tension from one side of his face to the other and then back again. "I haven't had the chance."

"I see," Jack says pleasantly.

I'm standing in the corner with my hands in my pockets, feeling like an outcast. On top of being fired, now I get the embarrassment of hearing people talk about it.

"So you don't know what was actually said in the hearing?" Jack asks.

"Well, I've certainly read the judge's account."

"Then FUCK YOU, you fucking child!" Jack roars. "How fucking DARE you call Baum in here before you know what the fuck's going on, you dumb fuck. How many times have you been across the street to see the supervision offices? Huh? When was the last time you were in a courtroom besides seeing your old man almost get indicted? What'd you ever do besides getting your name on a list? You fucking child."

Jack's voice is so loud that I have to look to make sure he's still sitting in his chair, and not across the room, yelling in the deputy commissioner's face. "Listen, Pirone . . ." Dawson says, trying to sound tough.

"No, you listen. You wanna get pushed around by the media, and set policy that way, I know people who work for the newspapers too . . ."

Dawson lowers his head and starts speaking rapidly like he's trying to slip his words through the barrier of sound Jack's putting up. "The fact remains that we have to have some accountability."

"You want accountability?" Jack says. "Then you can account for eight hundred probation officers walking off the job. You fire Baum and I'll stage a walkout that'll shut the town down. You'll have sixty thousand probationers walking around totally unsupervised. An invading army. How do you like that for a headline? You wouldn't just have the tabloids with that. You'd get the Times and TV news too."

A silence falls over the room. Dawson sits back in his chair and sighs, looking beaten. He picks up a pen and drops it right away.

"All right," he says to Jack. "What do you want from me?"

Jack looks down at his pudgy hand and sticks out his forefinger. "Number one," he says. "Baum gets his job back."

Dawson pats the pale, translucent hair on his scalp and looks pained. "That's going to be very difficult," he says. "People are very upset about this Darryl King business and they want to know who's to blame."

"Blame the judge," Jack says. "You got a very good press officer and he knows how to make phone calls. Tell everybody it was the judge's fault and we're still on the case."

"I guess I can try," Dawson mumbles. "We can have an administrative panel review the court proceedings."

Whatever that means. From the way he says the words, it's clear he doesn't know either.

"What else?" Jack says.

Now he's looking at me. I hold up my hands like I don't know what he wants. But he keeps looking at me and asking, "What else?" as if he expects me to present a list of demands.

"He's got his job back," Dawson whines to Jack. "What else does he want?"

"You've put him under obvious duress here," Jack says, suddenly taking the tone of a concerned family therapist. "I think Baum's entitled to some compensation for the shabby treatment he's received."

I start to tell Jack to knock it off, but Dawson's already asking me what I want to keep my mouth shut and not make a fuss. I can't think of anything too extravagant at the moment. "It'd be nice if I could have a couple of report days back at the office next week," I say. "With all the time I've been out in the field, I still have a couple of people to see and some paperwork to take care of."

"Done," says Jack. Dawson nods in reluctant agreement. "What else?" Jack asks me.

"No, that's enough," I tell him.

"Come on, you've been harassed by the administration. They owe you something. Take a comp day."

"I don't want a comp day," I say. "I'm already behind the eight ball in my work."

"Take the rest of the day off," Dawson interrupts. "I could use it too, with the headache I got."

46

Richard Silver put down the newspaper story he was reading about Darryl King and gave all his attention to the guy on the other end of the phone.

"You're not hearing what I'm telling you," he said.

"I guess not," said the guy from the personnel agency. He sounded like a kid, probably filling in for somebody regular at the firm. "You asked for a secretary who could type fifty-five words a minute, and so we sent you a secretary who could do that. I don't understand what the problem is."

Richard Silver leaned back in the chair behind his desk and peered out the doorway. His new secretary, Patricia, a matronly looking black woman in her fifties, was still out getting coffee.

"The problem is I asked for a front office type, and you sent me somebody who belongs in a back office," he explained.

"I'm not sure I catch your drift," the kid said.

"Oyshh," Richard Silver sighed, pulling out a desk drawer and putting his feet in it.

He looked down on his desk and saw the Chicago phone number written on a pink message slip. He closed his eyes and shook his head. Every time he thought about making that call, he wanted to reach for a Di-Gel. There were days when the whole thing made him proud of his ingenuity, and there were days when it made him feel cheap and ashamed. Today it was just getting on his nerves. The number on his desk was like an embarrassing stain on his clothes.

Meanwhile, the kid from the personnel agency was still sounding perplexed. "I don't get it," he was asking. "What's the difference between a front office type and somebody in a back office."

"The problem," Richard Silver told him, "is the tone."

"Tone?"

"Yeah, the tone of the person you sent me."

The kid from the agency was flabbergasted. "Was she rude?"

"Rude? No. Not at all. She's like Aunt Jemima. I'm just looking for somebody a little more Manhattan, and a little less Bronx."

"Huh?"

"Somebody with more of a front office demeanor."

The kid still didn't get it. Richard Silver looked up at the ceiling and calculated the chances that the kid on the phone might be black himself. Knowing this particular personnel agency, he decided the odds against it were about a million to one.

"Look," he told the kid finally. "Let me put it to you this way. I'm looking for someone who's a little bit more like you and me. You know what I mean?"

A few seconds passed. "Ohhh, I got it," the kid from the personnel agency said finally. "Whyn't you say so before?"

"Because that's not the way nice people do things," Richard Silver said. "So you send me somebody else next week."

"Somebody with the right tone."

"Yeah, this is a modern office I'm starting here," Richard Silver said before hanging up.

He took his feet out of the desk drawer and picked up the newspaper again. By the time he was done reading, Patricia was back with her coffee. He stood up and buttoned his suit jacket.

"I'm going to lunch," he told her. "And I'll probably be gone the rest of the afternoon. I'll call in later for messages."

"Yes, sir, Mr. Silver."

Just as he turned to go, he realized the Chicago phone number was still sitting on his desk. He picked it up almost daintily, folded it over once, and put it in his breast pocket.

"Patricia?" he said, stepping around the desk and heading out for the elevators.

"Yes, sir?"

"You have a nice day."

47

You'd think that once Dawson gives me my job back and lets me take the rest of the day off, I'd get in a much better mood. But I don't. All the way back uptown to my house, it keeps bothering me; people are going to think I wasn't doing my job.

It's more than just telling everybody what actually happened in Bernstein's courtroom. I have to convince myself that I did everything I could to stop Darryl from getting out. And in the back of my mind, this other crazy thought keeps coming back to me: That maybe there was something I should've done to turn Darryl around.

For the moment I'm feeling too mixed-up to figure that one out, so I try to use the free time I have to pull myself together, instead of doing paperwork. I put on *The Piper at the Gates of Dawn* by Pink Floyd and start working out, like I'm trying to get in shape for a fight with Darryl. I do one hundred push-ups and one hundred sit-ups and then I pump a twenty-pound weight seventy-five times behind my head and seventy-five times in front of my stomach. My muscles start to ache and I tell myself I'm never going to see Darryl again anyway. But I have to keep doing it.

After I repeat that whole routine a couple of times, I just sit by the window, drinking coffee and watching life go by for a couple of hours. This is kind of interesting at first, because I'm not usually home at this hour. I decide that the city has a secret daytime life. There's a discrete army of people out there who you never see out at night. As a group they tend to be older, slightly misshapen men and women, moving slowly and quietly down the sidewalk, dragging shopping carts behind them. Their faces are etched with a kind of gentle resignation and acceptance of life's disappointments.

After midnight, you see a completely different group around here. They're younger, they never wear shirts, they do a lot of drugs, scream at people going by, demand money, and generally are less quietly accepting of life's little disappointments.

Pretty quickly, I start getting bored and restless again. I don't know what to do with myself, but this big generator is roaring away inside of me. For a few minutes, I just pace back and forth, chain-smoking and telling myself I don't need a drink. Finally I decide to look at things as though I were one of my clients, and make out a list of goals.

I get out a yellow legal pad and write down number one. Finish those fucking law school applications. I've already made a stab at beginning an essay: "Having toiled for two years in the bloody, squalling emergency room of New York's criminal justice system, I now believe I am ready for specialized surgery..." Needs work, but it's a start. Number two is cut back on my drinking, as it's giving me a bad headache right now and clouding my thinking. Which leads me to number three: see Andrea again. Thinking about her is making me a little nuts. If she doesn't want to see me again, then so be it, but I have to hear it directly from her. Especially if there's a chance I can talk her out of it.

Number four is even more impractical, but it feels good to get it out of my head and on to the page: Find Darryl King and bring him back. I keep having this fantasy about what it would've been like if I'd been there for his big shoot-out with the cops. At least then no one could've said I didn't try.

For the moment, I decide to skip to number three and try to find Andrea. I've left a dozen messages for her over the past week without an answer. I always tell my clients it never does any good standing around waiting for life to happen to you, so I shower, get dressed, and go over to her house on the Upper West Side, unannounced, at eight o'clock.

Of course, the doorman in her old limestone apartment building says she isn't home, so I have no choice but to stake out the entrance of her building from the Mexican restaurant across the street. I know this sounds bad and maybe a little sick, watching her house the way the Field Service guys watch for a probation violator. But I need to see her so badly that it's like an itch inside my heart. I can't do anything else, except think about her.

The waitress comes over to take my drink order. She's cute, with long blonde hair and a low-cut blouse, and she gives me a big smile. But compared to Andrea, she doesn't do a thing for me, so I just order a Coke.

She brings over a basket full of chips as I keep looking out the window at the entrance to Andrea's building. At about a quarter past ten, I see a girl about her height come out of the lobby and toss her hair in that sexy way I was hoping to get used to. My heart starts to pound. Cars cruise by with their headlights throwing crucifixes of light across the restaurant's window. For a second, I lose sight of the girl coming out of the building. But then she steps out into the street light, and I see that she's white. I lean back in my chair and sip my Coke. Between Andrea and Maria Sanchez, I don't know what's up with me and girls who aren't white. Even Barbara Russo was kind of Mediterranean-looking. I wonder what a shrink would make of that. Or my father.

A mariachi band plays on the speakers and the waitress tells me that one of the specials is enchilada suiza, just like at the Tex-Mex place where Andrea and I had dinner that night. The man and woman in matching pin-striped jackets at the next table are talking about commodities futures. I get scared that Andrea might be out with Joel, the nasty yuppie she mentioned. Maybe all she's interested in is money. If that's so, then I never really stood a chance with her.

Another waitress comes by and asks me if I'd like to try the house margarita. With the mood I'm in, I have to hang on tight and say no. If I start drinking now, I'll be truly lost. I nurse my Coke for another fifteen minutes, and then I see someone I'm sure is her coming around the corner. I slap a five on the table and go running out. She's already crossing the street by the time I get outside. I go racing after her, as the light changes to red. A car almost hits me and the driver gives me the finger. I catch up to her on the corner and lay a hand on her arm.

"Steve," she says in a surprised tone that makes it sound like she's not sure if she likes the name or not.

"I was just in the neighborhood, you know . . ."

I don't get invited upstairs, but I do get her to agree to come for dinner on Friday. And that's enough to improve my mood and send me humming with anticipation for the rest of the dreary week I have to spend in the field. In fact, I may not even feel so bad next time I see one of those *Free Darryl King* banners.

48

The Probation Department quickly began to put the word out about what really happened in the Darryl King hearing, and by the next day the tabloids had stories that threw the blame for his release back onto the judge. Several of them specifically explained that it was actually a tip from Darryl's probation officer that led police to get a warrant and try to arrest Darryl. One source in the Probation union even went so far as to say that Darryl's officer was still actively helping the police investigation to find him.

The story was then picked up by an assignment editor for one of the local news shows. At 6:19, the show's anchorwoman delivered a rewritten version of the newspaper story. By now, a number of factual errors had crept in. The anchorwoman, who had light brown hair and bright blue eyes, stumbled once reading from the Teleprompter and then said Probation had taken over the Darryl King investigation.

"That's quite a turnaround, Jane," the show's coanchor, a blond man, told the camera.

"It sure is," Jane, the anchorwoman, said.

While the news was on, Joanna Coleman spoke with Darryl on the untapped phone line she had installed when she learned her regular phone was bugged.

"Check this shit out," Joanna said.

"What?" Darryl asked.

From his end of the line, he could barely hear the anchorwoman saying, "King's probation officer apparently has a personal stake in bringing the alleged gunman to justice..."

"They're saying your probation officer is the one who give you up," Joanna told him.

"I thought you said it was Eddie."

"Maybe it was the both of them."

The woman's voice on the television kept going on and on.

"Oh... I don't... Oh, I don't believe this shit," Joanna sputtered.

"What's she saying now?" Darryl King asked as a baby began crying on his end of the line. "Shut the fuck up back there!"

"She says your probation officer got a warrant against you and he be looking for you right now."

"Then he's one dead motherfucker," Darryl King said.

There was a very long pause. "Don't be talking that stupid shit on this phone!" Joanna angrily told her brother. "Don't you think like I told you no more? You're not visualizing. You be acting like a Taurus again."

"Whass up?" Darryl asked in a sluggish voice.

"I don't want any more bugs in my house! It's bad enough my other phone's bugged." She hung up abruptly.

Neither Darryl nor his sister was watching when a very agitated-looking police commissioner appeared on the eleven o'clock news insisting emphatically that his department was indeed still in charge of the Darryl King investigation.

49

I spend most of Friday getting ready for my dinner with Andrea, consulting an old cookbook I haven't opened since college to get the recipe for Chicken Fricassee with green peppers and tomatoes. I buy more than thirty dollars' worth of groceries, including endive, wild rice, a bottle of expensive wine, and a chocolate mousse cake for the dessert. I'm a reasonably good cook, but I know my limitations.

I borrow pots and pans from the old lady down the hall and use the chipped night table first as a carving board and then as the dinner table. It takes me five minutes to hack up the chicken, forty-five minutes to season it, and then I give it an hour and a half in the oven. As the sun goes down, I realize I need candlelight to make it a truly romantic dinner. I run to the occult bookstore down the street and buy six black candles with satanic pentangles on the sides. While the chicken cooks, I scrape the symbols off with a razor.

I put out my best and only table settings, and then look around and see the rest of the place is a mess. There are stacks of probation files and beer cans everywhere that I stopped noticing months ago. Maybe my father isn't the only one in the family who stockpiles things. I put the cans in a Hefty bag in the closet, stow the files in a kitchen cabinet, and finally throw out Barbara Russo's earring. I hope I won't be needing it anymore.

To my profound relief, Andrea appears to like the food. She compliments me on the dressing, which I didn't make, and the garlic bread, which I did.

When she sits back with a contented smile, I figure it's time to try to entertain her. "So did I tell you about the one we had in the field yesterday?"

"Which one's that?" she asks dabbing her mouth daintily with a napkin.

"Sharon Young. Sheila Young. Something like that." It's funny that I don't remember names as well in the field as I did in the office. "Anyway, she originally got picked up on a cocaine charge, and she didn't make her hearing, so we go looking for her again. Right? So we find her out on the street about a block from her house. I don't wanna think about what she's doing out there. But when we come up to her, she's like ... vibrating."

I do my best facial expression of somebody riding a cocaine buzz. Andrea nods like she understands.

"So we decide to bullshit her a little," I say. "We tell her that we're gonna take her downtown and have her urine tested right away. I know it's a little more complicated than that, but we're just trying to put a little pressure on her. So you know what she says?"

"No. What?"

"She says, 'Oh, I don't do cocaine anymore. But my boyfriend does. So before you test me, you all oughta know I give him head a lot of the time, so it may show up anyway.'"

Bill and Angel were in hysterics laughing when this incident happened, but Andrea's only smiling thinly. Maybe I'm telling it wrong. I try another story.

"Did I tell you about the crack dealer we picked up in the wheelchair..."

She holds up her fork. "Steven," she says coolly. "Do you think maybe you're spending a little too much time with those macho jerks in the Field Service Unit?''

"They're not jerks. They're my friends."

She goes back to eating her salad.

"You don't know what it's like out there," I tell her. "You need guys like Bill and Angel with you. I mean, we were at this one place near Mount Sinai when people started throwing shit at us."

"Was it a protest over that kid getting shot by the cop?" she asks.

"No, it was jealousy that we can walk around on two feet."

That came out a little sharper than I intended it, and she looks at me inquisitively with those gray eyes.

"You know what it is," I say, trying to explain myself. "It's this whole Darryl King thing. I'm just sorry I didn't duck when my supervisor gave me that assignment."

"Why?" Andrea asks.

"Because everything's gone wrong since then. I mean, first he comes into my office and goes nuts. Then he goes and violates on this car theft, which was what he did probably right after he killed that drug dealer in Harlem..."

Andrea puts her fork down. "Where'd you hear that?"

"Just out on the street... Anyway, you saw what happened when I tried to get him violated in court. And then he goes and shoots all these cops and then they shoot some poor schmuck kid and the city's in an uproar. So that's why I wish he hadn't come into my office."

"I see," she says.

"Plus, now, I had this disciplinary meeting on Tuesday morning because of what the judge said and I almost got fired..."

"Was this Deputy Dawg who did this to you?"

I laugh because I never knew anybody else called Dawson that.

"He's gross," Andrea says. "You know he tried to ask me out at the beginning of the summer."

"Is that right?"

"Yeah. But now he goes out with Cathy Brody."

"Really? Is he into that S & M business too?"

"Yeah," she says with a sweet smile, "they spend every weekend hitting each other over the head with free weights."

I knew there was a good reason I liked this girl.

"Anyway," I say. "This whole thing with Darryl has really got me kind of down. I mean, he shouldn't have been on probation in the first place. I'm not gonna change him."

"Why do you say it like that?"

"Like what?"

"With that funny look on your face."

I don't know what she's talking about. "Well, I'm not going to change him," I go on. "If anything he's going to change me."

"It sounds like he's done that already," she says, examining the remnants of the satanic pentangle on one of the candles.

All of a sudden I start feeling defensive. "What do you mean?"

"I mean, I hope you're not losing patience with all the rest of the people on probation. They're not all like Darryl, you know."

"I know. I know."

She takes a couple of mouthfuls of dessert and looks up at me. "You don't sound very convincing," she says. "When was the last time you saw one of your old clients?"

There I have her. "I'm seeing some of them next week," I say, reaching for a cigarette and then deciding I don't need it. "They gave me a special report day or two so I can come into the office and catch up on some of the work I fell behind on in the field."

"People at the office have been asking where you are," she says.

"Really? Who?"

"Well, like Miriam who I work with."

I picture heavyset Miriam, the secretary with the long fingernails and the Clark Gable mustache, giving me dirty looks in the legal department. "I thought she didn't like me," I say.

"Oh, she thinks you're kind of a skeezy guy, but she likes to know what everyone's up to. Especially after she saw all that stuff on television about Darryl King. She knew that was your client."

Who doesn't? I keep having these daydreams about bringing him in myself. But I guess that can never happen, so there's no point in mentioning it to Andrea.

"So where've you been?" I say, turning the tables on her.

"Well, you knew I was away for a long kayaking weekend with my family, right?"

"Kayaking?"

"Yeah, you know, it's like rowing," she says with a paddling motion. "I used to really be into guys who had those big muscles on the bottom of their arms from using the paddle."

I try not to let her see that I'm reaching around with my right hand and feeling the muscles on the bottom of my left arm. They're puny. Why don't the push-ups and weights build them up more?

"Maybe kayaking's only something we do in Princeton," Andrea says, drawing her knees up in front of her on the seat. "Do you do any sports?"

"I go to ball games sometimes." It'd be nice if I could somehow rustle up some tickets to take her to a Mets game, I think.

"How about swimming?" she says. "Do you ever go swimming?"

I don't answer right away, remembering the time my father threw me into the deep end of somebody's swimming pool when I was very small. I can still smell the chlorine and feel the icy water closing over my head. I see the watery blur of my father's image receding from me as I sink deeper. I shiver and try to wipe it out of my mind.

Meanwhile, Andrea's asking if I've ever been skiing. Where does she get these goyisheh activities? I try to imagine myself huddling with her around two hot chocolate mugs at a cozy resort. But the picture won't quite coalesce in my mind. I can see Andrea, the fireplace, the skis, and the preppy sweaters, but I can't put my own face in the scene.

I sense a distance growing between us. I can't afford the kind of life she's talking about. I wonder if she thinks I'm just a shlub from Flushing and that's the reason she's pulling away from me.

"So why've you been acting cold lately when I run into you in the halls?"

Her face goes blank. "What do you mean?" she says.

I try to be more specific with my questions, the way I would at work. "Why haven't you been returning my phone calls? I called you three times last week . . ."

"I was busy," she says vaguely, letting her eyes wander around the room.

I know I should ease off now and just let it drop, but I can't help myself. "And why'd you walk right by me in the hall the other day?"

She drops her spoon and her jaw clenches. "Don't talk to me that way, Steven," she says stiffly. "You're not going to find out anything by talking like I'm one of your criminals."

That stops me for a moment and I sink down a little in my chair. I can hear the old couple downstairs having another fight and throwing things around. I hope we don't sound like them already.

"You've got to learn to be more patient," she says in a more conciliatory tone. "This isn't one of your five-minute interviews at the office. I can't give you those kinds of definitive answers. My life isn't like that. Things change."

"I know," I say, trying to sound more casual. "But I still have to wonder what's gonna happen with you and me."

Her face loses its hard cast and she gives me a wistful smile. "I don't know, Steven," she says. "I wish I could tell you what was going to happen."

I take that as a sign that my heart is about to get broken, so I try to beat her to the punch. "I'm sorry," I say quietly. "I'm being an asshole. You wanna just forget the whole thing?"

"No," she says.

"Well, what do you want to do then?"

She doesn't say anything for a long time. She just keeps looking me in the eye from across the table. At first I think I must have a smudge of newspaper on my forehead or something.

"Hey, if you just want to call it a day, it's no problem," I say, trying to sound cool and breezy enough to take the pressure off her. "I can handle it."

She's still giving me that searching stare, like my face has something she's looking for. I'm becoming aware that the corners of my mouth have turned down without consulting me. I wonder if that's it. After thirty or forty more seconds, she finally gets up and walks over to my side of the table.

"What am I going to do with you, Steven?" she says, standing behind me and putting her hands on my shoulders.

"What do you mean?"

"You take everything so hard."

She rubs my shoulders for a couple of seconds and hums to herself. The summer heat is making my eyelids heavy and my back sweaty. There's an endless black sky outside the window. A dog barks in the distance.

"What do you say I take you to bed?" she asks.

She whips off her clothes and then mine, climbs on top of me, and rides me through the wee morning hours. I fall asleep with my arms and legs wrapped tightly around her, like I'm holding on for dear life. I wake up once with a dry throat and an urge for a drink. But I remember my list of goals, so I lie still until the feeling passes. I'd hate to have her wake up and see me guzzling whiskey now anyway.

Just before I go back to sleep, I hear a car alarm going off below my window. It blares loudly for a minute or two and then I hear it being driven away, its squall gradually receding into the night.

In the morning, I awake and find her fully dressed and ready to go. She's drinking a cup of coffee and looking through some papers on my desk.

"What're these?" she asks.

I wipe my eyes and struggle out of bed, pulling on a T-shirt and sweatpants. The dirty dishes are still in the sink and Mario Cuomo, a Persian cat who lives in the building, is licking the wineglass on the table.

Bleary-eyed and lank-haired, I make my way across the room and kiss her good morning. She hands me a cup of coffee and I see she's looking at my law school applications and essays. I'm tempted to snatch them out of her hands in embarrassment, but instead I start doing the dishes in the sink and try to casually discourage her from reading any more.

"I'm sure you won't find anything interesting there," I tell her, squirting around white dishwashing liquid.

"You didn't tell me you were applying to law school," she says, not taking her eyes off the page.

"Well, I haven't applied yet. I'm not sure if I'm going to."

"You know, this isn't bad what you wrote so far," she says. "Except maybe you should leave out that gory stuff about the emergency room of criminal justice."

"Tell you the truth, I don't think I'm gonna send that in."

She puts her hands on her hips. "Why not?"

I look down at the floor. "I don't know," I mumble. "It doesn't seem right for me. You know. Being a lawyer. It's like selling out or something."

She gives me a playful sock in the shoulder. "Can't win if you don't play, Steven."

"Yeah, I'll keep that in mind."

She adjusts a pink barrette in her hair. "I've gotta go study now . . . I had a blue comb with me. Did you see where it went?"

"Um, no . . . Listen, am I gonna see you again?"

She's still scanning the room for the comb. "Sure, Steven. Classes don't start till after Labor Day. I'll be around the office until then."

"That's not what I'm talking about. What I mean is, I'd hate to think I was just this thing you did over the summer. It's like, you know that old song, 'Will I See You in September?'"

"No," she says. "That's from before my time."

There's only about six years between us, but sometimes it feels like two decades. I can still remember the end of the 1960s; she's probably studied them in school. She smiles wistfully and takes my hand. "We'll see, Steven," she says, and kisses me tenderly on the cheek. Then she's out the door and down the stairs. From my window, I watch her cross the street. The coffee cup is cold in my hands. I wonder how I'll get through the rest of the day without seeing her.

50

Around midnight, a radio car with two cops came by the public pool in upper Manhattan. Nine kids were swimming. They'd all climbed over a locked gate to get in there. Two boys were trying to pull off a girl's bathing suit top in the deep end. Another boy was pushing his friend off the diving board. Eddie Johnson's body floated in the right lane, near the shallow end. The other kids just kept swimming around him.

After a minute spent arguing about whose job it was, the younger of the two cops waded in and tried to drag Eddie's body out of the water.

The cop who had not gone in the pool was outraged. "Hey!" he yelled at the other kids. "Didn't you notice this guy's dead?"

"Yeah." One of them shrugged. "But we're swimming."

A couple of the main arteries in Eddie's neck were cut and his face was slashed. The chlorine had faded the color from his parka. His blood drifted like red smoke in the blue water.

Part of a ham and cheese sandwich bobbed along the surface nearby.

51

Monday and Tuesday are my long-awaited report days, when I get to catch up on my paperwork and see some of my old clients before I go back out in the field.

Since my old cubicle is being used by somebody else, they've given me a ratty, unpainted corner office for the two days. Somebody's left an old *Sports Illustrated* on the desk, with a cover shot of a famous wide receiver dropping a football under the word "BUTTERFINGERS!"

I wonder if somebody's making a coy joke about the way I handled the Darryl King case. I would have expected other probation officers to be a little more understanding, but it's a cruel world, as Jack likes to say, especially when labor contracts are almost up. My guess is Deputy Dawson left the magazine here because he's still sore over the meeting with Jack.

I decide to ignore all the potential hassles and concentrate on work. Ms. Lang has arranged for me to see a couple of my old clients and the first in is Freddie Brooks, the homeless wino-junkie who's only reliable in keeping his appointments with me. He looks more worn-out than usual and he has these strange spots on his hands and arms. I hope it's not AIDS. Still, he's happy to see me and he gives me a screw-on bottle cap to remember him by just in case he can't show up again.

The rest of the appointments don't go as well. A number of my clients have strayed into trouble, mostly with crack, and I find myself being less understanding than before. The guys in the Field Service Unit have taught me to think like a cop, and it's harder than I thought it would be just to switch back to being a social worker.

When Scottie Austin, the thief from the Port Authority, shows up, I just turn him away. "Too late, my man," I say, closing his folder once and for all. "You already got violated."

After a while, the steady stream of repeat offenders starts to get me down. What was the point of me working with any of these people in the first place? The more I think about it, the worse I feel. The Darryl King thing threw me off-balance to begin with, then Andrea's got me reeling, and now I need a little reassurance. I'd like to know if I actually did somebody some good. I start going through my master list of clients and then I hit on Maria Sanchez's name.

I haven't seen her since the Fourth of July when I chastely brought her home, which was indisputably the right thing to do. So she seems like a safe bet to cheer me up. I go through my black book and find the phone number for her girlfriend's house on Edgecombe Avenue where Terry and I helped her move.

As I listen to the phone ring, I remember that she'll probably be out at school at this hour. So I figure I'll leave a message anyway.

But then the little girl who answers the phone tells me something in perfect English that makes my heart stop. She says Maria is not living there anymore. She moved out a week ago. It looks like she's pregnant again and she's certainly not going to school. The little girl gives me the new number. When I go to write it down next to Maria's name in the black book, I notice it's the same as the old number I crossed out for Maria's family's house, where her uncle molested her all these years. I read the number back to her twice to be sure. I can't believe this. My head's swimming. She's moved back in with her uncle and the others, in the house where she threw the baby out the window. I dial the number quickly.

The phone rings nine times before somebody picks it up. I hear the crash of the phone dropping and then being lifted again. "*Hola*," says a heavy, slurred male voice.

"Is Maria there?"

Dishes clatter and dialogue from a TV soap opera drones on in the background. "Who's looking for her?" the male voice says.

I identify myself and then there's a long silence. "*Chinga su madre*," the man says before he hangs up the phone.

I dial the number again immediately. This time the man picks up the phone after six rings. "She don't wanna talk to you," he says belligerently. I guess this is Maria's uncle. Scumbag. Lowlife. Degenerate. I fight the urge to curse him out right now.

"Can she tell me that herself?" I ask as a woman's voice begins talking in loud, rapid Spanish on the other end.

Maria's uncle grunts and hangs up again. I slam down my phone and punch the wall hard. "*FUCK!!*"

The place rattles and the Screamer across the hall yells at me to keep the noise down. I light a cigarette and try to think about what I should do. I could call Bill and Angel over at the Field Service Unit office and we could all drive up to the house and drag Maria out of there. I may have to get a warrant first, though.

I try her one more time. She finally picks up.

"*Hola*, Mr. Baum."

"Yeah, Maria." I try to sound calm and reasonable. "What's up? You living back there again?"

"Ah, yes, Mr. Baum. Could you do something for me please?"

"I'll try."

"Would you please not call again?"

"I don't understand."

"I can't talk to you no more." Her voice wavers as though she's about to start crying. "Please leave me alone."

She hangs up. I try dialing the number once more, but get

a busy signal. I try a second time, and the same thing happens. I call the operator and ask her to break in on the line, but the phone is off the hook.

I put my head in my hands. I haven't cried since the day my mother died but I feel like doing it now. I don't understand how she could do this to me. She's breaking my heart, going back to her sick old life with her fucked-up family. I tried to save her. I gave her my home number. I helped her move. I didn't even take advantage of her that night with the fireworks. I put myself on the line for her.

Fuck her. I can't do anything for her now.

I throw my chair across the office and walk out with other P.O.s bitching at me.

That night I don't sleep much. Things I should've said to her keep running through my mind. I construct an imaginary conversation in which I try once more to convince her not to throw her life away. I tell her that she has to talk to me because I'm her probation officer. But every time I try to imagine her side of the dialogue, it all gets too emotional and I have to start all over again. I watch sleeplessly as the green glowing numbers flick by on the clock radio.

I'm still feeling hurt and angry when I get to the office the next day. Just after eleven, I open my office door to get some fresh air. A couple of young black guys in sneakers and jeans are standing in the hall waiting for their appointment with another P.O. They're talking to each other about movies on television.

"I was watching *The Private Navy of Sergeant O'Farrell*," says one of them, who's wearing a Pittsburgh Pirates cap. "With Bob Hope..."

"And Phyllis Diller?" says his friend who wears a black Nike T-shirt and a Fade haircut.

"You see it?"

"Yeah."

"Man, that shit was bug," says the one in the Pirates cap.

"Yeah, I was buggin' out. You ever see, uh, *It's a Mad Mad Mad Mad World*?"

"That was some star-studded shit in that movie."

I try to ignore them as I look through my files.

"And did you see that program about Darryl K. on Channel Four?" the one in the Nike shirt asks.

I keep looking at the file I have opened on my lap, but the words are starting to appear backward. That's what happens when I can't concentrate. I find myself just waiting to hear what these guys are going to say next about Darryl King.

"Man, he popped those motherfuckers," says the one in the Pirates cap. "The rest of them come after him, they'll get popped too."

"Darryl K. all the way," says his friend in the Nike shirt. "Darryl K. will take no shit before its time ..."

I get up and slam the door on both of their laughing faces. From outside I can hear the Screamer warning me once more to stop making so much noise. "I'LL FUCKIN' HAVE YOU ON REPORT, I SWEAR IT, BAUM."

I ignore her and call the guard at the reception desk on the phone. "Hey, Roger, is that metal detector ever going to get fixed out there?"

On the other end of the line, I hear the buzz of the television and the sound of elevator doors opening and shutting. "Works as well as it ever did," paunchy old Roger says in a bored voice.

"I don't mean to sound paranoid, you know, but I'm a little worried about people coming in here with weapons after all this publicity about Darryl King."

"Like I said. Works as well as it ever did."

Enough is enough, I finally decide. I'm sick of sitting here and sick of these deadbeats coming in and out. I call Ms. Lang's office and leave a message that I'm going to make a field visit and I'll be back later. "She's not going to like that," the secretary says.

"She'll deal with it," I tell her.

I take another look through my files and make a quick decision about who I want to see. Charlie Simms. Charlie is the black kid from Washington Heights who I told Andrea about. He's the one solid success that I have left, I figure. When he came into my office two years ago after his first arrest for stealing a car radio, he was unsure of himself, and vulnerable to fast-talking hoods like his friend Rashid. Since then, Charlie's gotten married, gone back to school, and worked part-time with the Parks Department summer jobs program, which I got him into. At the moment, I probably need to see him worse than he needs to see me, if only just to remind myself there's some purpose to what I've been doing.

I put his file under my arm and catch the uptown express. Charlie's building is fairly easy to find in Washington Heights, even though I've never been there. It's just off Broadway, with a green cornice and a gray brick façade. I'm a little surprised how rundown it is. Charlie always led me to believe he lived in a nice place. But half the windows are boarded up and bricks are missing from the sides.

I hurry into the building before anything falls on me and run smack into a teenage black girl in a yellow smock dress coming out of a first-floor apartment.

"Sorry," I say. "You know if Charlie Simms is around?"

Without even pausing to answer, she turns and looks toward the blinding rectangle of sunlight at the other end of the dim hallway.

"Charlie!" the girl calls out. "Man's here to see you."

I see a head peek out of a doorway halfway down the hall and look toward me, barely long enough to register that I'm a white male, let alone someone he might know. Without warning, he goes shooting out toward the rectangle of sunlight.

"There he go," the girl in the yellow smock dress says.

I take off after him, down the hallway, through the rectangular doorway, and out into an alley between the buildings. Charlie is running ahead of me over landfill and garbage and anything else that happens to be lying there. Once he hits the street, I know I'll never catch him. I'm not even sure why I'm chasing him. This is supposed to be a friendly visit.

"CHARLIE!" I shout. "It's Steve Baum! Slow down!"

He pulls up short in front of a pair of aluminum garbage cans and waits for me to catch up with him. When I finally do see him up close, I feel my heart breaking for the second time in two days. Through his plastic-rimmed glasses, the sunlight reflects dully off his eyes. He's lost a tremendous amount of weight. His jeans sag from his waist and hang over his flat butt like a drape. His Patrick Ewing shirt envelops his torso. When I shake his right hand, I give it a good look. There's a dry burned crust of skin near his thumbnail. It's the kind of patch you get from flicking a lighter over and over to keep a crack pipe going.

"What's up with you?"

"Nothin'," Charlie mumbles.

"What do you mean 'nothin'? How long have you been smoking that shit?"

"I'm not smoking anything, man. I just say no. Leave me alone."

"You're not smoking crack?"

Charlie casts his eyes downward and shakes his head from side to side.

"Don't you fucking lie to me, Charlie," I say, shaking his folder at him, like it's a contract that's been broken between us.

"I'm not lying."

"No?" I take his sleeve and start to walk toward the street. "Okay, let's go then."

"Where we going?"

"Downtown. You're gonna piss in a cup and we're gonna do a test to see if you're lying and smoking crack. If you're telling me the truth, there shouldn't be any problem."

"Later for that bullshit," Charlie says softly. "You ain't got no machines to do tests..."

Actually, that used to be true, but just recently the department started getting the facilities to do testing. "Come on, let's go. I love to catch people lying..."

Charlie puts his hands up. "Forget it."

"Does that mean you admit you're smoking crack?"

"Yeah," Charlie says. "You happy now?"

"The opposite. Believe me."

Charlie sits down on one of the garbage cans and fingers the leather Back to Africa medallion he has around his neck. "Shit."

"What's the matter with you?" I say a little more calmly. "Why'd you run from me like that? You been in any more trouble besides the crack?"

"You got my file," he says into his hand.

I didn't bother looking at the file on the subway, but now I see he's gotten two hit notices since he was transferred to another P.O.'s caseload. He was arrested a month ago for a disorderly conduct in the Bronx. A week later, he was picked up for possession of a controlled substance in this neighborhood.

"Have you tried quitting?" I ask.

"Yeah..."

"How many times have you quit?"

Charlie holds up two fingers.

"What is it?" I say, slapping my thigh in frustration. "The responsibility? You were doing well. What's the matter? Couldn't you take the pressure?"

"What do you know about it?" Charlie sniffs.

"Not much, I guess. I thought you were tough enough to make it. I was wrong. You know you really disappointed me."

He looks away from me and scratches the back of his head. "What does this have to do with you?" he asks.

"What?"

"You say I 'disappointed' you. I let you down. What makes you so important?"

"Don't try to turn it around," I say, pointing at him. "We had a relationship..."

"Oh fuck you, man," Charlie makes a swatting motion with the back of his hand. "You're just like all the others, you just don't know it."

"All the other what? White people?"

Charlie smirks at me. "You said it. I didn't."

Wheels screech on the street and something I'm standing on cracks.

"Ah, don't punk out like that."

"You don't know what it's like," Charlie says heatedly.

"Yeah, yeah, yeah . . . You know, I hear that bullshit twelve times a day."

"And you still don't get it." Charlie rubs his nose. His face looks sucked out and lifeless. "You don't understand."

"Oh yeah? What don't I understand?"

"How hard it is."

"Ah, find me a Kleenex. I'm gonna start crying."

"Hey, you know something, Mr. Baum?" Charlie says. "I know exactly one guy from my block who's a success."

"Who?" I ask.

"Rashid." Charlie points down the alley and across the street. "On that corner last year, he started out as a lookout for one of the crack dealers on my block. He made a hundred dollars a day. Now he's out on his own, selling his own shit on the corner and he can make a grand on a slow morning." Charlie adjusts his glasses and raises his voice. "So you tell me why I'm gonna bag your groceries for three fuckin' dollars an hour at the Grand Union."

I can't think of anything to say for a long time. The sun beats down on the alley, making the air thick and the garbage stink worse. This is the argument I'm most afraid of. There's no honest answer for it.

"You'll just end up in prison or dead if you stick around the crack business," I tell him.

"Maybe," Charlie says in a voice that has nothing behind it. He's physically still sitting on the trash can in front of me, but his mind is down the street already. He'll probably buy two vials within five minutes of me leaving. His body begins to agitate like a test tube full of combustible elements.

"I thought you were a smart guy," I say despairingly. "Doesn't it mean anything when I say you're gonna die if you keep doing this?"

"If I die, I got no needs," he says, folding his arms and facing the wall away from me.

"Oh yeah? What if you go to prison?"

"Still got no needs. I'll have a home, three squares, TV."

"That's a bunch of shit," I say.

"And I'll be with my Muslim brothers." He gives the clenched fist salute.

"Oh, you're gonna be with them, huh? Don't real Muslims have strictures against drinking and doing drugs?"

Charlie waves his hands dismissively. "Let me tell you something, Mr. Baum," he says, somehow managing to sound both rote and angry. "White people say crack shatters lives and shit like that, but the real reason they don't like crack is because it's the black man's business. Ain't no Mafia or policeman getting our money."

"You got it so backward," I say with a sigh. It's like he's taken all the old black nationalist rhetoric and twisted it just enough to suit his own purposes.

"Y'all always act like you wanna help black people when you just wanna take shit away from us," he says fiercely. "You give our women birth control and say you wanna 'prevent cycle of dependency,'" he says in a nasal "white" voice. "But you just afraid of all these little black babies growing up to take over your world and rock your shit." He turns and jabs a finger right at me.

I've heard a lot of what he's saying before. I've even thought some of it might be true. But at the moment, it doesn't make much difference to me. He's throwing away all the good work we've done together and I'm starting to get good and pissed about it.

Charlie, in the meantime, is continuing his crack-fueled rant. "The Holocaust wasn't nothin'," he's saying. "My people are dealing with genocide right here in this country, and y'all still can't figure out why we can get behind Darryl King."

For some reason, this sends me right over the edge. I grab him by the collar of his sweatshirt and push him hard right up against the wall. "Hey, you know what?" I hear myself outing. "You know what? I give up on *you people*!"

For a second, Charlie looks kind of stunned, and then pushes back at me. I flash on the idea that he might have a knife in his pocket and I try to figure out what I'd do if he lunged at me. "You people?" he says, scrunching up his face. "What do you mean? You mean you niggers, right?"

"That's not what I said." I take my hands off his collar and back away from him. But it's too late.

Between "you people" and "you niggers," there's very little distance. Charlie knows it and I know it.

We move a little farther apart and give each other wary looks. The only sounds I'm aware of for a minute are both of us breathing and the blood pounding in my ears.

Gradually, the noise from the street begins to fade back in. No one pulled any knife here, but the damage has been done anyway. I scribble down the name and address of a drug rehabilitation program on a piece of notebook paper, but when I try to hand it to him, Charlie turns away. The physical contact involved in taking it from me would be too much like a handshake. Something I don't particularly feel like doing either. I leave the note on the nearest garbage can lid so he can pick it up himself.

"I want you to report to that place immediately," I say. "If you don't, you'll be looking at jail time for smoking crack."

"Yeah, right," he says bitterly.

We turn away from each other without saying good-bye. It's almost two o'clock and I hear myself mumbling, "Ignorant bastards," as I walk back through the alley. The girl who I saw before in the yellow smock dress is lingering in the building's doorway, giving me what you'd call an accusing look if that's what you were expecting.

I used to argue with the old saying "If you scratch a liberal, you'll find a guilty racist hiding underneath." Now, maybe, I'm not so sure.

52

Darryl King looked out the window. A brilliant day was in progress and a breeze blew through the screen. Twelve floors below, a group of small children screamed and frolicked in the spray from an open fire hydrant in the middle of the six-building city project called the Charles J. Stone Houses. Across a long stretch of brownish grass, several elderly women gathered on the benches, leaning on their canes and nodding solemnly at each other.

On the asphalt court, some fifty yards to the east, a half dozen young men Darryl's age were playing a furious game of basketball.

From his window, Darryl couldn't see the players, but he could hear the slapping sound of the ball being dribbled. He wished he could go outside and join the game. He tried to visualize what it would be like in his mind. He saw himself jumping high above the fray of scrambling boys and then above the backboard. As he descended, he reached back behind his head and jammed the basketball through the hoop so forcefully that the backboard slid down the pole and crashed into the court. Rival players and scantily dressed girls stared in awe at the devastation he'd caused.

His mother's voice, talking to someone on the phone, in-

...upted his reverie. "So who we want to go and kill that grand jury witness?"

"Let Aaron do it," Darryl told his mother to tell whoever she was talking to on the phone. "He did Eddie Johnson all right."

She went on talking and he shut his eyes tightly. "Moms, we got any ice cream? I'm hungry now."

She put her hand over the receiver and looked at him. "Honey, we just moved here," she said in a flat voice. She wore a Same Shit, Every Day T-shirt and a pair of gray stone-washed jeans. "I ain't had no time to shop...Since when you wanna eat anyhow?"

Darryl lumbered over to the refrigerator and took a look inside. All the food seemed old. With all the moving around and relocating since the big shoot-out, he hadn't done much eating anyway. Crack took most of his appetite away. It had him always agitated over one thing or another. He'd watch the news on TV or his mother would read the newspaper to him and he could hear his name and see his picture and he'd be glad that he was famous but then he'd think that these people who put these things on the tube did not know him and did not know about his mentality and the things happening in his head and he'd get enraged about their lies and start to break things.

"They don't know me," he said to himself. "No one knows me."

In between everything else, he kept getting images of his probation officer. He could not quite picture the guy's face in his mind, but he could still hear him saying, "Don't be late... Dooky," from the last time they saw each other outside the courthouse elevators.

But then the little glass pipe beckoned to him like an old friend waiting in his room. He'd smoke and smell the heady ether aroma and his heart would beat like a huge bass drum and he'd feel on top of things and in control again, even if he couldn't keep track of time or think things through so well.

The future was only the time between the last high and the next one. Hours and days would go by and he wouldn't sleep or eat. Then he'd crash for two days and wake up starving.

Instead of "visualizing" like his sister told him to, he'd sit in front of the TV for days, playing with the Nintendo games and watching the Channel 5 news at ten (to see if they would show his picture again). Other times, he just watched *Dallas* and *Dynasty* reruns. The plots he didn't care about, but he liked seeing the beautiful ladies and the big cars and the huge houses filled with nice stuff.

Sometimes that made him angry too, though. Especially when the commercials came on. It was like standing outside a candy store with your nose pressed up against the glass. They put the shit right in your face. Cars, women, airplanes, sneakers, diamonds, giant televisions. But they never let you have any of it.

The worst was the rich guy he kept seeing on the news. The one who always seemed to be flying somewhere in a helicopter or walking through some casino with a bunch of bodyguards. Every time Darryl saw him, he seemed to have a different woman with him, younger than the one before her. One time, the TV people even said the rich guy had a contract with his old wife that basically said he could fuck anyone he wanted.

Though they always claimed the guy did something else for a living, Darryl knew the guy had to be a drug dealer, because otherwise people wouldn't be falling all over him all the time like he had something they desperately needed. Darryl kind of liked the guy's style, except that the guy never seemed to be having that good a time.

Darryl decided if he ever had that much money, he'd really live it up right. He'd have all kinds of clothes. A different color warm-up suit for every single day. And a different chain too, instead of the same old cheap-looking red tie the rich guy wore every time he was on TV. Dinner would be at Red Lobster every night. And the other thing was he'd have as many ladies as the rich guy had, except he'd keep all of them. And if one of the old ones wanted to throw down and do the humpty dance again, he'd be happy to oblige. But the most important thing was that if they ever showed Darryl getting off a helicopter, he'd have a much bigger smile on his face than the rich guy.

All of that shit was waiting for him now. He had to just figure out a way to get to it. For now, they finally seemed to be settling in this apartment. The old couple they'd gotten rid of had kept the place clean and well-furnished. It had two bedrooms, two bathrooms, and a living room with a view of the plazas and the entrances below. This building was called the Fortress. Pops Osborn controlled it before he was killed, and it was still virtually impenetrable for police.

The "security team"—a group of young men paid by Darryl King's sister and Winston Murvin to act as lookouts in the lobby—could spot unfamiliar faces and call upstairs with warnings before the intruders could cross the plaza outside. If any strangers did get inside, a King family lieutenant on the eighth floor controlled the one working elevator and could shut it off at any point. With the time it took to climb the twelve flights to get to them, the King family could get rid of whatever drugs or weapons they had, sneak out of one of the back entrances—which had doors that only opened from the inside— and disappear before a raid got going.

Logistically, the building was a firetrap. Its sprinkler and alarm systems did not work and a dangerous, flammable residue coated the walls of one incinerator chute. But for drug dealers, it was a palace. Back when Paul "Stewy" Harris was running his operation out of the Fortress, a joint city-federal narcotics task force spent $303,174 on a massive sweep through the project. Vials of cocaine and guns literally rained out of the windows. Because of the strategic problems with the building's structure, the agents were only able to assemble enough evidence to support five felony convictions. Given the expense, the law enforcement agencies began to concentrate on other drug-infested parts of the city and the Fortress was left alone.

"When we eat?" Darryl King asked his mother.

"I dunno. What do you want?"

"I didn't eat for half a week." He patted the side of his stomach. "I want Ring Dings and Devil Dogs and then some Chinese food. Like takeout."

"You crazy. We can't let no delivery boy come here, Darryl."

"Fuck! When do I go outside again? I'm bugging out up here, Moms."

It was the most fucked-up thing. For the first time in his life, he was in a position to have some real money, but there was no way he could spend it. Somewhere downstairs, there was a brand-new Oldsmobile Cutlass Supreme that Winston had bought for him. He was even paying someone to wash it for him every day. But he'd never actually seen the car because he couldn't go outside now. He went over to the closet and looked at the custom-made white leather jacket his mother had bought all those weeks back. With the way things were going, he was never going to get to wear that either.

"You got only yourself to blame," she said.

He grabbed the jacket and walked to the door. "OUTTA HERE!"

"Darryl, you walk out that door, I swear I'll stab you right here and now." Her voice stopped him in his tracks. "Goddamn," she said. "Sometimes, I think you're same as you was when you was five years old."

"I WANNA GO OUT, MOMS."

"Darryl baby, if it was up to me, you be on the street right now. But the shit done happened already with those cops."

"It's 'cos of that probation officer," he grumbled. "Mr. Bomb. We gotta have somebody take him off the count."

"Aaron and Bobby are working on that," his mother said. "They'll get going. Now you just gotta relax here."

"When?" Darryl asked.

She sighed. "They know a guy, who knows another guy, who's got a cousin...I dunno. They'll work it out. They just got to get going, that's all. See if they wanna do him outside his office or follow him or what the fuck. So don't worry. They do it right."

"All right," Darryl said, scratching the back of his hand and looking around the room for his crack pipe. "I just wish they do it soon, that's all I'm saying."

"Why? You can't go out just because your probation officer's dead, right?"

"No. But it sure as hell make me feel better."

"Well, all right," Darryl King's mother said. "You wanna get high now?"

53

Naturally, the downtown train stops several times between stations, and this band of rowdy black kids keeps swaggering back and forth between the cars, hanging from the straps and menacing old people. Usually I just ignore gangs like this and read the hemorrhoid ads. But today, they've got me in a rage. After talking to Charlie, I'm in no mood for taking shit from anyone. I pick the one kid who seems to be the leader and just start staring at him.

He's got about seventeen thin gold chains wrapped around his neck. On his fingers, he has all these gold rings with different colored stones. Even his mouth is full of gold, though from the way the light hits his teeth, it looks like he's got a diamond implanted in one of his front caps.

In short, he's wearing what I clear after taxes. And I'm supposed to go back to my office and tell some little mother-fucker like him how to run his life.

No way.

For a while, he doesn't look back at me because he's busy putting his face near an old lady's ear and shouting. Then he notices me and smirks. I keep staring. He sits down on the bench across from me and his six other friends sit down next to him. Softly at first, he begins to tap out a rhythm on the edge of his seat with his index and middle fingers. His friends start to tap along with him. He looks at me and starts slapping the rhythm a little harder and a little more defiantly with his open hands, and his friends join in after him. I just keep my eyes right on the level with his. Finally he starts to beat the rhythm out with his fists and the rest of them do the same, and it sounds like war drums echoing through the stalled train.

I get up and walk over to him. For a minute, I just stand above him without saying anything. The drumming starts to die down a little. "You're annoying me," I say.

The drumming stops completely and the leader kid just looks at me, with his mouth hanging open a little. "Oh shit," one of his friends says. "My man Burn-hard Goetz."

They all laugh nervously as I go back to sit down, and when the train starts moving again, they all move on to another car.

I sit there simmering the rest of the way. It's a free country, I think, as the train grinds to a halt at 125th Street and a fat guy with a steel drum gets on. People like Charlie and Maria are grown-ups and they can do what they want, and deal with the consequences. I just don't know why they have to do it on my watch.

I start going over my list of clients in my mind to see which of them deserves to get their ass kicked. The steel drum guy begins to play a calypso version of "Rudolph, the Red-Nosed Reindeer." Right now, I feel like kicking his ass. Instead, I just glare at him until he moves on to the next car. The one name that keeps coming back to me is Richard Silver. Thinking about him makes me almost as anxious and uncomfortable as thinking about Darryl. Probably because—besides Darryl—he's the client who's most actively tried to undermine me and make me think twice about what I'm doing with my life.

I'd like to give him something to think about, but I'm not sure what pretext to use. That stuff his wife told me about money laundering sounded a little nuts, but I'm sure he's been up to something else. Then I remember he still hasn't done his community service requirement, which is as good an excuse as any to go over and bother him at his office.

The train pulls into the Columbus Circle station; I get off and walk a couple of blocks to his building on Seventh Avenue. Richard Silver Associates is on the thirty-eighth floor, so I take the elevator up, flash my badge at his puffy, blond secretary, and tell her to hold all his calls.

The secretary, who's in her thirties and wears enough hair spray and makeup for a heavy metal band and their road crew, buzzes him in his office while I stare at the white antiseptic walls and the postmodern furniture.

Silver comes tearing out thirty seconds later. But when he sees it's me, his face drops a little.

"Oh shit, I thought this was somebody important," he tells the secretary with some disappointment in his voice. "You almost gave me a heart attack."

"This is important," I say, walking around him and going right into his office.

It's both more and less opulent than I expected. He certainly has enough space—you could probably fit a helicopter in the room. The southern view goes on for miles and miles. In the distance you can see the World Trade Center's twin towers shimmering like a pair of switchblades in the sunlight. But he hardly has anything in the office, except a plain brown horseshoe-shaped desk, one big leather chair behind it, and two small leather-and-wood chairs in front of it. It's not so much cheap, as incredibly severe-looking. Sort of like Survivalist Chic. There are only three pictures on the wall and just two books on the shelf behind him, the telephone directory and *The Power Broker*, the biography of Robert Moses, the builder who I always thought personally mutilated New York City.

I'd say Richard Silver either just moved in or he has a very odd sense of self-esteem. With the rent he's paying, he can certainly afford more elaborate decorations. And then I look at the ceiling over his desk and see he's got a gold mirror up there, so he can look up and see himself. Why he'd want to do such a thing regularly, I couldn't say.

"So I guess I was just reading about your department," he says, seizing the offensive as he strolls back behind his desk. "How you've got an open-door policy for hoodlums. Right?"

He holds up his hands in mock sympathy and then gives me that long, silent look where you can't tell if his eyebrow is raised or not. I guess this is supposed to put me on the defensive, but I'm too pissed for that today.

"Speaking of fuckups," I say evenly. "I understand you still haven't been doing your community service..."

"Ooooo, that's bad, huh?" He sways playfully back and forth in his chair. "I haven't been brushing between meals either."

"I'm glad you think this is such a joke..."

"Well, really. I mean, did you come all the way up here just to bother me about this? Instead of going out and looking for these hoodlums you put out on the street. You could've called my lawyer. Or the other guy who's supposed to be my probation officer should call my lawyer."

This last part seems to stop him. "Hey, that's right," he says, reaching for the phone and putting his feet up on the desk, so they're right in my face. "You aren't even my probation officer anymore. What the hell are you doing here anyway?"

The way he says that makes me grind my teeth. I decide to taunt him back. "You know I saw your wife the other day."

"Oh yeah?" he says, feigning indifference while he looks at the phone and dials. "Did you fuck her or anything?"

"No, I just talked to her about this Goldman Resources."

I fully expect him to ignore me or make another wisecrack, but instead he puts the phone down and gives me his full attention. Only a muscle or two in his face have changed, but he looks gravely serious now.

"She told you that, huh?"

I glance up at the mirror above his desk and notice for the first time that he's got a little bald spot spreading across the back of his scalp. "She told me all about it," I say.

He closes his eyes and takes a breath. This is the last thing that I expected. I never for a second took what his ex-wife said seriously. But he seems genuinely stunned. It's like we were just sparring and I accidentally hit him with a knockout punch.

He presses a button on the phone and tells his secretary to hold his calls for a half hour. Then he points to one of the pictures on the wall.

"You know who that is?" he begins.

The picture shows a slightly younger, skinnier Richard Silver in a purple La Coste shirt with his arm around an older man who has a big nose and skin the texture of a deflated balloon's. They seem to be standing on the deck of a yacht.

"That's Jimmy Rose," I say. "He was your partner, right?"

"That's right. I met Jimmy years ago when he was leading the opposition to a housing project a number of us in the council wanted to put in Brooklyn. Probably before your time."

"I remember it, though," I tell him. "Sullivan Houses. It would've brought a lot of blacks and Hispanics into the area . . ."

"'Low-income families' is what it said in the bill." He leans forward on his elbow.

"Whatever."

"I'm glad you remember it, though. I thought it was an important project. So did Jimmy. He said supporting it would kill me. Politically speaking, of course . . . So you know what I did?"

"You chickened out," I say.

"I learned the value of compromise. I saw the opportunity to do great things with Jimmy. So I sacrificed a little bit of the present for the sake of the future."

I should be moving, but he's got that smooth seductive sound going in his voice again. He gestures for me to have a seat.

"Now, Steven," he begins calmly. "Do you remember the

little talk we had before about the importance of having resources?''

"Sure." To my horror, I'm beginning to see a little bit of
the sense behind what he's been saying all along, but I'm not
ready to agree to anything.

"Well, Steven," he says, "I'd like to talk to you a little bit
more about that right now."

54

The Dodgers' pitcher threw a curveball and Darryl Strawberry hit it foul down the first base line at Shea Stadium. The ball bounced once in the dirt and went into the stands just missing Richard Silver and his son, Leonard, in the first row.

"You should've caught it, Dad," Leonard said.

"You catch it next time," Richard Silver grumbled.

The Mets were losing 2–1 in the ninth inning and there were men on second and third with one man out. Most of the Monday night crowd was still there and a mild breeze was blowing out toward right field.

"You know your mother is causing me a lot of problems," Richard Silver told his son.

"Watch the game," Leonard said.

"You watch the game."

Valenzuela, the Dodger pitcher, threw a fastball that came in a little bit below the letters on Strawberry's shirt. But the umpire said it was inside, bringing the count to two balls and two strikes. The pitcher shook his head in disgust and Scioscia the catcher came out to the mound for a conference.

"What does she think she's trying to do to me?" Richard Silver said, turning in his seat and taking a bite of his son's hot dog.

"I don't know." His son didn't look at him but kept his eyes on Strawberry taking swings just outside the batter's box.

"You know I may end up in a lot of trouble because of something she told someone." Richard Silver stared at his son for a long time, but the boy didn't respond. "Do you think that's right?"

"I don't know," his son said as Strawberry stepped back in the box and the catcher went back behind the plate. "Watch the game."

Strawberry hits the next one foul down the third base line and it ricochets off the concrete steps a dozen seats to the left of us.

"These are great seats," Andrea says. "Who gave them to you?"

"Just a guy," I say. "Nobody you know."

She doesn't need to know anything else about it. I put the cheese spread from Balducci's back into the picnic basket she prepared.

"Did your folks used to take you here when you were a kid?" she asks.

"No."

"I thought this was just around the corner from where you grew up."

"No, I was born on the Grand Concourse in the Bronx," I explain. "My parents used to take me to a place called Freedomland when I was a kid."

"What was that?" she asks, reaching into the basket to put some cheese on a cracker.

"It was like the Disneyland of the Bronx, you know." It's a strain to remember what it looked like now. "I guess it wasn't anything special, but what did I know? I was like this really unhappy little kid and I had the time of my life at Freedomland; I remember all these little white kids running around with all these little black and Puerto Rican kids. We all took the bus home and sang songs together. Kinda like City College but better."

"Sounds like fun."

"It's the best memory I had growing up. In fact, I used to have this picture in my head of New York City being like Freedomland, with all these different kinds of people mixing and getting along."

I feel funny saying this after talking to Charlie and Maria earlier today. I'm not so sure about the melting pot now. I can't even bring myself to tell Andrea what's been going on with me, because I'm still struggling to work out what it all means. All I know now is that I don't want to give in to these bad thoughts I've been having.

"So what happened to Freedomland?" Andrea asks as a jet passes overhead.

"I think it went bankrupt," I tell her, "so they tore it down and put up Co-op City, the big middle-income housing complex. And all these Jewish people, like my parents, abandoned the Grand Concourse, which was like this really nice strip where they'd been living, and moved to Co-op City. Which left the Grand Concourse to these poor blacks and Puerto Ricans, who couldn't do anything with it, so they burned it down along with the rest of the South Bronx. And eventually the old Jews like my parents left the Bronx altogether. They ran away."

"You sound like you're ashamed of them," she says.

I turn back to the game. "Yeah, I guess I do."

Strawberry took a good swing at the next pitch, driving it high and deep down the right field line. The crowd stood and roared. The right fielder looked up. But at the last moment, the breeze pushed the ball into the foul territory in the upper deck, twenty rows away from where Detective Sergeant Bob McCullough was sitting with his family.

"Here's the best story I ever heard about a guy who lost his own gun," said his father, Captain Willie, sipping a Budweiser. "Johnny Riordan, used to be a sergeant at Midtown South, goes over to Fitzpatrick's on Tenth Avenue and gets absolutely stewed."

"Christ, but Johnny could do it too," said his daughter, Detective Katie McCullough, who had dark hair and very fair skin.

Bob McCullough tried to ignore the two of them and watch the game. But a sudden gust of wind blew up a little dust storm around the pitcher's mound and they had to take a break on the field. Captain Willie, a gray-haired bear of a man in his sixties, kept going with his story about Johnny Riordan.

"Anyway," he said with a belch. "Drunk as he is, Johnny manages to make it home. But when he wakes up in the morning, he can't for the life of him remember where he put his gun. He looks everywhere, but he can't find it. And his commander at the time was Hicks, so he knew there'd be hell to pay if they found out."

"Oh sure," said Detective Katie, slapping her knee.

Bob McCullough, whose father called him "Little Bob," nodded along as though he were amused instead of miserable. He hated it when the two of them traded war stories like this. And to top it off, his left leg still hurt where the bullet grazed him on the night of the shoot-out.

"So then Johnny comes up with a plan to save his own ass," Captain Willie said. "He goes over to the piers on the west side, finds a bum sleeping there, and throws him right in the drink."

"He doesn't!" said Detective Katie, with a shocked, delighted look.

"He does," said Captain Willie. "And then Johnny jumps right in after him and saves him from drowning. And in the next day's papers, it's HERO COP SAVES BUM for a headline. So nobody minded it when Johnny said he'd lost his gun in the rescue."

Captain Willie and Detective Katie threw their heads back and roared. Bob McCullough smiled weakly at them. His father clapped him on the shoulder.

"So you see, you needn't feel so bad about losing your gun to that nigger," his father told him with a chuckle.

"Thanks, Dad," Bob McCullough said as the Dodger pitcher finally began his next windup. "That means a lot."

Watching the game on television from the apartment in the Fortress, Darryl King sank down in his chair and put his face on the palm of his hand.

"Damn," he said, watching Strawberry. "How come they only got 'bout two niggers on this team?"

Strawberry wiggles his butt and waves his bat around. Andrea laughs and points. "That's so cute," she says, tugging on the binoculars I have around my neck. "I gotta see this."

I give her the glasses. "So you're having a good time now, right?"

"Of course." She squeezes my arm and looks through the binoculars.

"You like this," I say, pointing at the seats and the picnic basket. "You like these nice things in life that cost a lot of money."

She lowers the field glasses and gives me that mildly perturbed look. "Steven," she says. "There's nothing wrong with that."

"I wasn't saying there was."

Strawberry steps out of the box one last time and gives the third base coach a long look.

"Why's he doing that?" Andrea asks me.

"So that the other team will think the Mets have a play on," I say. "Like a suicide squeeze, you know, a bunt for the runner to come home from third. But never mind. They're not going to do that anyway."

"Why not?"

"Because that's Darryl Strawberry up there," I say, pointing. "They pay him to go up there and hit the ball out of the park."

The Dodger pitcher throws a high fastball and Strawberry smashes it toward the gap between the shortstop and third base. The crowd starts to yowl. But the shortstop scoops up the ball, looks the runner back to third base, and throws Strawberry out at first by a half step.

"Come on, let's go," Richard Silver said, rising out of his seat.

"There's one more out to go," said his son, Leonard, trying to get the hot dog remains out of his braces.

"They already blew their chance," Richard Silver told him, as he moved toward the aisle. "When an opportunity comes to you in life, you have to take it, otherwise it's gone forever. I was just saying that to somebody recently."

"Who?"

"Never mind." Silver pushed the blue Mets cap down over his son's eyes.

Leonard wasn't budging from his seat. "We can't go now, Dad. Kevin McReynolds is up."

Richard Silver looked down the line as the stocky left fielder settled into the batter's box. "He's a bum."

"He's my favorite player, Dad."

McReynolds swung at the first pitch and popped it up behind home plate. The ball was a white dot against the black nighttime sky. Scioscia the Dodgers' catcher threw off his mask and caught it easily, ending the game.

"Better find another favorite player," Richard Silver said, prodding his son to start moving toward the exits. "By the way, is your mother seeing anybody now?"

55

Darryl King was looking at his own reflection in the window-pane that night as he talked on the phone to his girlfriend, Alisha Watkins.

"I hate bagging up," said Alisha, who was small-boned, seventeen, and the mother of Darryl's two children. "I hate working. You know what I mean?"

"You hate working," Darryl King said on his end of the line. "You mean what you're doing now?"

"Yeah, I'm getting all drowsy from the fumes."

Darryl looked at the windowpane from a different angle and saw the reflection of his mother and his sister talking at the dining room table behind him. Women were always excluding him from the big plans now.

"I'm gonna get into the heavier weights," he told his girlfriend with phony confidence. "I wanna start dealing with kilos, you know. That's all I want to get with. That's it." He forgot what he was going to say next.

"You better stop smoking so much of that shit," Alisha Watkins said. "Your sister says she's ready to open up this new spot. She say she needs people to work for her."

"She told you that?"

"She didn't tell you?" Alisha asked.

Darryl whirled around to glare at his sister, Joanna, at the table. She kept pointing at her astrological chart and talking to their mother, ignoring him completely. Neither of them was telling him what was going on anymore. One of them said something that sounded like his name. Maybe they were going to give him up to the cops.

Sometimes it seemed like everything was out to get him. The police, the people on television, the slippery bathroom floor. Maybe his own family too. He could be being paranoid, but that didn't mean he was wrong.

"Yeah, I'm gonna open up a new spot too," Darryl said loudly. He hadn't thought of doing any such thing before and he was not sure if he wanted to do it now. But he raised his voice so his mother and sister could hear him.

"Yeah, I'm gonna get me some reliable people," Darryl said. "I'm not gonna pay them right away until we build up the clientele. I want about four spots, and we'd run for six months, man. I'm gonna fold that money, and that's it. I want a piece of land."

"Where?" his girlfriend asked.

"The building across the way here." Darryl pointed out the window as though Alisha could see him. From the twelfth-floor apartment in the Fortress, Darryl was looking at building B of the Charles J. Stone Houses. Its lights appeared blurred in the head-softening heat of the evening. "My family's got all this action in this building, you know, so I wanna expand. Get me a spot to start off that would bubble about ten Gs a day."

"That sounds like the right track," said Alisha, pleased by her boyfriend's new sense of enterprise. "You should get a little something for yourself. But you know when you first start something, it be slow," she cautioned him.

Again, Darryl lost his place in the conversation, and he started chewing his thumb. Maybe he was smoking too much crack. It was getting harder and harder to finish a thought now. Besides getting high, there were just two things he could think about for two minutes in a row these days. One was the movie

The Wild Bunch, which had several bloody scenes he watched over and over again on the VCR. The other was his probation officer.

He was beginning to think all his troubles began with his first meeting with Baum. Everything was wrong since then. He'd got caught breaking into Pops Osborn's car, he'd had to show up in court, he'd had the shoot-out with those cops, and worst of all, he had to stay shut up in the house like it was prison.

He reached down to touch his stomach and noticed there was a lot less of it than there used to be. He'd lost a tremendous amount of weight in these past few weeks, and all his clothes seemed too big now.

"How long you think it takes to knock off half a kilo?" he asked his girlfriend after a few seconds.

"Darryl, who you talking to?" his mother demanded in her lazy junkie voice from across the living room.

"Alisha, Moms."

"She ready to work for me?" his sister, Joanna, asked, without looking up from the dining room table.

"Maybe she work for me," Darryl King said.

"Maybe I work for myself," Alisha murmured on her end.

"Darryl, you can't be selling no drugs with the whole world out looking for you . . ." his mother said in a voice that trailed off into nothingness.

His sister stood up from her chair and came lumbering toward him. Her handcuff-sized gold earrings banged against the sides of her neck.

"Ever since you shot at those cops," she was saying, "we can't allow the workers to come out until ten at night. We don't get any money in the daytime." She was standing beside him now, nattering at him while he cradled the phone to his ear with his left shoulder. "And after all the bullshit we been through 'cos of you, you turn around and say you wanna go start your own business . . . Well, I think that is about the most selfish thing I have ever heard."

"Terrible," his mother chimed in from across the room. "And with Aaron looking for the probation officer for you."

"Fuck you," Darryl said.

"Darryl, don't you talk to your mother like that," Alisha said over the phone.

He felt overwhelmed by women and their disapproval.

A cop would not take this. A real cop. Like the kind he had in his head. Not like those suckers he shot at. Or the one he popped just before Christmas. A real cop would cuff these bitches and throw them in the squad car and beat both their butts with a television antenna. A crackhead would just stand there, feeling paranoid and trying to figure out if he wanted to jump out of his own skin or peel them out of theirs.

"You wouldn't talk like that there was a man in this house," his mother told him.

"I am the man in the house," Darryl King said.

He went back to chewing his thumb.

56

I'm sitting in the office between appointments on Tuesday, my second and final report day, when the phone rings.

"What're you doing?" the now-familiar voice asks me.

"Trying to make an honest living," I say. "Something you ought to think about."

"Why bother?" he says with a fatherly chuckle. "All that pressure. There're easier ways, you know."

"I know." I throw away the file of a client who got killed recently. "So are you doing that community service program like I told you too?"

"Central Harlem Boys' Club, I'll be there with bells on," Richard Silver says. "And have you thought about the conversation we had before?"

"Yeah, a little." I glance out the doorway to see if anybody might be listening in on this. "I haven't made up my mind."

"Why not?"

"I don't know if I'm ready."

"Remember what I told you about opportunity," he says in a quiet, assured voice. "Do you want to be a probation officer the rest of your life? That's what you have to ask yourself."

I must admit, he does have the gift for knowing his customer's soft spot.

"I gotta jump, Richard. Be good."

"Yeah, you too," he says.

57

Aaron Williams sat in the waiting room of the Manhattan probation office, touching the thin new mustache on his harelip as though he wanted to make sure it was still there. He wore a red Troop shirt, green shorts, white athletic socks pulled up to his knees, and a pair of blue-and-white Avia sneakers. He was looking for just the one probation officer, but now he couldn't remember the name.

Darryl said something about the guy having curly hair and a big nose. That didn't help much. All these white people looked the same to him.

Everyone expected a lot from Aaron now. He proved he had heart with the way he took care of Eddie Johnson with the razor blade at the swimming pool. And Eddie was a friend of his. But he was a snitch and Aaron needed the juice with Darryl and the rest of the crew.

But now he was getting angry and tired trying to recall anything Darryl and the others had told him about the probation officer. The only thing he could think of was that the guy had definitely disrespected Darryl by calling him "Dooky."

By early afternoon, he was wishing he'd stayed home in bed, looking at his Michael Jackson poster and enjoying the clean, strong ether smell from his pipe. He shifted in his seat so the gun in his waistband wouldn't keep sticking him in the back. He still couldn't believe the metal detector at the front hadn't picked it up, but everything around here seemed pretty broken-down anyway.

The other people in the waiting room noticed him twitching and cursing to himself. He went out of the building to smoke a vial and beam up. When he returned, the metal detector remained silent. The white court officer at the reception desk didn't even look up from his television to see him going by.

As he sat back down, the older men ignored him and went on talking quietly among themselves. The younger guys made fun of his harelip and women looked away as soon as they noticed it. He looked down and started tying and untying his sneaker laces.

Probation officers came and went past the front desk. More of them were black than Aaron expected. The whites all seemed pale and doughy to him. His mother said he needed glasses, but then why hadn't she gotten him any? She was always hassling him, but never doing anything about things she didn't like.

After another hour or so, Aaron began to notice that many of the probation officers and their clients were stopping to look at something on the table near the receptionist. When he got the chance, Aaron drifted over to take a look for himself.

From being in Family Court, Aaron recognized it as the sign-in table. More than a dozen white sheets were taped to the table, with a box of eraserless little yellow pencils on the side. Aaron knew that each sheet had the name of a probation officer on the top, and that clients were supposed to sign in underneath. If he could have recognized the name of Darryl's probation officer on one of the sheets, Aaron thought, he would have had a good start.

He could have stood there and seen which probation officer checked the sheet with his name on the top. Then Aaron would have been sure he had the right guy. He could have tracked the probation officer home from work and shot him in the head from across the street. It'd be easy.

But the plan would not work. Because Aaron Williams's

mother had not sent him to school regularly since the second grade and he could not read the names on the sheets or anything else. He looked around to see if there was anyone who might help him. But all he saw were unfriendly faces. Panic and shame went through him like electrical shocks. Everyone was looking at him. He was sure of it. They all knew he couldn't read. His heart started pounding and his face began sweating.

A very fat white man, wearing a fedora and a white polo shirt, came barging by. "Can I help you?" he asked.

Aaron could not speak. The fat man was looking right through him. He knew Aaron couldn't read. Aaron's mouth trembled and twisted. "What's the matter with you?" the fat man demanded.

Aaron backed away quickly, with his eyes cast down and his head shaking. He nearly fell over his own feet as he turned and ran for the elevators.

After Aaron got home, Darryl King and the others spent hours questioning him about what went wrong. It was Winston Murvin, Joanna's boyfriend, who finally got him to admit his reading panic. The others threw things and screamed at Aaron, but Winston took Aaron's face in his hands and smiled.

He said that Aaron was now the first man in the history of the drug business who failed to get ahead because he lacked a formal education.

58

Over the next few days, I find myself struggling more and more to hang on to some standard of patience and decency.

On the subway platform, I curse silently and clench my fists in anger. On the street, I'm getting rude and shoving people out of the way. And it's getting harder and harder to put on a civil face when I see Andrea after a day spent kicking ass in the field. Maybe I should consider this thing, Richard Silver's offering. At least that way I could afford one of those fucking ski vacations she's always talking about.

The last person who I should try and discuss this with is my father. He's busy stockpiling Gatorade in his basement for some imaginary race war. But you never know what's really driving you until you get there, so I call him and set up a time for us to go for a walk in Flushing Meadows Park.

He meets me early on a Saturday afternoon. Dozens of other men, all of whom look like divorced fathers, are playing with children they barely seem to know around the lake nearby.

"How come you never took me out like that when I was small?" I ask my dad.

"Ask a psychiatrist," he says sourly.

A sea gull flying over his head shrieks loudly. My father and I are wearing the exact same kind of blue windbreaker from Sears with the plaid lining, but for the first time I notice that I've developed two of his strangest old habits—not only do I carry a hundred things around in my pockets at all times, but I also never take my jacket off. He always said he kept his pockets stuffed and his jacket on because he thought he might get taken some place unexpectedly. Like Auschwitz or something. I don't know why I've fallen into doing the same thing.

"So what's it all about?" he says with his thick accent, walking a little bit ahead of me. "Why the big talk now?"

"I'm thinking about changing jobs maybe, and I wanted to talk it over with you."

"*Feh!*" He waves his arm and starts shuffling along again. "You want my advice now. I told you before not to take that *farchadat* job, but your mother raised you to be soft."

I hate it when he talks that way about Mom, but I don't feel like arguing about it now. A plane passes overhead and the traffic hums on the Van Wyck Expressway. The old man starts walking with the stiff-kneed gait of a man who's recently had surgery. Which he hasn't. We pass a lawn full of young people sunning themselves. More than half the women are wearing just bra-like halter tops and tight shorts, leaving their stomachs and thighs exposed. My father gazes across the landscape of flesh and raises a rigid arm and a clenched fist.

"Oh boy," he says. "If I were your age, ahhh!"

He nods as he navigates between the bike riders on the stone path called Robert Moses Walk, which leads to the World's Fair grounds. I wonder what I'm doing trading barbs with a crazy old man on a nice afternoon like this. The same question seems to occur to him at the same time.

"Enough standing on ceremony," he says. "What do you want from me?"

"Not much," I say a little sheepishly. "I just have some things going on in my life, and I wanted to see what you thought of them."

He plops himself down on a green bench along the side of the path and looks at me with mild curiosity. I notice his stomach is about the size of a small baby sitting on his lap.

I sit down beside him. "I'm seeing a girl now," I tell him. "She's very nice. You wouldn't like her, of course."

"Of course."

"But she likes nice things. She wants a good life. Things that cost money."

He sticks out his bottom lip. "So don't look at me," he says. "I'm retired. I don't have anything."

"Yeah, I know." Though I guess in some strange abstract way, I've been hoping he would suddenly turn out to be a millionaire, which would solve all my problems. "Anyway, she's come along at a peculiar time for me. Work's been very hard lately..."

He gives me a "what did you expect?" look.

"And then this other thing came up, which you can't tell anybody about."

He looks around in disbelief, with his sagging eyelids opened wide. "Who am I going to tell?" he says. "The mice in the kitchen?"

"It's just something that I'm trying to keep quiet."

He leans toward me a little. "What?"

"One of my clients is offering me a job."

My father is stunned. "Some schvartze's going to give you a job?"

"Well, who it is isn't so important," I say sharply. "He wants to keep his name quiet anyway. Anyway, the point is he wants me to...neglect my responsibilities. To look the other way."

"So?"

"So. I have a problem with that."

"Does this job pay well he's offering you?" he asks.

"Pretty well. Probably twice what I'm making now. But that's not the point even. I'd have some real power to do the things I want to, especially since he can't get involved directly. I could get to be like an assistant commissioner over at housing, or something."

He looks at me like he's suddenly discovered a dismembered animal sitting on the bench next to him. "Forget the housing, take the money," he says as if it's the most obvious thing in the world.

"I can't do that so easily."

"Why not?"

"It'd mean everything I tried to do before was wrong. I can't just give up like that."

His head goes up and down. Someone who didn't know him might think that he's nodding in agreement. But I know that my father actually just wants me to stop talking so he can interject his own vehement opinions.

"You wanna know what I think?" he says. "You wanna?"

"Sure. Yeah."

"Ideals are nice. I had a few when I was younger than you are now. But..." He clears his throat with a noisy hacking sound. "A man," he says finally, "does what he does..."

I can't bear to hear this again. The story about him almost killing the Polish carpenter in Auschwitz over a scrap of bread. The survivalist reduction of all right and wrong to his own material comfort. "I woke him up in the middle of the night and told him I would cut his throat from ear to ear with an aluminum knife while he slept," my father is saying. "They had him killed a little later anyway. He was too weak to work by then."

Whenever I hear this, it's like running straight into a brick wall. The same one I've spent my whole life trying to get past. I can't accept that I've ended up in the exact same place as him in spite of everything. "And you'd do just like me..."

"Hey, Pops," I say. "Skip it, will you? I know how it ends."

"You never understand," he mutters. "*I'm the only one.*"

I stop talking and just stare at him for a minute. "*I'm the only one,*" he said. It's like catching a glimpse of something shimmering out in the middle of the lake. Maybe the reason he's been this way for so long is because he feels guilty for surviving when so many of the other people he knew died in the camps. But the moment is over between us before it really gets started. He's already walking away and cursing me under his breath.

"You already know what you'll do," he says coldly as a softball rolls up to his feet. "Why ask me anything?"

A little boy, not yet four years old, comes toddling toward us in search of the softball. My father bends an inch or two at the waist, grunts in discomfort, and then kicks the ball past the little boy who has to go chasing after it the other way.

"I'm sorry," I say quietly.

"If you don't want to listen to me, why did you call me here today?" he asks before he clears his throat and spits on the stone path.

I have to think about that one for a while myself. Why ask him about something in which he has no vested interest? Why expect him to behave any differently now than he has for the past sixty-five years, or however long he's actually been alive? If I'd had a black client who had as hard a life and as many problems as my father, I'd probably just feel sorry for him. So why do I keep resenting the old man and picking on him?

When the answer finally comes to me, it seems so stupid and banal I want to crawl under the bench. What I want from my father is a scrap of affection, something to take with me as I go back out and face the world. But he's too old to change. He never was the affectionate type anyway. I know that, but I can't help myself. I sit there, feeling ten years old and helpless again.

More sea gulls fly past us and an abrupt wind shivers the trees. Somewhere in the distance, a brass band is playing. The sun glints off the Unisphere, two hundred yards away. My father zips up his windbreaker like he's getting ready to go.

"So that's it?" he says. "That's the big talk?"

"Well," I tell him finally. "I'm your only son and you're the only close relative I have, I guess. I just thought you might want to know what I've been up to."

"So." He stands up. "Now I know."

* * *

If anything, my talk with my father strengthens my resolve to hold out a little bit longer against Richard Silver. Instead, I find myself looking for more dangerous assignments at work, because in the back of my mind I'm hoping maybe I'll get hurt and that'll take away the pressure to make a decision.

When the sun comes up on Monday morning, I'm behind the wheel of the K car, fighting with Bill Neill and Angel about where we should go first. Bill wants to see a Colombian pick-pocket named Pablo in Washington Heights, because the guy used to be one of his clients. I want to follow up on a tip that there's an informant on St. Nicholas Avenue who's willing to talk about where Darryl King is, provided the reward money is real.

"Come on, Baum," Bill says as I make the turn onto West Street and head uptown. "We're supposed to leave all that Darryl King stuff to the police. It's their investigation."

"But the tip came from a probation client," I tell him.

"Who?" Bill asks.

"One of Cathy Brody's people," Angel explains. "I think she threatened him with a two-by-four."

"Anyway, it's our guy," I argue. "And no one said we're not supposed to follow up on our own leads."

"Ah, you're just pissed off because the judge made you look bad on this Darryl King case." Bill puts his leg up on the dashboard as we pass the meat-packing district and see the male prostitutes straggling back from the docks. "It's just politics."

"So what?" I say to him. "Are you scared?"

Bill sighs and stares out the window. "No, Baum, I'm not scared," he says. "I'd just like you to be the first one through the door this time."

The informant lives in a six-story gray stone building at the foot of Sugar Hill. Compared to a lot of the other places we've been, this is not too bad. It still seems like a working-class neighborhood with grocery stores and laundromats nearby and hardly any garbage in the street. In fact, I think I remember reading something about how the tenants in one of these apartment houses bought their building from the city and fixed it up as a co-op after their landlord abandoned them.

The informant's apartment is on the second floor and as Bill requested, I do the knocking.

After a couple of seconds, I hear someone moving around inside and a dog barking. Bill gestures for me to stand to the side a little and I start to get a little nervous. What if it's a pit bull in there that's going to come jumping out? Or worse, if this is somebody who knows Darryl King, we could be walking right into a hail of automatic weapons fire. Part of me wants to stop knocking and run downstairs right now. But the other part wants to stay and show it isn't scared.

Slowly the door starts to open a little way. The small oval face of an old man with dusky skin and avid eyes peers out at us. He won't remove the chain from the door. Instead, he insists on talking to me through the narrow space.

"Excuse me, sir, you called us," I say, starting to relax a little. "Didn't you?"

"Yes, I did," he tells me in a voice like a creaky hinge. "I believe I know how to find what you're looking for."

"Then why don't you just let us in?"

"I'd rather have you stay out there," he says.

From inside the apartment, that dog keeps barking. Sounds like a big dog. Maybe a rottweiler. Barking continuously, as though he doesn't need to draw a breath. I glance back at Bill and Angel and get a couple of indifferent looks.

"Sir, you have some information for us?" I ask.

"Yes, I do," he begins. "Now I wanna take you all back to Fort Bragg, North Carolina, 1943."

"Yes."

"A man buried a pair of shoes."

"Uh-huh."

I catch a whiff of something like old peanut butter wafting out of the informant's apartment. Behind me, I hear Bill mumbling, "Fuckin' wing-nut."

"Now you go there and you find those shoes," the informant

is saying. "And then we'll talk about the man you're looking for."

This has been a complete waste of time. If he didn't live here already, I'd slam the door on the old man. I should've known the offer of a Darryl King reward would bring out every crank in the city. The dog still hasn't stopped barking. I wonder if one of the neighbors is going to come out and shoot it.

"Is that it?" I ask.

"That's it," the man says. "You find them shoes, you'll have your answer. But let me know if you hear anything about some socks."

59

Darryl had been smoking crack and arguing with his mother steadily for two days. Now she was passed out in the other room and he was almost ready to crash.

He looked out the window in the kitchen.

The action was picking up on First Avenue. A man with hair like a bunch of corkscrews was pacing back and forth, steering people into a building that Darryl knew was a rival crack house. Many of the customers did not go far after leaving the brownstone. They just stopped in a doorway, took out their vials and pipes, and began flicking their lighters.

Darryl King could see the points of light going on and off, like fireflies in the night.

At about the same time, a woman named Thelma McDonald had a much closer perspective. She lived on the top floor of the brownstone and she could see the crackheads on the street directly under her window. Her two small boys, in first and second grades, had to walk past by them every day on their way home from school. But this night, there seemed to be more of them than usual. McDonald, a thirty-four-year-old bus dispatcher, called her local police precinct and asked them to send a car by.

* * *

Darryl King got hold of Bobby "House" Kirk and told him
to take care of the problem. Bobby rounded up a few of his
friends right away and they chased the steerer off the block
with knives and baseball bats. They directed the remaining
customers diagonally across the street to the Fortress, where
the King family's dealers were operating.

An hour later, the police car that Thelma McDonald had
requested stopped by outside the brownstone. By then, the
street was nearly empty and the cops did not notice anything
unusual. They drove off.

By nine o'clock, Darryl started feeling hungry again. For
what, he wasn't sure. He went into the back bedroom to ask
his mother to fix him something, but she was still facedown
on the pillow and she wasn't getting up anytime soon.

He started pacing back and forth in the kitchen. Getting
more and more useless and angry by the minute, the way he
used to in the foster home. It was her fault for letting him go
anyway. And now that she had him back, she expected him
to act like it was all okay and everything in between didn't
happen.

He opened up the refrigerator and looked through it. The
old people who'd lived here before had kept it well stocked.
They had greens, milk, catsup, cider, chicken, and macaroni
and cheese in a round plastic container. But they'd been gone
for weeks now and most of the food was spoiled.

He shut the door so the smell wouldn't be so bad and he
started going through the cupboards. Nothing much was there
either. Spices, tea bags, syrup. Then he saw the familiar orange
box that had the picture of the old black guy with the white
hair. Uncle Ben. He looked a little like the old guy who used
to live in this apartment. Darryl took the orange box out and
shook it. It sounded like it was still halfway full of rice.

He listened for his mother stirring in the other room. But

she was just talking in her sleep a little. Maybe she'd be hungry by the time she got up. And maybe if he had a hot plate of rice ready for her, she wouldn't give him so much shit. It was hard living close with somebody this way.

He stood there for a minute, trying to remember how they used to do it at the foster home. It didn't seem so hard. All you needed was a stove, some water and salt, and then it was almost as easy as making crack.

He rummaged around in the cabinets and found a big steel pot and filled it with water. A pigeon landed on the windowsill outside and looked at him suspiciously. He turned on the stove and set down the pot of water. Now came the ingredients. He emptied the box of Uncle Ben's rice into the pot and then found a salt shaker and poured that in for a while. The pigeon cooed like it was trying to warn him about something. Rice tasted kind of bland, he remembered. All of a sudden he wished he could've had something sweet instead. His mother always preferred eating candy bars. But they didn't even have cookies here.

It still didn't seem like enough for a whole meal. He went back to the refrigerator and opened up the freezer. There were a couple of white packages. He took one of them out and unwrapped it. Pork chops, frozen solid. He found a roasting pan in the cabinet and put them in. This part he wasn't as sure about, but it was worth a try. He turned on the oven and shoved in the pork chops.

The pigeon seemed to be nodding at him now. He sat down on an old wooden chair by the kitchen table so he could watch the stove. When he lowered his head a little, he could see the burner's blue and orange flames dancing off the bottom of the pot with the rice in it.

They were trying to hypnotize him, those flames. He felt himself getting pulled back into that dream again. The one where he was driving along in the Jeep through the middle of nowhere. No buildings, no streets, no sky. That's when a girl came up to him on the passenger's side of the car. She was really fine, like the girls in the M. C. Hammer video, with their flat little stomachs and their bouncing titties. So she got in beside him and before he knew it, she'd unzipped his fly and she was busy sucking his dick. It was really nice.

But then she did something really fucked up. She bit down on it. And then she lifted her head and it was still in her mouth. He got very scared, even though it didn't hurt yet. And here was something even more fucked up: When the girl spoke, she had his mother's voice. She said, "Darryl, what the hell you doing?"

He was about to start crying, but that made her angrier. "Darryl, what's up with this shit?" she shouted. "You trying to kill us all?" This time, the voice didn't sound like it was coming from a dream. It sounded real.

He slowly opened his eyes. There was smoke everywhere. He looked over at the pot on the stove. Streams of whitish gunk were coming down the sides and the lid was rattling a little. Most of the actual smoke was coming out of the oven. It smelled like a body was burning in there. He had no idea how long he'd been sleeping, but it was even darker than before outside now.

He rubbed his eyes and coughed a couple of times. Through the smoke, he could see his mother turning off the stove and throwing open the window. She was mad again.

"The fuck's the matter with you?" she said.

"Damn, that's a lot of smoke," Darryl grumbled. He still could barely see anything.

"It's a good thing them smoke detectors don't work in here."

"Why?"

She put her hands on her hips and hollered, "Because then they bring fuckin' fire department up here, and they'd find us and take us all away!"

"All right, all right," Darryl said, twisting in his seat, so he wouldn't be facing her voice. "Fuck you all. I'm never cooking again."

60

The disintegration continues.

After the episode with the shoe-obsessed informant and a couple of more routine field visits, Bill and Angel drop me off in Chelsea so I can look in on one of my other old clients: Ricky Velez, the little token sucker, who's attending an Alternative to Prison facility in the neighborhood.

They're supposed to be helping him with his reading, but instead they've got him finger painting and lip syncing to rap records at a talent show.

When I walk in, one of the bearded counselors is up on the stage, strumming a guitar and braying "Blowin' in the Wind" while dozens of bored young felons yell at him and throw things at each other. It's like a gruesome parody of what probation was supposed to be. After one of the little hoods gets up and starts doing a rap number about the importance of not missing your day in court and the excellence of Darryl King's marksmanship, I grab Ricky and drag him out of there.

I don't know if it's Darryl who put me off social work. I just know since I ran into him, things haven't been quite the same.

Just to end the day right, I get mugged coming in my building by a Hispanic crackhead with the sniffles. I don't see him waiting for me in the shadows. He just shoves me against the tiled wall and punches me in the nose before I know what's happening. I'm so busy holding my face that I don't get a good look at him as he takes my wallet and bounds down the front steps, almost jauntily.

Luckily, my nose isn't broken and the swelling isn't so bad, but I have this funny feeling inside. It's not that I'm angry or sad. I just feel different. And it isn't the mugging or the beating that did it. I think it was the sight of that pathetic bearded guy up with his guitar in front of the uninterested kids.

What's the point anymore? Fuck these people.

I fill out violation forms against Charlie Simms and Maria Sanchez.

"Are you sure you want to do this?" Ms. Lang asks me when I give her the papers the next morning.

"Why not?"

"I thought these were two of your favorite clients." She looks over her half glasses to peer at me.

"Used to be," I say, feeling the vinegar in my veins.

I take a good look around her office. It's not much bigger than my old cubicle, but she has all her degrees and graduation pictures up on the wall. I notice how young and pretty she was in her cap and gown. It's sad to see her sitting at the desk now, looking worn-down and defeated.

"So what happened with these people?" Ms. Lang asks, putting my papers into a wooden tray marked "Out."

"They fucked up."

She plucks the papers out of the tray and examines them again with her eyes narrowed. "You know, I think something happens sometimes to people who work here too long or too hard," she says in a slow, reflective voice. "They forget what they're supposed to be doing here and they take their frustration out on the clients. They see the symptoms, but they forget about the cause."

"What do you mean?" I say a little sullenly.

"Oh, they don't see the racism in the system," she says as

though it's something she's thought about so often that she doesn't get worked up about it anymore. "They don't see how our young black children go into schools that have nothing to teach them about their own people. They don't learn about Marcus Garvey or Crispus Attucks..."

I shift my weight from one foot to the other, feeling like I've been called into the principal's office. I'm in no mood for being lectured to. "Does all this go for Darryl King too?" I say with some impatience.

"Maybe. Maybe he'd be a different kind of person in another zip code."

"I doubt it."

"Well, I don't think anyone could say for sure," she says tolerantly.

This is all making me wince, which in turn makes my nose sting where the guy hit me. "So do you or don't you have a problem with the way I did my violations?" I say finally, stepping forward. "Because if you have a complaint, I'd like to hear it."

"No." She sighs, putting the papers down in the tray again and taking off her glasses. "I'm not accusing you of anything. I just hope you're not settling any scores here."

"Of course not."

"Good," she says. "There are too few good guys left. I'd hate to see you go over to the other side."

61

As the hour got later, the cars from New Jersey started coming in over the George Washington Bridge and driving up to the curb near the Fortress.

Two white guys in a black Trans Am pulled up behind a brand-new Oldsmobile Cutlass Supreme that was being washed by a crazy-looking black guy with a rat's nest of hair and a tangled beard.

The white guy who'd been driving the Trans Am got out and hitched up his chinos. He looked around nervously and then walked up to the crazy old man who was washing the Cutlass.

"Yo, mistah," said the white guy in chinos, who had a brush cut hairdo and wore a red New Jersey Devils hockey jersey. "You know where we can go cop around here?"

"Wha?" the crazy black guy sounded like he had rocks in his mouth. His eyes were clouded over and he was sweating profusely. He carried himself like something was broken inside of him, but he wasn't as old as he had first looked. At most, he was forty-three.

The other white guy had gotten out of the Trans Am and was standing next to his friend and the black guy. "We wanna catch a buzz, man," said the second white guy, who wore distressed jeans and Gucci loafers. "Where do we go around here?"

The crazy black guy looked scared and waved his squeegee at them. He was saying something that was hard to understand in his dull roar of a voice.

"What's he saying?" the white guy in the distressed jeans asked his friend.

"Sounds like 'blow dead bears,'" said the one in the Devils jersey.

"Your mother blows dead bears," said the one in the distressed jeans.

The black guy repeated what he'd been saying and pointed with his squeegee at the building's entrance. This time, the white guys understood him.

"He means, 'go in there,'" said the one in the Devils jersey. "You scared?"

"No way, man."

They thanked the car washer and walked into the building. They found a thirteen-year-old boy wearing a red terry-cloth Kangol hat leaning against the wall. Clearly the man in charge. The white guy in the Devils jersey negotiated with him for a few seconds and then slipped him three twenties. The kid sauntered off to a nearby stairwell, as if he'd suddenly lost interest in the white guys. They stood there side by side for a few seconds in the lobby, not even daring to look at each other.

The one in the distressed jeans began staring at the tangled yowls of graffiti on the walls by the elevators. "'D.K. All the Way,'" he read. "What's that mean?"

"I dunno," his friend told him.

By now the kid in the red Kangol had returned. He looked around and discreetly handed the guy in the red jersey a plastic bag with six vials of crack in it. "You all best get going," he told both white guys. "There's some dangerous types around here, man."

The two white guys walked quickly from the building and got back into their black Trans Am. As they started to pull away, the one in the Devils jersey leaned out the window and handed a five-dollar bill to the black guy who'd been washing the Cutlass.

"Thanks, dude."

The guy took the bill without a sound and they cruised up to the traffic light on the corner. "Were you scared in there?" said the one in the distressed jeans.

"No," said his friend in the hockey jersey. "Were you?"

"No way, man. That was fun."

"Yeah, let's come back again soon."

The one in the Devils jersey slipped a Bruce Springsteen cassette into the tape player. "Definitely, man. Definitely."

Back at the curb, the black guy who'd been washing the Cutlass put down his squeegee. He glanced after the New Jersey car's glowing taillights and stared up at the sky to make sure no one was watching him. Then he slowly took out the five-dollar bill he'd just been handed and gave it a good sniff.

Back upstairs at the Fortress apartment in the Charles J. Stone Houses, Darryl King was starting to get restless.

Hip-hop music was pounding out of the speakers in the living room and the sweet crack smell filled the air. The occasion was Winston's going-away party. The Jamaican was going to be taking Joanna to Miami to spend a week in the sun and pick up a shipment, leaving the kids with their grandmother at the Fortress.

Two dozen people floated around the apartment. Winston was whirling around barefoot to the music, with his dreadlocks flying through the air. Bobby "House" Kirk walked in and headed for the kitchen, muttering, "Everybody is on my dick," as he grabbed his own crotch. He'd just had a second letter *H* carved on the other side of his scalp and he was annoyed that nobody had complimented him on it. A damp, naked woman wandered in from another room. She'd been having sex with two dealers who refused to give her any more crack. She stood right in front of Bobby and pleaded.

"You want it, get busy, bitch," he said, unzipping his fly. She blew him for twenty seconds and then he gave her a crack pipe.

Nobody took much notice of Darryl, growing angry and intense, by the window. He'd been steadily losing sleep and weight over the past few days. "What I wanna know," he said very loudly, "is when do you all get going?"

" 'S what I'm saying," Aaron Williams lisped. With his broadening shoulders and hips, he was getting to be the same size as Darryl.

"And I'm telling you. P.O. or no P.O. I want that probation officer to go down!" He made a big sweeping arc with his arm and pointed down. "You understand what I'm saying?"

Darryl had not been outside since he'd moved into the apartment with his mother a couple of weeks before. The claustrophobia was making him crazy, and the twenty-five vials of crack he was smoking every day were not helping. He kept talking about the same things over and over again.

One was breaking off from the family and starting his own business. He'd said a lot of things to Bobby and Aaron about getting a new van, a shipment of Uzis, and some Israeli listening devices once he was free to move around. But what truly consumed him was the idea of his probation officer.

He could still hear Mr. Bomb's voice telling him, "I'm gonna personally send you to jail," and calling him "Dooky." But he was still having trouble remembering Mr. Bomb's face.

For weeks he'd been wrestling with the problem; breaking it down, reaching for its heart, tearing it out. He got rid of what other people called "common sense"; he knew that was just a distraction. Now he was dealing straight up with the truth. And the truth was that his probation officer was the reason he was confined. So Mr. Bomb had to die before Darryl could be free. Otherwise, he would just stay in Darryl's head, ticking away until he blew everything up.

"You wanna beer, D.?" Aaron asked, heading for the refrigerator.

"No, man, I ain't with that," Darryl told him. "I got too much shit on my mind already."

He was about to say something else about the P.O. when he turned around and saw Ernie Thompson, the guy who washed his car, staring at him with the squeegee still wet in his hand.

What Ernie wanted to say to him was simply, "When are you going to pay me?" But with his terrible speech impediment, it just sounded like he was imitating a garbage disposal and Darryl ignored him. "Atomic Dog" was playing on the stereo now and even more people were dancing.

When Ernie tried a second time to make himself understood, Darryl whipped around like he was about to hit him. "Man, get this motherfucker away from me," he said to no one in particular. "I can't stand being around people that are ill."

Ernie Thompson hadn't always been this way. When he was young, he appeared to be moving toward his destiny with the certainty of an arrow finding its target. He zoomed through the Head Start school programs in the sixties and four Ivy League universities had offered him full scholarships. He was on his way to becoming an engineer and a teacher, and his diabetes hardly seemed like an obstacle. But just before Christmas in his senior year, he'd run into some old friends and they convinced him to try shooting heroin. Since they were all junkies anyway, they barely noticed when he still hadn't woken up twelve hours later.

After he'd been in a coma for three days in the hospital, the doctors began to talk about what kind of brain damage he might have sustained. Most of his major motor reflexes were impaired in some way and his speech would never be the same. For the rest of his life, his basic intelligence was trapped in a mentally retarded man's body. Out of shame, he hid in his mother's house for the next twenty years or so, refusing to see or talk to old friends. It was only after his mother died a few months before that he was forced to leave home and get a job washing Darryl King's car for a hundred dollars a day.

* * *

Now, it was a week since he'd been paid and he was getting upset. Working for a drug dealer was hard enough on his pride, but having to beg for his proper pay was almost more than he could bear. He started tapping furiously on Darryl's shoulder, trying to get his attention. This time Darryl didn't hesitate. He spun around and in one quick motion hit Ernie just below the chin with his balled-up left hand.

Ernie went down with a loud gulp and for a moment, the party stopped and everyone looked over to see if he'd swallowed his tongue or something. Darryl was standing over him, like he was going to kick him in the stomach for good measure.

"Want some more?" Darryl said. "You want some more?"

As he lay there in a fetal position, Ernie kept burbling something over and over again that sounded like, "I can't find a land." But everyone knew that couldn't be what he meant.

"Dog-ass motherfucker," said Darryl.

Aaron helped Ernie get back up to his feet before he threw him out of the apartment. As he left, his voice was still saying that same thing. Darryl turned back to the window and looked down at the street, as if he expected his probation officer to come strolling up the block at any minute.

The music came on again. Aaron had returned and was standing beside him. "Hey," Darryl said to him. "What was the guy saying before?"

Aaron looked at him anxiously. "He say, 'You can't do that to a man.'"

"Oh." Darryl considered this for a second and then let it go. "Yes, I can," he said sadly.

62

"So did I tell you about the one we had today?"

"No," says Andrea. "What was it?"

"Another informant . . . Snake Man. We came to his apartment at noon and he was already drunk and slithering around on the floor in a trail of his own slime. He's only got one leg, I think. Bill was the one who wanted to call him Snake Man . . ."

We're sitting at the bar at a high-priced midtown hotel waiting for her parents to arrive. In the background, there's a murmur of low-key conversation and a Cole Porter song playing on the piano.

"Oh, why don't you just give up?" Andrea says.

I look in the mirror behind the counter. My hair's falling all over my forehead. I try to sweep it back, so I'll look presentable. My nose is still a little sore and one of my eyelids is sagging. As I close in on thirty, I'm starting to look more and more like my father. In the rest of the reflection, I see the bottles lit from behind and the way Andrea is looking at me. I hope we can get home early and make love tonight. Those have been the only times lately that I've felt anything at all. She runs her fingers up and down my arm and smiles at me. The piano player segues nicely into "Do Nothing Till You Hear from Me."

Maybe I could enjoy moments like this a little more if I wasn't thinking about Darryl King all the time.

"I think we're getting closer," I say.

She looks askance and smooths her black silk dress. "Snake Man," she says, as if the very thought of him makes her unhappy.

"That's my guy."

"You know you're starting to get a little weird yourself, Baum."

The bartender, wearing a starched white shirt and a black bow tie, asks me if I need another beer and I nod.

"Isn't it up to the cops to find Darryl?" she asks.

"Yeah, but I was the one who put all the work into the case."

She gives me an exasperated look but then decides not to pursue it. Just as well. It's too hard to explain to anybody. I notice a gold-plated cigarette lighter has been left on the counter. I flip the top and light my cigarette with the open flame. When Andrea looks away again, I drop it into my pocket.

"So what're you doing at work?" I ask her between drags.

"Nothing." She curls her fingers around a wineglass. "Just filing V.O.P. papers, talking to people. You know, finishing things off."

"That's right, you're going back to school...In a couple of weeks, right?"

"So that's another reason you oughta spend a little more time back at the office."

The bartender brings me a mug of beer and I drink about half of it on the first gulp. Across the room, the piano player is finishing the Duke Ellington song and going into the old Beatles' song "Ob-La-Di, Ob-La-Da [Life Goes On]." I wonder if he knows "Helter-Skelter." It might clear the bar, but it would make a lot more sense to me after the last few weeks.

That starts me thinking about the things that've been going on in the field lately, and as I'm sitting here, I find I just have to let out a little bit of steam. "I know you think it's stupid with Snake Man and all, but we are getting closer to Darryl," I say abruptly. "The informant who we're going to see tomorrow sounds dynamite."

"Oh, did you speak to him?"

"No, Angel did. We're seeing the guy in the morning at the Charles J. Stone Houses over by the river. Angel said the guy sounded great... when you could understand what he was saying. He had some kind of speech impediment, I think."

"And what makes this one so wonderful? Is he into oat bran or cactuses or something? You've talked to every other freak in the city. What's this one's specialty?"

"I don't know." I hear myself sounding grumpy and defensive about our little tipster. "This guy says he's actually seen Darryl and talked to him lately."

"Oh how interesting," she replies with a sardonic edge. "And what's been on Darryl's mind lately?"

"The guy says Darryl's been talking about his probation officer a lot..."

She laughs a little incredulously. "It's a good thing this doesn't feed into your vanity or anything," she says.

"Go ahead," I tell her, noticing I have a little grit on one of my contact lenses. "Act like it's a joke. I don't know why I bothered to tell you."

"Well, I don't think it's a joke," Andrea says with a sigh. "I think it's dangerous and I don't understand why you won't just let it drop."

"I can't."

"Why not?"

I look down the length of the bar and see a couple of older women on the way in, both wearing a lot of jewelry and makeup. "You wouldn't understand," I say, keeping my voice low.

"Try me."

"I don't know." For the first time in weeks, I start reaching down into myself and trying to figure out what's there. "It's like Darryl and I have this thing going on between us. And it's been going on all summer long."

"What's been going on all summer?"

I put the cigarette down and just watch it smolder for a while. "You know," I say, "before I met Darryl, I never used to get scared . . . I'm not talking about physical fear. I mean, scared because I used to be so sure I was doing the right thing with my life. But I don't feel that way anymore. I look around and I see everyone who I tried to help is going right down the drain like we never met. And that scares me."

"But there's only so much you can do for people, Baum," Andrea says, shaking her head. "You said so yourself. You can't expect them to change just because you want them to . . ."

"I know," I say, putting out the cigarette and gulping down my beer. "But what I worry about is what it's doing up here."

I put my finger up to my temple, like I'm pointing a gun at it. So much confusion whirling around up there. I try to douse it with the rest of my beer. Andrea's giving me the kind of look a security guard would give a suspicious package left alone at an airport.

"It's like . . . I'm turning hard inside," I tell her. "You know? I get so angry with them." I shake my fist in frustration.

I know people on the nearby barstools are turning to look at me, but I'm on a roll now and I can't stop. "I don't wanna be like that," I say. "But I'm in the middle of all this shit and what it's doing is changing me. You know? I went in there to change them and instead they're changing me."

She looks over my shoulder at a large well-dressed black man and a slim blond woman in a bolero jacket coming into the bar.

"I wanna tell you something," I say softly, staring straight ahead at my empty beer mug. "The other day, I went to see one of my old people. Charlie Simms, the one I told you about. And he starts saying this shit about Darryl and Jews and black people. And I don't know what happened . . . I just snapped."

"It's all right," she says, touching my cheek and looking back at the black man and the white woman who've stopped to talk to somebody at one of the nearby tables.

"It wasn't all right," I say, hitting the counter with my fist.

"I started yelling at him. He yelled back at me and we got into it . . . And the things I was saying to him . . ." I just stop short of telling her I almost called him nigger. "I mean, I really lost control there for a minute. I mean, I slammed him against the wall. I wanted to fuck him up. You know? I really wanted to hurt him . . . That's what was in my mind."

I sit back on the stool and shake my head. Andrea is looking bewildered, as if to say, where did all of this come from? I'm not sure myself.

"It's just these . . . bad thoughts," I tell her a little more calmly. "It's like I've been on this weird trip with Darryl. And I just want it to be over. I wanna settle things between him and me so I'll know where I am. And that way I can go on with the rest of my life."

She holds my hand, but I don't quite feel it. Mentally I'm in another place.

"Well," Andrea says, looking sympathetic and a little overwhelmed at the same time, "it certainly sounds like you need to get your shit together."

"Yeah, I suppose one way or the other, either Darryl or me will wind up getting our fucking head blown off and that'll be the end of it."

I feel a heavy hand on my shoulder and I almost jump off the stool. The black man and the white woman are standing behind me, giving me knowing smiles.

"Steven," Andrea says. "I want you to meet my parents."

63

"Sometime she just sleep for hour and hours," Alisha Watkins said, looking down at her two-month-old baby. "I think she never wake up. But then like other time...she just cry and cry, like she crazy or something..."

"Maybe she's sick," Darryl King's mother said indifferently.

They were standing by the kitchen sink, smoking cigarettes and drinking coffee cups full of Bacardi. It was just after eleven at the Charles J. Stone Houses. Darryl, Aaron, and Bobby were sitting at the dining room table, passing around a 9 mm and a Glock machine pistol. The two women were watching them carefully through the window-sized opening in the wall.

"Nobody else shoots Mr. Bomb," Darryl was saying once more. "That's my job."

Darryl's mother looked out at him and shook her head. "That's all he talk about now," she told Alisha in a hushed voice. " 'When are we gonna shoot 'im? How we gonna shoot 'im?' "

"He just concerned, that's all," said Alisha, who had her hair cut in a bowl shape and wore long eyelashes. "He just gotta lot of concern on his mind."

In the other room, Bobby pulled the cartridge out of the Glock and dropped it on the table.

"Don't you scratch that table, Bobby," Darryl's mother shouted from the kitchen. "You don't live here."

She took another sip of Bacardi and turned back to her son's girlfriend and the baby. "I just want for him to be happy, you know what I'm saying?" she told Alisha. "But sometime, I think he get so concerned he gonna go and shoot me."

"Darryl wouldn't do that," Alisha said, rocking the baby in her arms. "He got a good heart."

"Well, I know that," his mother said a little resentfully. "I just worry sometimes."

The air was getting dense and humid now, like a thunderstorm was about to break out. In the other room, Darryl was still talking to the others like he expected the probation officer just to show up on his doorstep. Bobby and Aaron were playing along with him so he wouldn't get mad again.

Two flies chased each other around a light fixture and the television showed people throwing a parade for a famous mobster who'd just been acquitted of trying to have a man killed. There were fireworks and champagne everywhere.

"Living large," said Bobby.

In the kitchen, Alisha was gently wiping the baby's head with a damp cloth. The child was still sleeping, but both her tiny fists were balled up like she was in a rage. "You think she look like Darryl?" Alisha asked.

Darryl's mother pursed her lips and looked down at her granddaughter. "She have his mouth," she said.

"Well, I hope she don't have his temper."

"That's for sure," Darryl's mother told her.

Alisha put the baby down on the table and saw it was time to change the diaper again. "I wanna raise my baby to be more like calm," she said, reaching for a tissue.

"Yeah, I wished I'd have done that too," Darryl's mother said, like it was something she'd just thought of. She drank the rest of her Bacardi and poured herself another one.

In the other room, they were almost finished loading the weapons and Darryl was saying that everyone in the organization should show up at the apartment tomorrow morning for a business meeting and strategy session.

"Nine-thirty," Darryl said.

"Why you put it so early?" Bobby complained. "I wanna sleep."

"So go to sleep early tonight," Darryl said. "You got a job now."

In the kitchen, Darryl's mother rolled up the sleeves of her yellow blouse she'd taken from the previous tenants' closet and looked over at her son's girlfriend.

"Well, I ain't gonna be around tomorrow," said Alisha Watkins as she got through putting on the new diaper and throwing away the old one. "I gotta take the baby to the hospital. The doctor say maybe she sick because I smoked crack when I was pregnant."

"So she's addicted?" Darryl's mother asked.

"Yeah, I guess," Alisha said. "I just hope my social worker don't find out. Then I will never hear the end of it."

64

For most of the night, I sit up in bed, studying Andrea's sleeping profile in the moonlight.

I can scarcely believe the symmetry of her features or the softness of her skin as she lies there next to me. I can feel the warmth from her body even when she's a few inches away. She tucks an arm under my side and rolls toward me with a slumbering sigh. Her cheek rests on my thigh, and her hair spills out across the bedspread. A garbage truck calls out in the night, but otherwise there's silence outside.

For a moment, I feel absolutely still inside. I never want to move again. I want to stay here in the sanctuary of this bed forever, feeling safe and protected, with Andrea by my side. Darryl King, Richard Silver, and the rest of the outside world can go to hell.

Andrea moans again and hugs my leg. I touch her face lightly with my fingertips. I still don't completely understand why she came home with me after the horrible things I said tonight, but somehow she's forgiven me.

I try thinking about what it would be like to live quietly with her. I imagine a parallel life, a route that I didn't take. One in which I somehow manage to get into the right school and get a good job. In which I marry Andrea and provide her with a home with a backyard and a car and kayaking vacations and anything else she wants. In which I come home from work before six every night and never lose sleep worrying about anybody else's problems besides my own or my children's. A family man.

It's probably a longer life than the one I'm living now, and certainly a happier one. I wonder if it's too late to call Richard Silver. What he's offering me can make all that real. So that I never have to go out and face the Darryl Kings of the world again.

But I don't reach for the phone, and as the clock near my bed flicks past 3:30 I start to get an uneasy sense of anticipation. Like a boxer the night before a fight or a soldier before a battle. The informant says Darryl's been talking about his probation officer. Angel says he believes the guy. We're getting closer to Darryl. I know it. It won't be long now. I feel like I'm standing on a precipice, looking down.

I start to get scared again and I tell myself it's not too late to pull back. I can try calling in sick and staying in bed with Andrea all day. We can lie there in the morning sunlight, giggling, making love, and planning a new life together while somebody else goes looking for Darryl King. But the more I think about it, the more impractical the plan seems. Even if I could convince Andrea to stay here, I know I'd feel guilty and ashamed if I didn't go with Bill and the others to find the informant. I started the Darryl King case and I need to have a part in ending it.

After that, I promise myself, I'll think about making a new life for Andrea and me. If she'll have me.

As the sky slowly lightens and birds begin to sing, my decision becomes clear. I have to go. I lean down and kiss Andrea's lips. Her breath is heavy and sweet and she sleepily puts her arms around me.

"Is it time already?" she murmurs.

65

Darryl King woke with a start and a loud throbbing in his ears.

At first, he thought it was his heart pounding double time from all the crack he'd smoked the night before. Then he realized somebody's car stereo downstairs had the bass turned all the way up, so it sounded like a giant heartbeat on wheels.

He was pissed about being awake. For a second, he thought about finding his 9 mm and firing a couple of rounds out the window. He'd been having a nice dream.

Now he couldn't remember what it was.

66

At ten o'clock, on a morning when the city seems dipped in bacon grease, I follow Angel, Bill, and four other field service officers into the lobby of Building C of the Charles J. Stone Houses. *The Fortress* is spray-painted above the entranceway in bold black letters. A forbidding name for another numbingly dull building in a numbingly dull city housing project. Three teenaged boys loiter by the front door, watching us carefully. One of them, a jumpy teenager with a flattop and a harelip, opens his eyes wide and goes dashing for the stairwell door. I think I've seen him somewhere before, but I can't remember when.

It gives me an uneasy feeling. "What do you think that's all about?" I ask, trying not to sound so hyped-up.

"Ah, he probably thought we're cops and he's carrying drugs on him," Bill Neill grunts. "For crying out loud, don't make a federal case out of everything."

I got myself up with three cups of coffee this morning and I've been riding on a wave of fear and adrenaline ever since. I almost threw a petty thief down a flight of stairs while we were taking him in a couple of hours ago, and since then everybody keeps telling me, "Cool out, cowboy." But all I can think about is Darryl and how I can't wait to get my hands on him. It's not even rational anymore. He's just this thing standing in the middle of my life, and I have to get rid of him.

Let's deal with them on their terms, is the way I'm looking at it now. They slap us in the face, let's kick them in the nuts. It's all right with me. I know the old way doesn't work anymore.

"Where's our police backup?" I ask.

"Hey, Baum," Bill says, furrowing his brow, "we're just talking to a potential informant here. If you're scared, you can sit in the car outside. It's probably just gonna be the guy who buried the rest of Shoe Man's shoes."

I point out where it says "D.K. All the Way" on the wall by the elevators. "Does that look like nothing?"

"Ah, people write all sorts of shit on the walls," Bill says. "If you grew up in a project, you'd know that, Baum."

I don't like him pulling ethnic rank on me like that. I wonder if this is the start of a subtle rift between us. "I'd still like to know where these cops are."

We just recently began taking special precautions on these investigative fishing expeditions. After Darryl's big shoot-out and the incident where the cop shot Jamal Perkins, there was a flurry of interdepartmental memos and a bunch of high-level meetings with the brass and community groups. So the other day, the commissioner declared that we should go out in units of at least four and have at least one senior police officer on hand when we go looking for Darryl. I guess they're worried that otherwise one of us might shoot another kid or something.

Bill frowns at me and tries to raise the police on his walkie-talkie. For a few seconds, all we hear is a snowstorm of static and then a cop's voice cuts through. "Where the hell are you guys?" he says. "We're waiting for you on the twelfth floor."

Bill clicks the radio off. "Okay, Baum? Good enough? Or do you need somebody to hold your hand?"

"It's all right, man," Angel tells me as he swats at a passing fly. "Bill's just being hump..."

While I cool out a little, Bill asks another officer, who's holding a walkie-talkie, if there's any further information about Darryl King.

"That King guy is probably a million miles from here," Angel says, pushing the "up" button at the bank of elevators. I notice the light doesn't go on.

"Now that is pure bullshit," Bill tells Angel as he lifts his injured left leg and hops up and down on his right leg to stay balanced. "That mutt has probably never been more than ten blocks from the house he was born in. Where is he gonna go? Mount Airy Lodge in the Poconos? Here is all he knows... You know that, Baum, don't you?"

"Sure thing, Bill."

Bill directs me to look out at the courtyard the way a college professor would direct a student's attention to the blackboard. "Given Darryl King's life experiences, I say he is still at large in this borough, if not this immediate neighborhood."

"You sound pretty sure." Angel hitches up his jeans under his bulletproof vest and Virgin Islands T-shirt. "Especially since they might have caught the guy this morning already..."

There was an unconfirmed radio report earlier this morning that said somebody answering Darryl's description got picked up in Brooklyn last night.

"Pure bullshit," Bill insists.

"Okay," says Angel. "Care to put ten dollars on a bet?"

Bill shakes his hand enthusiastically. "Remember," Bill says with a grin. "I'm not saying he has to be in this building or anything. Just the general area... like the Eastern seaboard..."

"Heh, heh, heh. You're fulla crap, Bill."

I notice one of the elevators seems to be stuck on the sixth floor and the three other elevators are completely out of service. I push the buttons three more times before I give up. "I think we're gonna have to use the stairs," I say.

Everyone groans, except for Angel, who grins and slaps his taut, muscular thighs. "I run up and down stairs like these five times a day," he says, reaching over to pat Bill's ample stomach. "Unlike certain members of this unit who exercise primarily by opening and closing the icebox..."

The seven of us head for the stairwell. The higher we go,

the more evidence we find of insane and dangerous behavior. By the second floor the air is stinking from recently smoked crack and sprayed urine. The graffiti on the walls is unintelligible. Nobody could mistake this for art anymore. It's just bits and pieces of angry, throttled language. "XMCREW"—"DJC34"—"EHWRT." Like the artists got too deranged to put their ideas in any kind of order.

What's really extraordinary, though, is the vomit. It's caked on the walls, as though somebody threw up on the floor and then picked it up and put it there with his hands.

"How far do we have to go?" Bill asks me on the fourth-floor landing, which is strewn with crack vials.

He grimaces and grips the banister as he lifts his left leg slowly. For a moment, I smile because Bill looks like an overweight ballerina doing a bar exercise. But then I realize how much it must hurt to climb all these stairs with his wounded leg.

"Twelfth floor," Angel says for the fifth time this morning.

"Why couldn't he meet us at the bar around the corner from work?" Bill asks.

"I don't know. I guess he feels safer here," Angel says, sprinting ahead of the rest of us. The guy's in incredible shape, even for a former lightweight fighter. He must never drink beer at home or something.

"Well, if he does have anything to tell us," Bill says, "he won't be safe for long. Everyone in this building will know we came by to see him." He steps over a turd and a spent bullet shell on one of the steps. "Fuckin' animals," he mumbles.

"It's our job to keep 'em locked up, Mr. Bill," Angel says over his shoulder.

"Bullshit," Bill tells him.

From the floors above us, we can hear the echoes of feet shuffling, doors slamming, and voices squealing. Between the fourth and fifth floors, we pass this strange-looking guy with a tangled beard and squeegee, who's just standing there, pointing upward, like we need him to tell us where we're going.

Then he looks at us like we owe him a tip or something. Fuck him too. By the seventh floor, the stuffiness is getting to me and I find myself short of breath. Bill uses the break as an opportunity to light another cigar.

I look around at the cracked steps and broken railings. Bill blows out another heavy cloud of cigar smoke and the rest of us begin to choke and cough.

"You guys didn't smoke, we'd be there by now," Angel taunts us as he heads up toward the next flight.

"If the people didn't smoke crack, we wouldn't have to come at all," one of the new guys in the unit says. Another of the rookies yodels like a Swiss mountain climber.

"Oh, shut the fuck up," Bill says, rubbing his wounded knee. "Look at this, Baum. Angel and me are surrounded by idiots."

"You know something I just realized, Bill?" I ask. "This is the building Lee Harvey Oswald lived in when he stayed in New York..."

"Really?" Bill asked.

"Oh yeah," I tell him with a straight face. "He sang in a doo-wop group called the Red Squares. You knew that, Bill, didn't you?"

Bill looks at me carefully for a second and then waves his cigar in disgust. "Oh, you're fulla shit too..."

Everyone else starts laughing and Angel whacks me affectionately on the shoulder. Even Bill smiles.

"Onward and upward, Private Vasquez," Bill says, trudging up to the next flight.

"Whatever you say, General Custer." Angel salutes.

A few minutes later, we arrive on the twelfth-floor landing. Bill clasps both hands around the butt of his gun, glances through the porthole, and shoves himself out into the hall. Angel gives me a look like he thinks Bill is being a self-conscious show-off. The rest of us spin out after him, one by one.

67

Darryl told his mother to get his great-grandmother out of the apartment. "Aaron says they're coming upstairs right now," he said. "She's making too much noise."

Ethel McDaniels, his seventy-six-year-old great-grandmother, was holding on to the frame of the kitchen doorway as Darryl, Bobby, and the dozen other young men handled their guns. The old woman was too scared to stop crying.

"She'll be all right," Darryl's mother said.

"Tell her to shut up or I'll shoot her."

Darryl's mother went over to hold her grandmother's hand and stroke her trembling gray head. "Don't mind him, Grandma," she said. "He's just feeling hyper."

"Bobby," said Darryl. "Go see what's up."

Bobby Kirk shoved his .45 and his 9 mm into the tight waistband of his broad jeans. He straightened the thick gold chains around his neck, opened the apartment's front door, and stepped out into the hall.

68

The first thing I hear on the twelfth floor is the jangling of necklace chains. The first thing I see is an enormous young guy wearing the chains and a nameplate ring. Two big H's are carved in the hair on either side of his head.

"Oh look at this guy," Bill mutters.

The big kid starts to amble down the airless, seaweed green hall. Almost all the doors have triple locks, I notice, and are covered with chipped black paint. The same television game show seems to be playing inside several of the apartments. A few crack vials and broken light bulbs lie on the sticky black-and-yellow-checked linoleum floor. Behind the big kid with the chains and the H's in his hair, a little girl with bare feet lugs what appears to be a bedpost into the incinerator room. It strikes me as an odd way to get rid of an old bed, but then I don't live here.

Daniels, a pink-cheeked new guy with the Field Service Unit, keeps stepping on the backs of my sneakers. Since the cops don't seem to be here, Angel takes three of the other officers around the corner and down another hall looking for them. After a few seconds, I faintly hear Angel's voice saying, "Not Building D, Building C. You schmucks are in the wrong building," into the walkie-talkie. I guess it's going to take that backup unit a while to get here. Just as well. Once they arrive, they'll take over and make us the backup unit.

Now it's just Daniels, Bill, and me.

"Hey, homeboy," Bill calls out to the big kid in the chains who's standing less than fifteen yards away from us. "Where's da man?"

I'd shudder if I heard a white cop talking this way. Even coming from a black social worker like Bill, I find it a little unnerving.

The big kid in the chains gives Bill a blank look. "I said, where's the man?" Bill repeats. "D.K., homes. Darryl. Where he at, homeboy?"

The big kid takes a huge step forward and looks at the gun in Bill's hand. "Who you talkin' about?" he says unconvincingly.

"An actor," Bill says out of the side of his mouth. "That's very cute. 'Who you talkin' about?' "

"Bill, I don't think this is our informant," I tell him. "You better stop fucking around."

The guy in the chains takes another step and puts his hands behind his back like he's had a lot of practice wearing handcuffs.

"We're looking for somebody who can tell us about Darryl King," Daniels, the rookie, asks in a loud, gawky voice.

I close my eyes in embarrassment. Maybe it's true, I think. Maybe social workers and probation officers don't have any business pretending to be cops.

I hear a door opening behind the big kid in chains, about thirty feet to our right. For a moment, we get distracted by the sound. The kid with the chains takes his hands from behind his back and assumes a shooter's stance. He's still pretty far away from us. Even with my contact lenses in, he's like a figure on a TV screen. In his right hand, he has a gun with a long barrel. He begins firing it.

The door down at the right end of the hall opened a little more and Darryl King peered out at the gunfire. Then he pushed a fourteen-year-old boy known as "Life Knowledge" out into the hall. "Life Knowledge" was part of a youth gang who called themselves gods and considered themselves to be invincible. His gun, however, was a Raven .25 caliber worth less than seventy dollars. He fired it once and the handle came apart in his hands. A slug from Bill Neill's .38 service revolver tore through the boy's forehead and Life Knowledge fell to the floor, dead.

Behind one of the other apartment doors, a baby cried and a game show audience cheered wildly.

Daniels, the rookie, turns around and runs down the other end of the hall, shrieking that he's going to get Angel and the others.

The big kid with the *H*'s in his hair continues to fire his 9 mm Browning wildly. Bill and I return the shots and look desperately for cover. One of Bill's bullets grazes the left side of the big kid's rib cage and the big kid does a half-turn downward to the floor. He steadies himself with his left hand against the cinder block wall, and with his right hand, he squeezes the trigger of the Browning again.

Bill falls over backward with blood gushing from a spot near his chin.

All of a sudden, this whole thing doesn't seem like it's happening on TV anymore. It's sickeningly real. I've got my back flat against one of the apartment doors. I start banging on it with my elbow and pleading with the person inside to let me in to safety. I hear the door at the other end of the hall open once more, and the gunfire resumes.

I bang harder on the door I'm leaning against. "Please let me in, dear God. Please."

"It's not locked," a weak voice finally tells me from inside.

But by then I'm so crazed with panic I can't figure out if the door opens to the outside or the inside. I just keep yanking on the doorknob, because I'm afraid that if I stop long enough to figure it out, someone will come up behind me and shoot me in the head.

I'm out of bullets. Bill Neill is lying there, bleeding on the floor. And I still can't get the door open. My breathing sounds so frenzied that for a second I think it's someone else doing it. Finally, I look right at the metal doorknob. I twist it the wrong way and it doesn't move at all. I try it the other way and the latch clicks. But before I can press my weight on the door, I feel the presence of someone standing directly behind me.

I turn and see Darryl King pointing a .45 right at me. If I hadn't spent so much time looking at his picture over the past few weeks, I wouldn't have recognized him.

His appearance is shocking. He's preternaturally thin now, like a wire sculpture. His sunken skin looks like it's been melted over his skeleton. His head is completely out of proportion with his once-solid build and his limbs seem elongated and frail. He wears a soiled brown T-shirt and rumpled green velour slacks. I've seen a lot of crack addicts, but never anyone so utterly deformed by the habit. Darryl is all bulging eyes and big hands. It's as if he's been boiled down to his fiercest essence.

He puts the barrel of the gun right up to my temple. "You gonna die now," he says.

Three other young guys stand behind him, shaking their heads slowly. I can't believe my life is about to end so abruptly. It doesn't make sense. It's not my time. There hasn't been enough of a build-up. I feel angry and cheated.

"Hey," I say.

But none of them answer and I see Darryl's about to press down on the trigger. I hold my breath and the blood rushes to my head. I want to pray but I'm too confused.

"What's going on, Baum?" I hear Angel asking from the other end of the hall. His tone is meant to be reassuring.

Darryl grabs me by the arm and turns me roughly so that I'm facing Angel and Darryl is standing behind me with the gun to my head. I smell vomit, crack, and cigarettes on his breath. I start to gag and Darryl digs his nails into my arm.

"Okay, everybody should just chill the fuck out a minute," Angel says firmly.

"FUCK YOU, MAN!" Darryl King screams. "I AM RE-
LAXED!"

With the halt in the shooting, people are beginning to peek
cautiously out of the doorways up and down the hall. I can
see how terrified they are, but my insides feel bound up in
catgut and thorns. The short hairs of my left temple catch on
something at the end of Darryl's gun barrel and I wince as a
couple of them get pulled out.

"WHAT'RE YOU MAKIN' A FACE FOR, MAN!" Darryl
screams senselessly at me. "YOU THINK THIS IS SOME
KINDA FUCKIN' JOKE?! I BLOW YOUR FUCKIN' HEAD
OFF!!!"

"All right, let's take it easy now," Angel says, taking tiny
steps forward. "Let's chill, people . . ."

"FUCK YOU! I KILL HIM IN THE FUCKIN' HEAD, MAN!!"

Angel and the three other field service guys have their guns
trained on Darryl and his gang. Darryl's men are looking at
him strangely, as though they're afraid he might actually pull
the trigger on the spot and get them all killed.

"Darryl, don't you do nothing stupid," a woman's voice
calls from down the hall behind where we're standing.

"SHUT THE FUCK UP, MOMS!" Darryl yells. "ELSE I KILL
YOU NEXT!"

I hear Darryl's mother complaining to somebody else in the
apartment about her son's lack of respect. Angel makes a deliberate show of moving back the safety catch on his gun. The
other officers follow his example. "So let's work this out,"
Angel says, advancing a few more steps toward Darryl.

"Back up, chump," says the skinny fourteen-year-old kid
with the flattop and the harelip who I saw before in the lobby.
Only now he's carrying an Uzi.

"Come on, man." Angel holds out his free hand like a peace
offering. "Let him go."

Now I see what a fearless motherfucker he must've been in
his street gang days.

"I'M GIVIN' THE ORDERS," Darryl King says, banging the
side of my head for emphasis. "YOU TAKE 'EM."

A single dingy light bulb hangs from a loose ceiling wire just a few inches in front of my face. From somewhere to my left, I hear Bill Neill making gurgling noises. I hope he's not dying. I can't even look down at him on the floor because Darryl still has the gun to my head. No one's paying much attention to the kid in the Life Knowledge T-shirt who came out of the apartment with the shitty little gun. I happen to catch a single glimpse of him as Darryl swings me around. He's lying face-down in a widening puddle of blood.

Angel asks Darryl if he'll at least back up a few steps so they can reach Bill's body and get him emergency medical treatment. Darryl remains unmoved. "This here is our prisoner," he says, lowering his gun to my jaw.

"Prisoner of war," says the big kid with all the chains and the H's in his hair. He's clutching his side where Bill's shot must've just grazed him.

"Prisoner of the crack wars," someone else says. One or two people laugh.

Darryl wraps his free hand around my neck and begins pulling me backward toward the apartment he emerged from. The bile rises in my throat as my black sneakers squeak on the floor tiles.

"Hey, man, where you taking him?" Angel calls out. "Don't make it hard on everyone, Darryl . . ."

I feel like I'm getting dragged down to hell, far away from the world of the living. Everybody in the hall is yelling at each other. Their voices blend together in my ears and their words are indistinct—except somebody keeps saying, "Take no prisoners," loud and clear. Darryl tightens his stranglehold and my eyes roll back into my head. I black out for a moment.

When I come to, I realize I've been pulled back into the apartment at the south end of the hall. I'm dropped on the carpet and somebody puts a knee on my chest.

"STEP OFF, MAN!!!" I hear Darryl shouting. "STAY BACK!!! WE KILL THE FUCKIN' HOSTAGE RIGHT HERE ON THE RUG!!!"

"Whatever you say, man," Angel's voice says from some-where out in the hall. "Let's not do anything we'll be sorry about."

"No, I won't," Darryl says with sudden calm.

There's a protracted silence and then a long fusillade of automatic weapons firing from the apartment out into the hall. When the shots finally cease, I hear the voices of Angel and the other Field Service guys fading and the scuff of their sneakers getting lighter as they retreat down the hall floor.

"Yeah, that's right," says the big kid with the chains and the H's in his hair, lowering himself into a large chair and trying to pull his bloodied shirt off. "Run away, faggots."

"Chicken," somebody else says.

Still lying on my back, I look up and see two women's faces. One appears to be in her seventies; she wears heavy glasses and has a sad, wrinkled mouth. The other woman I recognize from court as Darryl's mother. She appears uninterested in anything going on around her.

"This is my probation officer, Moms," Darryl says.

"He behind enemy lines," adds the big kid with the chains and the H's, who's having some trouble breathing.

"Yeah," Darryl's mother says to me. "You in another country now."

69

Richard Silver was lying on his back in the Connecticut house.

The place was beautiful, he had to admit that. There were vistas almost everywhere you looked. A skylight overhead revealed a bright sun and a cloud formation that looked like the Hindenberg. The window on the right led your eye to the swimming pool. The window on the left opened onto the woods. Something was stirring behind the trees.

Richard Silver rolled to his side. The problem with being able to see everything was that then you didn't feel like going anywhere.

This is what life was for, Jimmy Rose used to say. You made money so you could get away from all the things you hated in the city. The noise. The pollution. The guy coughing phlegm all over you on the subway. The half hour wait for a table at The Palm. The hoodlums on the street. The indictments. The probation officer who he'd been talking to. The investigators from the U.S. Attorney's office in Chicago who Larry said were going around asking questions the last week or so.

Somebody was talking.

Better not to think about all that now. What was the point

of coming up to a place like this on a weekday unless you were going to relax? Through the window on the left, he could see that something definitely was moving behind the trees. Maybe a deer. He started feeling hot. The skylight above him was a magnifying glass on the sun. Why didn't anybody think of that when it was put in?

He opened another button on his blue Paul Stuart shirt. It was funny the way they made these things without buttons on the wings of the collar. He remembered the blue cotton oxfords from Brooks Brothers he used to wear in the sixties. There was something kind of earnest and preppy about them, but they had a slightly rougher texture, which made them look good with jeans. You could honorably wear one to a community meeting in Harlem and then grab a tie out of the glove compartment and go to City Hall if you had to. A Bobby Kennedy kind of thing to do. Bobby was always good with the "out in the streets" bullshit. You had to give him that. And the girls.

He remembered wearing a shirt like that when he walked the streets over the long, hot summers in Harlem. He could still feel the fabric sticking to his back when he got all tired and sweaty. Of course in those days, when he tucked his shirt in, it was like a bed sheet stretched tight over the firm flat expanse of his stomach. Now it was more like a ship's sail billowing in the wind. He had to get back to the gym soon.

He hadn't worn a shirt like that since he threw his lot in with Jimmy Rose on the Sullivan Houses deal in Brooklyn. Lose the Young Democrats look, Jimmy told him, you make me nervous. Get yourself some wing tips and a manicure.

It'd been years since he'd thought about any of that. The Hindenberg cloud moved on and the sun got stronger. He heard something rustling outside again. This time he stood up to see what was coming through the trees. Twigs snapped and branches parted. It was the guys coming to clean the pool. Suburban scum in T-shirts and jeans. One of them was carrying the long pole with the net on it. The other was dragging that filtering machine that made all the noise. He'd forgotten this was their day to come in. He wouldn't have bothered driving up if he'd remembered.

Richard Silver decided he might as well turn on the television again and find out what was going on in the city. He was never going to get any peace now anyway.

70

"All right, spread 'em!" says Darryl King.

"Open his mouth! SOMEBODY get his mouth open!"

At least four pairs of hands are frisking me now as I lie down flat on the floor, hands behind my head. Only people who've been arrested and slapped around by police all their lives could have this much enthusiasm about playing cops.

"You have the right to an attorney," says one of them.

"Somebody please open his mouth," says Bobby, the big one with the *H*'s in his hair, who's standing right by my head. A little bit of blood is leaking through the side of the shirt he just put on. Now he's furious and waving a gun at me like he knows just where he'd like to put it.

The rest of them ignore him and take my gun, cigarettes, Silly Putty, and my bulletproof vest. I happen to look over and see a bunch of other people sitting over on the couch, watching television, like what's going on here couldn't possibly be as interesting.

Darryl is crouching over me, pointing my gun right in my face. And as he holds the power to end my life in his hands, what he says to me is: "Yo, blood clot, what's up?"

I used to have a very immature idea of what death would be like. Somehow, I thought that all the people who'd mistreated me in life would jam into a great synagogue somewhere, bow their heads in unison, and say how sorry they were that I was gone.

I never dreamed it would end in a poorly maintained Harlem housing project, with a group of bored-looking black people sitting around watching white people do aerobics on TV while a belligerent crackhead grinds his broken yellow teeth in my face.

I suddenly have a vision of myself lying facedown on the green carpet with a bullet in the back of my head and a spreading stain where I've lost control of my bladder. One of those forsaken corpses you read about sometimes in the newspapers. Darryl steadies his aim with the gun and I start to get really scared.

My throat feels dry and my contact lenses are poking me again. I dearly don't want to die. But I know that if I show any emotion, I'll lose all control.

"Over here," someone says.

They bring me over to a chair in the middle of the room and surround me. I guess they want to make sure nobody can take a shot at any of them without the risk of hitting me, but they need me close enough to the window so the outside world can see I'm in immediate danger.

A heavy mingled aroma like burned meat and crack hangs in the air. So far, I've counted about a dozen people floating from room to room here. Most of them still aren't paying much attention to me. One of them gets up and changes the TV channel to The Price Is Right. A couple of the others stare listlessly out the windows, like the people in a mental health commercial. Two small children are roughhousing in one of the back bedrooms.

A couple of quieter minutes pass and I start to wonder what they're doing outside. The last thing I heard was something that sounded like bodies being dragged away in the hall. I hope Bill's not dead. It gets me thinking about the way he looked lying on the floor with the gunshot wound, and my features start moving around my face. I have no idea what it looks like to anyone else, but Darryl clearly doesn't like it.

"Don't be looking that way," he says. He shoves what used to be my .38-caliber service revolver right in my face. "You remanded," he says.

I can't tell if that's supposed to be a joke or not. Beyond the sights of the gun, his face is a death mask with its hollow eyes and rictus grin. Looking at it, its hard to believe that this is where I wanted to be. Dealing with Darryl in Darryl's world on Darryl's terms. I'd ask myself what I've done to deserve this, except that I was the one who insisted on coming here.

With the hand not holding the gun, Darryl begins to play with himself, fumbling with his genitals in a grim, unconscious kind of way. After a while, he gets tired of it and starts fooling around with an old-fashioned flip-top silver lighter. I think of the lighter I snatched off the bar last night when I was with Andrea. At the time I wasn't sure why I took it—a momentary larcenous impulse, I guess. But now it reminds me of Andrea and I feel a little ripple inside because I'll probably never see her again.

Then I start missing things I never even liked before. Like walking to work from the subway in the morning. I used to hate that walk before, because it took me under that scaffolding with filthy water dripping down. But now I miss that walk like crazy. I wonder what I could've done differently. Maybe if I'd kept the window open the night it rained a couple of weeks ago, I might've caught a cold and been out sick today.

Darryl's voice jolts me back into the present tense.

"Get your legs under the chair," he says, putting one of my cigarettes in his mouth and setting it on fire with the lighter.

"Why?" There's hardly any room.

"Just do it," he says. "My house, my rules."

He keeps flicking the gun's safety catch on and off, finally leaving it off and turning the gun sideways to examine its chambers. When he's satisfied that everything's where it ought to be, he points it straight ahead so that its muzzle is less than six inches from the bridge of my nose.

"Darryl, what're you doing?" his mother asks, like she'd

just caught him raiding the refrigerator before dinner.

"What it look like?"

"Well, I just hope you don't think you're gonna shoot that man right here now..."

I keep my eyes shut and take deep breaths.

"Darryl," his mother repeats. When I open my eyes again, I see she has her hands on her hips. She's as thin as her son, but she seems drained by heroin, not crack. "Don't you try and shoot that man..." she says lazily.

"Why not?"

"You shoot him, what's gonna happen to us? You ever stop and think about that?"

"No," Darryl says barely acknowledging her.

"That's 'cos you stupid, like your sister said." His mother opens a can of diet Slice orange soda and takes a long drink. Her elbow forms a jagged angle off her body. "The only reason they ain't come through that door already is 'cos we have a hostage."

"I know what time it is." Darryl's face contorts and he takes two steps back and punches the wall, leaving a crushed-in mark. The other guys surrounding me with guns look at each other like they're truly impressed with his ability to express himself.

"What's the matter with you?" his mother asks.

"You called me stupid."

She reconsiders. "Well, I don't think you stupid," she says with a sigh. "You just smoke too much shit and you don't think straight sometimes."

"Well, all right."

Darryl's mother looks at me. "What's his name again?" she asks Darryl like she's inquiring about a new household pet.

"Mr. Baum." Mr. Bomb, it sounds like.

"Is he Jewish or something?"

"I dunno." Darryl cocks his head to one side as he looks at me. "Are you Jewish?"

"Yes," I say, and immediately regret answering.

"See?" says Darryl's mother.

"What?" I say.

"Nothin'." She finishes her soda and goes back to the kitchen.

A single bead of sweat slides down my face and a truck sighs outside. For the first time, I'm aware of people's voices coming through the windows. There must be hundreds of cops and emergency service people downstairs, making plans and waiting to see what's going to happen. Darryl shifts the gun over to his right hand and puffs away on my cigarette. It looks like a bomb's fuse burning down in the corner of his mouth. After three long last drags, he spits it out on the floor and looks after it.

"Fuckin' Marlboros, man," he says. "How can you smoke that shit?"

71

SLOW MOTION RIOT

Darryl left Aaron to guard the hostage and went into one of the back bedrooms just as the noon news was starting on television.

His mother was lying on the charred mattress he'd accidentally set fire to when he fell asleep smoking crack a couple of nights back. With her eyes closed like that, she looked dead, and watching her, he got sad. It started him thinking about the foster home again and how it was being away from her. He kicked at the balled-up newspapers and matchbook covers lying on the floor. Then he noticed she didn't seem to be breathing and he began to panic. For a couple of seconds, he stopped breathing too.

His hand went back down into his pants. But nothing much was happening there, so he grabbed the crack pipe off the night table under the window and tried to light it with his propane torch. The spout was broken, though, so he had to use the silver lighter he'd found before. His hands were almost shaking too much to keep the flame steady, but soon the strong blue crack smell filled the room and woke his mother. She rolled her bloodshot eyes from the TV to Darryl taking long hits off the stem.

"Look like you suck on a glass dick," she told him.

One of the TV ladies was on the screen. She was the type

that looked fine sometimes, and not too good other times. Today she was okay. She was standing outside by a red brick
wall while a posse of kids were jumping around behind her
and waving at the camera.

" 'S a long day," Darryl said.

His mother sat up slowly and blinked her eyes. She looked
so much older all of a sudden. He wondered if just having the
probation officer in the apartment had aged her. When Mr.
Bomb had first shown up like that this morning it was like a
dream coming true. Now it was turning into a nightmare.

"What time is it?" his mother asked him.

"I don't know." Darryl just looked at her.

The lady on the television was saying something about a
standoff and the police. The sun was hitting one side of her
face and a shadow fell over the other side. One of the homeboys
jumping around behind her looked like he was about to grab
the microphone out of her hands and do his own personal
version of the news.

"I like to change my clothes," said Darryl's mother. "I been
sleeping in these."

Through the doorway, he could hear the sound of the probation officer asking Bobby for something.

"I don't even remember the last time I had my hair done,"
his mother said, pulling on the lank part in the back.

Darryl didn't hear her. He was busy trying to recognize
somebody on the television screen. A little kid he'd seen running around the hallway outside. Now the kid was jumping
around near the TV lady and the brick wall. He looked again
and thought he saw Ernie, the car washer, lingering around
the edge of the scene.

He started watching more closely to find out how Ernie got
to hang out with the TV lady. Maybe Ernie dropped a dime
on somebody or something. Slowly, he began to recognize the
brick wall on television as the one downstairs. They were
doing the show right now, right outside the Charles J. Stone
Houses.

"Again, all our information is very preliminary," said the TV lady, who had on a lot of lipstick and small earrings, "but we understand at least one field officer is being held hostage in the apartment."

Darryl's mother opened her mouth a little. The TV camera swept slowly around the courtyard outside, showing hundreds of cops standing ready. They looked like they were about to go to war in a science fiction movie. Most of them had on riot helmets and carried Plexiglas shields. The TV lady said they were just waiting for the order to go ahead and break down the door of the apartment.

"Don't believe the hype," said Darryl.

But then the camera began to rise, passing all the people hanging out the windows, and finally pointing up at the roof. More than a dozen guys wearing SWAT team caps and carrying high-powered rifles were scurrying around for position up there.

"Now look what you done," said Darryl's mother.

"What?"

"I told you, you should've talked to the man who called before to negotiate."

"Ah, he was another sucker," Darryl said.

He heard another siren going down the street outside. A split second later, the same sound was coming out of the television.

"We should've done Mr. Bomb when we had the chance," Darryl mumbled, taking another hit off the pipe. He put it down on the table, next to the ether tank he'd been using to get rid of the impurities in cocaine.

"Then they just come right in and kill us all," his mother said once more. "Like at Attica."

He didn't know what she was talking about. He had a lot of friends who'd been upstate at Attica Correctional Facility and it didn't sound any worse than Auburn or Greenhaven or any of the other prisons. It was mainly being locked up. Like he was now. He asked his mother what was so special about Attica.

"Don't you remember?"

He shook his head, but kept his eyes on the television.

"I guess that was before your time," she said. "The brothers had themselves a uprising there and took some hostages."

"Yeah? So what happened?"

A cloud seemed to pass in front of her face. "Well, I don't remember all of it," she said vaguely. "I think the police went in and killed a whole mess of the brothers. Like, I think your uncle Willie was there."

Darryl shrugged. He never even knew he had an uncle Willie.

"Anyway," said his mother, sounding more sure of herself now. "After the police went in, they took the rest of them inmates that they didn't kill and made them strip buck-naked and crawl through the mud."

She nodded, relieved she had at least part of it right. Darryl just stared at her.

"That's fucked up," he said.

"'S why I don't want that to happen to us," his mother told him. "I already been to prison."

Darryl looked over at the television. They'd cut back to the studio where a guy, wearing a tie and a lump of curly hair on his head, was saying they'd have more on the hostage situation later. He also said there'd be a report about whether that cop was going to get indicted for shooting Jamal Perkins. A commercial came on with a lady in a white headband drinking a cup of tea.

"That's all it is, Darryl," his mother said. "When that man calls back to negotiate, you all better have something to tell him that won't get us throwed back in jail. Because I cannot stand it."

"Fuck, Moms!" He made a move to punch the wall again. "What'm I supposed to do?"

"Get a holda yourself. I always said your temper was going to get the better of you," his mother said sharply. "Now get on outta here. My program is coming on. *The Young and the Restless*. That bitch Nina be doin' it again."

72

For fifteen years, Lieutentant Jerry Lawrence had been one of the lead hostage negotiators for the New York Police Department. In that time, he'd been to every neighborhood in the city and talked to failed bank robbers, husbands who'd kidnapped their ex-wives, crazed mothers grabbing their children in custody disputes, and every other kind of desperate person in a desperate circumstance. But in the end, it all came back to his friend John, who was one of the guards who'd been taken hostage at Attica.

The two of them had grown up together in Valley Stream and played next to each other on the high school football team. So after Lawrence got back from the Marines in September 1971, he went upstate to visit his old friend, who'd started working at the prison earlier in the year. But instead of being able to hang out and drink beer with his buddy, Lawrence wound up watching television at the house near Attica, as the twelve hundred inmates took over the prison and grabbed his friend John and thirty-seven other hostages.

Long after all the shooting was over and the bodies were carried out, Lawrence found himself thinking about how everything could've been handled differently. They could've tried to reopen negotiations and get a new list of demands. The governor could've shown up and stood outside the gate.

A thousand other scenarios kept playing themselves out in his head over the years. The whole thing stayed with him after he got to be a sergeant in the Brooklyn robbery squad. It was how he wound up talking his way out of a supermarket stickup that'd turned into a hostage situation in East Flatbush.

His technique had pretty much stayed the same. It always just boiled down to him and the guy on the other end of the phone. All the rest of them—the brass, the zone commanders, the specialized units with their surveillance equipment and backup negotiators, the media, the wandering by crazies—just faded away. "It's just him and me, like a Clint Eastwood movie," he'd lie to other cops afterward. His former wife was a little closer to the mark. "It's like therapy," she said. "Except you can't be sure which one's the nut."

What you had to do was get the guy to trust you. Even if it meant staying on the phone or sitting on the other side of a door for nine or ten hours straight. You lost him even for a second, he'd kill them all and it'd be your fault. If he said he saw a little green man in the corner, you'd better not say you did too. Otherwise, he'd know you were full of shit, like the rest of them, so why not end it all? After you'd been talking to him long enough, though, you started to feel like you knew the guy better than his best friend did. Sometimes it wasn't just feeling sorry for him. You genuinely started to like the guy. Which made it too bad if it came around later where you had to blow him out of his socks, but you tried not to think about that too much.

At first, the situation with the probation officer and Darryl King didn't seem too impossible. It was true that King's people weren't allowing anybody up to the twelfth floor, where they were holding the hostage, and the tenth and eleventh floors were also out-of-bounds. But there was a makeshift command post set up in one of the apartments downstairs and they were trying to fix up a direct telephone line to the hostage takers, even though the cables around here were old and hard to work with.

However, the biggest pain at the moment was that Detective

Sergeant McCullough from the two-five hanging over his shoulder. The writer. McCullough said he wanted to be there because he'd been wounded by Darryl. But Lawrence figured he just wanted to hang around taking notes, so he could get a movie deal later.

The previous efforts to get a dialogue going with the hostage takers had failed miserably, so when Lawrence dialed the phone and got Darryl King in the middle of the afternoon, he decided to start off with the soft sell.

"How's it going, kid?"

"What do you mean?"

"Just checking in," Lawrence said casually. He glanced at the red-and-green finger painting hanging on the kitchen wall. There were children's drawings all over the apartment. "Just making sure everybody's cool."

"Yeah, what's the matter with you, man? Somebody got a beef?"

"No, not at all."

"Because if somebody got a beef, I got my finger on the trigger," Darryl told him.

Lawrence recognized the cocaine arrogance with a little bit of fear around the edges. The kid had probably been sitting up there, smoking crack all day. Time to lay down some ground rules.

"I'd like to make sure the hostage is okay," Lawrence said calmly, pulling on one of the waxed ends of his mustache and looking at McCullough hovering nearby. "Can I talk to him?"

"Fuck you. No."

"Well, maybe I could just hear his voice or something."

There were some bumping sounds, like Darryl was walking around with the phone in his hand. "Say something," he told somebody on his end.

"Something," a faint voice said in the background. "What else do you want me to say?" It sounded like a white guy with a bad hangover. Lawrence assumed it was the probation officer, but since he'd never actually talked to the guy, he couldn't be sure.

That was about as good as they were going to get at the moment. They could try to use the telescopes a little later to reconfirm the probation officer was okay. For now, the thing was to try to get some demands on the table.

"Do you have a list of what you want?" Lawrence said once Darryl was back on the phone again.

"I demand my shit from my old house."

The kid honestly didn't seem to understand that he had them by the balls now. Lawrence kept trying to pin him down on specifics. You were always better off if you had a goal to work toward. Otherwise, it was all just endless vamping until somebody got killed.

"What do you want in exchange for releasing the hostage?" Lawrence asked patiently, sitting on the kitchen counter and adjusting the bill on his baseball cap.

A group of voices all started speaking at once on Darryl's end. It sounded like all of them were giving the kid static.

"All right, you all shut the fuck up before I decide to shoot somebody," Darryl was telling them defensively.

Lawrence tried shouting, "Calm down," into the receiver. He thought he saw McCullough make a move for the phone, and he got ready to shove him out of the way. McCullough was about five years younger and two inches taller, but he was a little thick around the middle.

"Let me talk to him," he said to Lawrence.

"Get lost," Lawrence told McCullough, preparing to draw his gun if he had to.

All at once, the voices on the other end stopped talking and it was just him and Darryl again.

"All right," Darryl told him. "What I want is a key."

"A key to what?"

"Make it two keys, and I want my Olds..."

"Wait a second." Lawrence took off his cap for a second and wiped his forehead with the back of his wrist. "Are we talking about two kilos of cocaine here?"

" 'S right," said Darryl. "It's a business." Lawrence couldn't tell if the kid was crazy or kidding. "And I want a helicopter so I can fly the shit to Cali," Darryl went on.

"Cali in Colombia?"

"Cali is California, man," said Darryl. "I know some people there, who can set it up right. So you get me the two keys and the copter and you bring my Cutlass around front so my man Aaron can drive it out west."

He was acting like this hostage situation was an investment opportunity. Lawrence wondered if the kid had thought about any of this or if he was making it all up off the top of his head. "Is that it?" he asked Darryl.

"Yeah, man, and you get together about a half million in cash and then we'll talk. You got until midnight, man."

Lieutenant Lawrence covered the phone with his hand and said, "Bullshit," to everyone else in the room.

There had to be thirty people jammed into this small space. It was like the circus clowns all trying to get in the car. Half of them were like that stooge McCullough and didn't have any business being there. Lawrence closed his eyes and pretended all of them were going to disappear in a puff of smoke.

Somewhere, on one of the rooftops outside, there was a cop holding a high-powered rifle and smoking a cigarette. The designated shooter. He'd be the one to end it all, if it came to that. Until then, it was Lawrence's ball game.

"All right," he said to Darryl. "Let's get serious now."

"We are serious," Darryl said in a hoarse, enraged voice. "We prepared to die here."

The words brought Lawrence back to Attica. He remembered the inmates on television chanting the same thing and refusing to compromise on any of their demands. Unconditional amnesty with flights to "nonimperialist" countries for the inmates who wanted it. His friend John's brother had said, "They think they're gonna get out of this, but they won't." He didn't know the half of it. Four days later, the governor ordered in the State Police with their guns and riot gear. Twenty-nine inmates died that day.

What nobody expected was that his friend John and nine

of the other hostages would get killed too. Who could've predicted they'd get shot by the State Police when they moved in? But that's what happened when you did these kinds of big operations with a lot of confusion and bullets flying around. The wrong people got hurt.

He hoped the same thing wouldn't happen now with the probation officer, but he'd given up looking for guarantees in life that day at Attica.

"I'll call you back later and see if you're ready to talk sense," he told Darryl.

73

Outside the living room window, the sun is going down and the TV klieg lights are coming up. Long shadows appear on the apartment's walls and ceilings.

Assuming this is the last place I'll ever see, I take a good look around. Whoever lived here before did try to make it into a respectable middle-class home, with slipcovers on the couches and chairs and a white lace cloth on the dining room table. They even have two elaborate candelabras.

In the corner, I notice a five-foot-high wooden cabinet with glass windows in the corner. Its shelves are lined with copies of the Old and New Testaments, books of religious songs, and figures of Jesus. Several eight-by-ten photos are arranged on a shelf underneath the books. The people in the pictures must've lived here before, and Darryl and the others must've chased them out.

I squint to get a better look at the photos through the glass. They're arranged in chronological order, like a little history lesson. In the oldest picture, a determined-looking black man is dressed in a World War II private's uniform. In another shot from the 1940s, a woman is standing in what looks like an armaments factory with her co-workers. Later pictures from the 1950s have the man dressed as a bus driver, and the woman dressed as a nurse. As the progression goes on, a young woman, who must be their daughter, starts appearing in many of the pictures with them. As the photos change from grainy black-and-white to glossy color, I watch her growing up: from a high school graduation, to a wedding, to a beach holiday. But the pictures of her seem to stop a couple of years ago, when she's about thirty-three. I wonder if she died or something.

The last photo on the shelf is the most recent and the most touching. It shows the bus driver and the nurse as an old couple, in their best Sunday clothes, standing on either side of a young boy with a bright toothy smile, who's obviously their grandson. They're proud people who've spent their whole lives working hard and wound up in this shitty housing project built by someone like Robert Moses or Richard Silver and overseen by bureaucrats like me. The boy is their hope for the future.

Now they're all gone and Darryl King and his friends are left in their place. The glass in the cabinet is cracked, the couch slipcovers are ripped, and the lace cloth is stained with what I first thought was red paint, and I now realize is blood. There's a window-sized hole in the wall, opening out on the kitchen. I can see scales, piles of money, bags of crack vials, and ether tanks spread around. The dining room table is covered with Uzis, .45s, and various other automatics and semiautomatics. The door to the back bedroom has been removed and instead there's a white sheet hanging there, so the place looks like a real den of iniquity.

I notice a white telephone cord stretched around the sheet and into the back bedroom, where Darryl's been negotiating with the cop for a few minutes. I can only make out bits and pieces of what he's been saying. There was one hopeful part where he sounded all blustery and entrepreneurial, but then I hear him say, "We prepared to die here," and a long silence passes. After a couple of more minutes, the phone cord draws up and Darryl walks out, grinding his teeth again.

"So what'd he say?" I ask him as he starts to walk by me on the way to the kitchen.

He gives me the kind of look a woman would give her ex-husband during a divorce proceeding. Like it's inappropriate for us to be talking to each other.

It's been like this for hours, with hardly anyone talking to me. If it wasn't for the sun, I'd completely lose track of time. They've gotten much more militant about everything; taking shifts holding the gun on me and even putting a blindfold on me a couple of times, for no particular reason other than it's what one seems to do when hostages are around. Eventually they decide to leave it off.

Across the room, by the glass cabinets, I see three girls teaching each other a new dance step and two boys practicing paramilitary maneuvers with their Uzis. It's hard to tell if they got all this from old film clips of the Black Panthers or *Rambo*.

I'm bored, my head aches, and I'm dying for a cigarette. I hope nobody asks me to stand up quickly, because after sitting here all day, I don't think my legs will hold up. And worst of all, my bladder is about ready to burst.

I look over at the couch near the television. A really pretty little girl, about four or five, with pigtails and a gap in her teeth, is sitting between the old lady who's trying to do some knitting and a little boy of about six who's sliding some Sesame Street toys across one of the armrests. The three of them have been around the periphery of my attention all day. The little girl keeps looking back and forth, like she can't decide which is more exciting, the toys or the knitting. It seems like they all wandered into the wrong apartment.

In my isolation and mind fog, I start to have strange thoughts.

Like about black people. I start remembering how my father always said black people were coming to get us when I was growing up. But then as I got older, the black people I met weren't like that. So I guess in some way I've always thought these weren't the black people my father was talking about.

In one of the other rooms, somebody is listening to a radio broadcast of a Black Muslim minister preaching his doctrine about the races.

I wonder if somebody told Darryl about white people coming to get him when he was growing up. What do Black Muslims call us? Devils. I guess if somebody grabbed my people, threw them into chains, and shipped them as slaves to a strange, unfriendly land, I might think they were devils too. It's certainly the kind of thing the Devil would do.

In the other room, the Black Muslim minister on the radio is saying the white man's time on earth is almost up.

I start to imagine the building we're in is a gigantic skull and I'm trapped inside it and not allowed to communicate with anybody on the outside. So the thoughts inside are getting into a rage, knocking me around and building up pressure. If they aren't let out soon, the whole skull will explode.

After a while, I notice Darryl and the others are going around the apartment, collecting spray cans and lighters. Maybe they've hit on some new way of smoking crack. Once every few minutes one of them says something loud, angry, and not completely sensible. I start getting worried that the drug is making them too crazy. I hope they don't just decide to shoot me without regard to the consequences.

The only one who doesn't seem ready to detonate any moment is the small old woman knitting next to the kids on the couch. She wears a sagging gray cardigan, brown slacks, and plastic-rimmed glasses with silvery wings. Her hair is a wiry mass of gray and black strands dyed at random. She was probably quite beautiful once, but now her face is well-mapped with deep wrinkles receding toward her small flat chin.

She gives me what seems to be a sympathetic look. Next to her, several of Darryl's teenage lieutenants are fingering their guns and watching a cop show on television like it's an instructional film. I smile at the old woman, but Aaron, who's guarding me with an Uzi, catches the look.

"What're you smiling at?" he says.

I'm so surprised at being spoken to that I sputter before answering, "I'm just a stupid asshole."

The answer seems to satisfy Aaron for the moment. The

phone rings and more voices blare from the megaphones outside. I can hear Darryl arguing with his mother in the kitchen. More crack is burning and everyone's sounding much too excited. More police sirens wail outside. I hear somebody mention a midnight deadline and my palms start to sweat.

In all the confusion, the old woman on the couch pushes herself to her feet and comes over to me. Aaron, sitting on a wooden chair a yard away, hardly looks at her.

"How you doing?" she asks in an odd, high-pitched voice that strikes a chord in my head.

Her right hand flutters like a paper caught in a sudden updraft and her fingers come to a rest on her brittle-looking collarbone. She must be Darryl King's great-grandmother, who I spoke to on the phone just before that day in court. I remember the desperate note she wrote to me and decide it's safer for us not to acknowledge that we've spoken before. An ally. Maybe.

She puts her hands behind her back and looks down at me like I'm an old friend she just spotted on a park bench.

"Lovely night," she says pleasantly.

Behind her, I see a thirteen-year-old kid in a red Kangol hat trying to jam his gun into another boy's mouth. After a couple of seconds, he takes it out and points it at the ceiling. If he fires it now, all the cops will probably come crashing in, shooting, and we'll all get killed.

I try to contain my voice and insides. "Lovely," I say as the boy finally lowers his gun. "Will you be getting outside at all?" I mean, would you help me escape?

"Well," she says. "No, I don't think so." It occurs to me that she's not allowed to come and go as she pleases either.

Someone outside keeps chanting Darryl's name over and over on the megaphone and a searchlight swings through the windows. Darryl's great-grandmother—whose name is Ethel McDaniels, I recall—continues to act as though nothing out of the ordinary is going on.

Time is running out. My kidneys are killing me. It feels like someone's trying to blow up a parade float in there. The kid in the red Kangol hat is sipping a beer and flicking a straw at

me. Little droplets land on my face. It's his homemade torture.
I look at the guns on the kitchen table and think about using
one to shoot him and then Mrs. McDaniels's great-grandson,
Darryl.

I watch the little boy and little girl chase each other out of
a back bedroom, yelling, "Yiii, yiiii!!" as they go. They disappear into the bathroom and my bladder feels like it's getting
swollen to about twice its normal size.

"Who are those kids?" I ask the old woman, trying to get
my mind off the pain.

"They belong to Darryl's sister," she says in that voice that
makes everything sound either cheerful or completely dev-
astating. "LaToya and Howard."

Aaron is resting his Uzi on his knee and looking at me
impassively through narrowed eyes.

"So what the hell are they doing here?"

"Oh, they was just left," she says. She looks kind of sad
about it. "You know the family wasn't always like this," she
tells me. "Not back home. Because we didn't always live in
New York, you know. The McDanielses, they come from Lee
County in Arkansas. The boy's great-granddaddy was a..."
She smiles to herself. "Oh he was a very articulate man." From
the way her face lights up, you can tell she admired him for
more than just the way he spoke. They must've been happy
together.

"He was gonna be the first engineer in Lee County," she
says, "except they didn't hire colored folks for engineers then
... So that's why we had to come to New York."

It almost sounds like she's trying to defend the family reputation against what's going on right here in the apartment.
"But what it was, was we thought we had ourselves a house
in Brooklyn," she says. "It was gonna be near the good schools,
because it was gonna be an integrated neighborhood. You
know what I'm saying? They'd pick up people's trash in the
streets. And then, what happened is they went and didn't build
those houses."

She looks around at the mess here like it's the direct result.

I wonder if the place she's talking about is the Sullivan Houses, the low-income project in Brooklyn that Richard Silver backed out of in the 1970s. A few weeks ago, I would've blamed him for all this; I mean, what can you expect if you have people living apart from everyone else, in poverty? But I don't have the time or the inclination to think that way anymore. I wouldn't want Darryl King growing up next door to me either.

"Yes sir," Mrs. McDaniels is saying, "the trouble started with the boy's mother. She just got bored being poor all the time. She had to be that star, runnin' in the streets."

Darryl walks into the room, waving his arms and jabbering half coherently. I try to ignore him. But I need to piss so badly that tears are forming in my eyes.

"Listen," I say to Aaron. "Will you please just let me go to the can this once?"

Darryl happens to hear me as he walks by. "You want permission?" he demands. His eyes look tired and there's a thick white crust around his mouth.

"Yeah."

"Permission denied," Darryl says, taking control amidst all the confusion. "Shit in the chair . . . And if you get any on the seat, I kill you."

All this rage breaks loose in my mind. Before I can get a grip, I hear myself saying, "How about I just piss on you?"

As casually as a tennis pro approaching the net, he steps forward and backhands me across the mouth. I go falling over sideways while he heads off to the kitchen. As I lie there on the floor, bloody and humiliated, I realize I've never hated anyone as much as I hate Darryl right at this moment. It's a primal, consuming fury unlike anything I've ever felt before. I can't hear anything except a sound like a subway train going right by my ears.

The kid with the straw keeps flicking droplets of his spit on my face.

I let out a howl. Everything from before means nothing now. I only care about one thing. I want to blow Darryl King's head off. And I pray that I'll live long enough to do it.

I get back up on the chair, but within two minutes I'm on the verge of losing all control of my bladder. Just then, Darryl's great-grandmother turns to Aaron.

"Let him go to the bathroom," she says abruptly.

"No way," Aaron tells her, a gold tooth peeking through his harelip and wispy mustache. "I got my orders."

"Oh, Aaron, stop this foolishness. Take the man where he wants to go."

Aaron shakes his head emphatically. "Darryl said no."

"I'll talk to Darryl," Mrs. McDaniels says, pointing a bony finger at Aaron.

The boy is weakening. "Why you care about him?" Aaron asks, looking at me.

"Just do it," she says.

Reluctantly, Aaron hoists me up by the elbow. After sitting down the whole day, I get dizzy from standing up so fast and my legs nearly give way under me. I steady myself on the slim boy's shoulder and allow myself to be led to the bathroom, too bound up to even look back in gratitude at Darryl's great-grandmother.

I have my fly open before I actually enter the room. I put my hand against the wall as I lean over the toilet. The piss shoots out of me like a flame, gas follows, and I moan out loud with relief. I keep a powerful stream going for at least three minutes while Aaron presses the Uzi against the base of my skull. As I continue to empty myself, I notice a pair of cockroaches racing down the bathroom wall.

Then I smell something awful coming from another part of the bathroom. I turn my head slowly with the gun following it. The bathtub is full of feces.

"Oh Jesus," I say, ready to throw up.

"Looks bad, huh?" says Aaron.

The two small children come running in. They're both cute kids with round, shiny faces and high-pitched giggles. Their clothes are soiled and smelly, though. The boy wears shit-stained jeans and a red shirt that looks like he hasn't taken it off for days. The little girl, LaToya, has on a pair of blue pajamas with smiling gray elephants and a wide yellow stain on the front. Her little legs are like matchsticks.

I realize the two kids are as used to playing tag around crack dens as other children are used to playing in country fields.

When they see me watching them, they suddenly stop. The boy lowers his jeans to his ankles and prepares to take a dump over the side of the tub. LaToya, the little girl, who wears her hair in pigtails, raises her fingers to her lips and gives me a melancholy look.

"You wanna see Big Bird?" she asks after a couple of seconds.

"Who?"

She stretches out her hand like she wants me to take it and follow her somewhere. Aaron pushes her hand away with the muzzle of his gun, but she doesn't get discouraged.

"Mom say Big Bird 'sa big Muppets," she tells me, the words whistling through the space in her teeth.

I'd noticed her brother playing with Muppet toys before. She must have some of her own in one of the other rooms.

"That's your Big Bird?" I say. "I thought Big Bird was on a TV show."

She nods wildly. Aaron is half bored, half listening, not making any effort to interrupt.

"What day is the show on?" I ask, playing for time and trying to figure out if there's another way out of here.

She looks at me blankly. She doesn't know the days of the week. I smile to show her that's okay.

"Mommy say they got Big Bird downtown, but she can't take me."

"Why not?" I can't tell if she means there's a movie with Big Bird in it or a stage show at Radio City or what.

"Mommy say she too busy," she says. She gives me a little coquettish smile. " 'Ould you take me?"

Even Aaron seems interested in what I'll say to that, peering at me over the sights of his gun.

"Sure, I'd take you," I say.

Aaron shakes his head like maybe he'd like to go too. But the little girl studies my face for a minute and her smile disappears. "No, you don't," she says softly. "You don't take me anywhere."

She hardly knows me and already she's disappointed in me.

"Well, I'll try," I tell her.

Aaron motions with his gun that he wants me to leave. The smell was starting to get to me anyway. But before I go, I notice the girl has a little purplish bruise on her left cheek.

"Hey, what happened to you there?" I ask, pointing to it.

She looks up at me and puts her finger to the side of her head.

"Crack," she says.

She goes running out of the bathroom, leaving me completely confused. Maybe she meant a crackhead did this to her. Like Darryl or one of his friends. Or maybe crack was the sound she heard when she got hit. But there's another possibility, just barely edging into my mind. Maybe she meant somebody gave her crack and this is what happened to her when she got high. I know that couldn't be, but now I can't shake the idea.

It's that look she gave me. The one that said: You may think this is a hard place to be right now, but try growing up here.

74

Darryl's mother was crying when he came back into the bedroom.

"Oh, Darryl, we gonna die," she said.

"What the fuck, Moms."

The television was still on. It showed night outside their building. This time there were gas masks, ladders, and assault rifles all over the place. The sidewalks around the Fortress were packed with black and Hispanic mothers, fathers, and children—many of them residents of the building who'd been chased out by the King family posse and the cops who'd arrived on the scene. Concession stands were set up near the curbs to sell fried meat and Malcolm X T-shirts.

The picture on the TV suddenly turned black-and-white. It looked like one of those old-fashioned movies. People were running around, like a riot was about to start. Then there was a lot of smoke and it was hard to see what was going on. They cut to a picture of a black guy lying facedown on a concrete floor near a pair of binoculars. Next there was a white guy on his back in the mud with his arms spread out and a bloody bandage over his face.

" 'S a war," said Darryl.

More tears streamed down his mother's face. " 'S not a

war," she told him. "That's Attica. That's what they say is gonna happen with us."

Darryl stared at the screen, but the black-and-white pictures had vanished like it was all a bad dream. The TV lady was on again, saying something about how they'd return to the scene before the midnight deadline and now it was back to the studio. Darryl was starting to feel drowsy. He sat down next to his mother on the bed and reached for the crack pipe on the night table. There was a story about an airplane crash on when he flipped open the top of the lighter.

"Darryl, we gotta do something," his mother said through her sobs.

He tried thinking about the future, but it didn't work anymore. He couldn't visualize it. Too much going from one high to the next. Even now, his mind kept wandering back to how he'd like to beam up. If only he could get his hand up to light the pipe. But sleep was draining away his energy and his arm started to fall. His eyes closed and the lighter slipped between his fingers.

It fell on the carpet with the top open and the flame still going. On the television screen, the anchorman said they'd just learned that the cop wasn't going to be indicted for shooting Jamal Perkins. Darryl's mother began to weep a little louder and a little harder. She looked over to say something to Darryl, but he was already sleeping. When the commercial came on, she punched him in the shoulder and told him to get up.

His eyes slowly opened and he gave her that look that made her fear for her own life again. "There's things I wanna tell you," she said.

"What?" He bent over and picked up the lighter, without noticing where its flame had licked the carpet fibers and started them smoldering.

"I hope you don't think you getting high now."

He lit the pipe and took a long hit. His face closed up and his body shook a little. "Relax, Moms," he said.

She started to dry her eyes with the sleeves of her blouse. "In four hours is midnight," she said. "And they gonna come for us."

"Well, I ain't gonna give up now," he said sullenly.

"Well, I ain't asking you to," she snapped at him. "Your father couldn't do prison time, so you couldn't neither."

He was going to say something to her about that, but now he couldn't think of what it was. The newspeople came back on the TV and did a story about sea cows mating at a zoo and the New York Yankees.

"There's things I want to tell you before I die," his mother said more softly.

"What?"

"I don't know." She looked up at the ceiling for a minute and he could still see where the tears had left their tracks on her face. The voices outside seemed to be shouting his name out.

"I ain't worked it all out yet," she said finally. "But there's things I wanna say to you about life."

He rocked himself up onto his feet. "Well, I ain't dead yet," he said. "I'm gonna get us outta here."

"Well, what nonsense you telling me now?"

"We're gonna get out and start making that crazy money."

The confident way he was talking made her want to start crying again. But he was already waking himself up and working himself into a mood. "This a opportunity," he was saying. "We got the whole world in front of my hands."

She screwed up her mouth skeptically and put her hands on her skinny hips. "Well, tell me how you figure on that."

"Motherfuckers got to give me what I'm asking for," he said, clapping his hands together like an athlete about to take the field. "We still got the hostage here."

His mother began crying again, but by now Darryl was fed up. He flapped his hands and started to walk out of the room. His mother threw a balled-up Kleenex after him. He stopped in the doorway and looked back in, wrinkling up his nose.

"You smell something funny?" he asked.

"Only you," his mother told him.

75

Ever since it said on TV that the cop who shot Jamal Perkins wasn't going to get indicted, I've been waiting for the explosion in here. For a couple of hours things have been degenerating. That kid is still flicking droplets on my face and the one called Bobby "the House" is wandering around in shades muttering, "Violence, ultraviolence," over and over.

Most of the lights have been turned down and in the flickering blasts of illumination from the television set, I can see four of Darryl's other lieutenants hovering around the dinner table, which is just two or three yards from the front door entrance. The table is covered with guns and set up so that each kid can grab one on his way out, just as other boys their age grab a hat and mittens heading out for school on a cold winter's day.

It's almost a relief when Darryl comes out of the back bedroom with his mother, though my mouth still hurts where he belted me before. At least with him around I know I'm dealing with the real power around here, not just a dangerous functionary who'd pop me for no good reason. I have a feeling things are coming to a head quickly and no one's ready for it. The voices outside seem to be getting louder and the lights appear brighter. I guess it's almost midnight now. Once the deadline arrives, the forces outside will have to try crashing in, or Darryl and the others will have to try crashing out. Either way, I'm probably dead.

I start talking, as if words themselves can keep me alive.

"Hey, what's going on out there?" I ask Darryl.

"Yo, shut the fuck up, man. Who asked you?"

He looks over at Bobby, who's holding a gun on me, like he's about to give him an order. "Hey," I say, bracing myself. "I was just looking for information."

Darryl turns up the side of his mouth. "Oh that's all," he says, balling up his fists and taking a step toward me. For most of the day I've been avoiding looking him in the eye, kind of the way you don't look at people on the subway. But now our eyes meet and it's like wires crossing.

I've never known there could be such violence in just a look before. There's no white showing in his eyes, only huge, angry pupils staring out of a ruined face. He's got that horrible crack breath again and two lines of sweat are coming down his brow.

Normally I'd be too scared to say anything, but with the way things are going I better take a shot at it. "So did you talk to the guy?" I ask.

"Who?"

"The hostage negotiator."

He smiles like everything's under control.

"What's so funny?" I ask, looking back to the bedroom where he's been with his mother.

"I'm about to get paid," he says.

An old subway mugger's line. I'm starting to wonder if he has any real sense of what's about to happen here.

"So what'd you say to the guy?" I ask.

"I gave him my list."

Darryl looks around at everybody else in the room like they're going to confirm that's just what they discussed.

I try not to let my hopes get up too high. I'd thought his last few conversations with the hostage negotiator had gone badly, but now he's acting like they might've worked out a deal. Maybe he's somehow managed to seize the moment and act rationally.

"So what was on your list?" I ask him.

"Business equipment," he says.

That stops me cold and I look at the others to see if they have a clue as to what he's talking about. In the red light from the TV, his mother looks like she's trying to shrink down and lose herself in the folds of her blouse.

"Business equipment?" I say. "What does that mean?"

"Equipment to start my business," he explains. "They're gonna give me a helicopter, and two keys, so I can get started up right up . . ."

My sense of hope is fraying, like an old cable carrying too much freight. "They're not gonna give you dick."

"Yes, they will," he insists.

One of the other kids comes over to take Bobby's place, holding the gun on me. I don't know this kid's name, but he's about sixteen and he wears an NWA baseball cap with the bill turned sideways. He's only a couple of years younger than the inmates we just saw in the film clips of Attica, who were holding knives on the hostages when they got shot themselves.

What they said on TV was that the prisoners and the authorities couldn't agree on the demands and, after a while, the state just had to reestablish order, no matter what the cost was to lives. It's about to happen again here if we don't watch it.

"Didn't you talk to the guy about amnesty?" I ask Darryl, figuring he must've seen that part of the television report.

"Nope," Darryl says. "Don't have to."

"What did he say?" I hear Darryl's mother asking somebody in the corner.

"You mean you didn't even talk to the guy about letting me go in exchange for some leniency?" I say. At this point I stand up in front of Darryl, just to make sure he's listening to me.

"Sit your ass down," he says.

"Didn't you talk to him about doing a deal with the judge?"

"Nigger, sit your ass down."

The guy in the NWA cap puts his hand on my shoulder. All the other people who've been milling around, doing drugs, and watching TV stop talking and start watching us more carefully. Like something really serious is about to happen. I sit down slowly.

"Damn," says Darryl, rocking from side to side, and spoiling for a good fight.

My scalp tingles like my hair is turning gray while I'm sitting here. "Listen," I say, "you gotta try and call that guy back. He's gonna make this deal."

"Why the fuck don't you call them?" he says, bellowing the words down into my face.

"Because you won't let me."

" 'S right," says Darryl. " 'S my motherfuckin' house. Who asked you to come up here?"

"Nobody. You broke the law."

"What law?"

"Come on, you know what law," I say, trying to keep the discussion reasonable. "Like the law against shooting cops."

"What law's that?" he says, throwing up his hands. "Motherfuckers come in my house and tear shit up. They threaten me with violence. Shoot them guns off. What law's that?"

" 'S right," says a voice from the darkness.

"You tell 'im, D.," adds Bobby.

"That's not what it is," I say, fumbling the words. "That's not the reality of it."

"*Reality?*" Darryl's voice goes up and his head jerks back. "Motherfucker. Lemme tell you about the reality. You come around here talking about the *law*. But there be your law and the law of the jungle. You know what I'm saying? See, you in the jungle now, Mr. Bomb."

"Yeah, yeah, yeah." I turn halfway away from him in my seat. "I know all about that."

"No, you don't. You think you know. Because you sit in your office, and you be the law and the rest of us be niggas. But now you come in my house. Right? You in my supervision. So you respect my law. Understand what I'm saying? You not any better than us. You the nigga here."

In the dark, one of the boys makes a hissing noise and says, "Aw busted . . ." That gets a short laugh out of the others without really cheering anybody up. "Say it," someone else chimes in. It's like a disillusioned revivalist meeting where no one can quite find the spirit. But in the blue radium flashes of television light, I see at least a dozen pairs of worried eyes looking around, just as afraid as I am.

"Well, I'm sorry you feel that way," I say slowly, trying hard to keep the fear and anger out of my voice. "But what you're talking about isn't the same thing."

"Why the fuck not?"

"Because I didn't kill anybody. I don't come to your neighborhood and rob people."

"But you put the shit right in my face!" Darryl yells. "You put the shit right in my face!" He's pointing furiously at the television, like it's the whore that's led him down the road to temptation. "I seen it right there. People be making all that crazy money. People flying with helicopters, and their boat, and driving around in the limos. And with the females. I seen it right while I was sitting there." He kicks the chair I'm sitting in. *"You put the shit right in my face and tell me I can't grab for it."*

" 'S the system," I hear Darryl's mother muttering.

"They doing it to us again," someone else calls out.

"Conspiracy," says Aaron, adding his voice to the growing uproar.

"The way they want it," says Darryl's mother loudly.

"Genocide," says Darryl, using the word like it's something he heard on TV.

"Oh, fuck you," I say, rising to my feet. "Who told you to put a needle in your arm? Who said go smoke twenty-five vials of crack. If I gave you rat poison, would you do that too? Why's it always our fault?"

"BECAUSE IT IS!" says Darryl. "YOU PUT THE SHIT RIGHT IN MY FACE!!"

For Bobby, this is the cue to take leave of his senses and he starts raving at me too.

"YOU WERE THE ONE!" he shouts. "YOU BROUGHT DIS-EASE INTO THIS HOUSE! YOU EAT PORK! AND THE PORK EAT WORMS! AND THE WORMS EAT DIRT!!! NOW there's worms in this house. This used to be a CLEAN HOUSE."

"Bobby," says Darryl in a quieter tone. "Chill, man. 'S just life."

I'm standing in the middle of the darkened room, and Darryl's prowling around me. In the flashes of television light, I can see the rest of them in a loose circle around us, but I can't make out any of their faces.

"Motherfucker tryin' to tell me how to negotiate," I hear Darryl saying, like he can't believe I had the nerve to second-guess him before.

"THAT'S RIGHT!" one of the others cries out. "THAT'S WHAT HE TRY!"

Now Darryl's standing right in front of me and snarling. "Let me ask you something, Mr. Bomb," he says in a low voice. "What give you the right to tell me what to ask for when I'm in negotiations?"

"It's my life too," I say.

"But what give you the right to tell niggers how to live?"

The rest of them yell out their approval. "THAT'S RIGHT! THAT'S ALL RIGHT!!"

"Well . . ." one deep voice keeps saying.

"The earth is gettin' too far from the sun," an older woman's voice calls. I can't see who it belongs to.

"I'm not trying to tell anybody anything," I explain.

"Yes, you are," says Darryl, pointing his finger accusingly. "Yes, you are. You trying to say we should go beg when we in the position to get something for ourselves."

"That's not true," I tell all of them. "I'm trying to help."

"Now that's bullshit," says Darryl's mother.

"Yeah, right, Mr. Nice Guy," Bobby taunts me.

"You trying to short us again," Darryl says.

"No, I'm not," I say, putting up my hands defensively, like one of them's about to take a swing at me out of the darkness. "I'm just trying to keep us all alive."

"You trying to take the shit out of our hands when it's ours."

"Jew-Man," another voice in the dark says.

"All right!" I shout. "All right! The hell with all of you. Stick to your stupid, goddamn unreasonable list of demands and keep trying to sell crack. You're all going down in flames anyway."

"Well, there's at least one white motherfucker going down with us," Darryl says.

They all start roaring at once. "EEEYAHHHHH!!! MISTT-TERNICEGUY! FFUGGGIMMMUPP!" I feel like an actor on-stage being booed by an invisible audience beyond the footlights. I hear the clatter of a gun being picked out of the pile on the dining room table. There are sounds of laughter and hands slapping.

"Right?" Aaron is saying. "Right?"

"You tell 'im, Darryl," says his mother.

"What'd he say?" the little girl, LaToya, is asking.

"EEEEEEEYYYYEEE AAAAHHH ! ! ! MISSSSSTERRRR NICEGUYY! ! ! !"

"TELLLIM D! TELLIM!"

They're getting louder and louder now. It's starting to sound like a victory celebration in a high school locker room.

In the meantime, the light in the room has gone flat. The regular program on television must have gone to a blank screen before switching to a commercial. It's hard to see anything now and almost impossible to pick a phrase out of the racket Darryl and his friends are making. All it sounds like is "pop that five-o" and a lot of indiscriminate "motherfuckers."

All the air feels used up in here. A vein pulses in my brow and I take a small step forward into the darkness. A hand grabs my elbow and something brushes against my head. I don't know what it is, but it has teeth.

I duck away from it, but it comes back again, landing on my forehead and raking across my scalp. It doesn't so much hurt now, as promise to start really hurting in a second. I begin struggling to get away, but somebody has my other elbow and the thing touches my head once more. It's hard and cold with jagged edges. I get scared it's going to start ripping through my scalp at any moment.

"Get that fuckin' thing away from me!" I scream.

"Huh," somebody says. "He mad."

Just then, a commercial comes on the TV, making the light a little brighter, so I can finally see what's been touching my head. It's the kind of big African-looking comb I've noticed black kids using on the train and outside the office.

Darryl sees me staring at it and he gives me his rictus grin again. "I just want you to look pretty before you die," he says, flourishing the comb like a downtown stylist.

The rest of them start giggling hysterically, as though this was some great high school prank we've all been in on. But to me it's been more like a gross violation and I reach out and give Darryl a good shove with both hands. He goes back a step or two, and for a second he just seems stunned. As the TV starts to flicker like a strobe light, I see his eyes open a little wider. Somebody takes a deep sniff and somebody else mutters, "Oh shit."

Without any further warning, Darryl charges me like a bull and shoves me back with all his might. Instead of letting me fall over, though, somebody catches me from behind and shoves me back toward the center of the circle people have formed. As my trajectory carries me forward, I stick out my arm and hit somebody standing on the side. I think I've just smacked him in the mouth. Maybe hard enough to draw blood.

Again, I'm caught before I hit the floor and somebody standing in front of me pushes me backward. It's like a malicious version of the old kids' game of Trust, made even scarier by the way the flickering TV light breaks up what you see. All you can make out is somebody's gesture or expression, frozen in time, but not what led up to it or what's about to follow.

Everybody's getting too frenzied with all the shoving, breathing, and cursing in high, crazy voices. I start thinking one of these guys is bound to have a knife, so maybe he's going to just reach out and puncture me as I go flying by. I try to grab a hold of something and steady myself, but my arms just flail out uselessly. With each shove, the game is getting more out of control and violent. I feel the blood sloshing around in my head and the dampness on my back where their sweaty palms have been touching me. If I don't kill one of them right now, they'll kill me.

Suddenly there's a flare-up of light from outside, and I see Darryl's face again, just a foot or two in front of me. If I had a gun right now, I'd shoot him. But it might be easier just to kick him in the balls and step on his head when he's down. I picture grinding his bloody face into the rug and hearing the crunch of bones in his neck.

But just as I begin to raise my leg, the phone starts ringing and everything else gets very quiet all of a sudden. For what seems like an hour, the only sound is that phone. It must ring at least a dozen times. The cops calling again. Trying to find out what's going on. Or maybe offering one last shot at getting us all out of here alive. The others look at Darryl expectantly, as if he knows just what to do. But he stays rooted to the spot, not even looking over at the phone. Turning his eyes away, like he's afraid to see it ringing. I feel a slow ache spreading across my chest.

The phone stops ringing.

With the break, everybody seems to chill out a little. The sounds from outside have also stopped and the bright light is gone. A different kind of tension makes its way around the room. Everyone's thinking the same thing: I hope they don't come rushing in now and kill us all.

"Why everybody stop talking?" I hear LaToya, the little girl from the bathroom, asking from somewhere behind me. "Are we apposed to be scared?"

I think about the bruise on her face and feel a little cold inside.

On the other side of the room, somebody lights up a crack pipe. It makes for an eerie scene, with the lights down. The sound of the cocaine burning and crackling seems about ten times louder than normal. Almost like twigs snapping next to your ear. This must be what it's like being out in the woods when you know there are bears nearby. I think about my mother and how she tried to get me to start praying when my father wasn't around. I'm sorry it never took.

"You know that was probably the hostage negotiator trying to call you just now," I say with a sigh escaping from somewhere deep inside of me.

"Yeah," Darryl answers flatly, as though I'd just said something boring about the weather. He just doesn't give a shit.

My eyelids are heavy and my brain feels sodden. I'm starting to realize how very, very tired I am. I don't even know if I'd mind them finishing it off once and for all now.

"I dunno, Darryl," I tell him, "I spent all this time trying to understand guys like you, and in the end, I guess I don't have a clue."

"No one knows me," he says bitterly. "Understand? No one. Not in my mentality. You wanna be me? You wanna know how I feel? FUCK YOU! THAT'S HOW I FEEL!!"

It's useless. I tell myself I'm dead already and it doesn't matter anymore. I don't know why I even bother saying anything else; the words just come out. "Well, I was going to say you could try calling the guy back," I tell him in an exhausted voice.

Darryl doesn't say anything. He just breathes out loudly.

"You wrote down his number, didn't you?"

There's a long silence. And in the weak light I see Darryl give me that half hurt, half resentful look that I've come to recognize over the years at Probation. It's the way illiterate people look at you when you ask them if they can read.

I don't know whether to laugh or cry or find a way to blow my brains out.

For the first time in his life, Darryl King has some real power. Not just to chase some rival crack dealer off his corner. He can bring the system to its knees, right here and now. He's got the authorities and the media listening to him. He can demand amnesty or he can call for justice for Jamal Perkins, or ask for safe passage for his family to get out of here, or whatever the hell he wants. In the end, he might get only part of what he's asking for or none of it, but he can at least get everything to stop for a while and make his voice heard.

But none of that will happen. Because Darryl King doesn't have what it takes to go up against the system. Because the system never gave him the equipment to do it. He never got the basic skills required to write down a phone number. And even if he could, he never stood much of a chance anyway, with everything else that's happened. As he stares toward the living room window, looking a little overwhelmed, I could almost feel sorry for him. But I can't afford sympathy anymore. That side of me is dead and I need it to stay dead. Darryl is ready to kill me at any time, and I have to be ready to kill him. A man does what he does to survive, my father said. For the first time, the words come alive to me.

From outside, I start to hear something familiar, getting nearer. A fierce fluttering noise. A cool breeze stirring the unbearably hot night. The curtains on the window shimmy slightly. It's the whir of a helicopter's propeller, closing in on us. The gust of air blows dollar bills and rolling papers all over the place.

"What'd I tell you?" says Darryl.

For a second, I can almost believe they've given in to his demands. But then I realize it has to be the opposite. They're probably making a last fly-by attempt to see if they can get a shot at Darryl or one of the others before they break down the front door. Or maybe it's just a distraction.

"Come on, Moms," Darryl says with a burst of boyish enthusiasm. "They gonna land it on the roof for us."

As the searchlight sweeps through the apartment, I see her looking more glassy-eyed than ever. "What?" she says.

Just then, the TV picture dies and the room gets completely dark. There's a mood of hushed anticipation, like a surprise birthday is about to begin, but I feel dread eating away at the pit of my stomach. I remember seeing a movie where the cops cut all the electricity in a building just before they moved in on a hostage situation.

"Darryl, what happened to my program?" his mother says. "I was just watching."

I hear the first explosion and see the first flash of light through the white sheet hanging in the bedroom doorway. I can't imagine how the cops got through the window back there without anybody noticing. There's a second, louder explosion. The impact makes Darryl stagger and it shakes the chair out from under me. Darryl's great-grandmother comes out of one of the other back rooms with a teacup and saucer rattling in her hand. Everyone gets down on hands and knees and starts screaming at the same time.

Darryl's hoarse voice rises above all the others. "NO ONE KNOWS ME!!"

I look up and see the bed sheet hanging in the doorway is on fire, but there aren't any cops coming out. It's not a raid. Somehow, something back there must've ignited and hit an ether tank or something. Now the whole apartment is flashing over. It's like someone's turned on a giant blowtorch. The fire from the bed sheet catches the carpet in this room and soon there's heavy black smoke everywhere.

I feel the heat on my skin as I roll onto my stomach. It's not quite as bad down here yet, but the flames are racing along the paint on the walls and most of the furniture is burning.

"HELP ME PLEASE!" a woman's voice keeps calling.

I raise my eyes and see Darryl's mother getting consumed by fire. Her legs and her back are smoldering. Bobby Kirk grabs a tablecloth to try to smother her, but it's already caught fire and his hands get scorched. I start coughing and choking on the smoke as I crawl around on my hands and knees, looking for the front door.

I see the dining room table is still covered with guns. An idea flashes through my mind about grabbing one and turning to look for Darryl. But then I hear my father's voice in my head, telling me to survive again, and I keep looking for the front door. It can't be far from here.

Something falls on the carpet in front of me and a small fire starts in my path. I go down on my elbows and shift direction. As I turn, I see the glass-and-wood cabinet with the old tenants' family pictures and Bibles glowing from the heat. Soon the flames begin to lick at the walls around it and the cabinet collapses.

Tears are forming in my eyes and my contact lenses are starting to dry up and crinkle under my eyelids. I'm getting confused and disoriented. I spin around several more times, trying to find the front door, and put my hand in a pile of bobby pins and toothpicks. In a momentary clearing, I see Aaron yanking open what I know to be a closet door and jumping in.

The smoke is beginning to blind me. There's no thing or landmark to tell me where I am in the room, but I try not to panic. I spin around again and crawl along for a few more steps before I run into somebody. A living body. I reach out and touch a frail bony arm and a weak shoulder. It's impossible to see a face with all this smoke. Whoever it is feels down my arm and then takes my hand, like we're going to try to make it to the door together. The grip is warm and reassuring, what you'd expect from someone who's raised children.

"All right," I say hoarsely. "Let's do it."

We begin to move in the same direction, away from the main source of heat. The smoke starts to change direction and a little clearing forms ahead of us. My hand is released and I look up for the first time to see Darryl King has been the one holding it.

He just stares at me for a long while as we face each other

on our hands and knees. There's something oddly pacific in his eyes. Like he's going to ask me to join him in a silent act of communion. But I've already been through all that and my mind is made up that I will try to kill him, even if it means using my bare hands to strangle him.

I reach for him, and at the same moment his hand comes shooting out at me. My heart stops. But instead of grabbing my throat, his hand lands on my shoulder and roughly shoves me out of the way. Without giving me another look, he turns and starts to crawl off, like he's trying to find another way to the door. I notice flames riding up his back and climbing his neck, on their way to his brains. I think for a second about going after him, but my skin is starting to prickle, and if I don't get out soon, it'll bubble off my bones. There's a constant deep rumbling everywhere, like the sound of a fireplace amplified ten times over. I keep plunging ahead.

As I go to my left, I become aware of a loud, piercing shriek. Someone else is burning to death very nearby.

I open my eyes wide and the stinging is almost more than I can bear. At last I focus. LaToya, the little girl I'd seen in the bathroom before, is lying on her back about three yards away. What looks like a small bonfire is burning on her stomach and she's trying to beat it out with her bare hands.

A smell like hair frying fills my nostrils and I see the little girl giving me a pleading look. She opens her mouth as though she's going to say something to me, but nothing comes out.

I put my hand out and realize I'm touching the front door. The knob is surprisingly cool to the touch. I turn it, but the door doesn't open. That's when I notice a smaller knob for the lock underneath and a chain about a foot above it. In the seconds it takes to undo them, my lungs fill up with more poison and my chest feels like it's about to burst.

I finally get the door open and go lunging out into the hall, landing at a funny angle. It feels like I've broken my ankle, but somehow I'm managing to keep the door open with it. I'm lying there, looking back into the apartment. I hear people screaming and the crackling sound of fire eating more of the paint off the walls. But all I can see is more heavy toxic smoke coming out, choking me and burning my eyes. It's like staring into the abyss. I'm about to pass out at any minute from the fumes. This must be what hell smells like.

The little girl's voice cries out and I hear someone who sounds like Darryl shouting. Just then there's a powerful blast of air and the door starts to close, pushing my foot out of the way. The set of muscles that I was sure would have kept it there, propping the door open, don't respond anymore. Something over the past few minutes, hours, days, weeks, and years has worn them down. My foot moves just a little more out of the way and the door slams shut.

Everything goes black for a moment and my head hits the floor. The roar I've had in my ears is muffled. When I open my eyes again, the hall is filled with smoke and more is starting to seep out from under the front door.

I look over and see a bunch of Emergency Service Unit cops coming through the stairwell door, followed by a couple of firemen in black turn-out coats and helmets. They look like huge dark moths hovering there.

"How many of them still in there?" the fireman with the extinguisher can asks me.

"I don't know."

Most of the cops fan out through the hall with their weapons drawn. Only a couple go to help the fireman with the ax and the iron crowbar who's trying to get the apartment door open. "It's a snap lock," he says. "Half of them are probably baked already."

If your heart gets broken too often, it doesn't work anymore, I told Andrea. A man does what he does to survive, my father told me. You're not any better than me, Darryl said. I listen for the little girl's voice, but I don't hear it anymore.

"You must've been the one nearest the door," the fireman holding the can says as he moves to help his partner and the others.

"I must've."

I start coughing again. It feels like I'm about to spit up a lung. The skin exposed on my arms and legs looks charred and blackened in the places where it isn't red and swollen. My face feels numb and the inside of my chest is seared, but I am alive. And in that moment, I know that I am truly my father's son. I wonder if I will ever stop hating myself.

76

With the car in the shop and the time running late, Richard Silver and Jessica first tried to catch a cab going downtown. But it was snowing hard and traffic was bad, so for the first time in more than twenty years, Richard announced he was going to take the subway.

"Why the hell not?" he said. "I practically helped build the fucking thing. Aren't I entitled to something on a day like this?"

The line for the token booth at the Eighty-sixth Street station was much too long, though, and he had to buy a couple from a desolate-looking guy with swollen lips standing by the turnstiles.

"Bet he doesn't pay taxes," Richard Silver said, pushing through.

"Good," Jessica replied. "Maybe it'd be a good job for you when you get out."

They walked down a flight of stairs to the platform where the express train was supposed to pull in. The shopgirls and secretaries were standing around the steel pillars. A guy in a long moth-eaten old coat was asleep on the wooden bench. The man next to him was picking his nose and reading the *Racing Form*. The graffiti above their heads said: "Jesus Died for Your Sins, What Have You Done FOR HIM Lately?"

"Some life," Richard Silver said. "You know I helped them fix up this station when they had Gimbel's here."

"I still can't believe they gave you three years for money laundering," Jessica told him.

The local train went by upstairs and he didn't say anything.

"Why did Larry's cousin set you up like that?" she said. "You didn't do anything to hurt him, did you? You just offered him a deal."

"Ah, he was just a lousy bank manager," Richard Silver told her with a wave of his hand. "He's got his own problems. It was that probation thing that killed me. If I hadn't had that violation and that prick Baum hanging over my head, I would've had a shot at working out a deal with the feds."

"Is that what your new lawyer said?"

He grunted and undid two of the buttons on his gray cashmere overcoat. "Yeah, well, I'll tell you something about that guy Baum. I had him about *this far* from making a trip to the Cayman Islands for me." He showed her the distance with his thumb and index finger.

"He didn't go for it?"

"What do you want, he's a social worker," he said, shrugging in exasperation. "Anyway, it's no wonder he cares so much about the blacks. He's starting to look like one of them. I think he was in a fire or something."

Richard Silver noticed a broad-shouldered black man in a business suit staring at him and realized he'd been talking much too loud. "You should watch it," Jessica said.

A beam of light appeared from the end of the tracks and began to grow larger. The distant rumble soon turned into a metallic roar and when the train pulled into the station, people's faces were pressed almost right against the windows.

"It's too crowded," said Richard Silver. "Let's wait for the next one."

Jessica looked down at her watch. "You're due at the marshal's office in fifteen minutes. We better not."

They shoved their way onto the train and the closing doors caught the back of Richard's coat. He turned around and got a face full of garlic breath from the Puerto Rican man with greasy hair and intelligent eyes, who was standing next to him. To his left, a fiftyish black woman with her hair in curlers was giving him the kind of angry look he'd come to expect from people who'd seen his picture in the newspapers lately. The car was a hellish sweatbox.

"Can I get some room here?" he said.

No one budged. Everywhere he looked people were packed up right against each other. Jessica was nowhere to be seen. He tried to elbow his way in a little farther, but he first felt some slight resistance and then a rough shove that almost put him on the floor. To steady himself as the train heaved forward, he reached up and grabbed an overhead strap. Somebody behind him poked him in the ass with something long and stiff.

He hoped prison would be a little bit better than this. But as the train continued its inevitable journey going down, he knew it wouldn't. By the time they'd passed the Bloomingdale's stop, he'd even given up hope of finding a seat. He'd just stand there, numb and tired on his feet, like everybody else in New York.

77

Sometimes, when I'm standing in the checkout line at the local Grand Union, I still get strange looks from the housewives because of the patches of seared, discolored skin on my ears, neck, and forehead. But I'm getting used to that, and it doesn't bother me so much.

My life is quite different from the way it once was. I live on the second floor of a small, but cozy wooden house just outside Camden, New Jersey, where I attend Rutgers University Law School. I often spend part of the weekend working on the garden in the back, and I plan to put in a row of tomatoes in the spring. At night I go to sleep to the sound of cicadas and crickets rather than crackheads and M-80s exploding down the street.

Overall, I would have to say I am grateful for my new life. After all the turmoil and violence in the city, I appreciate the subtle nuances more: a cup of coffee in the morning, a mildly amusing story in the newspaper, strands of my hair on the brush in the bathroom. With the ninety-seven-thousand-dollar settlement I got from the city after the fire, I have relatively few money worries.

Still, there are times when I feel a sadness lurking underneath and an emptiness inside. The other week I went to my cousin Jerry's wedding in Hackensack and one particular part of the vows kept tolling over and over in my head. Forsaking all others. In some sense, I believe I have forsaken all others by leaving Probation and New York City.

The last time I stopped by the office to pick up some papers, I ran into Jack, my old union rep. As a favor, he looked up how some of my old clients were doing. Ricky Velez, the ex-token sucker, got a job bagging groceries at a neighborhood Food Emporium and eventually moved up to assistant manager. Not a major accomplishment, I suppose, but something. On the other hand, Charlie Simms stayed addicted to crack and Maria Sanchez remained with her family. So they both wound up in jail.

"Do you see that girl anymore?" Jack asked me as I was on my way out.

I stopped and started to say yes, but then I caught myself and realized he was talking about Andrea, the law student I'd been seeing that summer. In fact, I don't see Andrea anymore. It became very difficult for me to be around anybody in the months after I got out of the hospital. But I am still seeing the other girl. The one I neglected to save that day in the fire.

In the middle of the night sometimes I'll see her face and I won't be able to sleep. I'll rise from bed and fix myself two or three stiff drinks. When that doesn't work, I get in the car and drive aimlessly for hours with a beer in my hand and the radio on at full blast. Going seventy-five miles an hour on the New Jersey Turnpike, I feel free and lost in a way I never thought was possible from growing up in the city. But I can't get the girl out of my mind.

One night just before Christmas, I find myself driving drunkenly through Weehawken, a small industrial town near the Lincoln Tunnel entrance. As I cruise up a street called Boulevard East, past rows of one-family brick houses and modernized Victorian homes, I take careful note of all the dependable old American cars with names like Mercury and Ford sitting out front. Just then, the road turns steep and crooked, as though it's about to reveal something surprising. When it does, it's enough to make me stop the car and get out.

What it is is a view of the city that I've never seen before. Across the river, the Manhattan skyline is shining like a string of Christmas lights in the night. It takes my breath away. I see the old piers thrusting out at the water and the top of the Empire State Building reaching for the starless sky. The World Trade Center towers rise from the south end of the island and the anonymous projects are fading off to the north. Huge new glass-and-steel towers are blocking out other old familiar parts of the horizon.

Just to get a better look, I walk past a shady park and wander into a small concrete plaza area overlooking a marina. I think I remember reading once that Alexander Hamilton got shot around here, but at the moment all I see is a couple of stone memorials to veterans of foreign wars in the middle of the plaza. An American flag hangs from the porch of a house behind me, even though the sun went down hours ago. Somebody must've had to get out of town in a hurry and just left it up there.

I stumble once or twice in the dark and make my way over to the fence at the outer edge of the plaza. I look down once and start to get dizzy. This whole thing seems to be set on top of a high stone wall, towering over the shoreline, like an ancient barrier designed to repel hostile forces arriving by water. I find myself leaning against some kind of metal contraption just to get my balance. It's one of those old-fashioned viewing machines, with the steel mask on top that you look through. Its sad impassive eyes are pointing toward Manhattan. The sign underneath them says: "25 cents. BRING DISTANT POINTS OF INTEREST WITHIN CLOSE RANGE WITH THE USE OF THIS MACHINE."

I finish my beer and check my pockets, but I don't have a quarter. I squint once more at the skyline. During the day there are ferries from here, but right now, it seems like it's a world away. Somewhere across the water, somebody is getting laid, somebody else is getting shot, somebody's getting ripped off, and somebody's getting high. The city is a slow motion riot, destroying itself piece by piece, and I don't have a place in it anymore. It's like looking at a family portrait of people I'll never see again.

A dark cloud passes in front of the moon and an airplane glows like an ember falling from the sky. The world keeps going around faster all the time. A chilling wind whips through the air, rustling the trees and the American flag behind me.